2008 WOW ANTHOLOGY

By contributing members of
Wizards of Words
A nonprofit organization

www.wizardsofwords.org

ISBN13: 978-0-9791701-1-9

The opinions expressed and level of research to support fact in any of the following stories are solely the responsibility of the individual authors and do not reflect the collective opinions, judgment or beliefs of the WOW organization. Any questions or comments may be directed to the individual author through his/her website listed after his/her story.

When you purchase this book, the net profit goes to providing funds to produce workshops and seminars at WOW conferences and to writers who apply for financial assist in order to attend WOW educational events.

Published by:

R.J. Buckley Publishing
1451 E. Poncho Lane
Queen Creek AZ 85243

www.rjbuckleypublishing.com
rjbuckleypublish@aol.com

DEDICATION

This book is graciously dedicated to the members of Wizards of Words and especially to the 25 published authors who contributed their diversified writing talents in order to produce this unique endeavor.

Thank you, my Fellow Wizards!

Rebecca Buckley, CEO
Wizards of Words

"All art has this characteristic – it unites people."
Leo Tolstoy

TABLE OF CONTENTS

A Collection of Short Stories

BREATHE

By Kevin Lucia

"What if no one likes me?"

Smiling, hair tie clamped between his teeth and pulling several stubborn hairs into place, Chris replied, "That's ridiculous, sweetie. You're the world's best friend."

Seven-year-old Madison frowned, chewing her bottom lip as she watched her favorite show about the lions who owned a whole library. "Everybody at St. John's is so different. What if I don't–"

"Fit in?" Chris held the base of the ponytail between his thumb and forefinger, whipping the hair tie out of his mouth, wrapping it around the pinched hair. Finished, he sat back on his heels to inspect the results.

The ponytail on the right stuck straight up like radar antenna; the newly finished one on the left drooped towards the ground. *Great, my daughter looks like a lopsided alien.* Shaking his head, he re-applied himself to the left ponytail to match it with the right one.

Madison spied her reflection in the television and frowned, "Daddy, that's not right at all."

Chris laughed quietly, "It does look a little weird, doesn't it?" He gently pulled it apart.

"Yeah, and if I have weird hair on my first day in school, I'll stick out like a big old freak," Madison quipped forlornly, her face far too serious for someone so young.

Chris sighed. Madison was bright for her age and had always exuded a slightly more mature air than the other kids, but she hadn't been herself for months. He missed her ear-to-ear grins and belly-shaking giggles, which had been absent since the accident.

He got them out of her occasionally; she was "daddy's girl" after all and he still had the magic, but for the most part his silly, exuberant, hyperactive little girl had turned into a dark-eyed waif repressed by sadness unfit for her youth.

Chris's stomach twisted. Death did that to people, especially seven-year-olds. He worried because she wasn't grieving, compartmentalizing her sadness just as effectively as an adult. It was human nature to cry, rage, and despair at the loss of someone vital, like a little girl's mother. But so far, Madison hadn't shown much emotion. She'd descended into a rock-like seriousness eating Chris's heart away just as much as any amount of crying could.

Another clump of hair slipped through his fingers, and he pressed his lips together while working doggedly at her ponytail, as if he could balance the cosmic scales by fixing them.

"I'm gonna stick out like a big sore thumb," Madison pronounced with the sage wisdom of a second grader.

"Why do you think that?" *Twist ... twist ... oh, geez ... that's not even close.*

Madison shrugged, fidgeting slightly. "Lots a reasons. They're all Catholic, and I'm P'esbyterian."

"It's Pres-byterian. Hold still; I don't want to make you bald on your first day."

Madison smirked ,"Not funny, daddy."

Chris caught a flicker of her old self and snorted, "I certainly thought so." He gathered more hair between his fingers. "Catholics aren't that different, Madison; it's not like they sacrifice cats—"

"Yuck. That's gross!" Madison made a face.

"And we all go to church on Sunday, right?"

"Yeah, but they have all those weird prayers and the communion wafers are yucky."

Quick fingers not quite nimble enough fumbled, dropping the hair tie. "Nuts." He scooped it off the floor and asked, "What else?"

Madison considered. "Most of those kids are rich. We're not rich."

Chris answered ruefully. "No we're not, honey, but we're certainly not poor, either."

"Yeah, but we're still not rich. All the kids looked at me weird when we visited. They think I'm poor."

Chris frowned in disbelief. "Madison, how can you possibly think that?"

"Cause they looked at me with their noses wrinkled, like this," she said as she gave her father an example in the television screen's reflection.

"Be careful about squinching up your nose, it might get stuck that way."

Madison exhaled noisily. "Uh uh, daddy. I asked Ms. Truman that at Bible Class last Sunday, and she said that's not true."

Chris laughed. "Yeah, right. Have you looked at Ms. Truman? She obviously didn't listen to her parents when they told her that."

Madison's face melted, her delicate hands flying to her mouth, as if God would punish her for laughing. "Dadd-ie," she huffed between giggles, "tha-that's n-not nice."

Chris allowed himself one more grunt, figuring he was toeing the line at ripping on his daughter's Sunday School teacher. "But so true," he whispered under his breath. He cleared his throat and said, "Well, that can't be all. What else?"

Madison's laughter faded as she looked down at her blouse and skirt, "Well, I'm not in dress code either. I'm supposed to be wearin' a green plaid skirt with a green sweater, and I'm all blue instead."

Chris started, because he'd forgotten to discuss this with her. "Well, I talked to Sister Rita, and she said because you're a late register you can wear any solid color skirt and blouse for the rest of the first marking quarter until your uniforms come in." He twisted the hair tie again around her ponytail. "How'd you know about that, kiddo? I didn't mention it because—"

"'Cause you forgot?"

"No," Chris said quickly, trying to save face while scrambling to hide his embarrassment at getting caught by a seven-year-old, "I just didn't want you to worry. Besides, how'd you find out the dress code colors?"

"The student handbook says so."

"What student handbook?"

Madison sighed theatrically. "Dadd-ie, it came in the mail two months ago."

Chris frowned, confused. "How'd I miss that?"

"'Cause you're the funny, messy one, and Mom's—"

Mom's the organized one.

The thought fell unfinished into a gulf of silence yawning between them, swallowing up their brief moment of levity. Chris' heart clenched as he saw the expressionless mask slip over his daughter's face. He swallowed tightly. Licking his lips, he barely managed, "Well, it's not a problem. Sister Rita told the teachers all about it."

"I'll still look different," Madison said in a flat voice, "and kids'll say stuff."

"Well," Chris said lightly, trying to re-inject the light feeling of the moments before, "if they do, just tell me, and we'll have them arrested for being meanies."

Her eyes flickered slightly, but her face remained impassive, stone-like. "Daddy, people can't be arrested for being mean."

"Sure they can," Chris replied as he unwound the stubborn hair-tie and reapplied it for what he desperately hoped was the last time.

Madison's lip gave a slight tremor upwards, but no smile. "Nuh-uh."

"Sure can; says so right in the student handbook."

The little girl shrugged her shoulders in a gesture so dismissive and grown up it made his heart ache. "Doesn't matter anyway."

Chris frowned at both pony tails, sure this time they were at least a little even. *Oh, for Pete's sake, now the right one is messed up.* "And why not?" he asked as he untied the hair tie from the right ponytail.

"Cause you're a writer, not a policeman. You can't arrest people."

Chris chuckled lightly at her precociousness. "Oh. Well, I'll make a citizens' arrest, then." He wound the tie around the right ponytail, tugged them both lightly upwards one last time, cocked his head, closing one eye as if judging a famous work of art, and then sighed. "Okay kiddo," he said, snatching a mirror and handing it to her. "How does that look? It's not Hillary Duff, but it's not Oscar the Grouch, either."

"Daddy, Hillary Duff's so … so yesterday." Madison looked in the mirror, squinted her eyes and shrugged. "It's okay."

"All right," Chris said, turning her around by the shoulders. "Let's make a last minute check and see if all the lights are green—"

"Are you going to die someday too, Daddy?"

A flash of saddened anger filled him at Madison's sudden, impromptu query, threatening to erupt like a geyser long held in check. He was angry that Miranda had been taken from them and that Madison had to wrestle with questions of mortality no child should have to face. Struggling to keep it from showing on his face, he reached out and grasped her tiny shoulders, squeezing firmly, careful not to hurt her. "No, sweetie … God, no. Not any time soon."

It was a lie; because there was no way he could promise that, and the worst thing was, he could see in Madison's eyes she knew it was a lie, too.

A small shake of the head, "But you can't say that," Madison whispered. "Remember when Peanut died last year?"

Chris frowned; he remembered the small tiger cat had passed away shortly after school let out, and Madison had been inconsolable for days. "I do, sweetie."

Madison stiffened a little as she spoke, "I asked Mommy that night if she was going to die; and she promised she wouldn't for a real long time; she promised."

A black hole opened up inside as Chris struggled to contain the swirling emotions in his gut. He exhaled a sigh filled with every ounce of grief that had tormented him the last few months, and he reached out, cupping his daughter's face lovingly. "Honey, I'm so sorry."

"So how can you say you're not gonna die for a real long time? Mommy said that, and–"

Chris swallowed thickly, and realized he had no answers for her; and also realized part of him had been secretly glad for Madison's past silence, because it spared him these questions. He blinked back hot tears as he said thickly, "Sometimes I forget how smart you are, kiddo." He patted his thigh. "Are you too old to sit in dad's lap?"

Despite the heavy-hearted atmosphere, Chris almost laughed as Madison said with a leery look, "I'll just sit next to you, 'kay?"

Chris smiled. "Good enough, pumpkin." His daughter scrambled her way onto the couch and Chris seated himself next to her, arm holding her close. She apparently decided she wasn't too old to snuggle, and a pleasant warmth filled Chris's stomach as Madison nestled under his arm.

"Honey, I'm not going to pretend I know more just because I'm a grownup. Bad stuff can happen anywhere, anytime. We could hide out here for the rest of our lives, but something bad could still happen to us here. It's part of life; we have to try our best not to worry about it. If we spent all our time worrying about the bad stuff in life, we'd never enjoy the good stuff."

Madison crinkled her nose in confusion, snuggling closer. "I don't get it."

"Well, take Peanut. What if we spent all our time being sad about her?"

Madison's brow furrowed with silent thought. "We'd be sad all the time and never get another cat."

Chris nodded. "Right. We'd never be able to enjoy another pet, because we'd be so sad about the one we lost, even though there are probably lots of great other pets out there we could have fun with someday."

Madison sat up, peering at Chris suspiciously "Are you gonna get a new mommy someday?"

Chris laughed even as his heart ached, "God no. I don't know if I'll ever be ready to do that."

Madison flounced back onto the couch with fiery, juvenile determination burning on her cheeks. "Good," she whispered under her breath, "Me neither."

"But the point is not really about replacing Mom, because we'll never be able to do that," Chris managed despite a dry throat. "It's about living after bad things happen. We can't be so scared of more bad things that we miss all the good things too." He paused, brushing his daughter's bangs off her forehead and added huskily, "I don't think Mom would want us to do that."

Madison sniffed, a solitary tear trailing its way down her rosy cheeks. "Me neither," she whispered, "but how do we do it?"

"Do what, sweetheart?"

"Be happy after mommy."

Chris sat silently for several seconds, feeling horribly inadequate to answer her. He exhaled a long, hard breath and slowly said, "You don't pretend not to care. It's important to feel things and let them out, so feeling bad isn't bad."

Madison cocked her head, looking at him with such inquisitive eyes, it was easy to mark her older than she really was. "How come we gotta let it out? Won't that make us feel sadder?"

Chris sighed, ruffling his daughter's hair and looking out the window. "At first, yes. But we can't hold it in forever; because it will build up, and then when it comes out, it's even worse." He leaned back a little and met Madison's dark-eyed gaze. "What happens when you shake up a can of soda?"

Madison blinked, a small light coming to her eyes. "When you open it, everythin' explodes all over."

Chris nodded. "The same thing happens to us if we hold it inside too long." He paused, searching her eyes carefully. "Do you understand?"

Madison looked down at her hands as she twisted her blouse's hem. "I guess so," she whispered, "a little." She bit her lip. "Do I gotta cry?"

Chris chose his words carefully, instinctively sensing this was a moment that couldn't be forced, and was better off left to develop on its own. "Yeah," he whispered, "everybody cries; it's perfectly okay." He paused before adding, "Cry when you're ready, kiddo. No rush."

"I wanna be a big girl, though."

"Sweetie, you are a big girl."

Madison looked down, kicking half-heartedly. "I heard a song on the radio last summer; about how big girls don't cry. I wanna be a big girl daddy; I don't wanna cry."

Chris allowed himself a wry chuckle. "Honey, Frankie Valli was many fine things, but a psychologist he wasn't. You can be a big girl and still cry."

"Promise?"

He kissed her head. "Promise."

"I'm not ready to cry yet. Okay?"

He squeezed her affectionately again. "Like I said, kiddo, cry when you're ready."

"Kay." She sniffed once and asked, "Can you fix my ponytails? They look weird."

Chris laughed, a small fire blooming in his heart at his daughter's impish grin that had been gone for so long. He gestured with exaggerated flair, "Of course, m'lady; I'm at your service."

Madison grinned, the dimples on her cheeks defrosting from a long winter as she slid off the couch. Chris resumed work on her beleaguered ponytails as the following minutes wove themselves together into a tapestry of love, remembrance, and connectedness.

Even though Miranda was still gone, the pain buried deep inside, Madison was there and so was he, and they were together. All things were right in the universe, even if only for this slice of time as a father braided his daughter's hair.

♦♦♦♦♦♦♦♦♦♦♦♦♦

Kevin Lucia writes for The Press & Sun Bulletin, a Gannett News Publication, and his reviews and interviews have appeared in Infuze, Title Trakk.com, Nappaland Internet Magazine for Families, and The Suspense Zone. His short fiction has appeared in Liquid Mind Dreams, Millennium Science Fiction Magazine, The Relief Journal, Infuze, All Hallows, and the EditRed Anthology "City Smells".

He resides in Castle Creek, New York, with his wife Abby, daughter Madison and son Zackary. He teaches high school English at Seton Catholic Central High School in Binghamton, New York; and is currently pursuing his Masters of Arts in Creative Writing at Binghamton University.

Kevin's short story "Making a Difference" placed in the 2007 WOW Short Story Contest.

www.kevinlucia.net.

THE FEVER

By Jeffery S. Miller

DAY 1

I arrived from boat on the Pickens Bay. The Amazon Rain Forest is beautiful and it surpasses all of the extravagant wonders I have seen the world over. Doctor Tina Brown of Holliman University was right when she told me I would see things of untold wonder. Trust me when I say she wasn't lying.

I had no idea it would be this humid. Of course, people told me about the heat of the tropics and I'd even read the reports; but this heat cannot be captured by words. Trust me when I say it is beyond hot. I traveled on foot to meet the others in my search party. Safety was my primary concern in crossing the terrain and anyone who knows me can verify it.

Doctor Leonard McCain informed me at the camp of the mysterious *Frog Plant,* which is the reason for me being here, that the *Frog Plant* supposedly contains psychedelic and medicinal properties in its DNA makeup. If the reports are true we have discovered the cure of the century, perhaps of the millennium. Doctor Brown even hypothesized on the plant's ability to cure cancer. It isn't supported by facts, but the locals claim to have used the plant in small dosages to cure all sorts of ailments. My imagination runs wild at the possibilities we may uncover. Doctor McCain was quick to tell me that some locals have died by merely coming into contact with the plant.

We will venture out in the morning to meet with the others who have congregated with the local tribe, so I will find out more about it then. By nightfall tomorrow, I'll write more in my journal.

DAY 2

Doctor McCain and I traveled further into the Amazon Forest today. It was quite a hike. We had a guide, but I can't pronounce his name and I don't even dare to try to write it. He seems nice enough, but he doesn't speak English and I don't know his tribal affiliation. In fact, I don't know a heck of a whole lot other than what happened today.

We arrived in the tribal territory around midday with the sun beating heavily through the leafy canopies. My first impression of the tribal leaders was kind of eerie. The main guy, who was a chief, pointed at me and threw a rock down by my shoe. I asked Doctor McCain what was the problem and he relayed the reason for chief's hostility, in English.

"He knows you're not a medicine man," he said.

He meant doctor when he said medicine man. People who are familiar with this report already know I'm not a doctor. I am just a journalist writing back to the University. I guess the chief didn't take kindly to a white man without a doctorate. I have no idea how he knew, it's not like people here wear white lab coats.

The chief called for a runner to deliver Doctor McCain and me to the location of the *Frog Plant*. The rest of our party was nowhere to be seen. I don't know how the kind doctor felt, but I found it quite unnerving that the tribal people don't wear clothes and they run around chucking spears at things. I think maybe I should have done more research about the people of the Amazon before I agreed to traipse off into the forest looking for a bizarre plant.

DAY 3 - Morning

We camped overnight with the tribal people. The bedding is dreadfully uncomfortable. I do hope we don't stay another night out here in this maddening heat. I awoke to a large python slithering by my sleeping quarters. Upon the sight of the thing, I jumped and shouted like a darn fool.

The chief was awakened by my childish behavior and threw a fit when he realized I was dancing and shouting over a large snake.

One of the tribal members blew a dart and the snake stopped moving. I asked Doctor McCain what was in the dart to stop the snake. He said it was traces of the *Frog Plant*. I don't know much about medicine, but how safe can a plant be if it can instantly kill a giant snake like that? The plant would have to be tamed somewhat before anyone could fully experiment with it on a human being. This isn't coming from a doctor, mind you.

This morning some of the tribal people skinned the snake. I say skinned because I don't think they have scales. As they hung the snake from a large tree branch, I watched as they used torches to burn the flesh as if to cook it. My assumption was right and they even offered me a bite from the hanging snake. It is needless to say, I declined the dinner invitation.

DAY 3 - Midday

The other doctors returned to camp with samples of the *Frog Plant*. The tribe was astounded by the amount they had brought back with them. They hadn't returned with one or two plants, they had gathered a large collection of it.

DAY 3 - Nightfall

Many members of the tribe have stolen samples of the *Frog Plant*. I sit on the ground watching them as if they are in some sort of ritual. Some are dancing and some are acting bizarre. One of the members just grabbed my hat and ran off with it. I do hope he returns it. Okay, he just brought it back to me. This is one of the most bizarre scenes I have ever encountered.

I just saw a woman ingest parts of the plant and she is acting as if she is in a trance. I will pause for a moment to see how long she will stay in the hypnotic state.

I have been watching the woman for almost twenty minutes and she is, as the younger people say, *stoned*. She hasn't moved a muscle and is staring heavily at the fire the locals have started. I'm not sure where the doctors are, but I am a bit terrified. I dare not make any sudden movements. I wouldn't want to startle any of them during their ritual. When I get back to the university, I'll be happy to reenact their jerky movements for further study.

DAY 4 - Midmorning

I slept on the ground once again. No snakes hindered my beauty sleep this time. I asked Doctor McCain if he had heard the ritual performed by the tribe. He replied he knew of it, but was not at camp. The doctors were doing research on other topics.

When quizzed of the other topics, he replied, "Mister Booth, we don't work all of the time."

I do not know what was meant by that statement.

While we walked across the jungle, we came to a large hill. The pathway had been made for us. Halfway up this hill, something managed to sting my left calf. I don't know what the creature was, but whatever it was, it was capable of stinging through denim. I became weary as we marched onward.

I now lie somewhere in the jungle recounting this. I have become definitely ill. My leg is swollen. Sweat is pouring out of me at a fast rate.

Doctor McCain is trying to keep me hydrated. I am not well at all. I have a fever. Hopefully a little rest will take care of my situation. If I'm not any better by morning, I will have to return to the research station.

DAY 5 - Midnight

Doctor McCain called for members of the tribe to take me back to the research station. I vaguely recall the return trip. My consciousness must have faded in and out. All I know is that I am being seen to by a nurse, named Betty Wellford. She seems to be good at what she does. She has given me some medication, but I don't know what it is. I am barely able to write this.

I will continue to write, thanks to the urging of Doctor McCain. He said an unknown insect species may have bitten me and further research would be required. I am to document my sickness. I don't know how well I'll do because sickness has overtaken me with a full head of steam.

DAY 5

I do not know how long I've been in this jungle. I am guessing it is day five because I last wrote at day four, I think. I am becoming weird. I do not know how to describe my feelings. Never has an ailment affected me as much as I am afflicted now. I think I'm seeing things. Either I have become unaware of my surroundings or I am hallucinating. A spider monkey just crawled across my chest as I lie on my cot.

Not wanting a wild monkey on my body, I attempted to swat the poor creature. The creature slapped my chest and ran off. It is not the creature's fault, for he is just an animal. I can hear the small creature as I write. It is screaming like a banshee and my nurse is nowhere to be seen.

The birds of the Amazon seem to be at rut, if there is such a thing. I recall the days when I would deer hunt in the woods of Arkansas. Deer would have a rut season. So why can't birds? Oh, what am I saying, birds don't come in rut. They have a mating season. Stop this! I must stop this madness! I believe I am losing my mind. I'll call the nurse.

After four attempts at calling Miss Wellford, she still hasn't shown up. I need a drink. Curse the Amazon! I have spilled the contents of my water pitcher. Please forgive me if my words come across as total nonsense. I am at odds with my own well being. I want to be a good little Indian and finish my documentation. The chief told me to. I do not want to let him down.

What's the use? Why am I writing this nonsense? I must be mad! I have become crazy; thanks to the little bitty bug that has bitten me. The heat is overwhelming. I feel as if I will die. I am in pain and cannot lift up to see my leg. Oh, the pain in my leg has been numbed. Maybe the nurse heard me when I called for her and gave me a shot. I don't know. I am determined to write. I will not let a spider monkey nor a nurse interfere with my journalistic duties.

I am petrified now. Cautiously I write my words down on this paper. I hope this is a hallucination. Fear has overtaken me and it is all I can do to write. This could be the end of me. A leopard is right outside. I can see him through the mosquito netting. If I die, send this report to Holliman University in care of Doctor Tina Brown.

DAY 6

I feel somewhat better, but the fever comes and goes. The leopard isn't here now. I can't say for sure if it was a hallucination or not. I guess I slept right after the sighting. I woke up and had my journal on top of my chest. I look back to see the things I have written and it is wild.

My head is hurting. I need more water. I just tried to get out of my bed, but I couldn't do it. There is no way I can stand on my left leg. I am in a world of hurt. The leopard would have taken me for an easy lunch. A person does not know fear until they are helpless in a dire situation. This, my friend, is a dire situation.

SOMETIME IN THE DAY

My fever has returned. I don't recall going to the bathroom, I smell an awful stench and it must be me. The Amazon is brutal for an American who is used to civilization. There are no showers here. I am not crazy enough to bathe in one of the rivers. Brine might swim into one of my orifices and begin to devour me from the inside out.

I was able to move my hand and now I am happy to report I have not had a bowel movement nor urinated. My body controls must be working somewhat. I would guess I am sweating so much that I haven't had the need to relieve my bladder. Food is nowhere to be seen, but there's a lot of whiskey. When I see my nurse again, I'll request a stiff drink. It may make my condition worse, but I refuse to be in so much pain while I am sober.

Curse it! The spider monkey is back! This time I am going to play with him. If he gets too close to me, I'll wring his neck! What am I saying? I can't hurt the little monkey. He just wants to play. No, I'll kill him. No, I won't! I don't even know what I'm doing. It must be the fever.

I decided to allow the monkey refuge on my chest. He stinks, but no more than I do. The monkey patted me on the head and I tried to stop him. The little bugger slapped me across the face. I slapped him back. The process repeated itself over and over again. Here I am, a grown man, returning face slaps with a spider monkey.

The spider monkey has returned. He has a glass of something. I'll try to get whatever he has. Well, he just drank it all. Now I have no chance of getting it.

The monkey just spoke to me. He said, "Don't look at me."

I swear, the monkey is talking!

I just attempted to stand again. I fell and hit my head on something. It was hard whatever it was. This is getting ridiculous. A talking monkey? I will kill that monkey for sure! He caused me to hit my head on this stupid thing where the nurse keeps her stuff. The monkey is running around my tent. He's not talking now, he's screaming.

The monkey made a mistake of running into me. I made the mistake of grabbing him. The bugger bit my right hand. What if I get rabies? I'm going to be laid up for God knows how long now. What diseases does a monkey carry?

DAY 6 – Night . . . I think . . .

The nurse has bandaged my hand. She said she heard a monkey screaming from the area earlier in the day. I asked her where she had been and she replied, "I have to pick up supplies, you know." She was kind of rude about it.

I can't help it! I'm stuck here in the stupid jungle with a monkey bite and insect sting. If she has a problem with being a nurse, get her out of here! I don't need her!

I was perhaps a little irrational when I wrote the preceding paragraph. I'm not against the nurse, but I think she should show some manners. The nurse was agreeable to bring me some whiskey. If I have my say over it, I'll drink my pain away.

God! That was terrible! I've never drunk whiskey before. My first shot just went down. I'll continue to drink it though. I refuse to be sober dealing with this pain. The mosquitoes are bad. I've been bitten a bunch of times while I'm drinking. I remember the first shot's taste and now I can't even taste the stuff. I must be drunk.

Yeah, I'm drunk. I hope you can make out my handwriting. Who is *you*? I don't even know *you*. *You* is the person at Holliman University. I must admit I'm having a good time. Why am I even here? Oh, yes. The *Frog Plant*. I wish the tribal chief would bring me a leaf or two. That could be fun.

I am stricken with a fever, drunk, and doped up thanks to Betty. I don't even know what I'm saying now. You're not saying anything, you fool, you are writing. Now I am laughing at myself. I'm even talking to myself in my journal. The drunk man says you're not talking, you're writing. He doesn't sound drunk, does he? No, of course not. He sounds like a wise man.

I am getting depressed now. Perhaps the drunk man has been too much for my fragile mind. I'm thinking of my high school sweetheart, June. I am thinking of June. June, only if you could see me now. I am a big shot journalist traveling the globe for Holliman University. I wonder where June is? Perhaps she's married and has a bunch of children. I would venture to bet she lives in a trailer house. Some of the rich trailer trash call them mobile homes. It's still a trailer, though. A man once got insulted in Amarillo because I asked where Ivory Trailer Park was located.

He said, "Son, it's not a trailer park, it's a mobile home division."

What a fool! He believed it was a mobile home, but I knew it was a trailer. Texas knows it's a trailer. America knows it's a trailer. If you find that old man, tell him it was a trailer park. Tell him I told you to say it.

This is crazy.

DAY 7

I woke up in the afternoon. The whiskey, drugs, and pain have really taken their toll on me. I haven't seen the little spider monkey. If he comes back, I'll tell him his new name. I named the little bugger. His name is Troy.

The Jaguar returned, I think, or is it a leopard? I don't know. I'm just writing because I have no strength to go back to see what I have written. I am just writing whatever comes to mind. That's what the good doctor told me to do.

I wouldn't wish this condition on my worst enemy. I am becoming delusional. Actually, I'm not becoming delusional, I am delusional. The mosquitoes are driving me crazy. I need to shave and the humidity is killing me. I'm going to remove some of my clothes. I am burning up.

I took off my shirt, but kept my pants on. I wouldn't want to give Betty a thrill. Now I know why these crazy locals don't wear any clothes. It's definitely too hot for clothing, especially when you have a fever. I need more whiskey because the drugs seem to be wearing off. My hand is pounding where Troy bit me. These monkeys should learn to stay away from humans. He's lucky I don't have a gun; I'd blow him from here to kingdom come. Actually, I would like to have a gun in case the leopard or Jaguar comes back. I'm not going without a fight.

DAY 7 - Night

Betty came to read me the newspaper from America. It was old news, but news to me. I asked her how long I've been under her care, but I didn't hear what she said. I think my hearing is going. While she read the political pages, I couldn't hear a word she said. All I heard was ringing. I swear, I'm not doing well.

Betty just left. She got mad because I kept asking her to repeat herself. I've never seen such a temperamental woman. She has red hair; I've heard things like this about red heads. I never thought they were true though. She left some whiskey nearby so you know what I'm going to be doing all night.

I'm four shots into the new whiskey bottle. This must be a different brand, because it's smooth. It doesn't have a jagged edge like the whiskey last night or whenever I last drank it. I just had two more shots and I'm feeling good. The drunk man feels no pain. Bring it on, Troy! I just shouted into the jungle. I don't care if I awakened Betty. She can get over it.

I'm starting to think Doctor McCain is a bum. He hasn't come to check on me once since he brought me here. I know he's a hotshot doctor, but he should show some compassion for a patient. I know I'm not his patient, but maybe I am. Who does Betty work for?

I'm starting to think I'd be best looked after in a medical ward. I shouted for Betty to take me to the hospital, but she was peeved I awakened her. Fine, just fine! I'll die here. I don't care. I'm in the Amazon Rain Forest and I'm going to die of fever or whatever I have. I'm not a happy camper tonight. I'm ready to fight. I wish Troy would show up. I would wring his little neck this time.

Even if the Jaguar or leopard shows up I'll fight him. This whiskey makes me want to fight. I just looked at the brand and it's a man's name. I can't read very well. I'm just writing on instinct. My eyesight is blurry and I am hateful. I'm not sure if it's the whiskey talking or the fever. It could be the drugs, too. I'm not sure, because I'm just a journalist.

DAY 8 - I'm guessing

I'm ready to die. I have a tremendous chill in this tropic heat. I'm not real sure how much longer I can stand it. I'm ready to start walking. If I fall down, just leave me there. I'm ready to die. Mark my words, when Betty's gone, I'm sneaking out of here. I'm going home to America.

DAY 8 - Night

Betty's sleeping. I'm going to leave now. I will take all of the whiskey I can carry. On second thought, I won't. I'll just drink a bunch of it before I head out. I managed to sit up in the cot. I injected myself with something. I don't know what it was. I'm feeling like I'm on cloud nine. I'm going to leave my journal on the cot. When you find this, send it to Holliman University in care of Doctor Tina Brown. Betty, it's been nice knowing you, but you're rude. I hope you show more compassion to your next patient. I will not tolerate any more of your rude behavior. I'm leaving now.

Doctor Tina Brown,

I am sending this to you as Sean Booth requested. The details are in the journal. He left and Doctor McCain found his lifeless body about a mile from here. I tried my best for this man and I don't blame him for his unfounded comments in the journal. He was sick and we will make arrangements to send his body back home to America.

Signed, Betty Wellford

♦♦♦♦♦♦♦♦♦♦♦♦♦

The author Jeffery S. Miller enjoys a good story. Robert Anton Wilson, Kurt Vonnegut, and H.P. Lovecraft are his literary influences. Miller enjoys experimenting with his writing style. From horror to comedy to the speculative genre, they have all worked their way into Miller's repertoire.

Jeffery was born in Conway, Arkansas and currently resides in the silver state of Nevada. To his credit he is the co-inventor of the Davis-Miller Clear Mailbox which led to Miller's terrestrial radio show on the Little Rock airwaves.

Many of his short stories are featured on Amazon.com along with two novellas. Miller enjoys spending time with family and his canine buddies.

www.freewebs.com/jefferysmiller

BLACK EYES AND BLUE TEARS

By Vicki M. Taylor

I lay face down on a sun-drenched beach. A deeply tanned stranger with a dark mass of shoulder-length hair strolled toward me. We locked eyes. He knelt down next to my towel. A slow smile turned his sharply angled face into a friendly welcome. He offered to rub lotion onto my back. I didn't resist. His strong, capable hands smoothed sunscreen onto my warm, bare skin. I practically purred beneath his touch.

His firm hands gently massaged my tight shoulders. Ah, this was exactly what I needed. I melted under his soothing stroke. I wiggled my backside between his bare legs, begging for more attention.

"Miss Anderson?"

He whispered my name into my ear; his hot breath tickled my hair. I sighed softly. The sharp scent of Hi-Karate burned my nostrils. Absently, I rubbed at my nose.

"Miss Anderson!"

I leaned my head back. Closer to his voice. His breath reminded me of . . . coffee. I wanted to see his dark, smoldering eyes. I opened mine and stared right into–

"Professor Stanton!"

The rest of the classroom burst into laughter. A red hot flush crept up my neck and settled into my cheeks. I didn't need to touch my face to know I looked like I had just received an instant sunburn.

"Welcome back, Miss Anderson. Nice trip?"

"Uh . . . I, uh . . . that is, I mean—"

"Yes, well, we know what you mean, Miss Anderson."

"Sir?" Oh, God. Did I say anything embarrassing while I napped?

"You were just going to explain to the rest of the class what the 'law of thumb' meant in the 1700s."

I sunk deep into my chair, wishing I could disappear. Sometimes life just wasn't fair. I prayed for a quick end to my torture. Anything. Flash flood, hurricane, terrorist attack, I wasn't picky at the moment. A full thirty seconds clicked off the clock before it happened.

"Brrr-rrr-nnnngg"

Saved by the bell! My prayers were answered. End of class. Students sprang from their chairs as if released from tightly wound springs. They bolted for the door. Relief washed over me.

I quickly gathered my books and backpack, then flashed a winning smile at my professor of Sociology. "I'll have to get back to you on that, Professor Stanton."

"You do that, Miss Anderson. I'll expect it on my desk tomorrow morning, in no less than five hundred words."

My smile vanished. My shoulders slumped. I cast a furtive glance toward my best friend Sara. She shrugged her shoulders as if to say don't look at me, you were the one caught sleeping.

"Good day, Miss Anderson."

"Yes, sir."

Sara and I filed out of the classroom behind the last of the students and made our way through the crowded hallway into the warm sunshine.

I squinted into the bright sunlight and breathed deeply. Classrooms always smelled like dirty feet to me.

"God, I can't believe I fell asleep in class again."

"What's up with you, girl?" Sara asked as she pulled her backpack off her shoulder and rummaged through it while we walked to the parking lot. Classes over for the day, we planned on spending the rest of the beautiful day on a real beach, not unlike the one I was daydreaming about.

"I dunno." I shrugged as best I could with the weight of my backpack. I guess I deserved that extra assignment Professor Stanton gave me, but he just doesn't understand what I'd been going through lately.

"That's the second time this week, you know. Shit! Where is it?" Sara searched frantically through her disorganized bag. "Damn it. Where are they?"

"Sara, why don't we stop for a– watch out!" It was too late. She walked right off the edge of the sidewalk and tripped over a small, thin girl sitting on the curb.

"Oh my God, are you OK?" Sara stood and pulled the girl up with her. "Did I hurt you? Bloodied? Bruised?"

I noticed the girl wasn't really very young, just small. Fragile popped into my head. I picked up the cause of Sara's distraction and zipped it to prevent Sara's life from scattering.

Sara, oblivious to what she had been searching for, focused her attention on the girl. She smoothed and straightened, brushing bits of grass and gravel from the girl's shirt. "Jeez, I'm sorry, I wasn't watching where I was– my God! Did I do that to you?" Sara held the girl's sleeve and stared at her arm.

"No, please. I'm fine. Leave me alone." The girl pulled away trying to cover her arms at the same time. Her fingers played at the frayed ends of her shirt, like nervous little butterflies. She ducked her head, refusing to make eye contact.

I stared at her arm too. Both of them. I saw bright blue-black bruises encircling her narrow wrists and arms before they disappeared from my sight under the worn shirtsleeves. No way had Sara caused that damage. Before I could stop, a low whistle escaped from my lips.

Ever concerned for wayward puppies and lost souls, Sara, the "touchiest" person I knew, put her hand on the arm of the girl and looked into her eyes. "Oh, girl. You need to get those checked."

"I said I was fine." She pulled her arm away at the same time tossing her long blond hair over her shoulder. She stiffly turned to go. We'd been dismissed.

Sara and I exchanged glances.

"Whatever, OK? I'm sorry about walking into you." Sara took her backpack from me, turned away, and headed for my car. I gave the girl's small, straight back one more look and followed Sara.

Neither of us said anything until we settled into the front seat of my year-old Mustang convertible enjoying the air-conditioned breeze.

I left the car in park, lowered the thumping tunes coming from the radio, and turned to Sara who had gone back to rummaging in her backpack. "Weird, huh?"

"Yeah. Finally!" She pulled out a pair of sunglasses and held them up in victory. "Yes!"

"Is that what you were looking for?"

"Yep. Gotta look cool in my shades while we cruise the boulevard in your fine new auto-mo-bile." She tossed me a large, sassy smile as she settled her sunglasses on her tiny, upturned nose and tossed her long curly dark hair. She turned up the radio until I could feel the thumping bass deep down into my very core.

We both laughed at her silly joke. I pressed the button to let the top down. We threw our cares to the wind as we headed for the beach. My best friend was also my weirdest friend, but I wouldn't trade her for anyone else in the world.

The stars in the night sky sparkled like tiny pinpricks of light shining through black construction paper. The moon shined brightly from its high perch above the water.

I curled my legs under me as I sat on a wicker loveseat and I breathed in the salty air. It smelled good. A kind of brackish, fishy, sandy smell. Only the Gulf of Mexico had that smell. It smelled like home.

I loved my little beach house. I was far enough from the water to avoid the rising surf during the occasional storm but close enough to hear the waves lapping at the crushed shells that lined the beach.

I'd finished Professor Stanton's punishing assignment hours ago. I went into lengthy detail about the English common law that decreed a husband had the right to punish his wife with a whip so long as it was no bigger than his thumb, hence the "rule of thumb." He should be satisfied that I'd learned my lesson about sleeping in class.

At least, I hope I learned my lesson. God, I had to start getting some sleep. I stretched my legs and leaned back into the cushions. I'd been sitting and listening to the water as I read more of my mother's journals. I couldn't put them down. They were the reason I slept in class.

Night after night I'd reach for them again, re-reading her words; imagining her life. Trying to comprehend the life she lived with my father until she snapped and killed him. What was their existence like? What made her stay? What made him beat her? Why? So many unanswered questions. I probably would never know the real answers. My only hope was that I could eventually help others before they ended up like my parents.

I put a lot of my hope into learning as much as I could from my new classes. After I changed my major last month, it was all I could do to keep from plowing ahead of the class material to get to real situations. So far, all I'd gotten out of the classes was that studying psychology and sociology meant a lot of reading and quoting theories. I wanted real answers - real answers from real people, not people who'd been dead a hundred years.

I pulled into the school parking lot the next morning much earlier than usual.

"Hey!" I shoved my watch into Sara's face. "What's going on? Look at this. We're early!"

Sara pushed my hand out of her face and stuck her tongue out. "Oh give me a break. I'm not always the one who's late."

Getting to class early is a great plus, I thought as I drove through the parking lot toward the front. I can park a lot closer to the building. Cruising through the first two lanes of cars, I searched for an empty spot. Suddenly, the car in front of me slammed on its brakes. I hit mine too, nearly toppling Sara from her seat.

"Shit!" Sara sputtered. "What's the big idea?"

I threw my hand in front of her to keep her from hitting the dash. "This idiot in front of me slammed on the brakes."

"You should have hit him, it'd serve him right."

"Yeah, you say that now, let's see what you say when it's your car. Florida is a 'no-fault' state. I'd have to pay for my own damages."

"Can you get around him?"

"No, he's stopped in the middle of the lane. So much for getting to class early." I tapped my horn hoping to make the person in front of me notice he was blocking the way.

The passenger side door opened and a cloud of blond hair floated out. Something familiar about the hair made me take a second look. "Hey, Sara. Look. It's that girl from yesterday. You know, the one you tripped over."

"Oh yeah, so it is. Huh. Blow your horn again."

"Wait, look." I motioned for Sara to watch. The girl leaned into the car, as if to get a kiss goodbye. Instead, she was hit full, across the face by the man behind the wheel.

Sara and I both gasped. We turned to each other, amazed at what we just saw. "Did you—"

"Did he just—"

We both started talking then stopped at the same time. "Incredible." I said.

"I can't believe that just happened." Sara held a hand to her lips as if she felt the sting of the slap the other girl received.

I slammed my hand down on my horn and let it wail. The blond turned quickly and then said something to the man in the car. He flung his hand out his side window and sent a single finger gesture in our direction.

Sara opened her window and yelled, "Oh, big man. Beat up little girls. Move your fuckin' car."

Between my horn blowing and Sara's mouth, we'd drawn a little crowd. I could see the blond gesturing to the man in the car. It looked like she was trying to get him to stay in the car and leave.

Adrenalin pounded through my veins. I almost wanted him to get out of his car and threaten us. I blew the horn again, just for good measure. The blond turned and looked at me. Her eyes wide with fear. I let go of the horn. Something inside of me twisted.

"Sara," I said without losing eye contact.

"Huh?"

"Get out and go make sure she's all right. Get her away from the car. And Sara, don't you go near that car." I added. I knew Sara would intervene if it got ugly. I wanted to find a parking spot quickly.

"You got it. That son-of-a-bitch isn't going to hit her again."

"Sara."

She stopped to turn as she shut the door. "Charlie, don't worry. I'm not going to do anything stupid. Neither is he. Not with all these witnesses."

"Be careful."

"I will. Go park the car. We'll be waiting for you by the fountain."

I could see Sara sitting next to the girl with the blond hair and a small crowd around them. Sara still looked furious. I hurried over.

"Hey," I motioned to Sara. "I waited and parked my car after I watched that guy leave campus. She all right?" I tilted my head in the direction of the girl staring at the ground. She didn't even lift her head to acknowledge that we were talking about her.

"Yeah. I think so. SherryLynn, meet Charlie."

"Hi, SherryLynn." I put out my hand to shake hers. No response. Maybe it was the crowd. I turned around and addressed the curious group that had gathered. "Hey, why don't y'all just go on and leave us alone. There's nothing to see."

As soon as the last of the lingering crowd wandered away, I heard a small voice.

"Thank you."

"You're welcome. Do you need to go to a hospital or something?"

"No, I'll be all right." SherryLynn gently touched her face. She winced as her fingers met the swollen flesh. I watched a vacant look pass over her crystal-blue eyes. Something inside of me told me that this wasn't the first time she'd been hit.

Sara was more direct and to the point. "Who was that son-of-a-bitch? Your husband? Has he hit you before? Should we call the police?"

SherryLynn shrank from Sara's demanding barrage of questions. She shook like a scared rabbit caught in a snare.

"Sara." I placed a calming hand on her shoulder. She got the message. "Why don't you head into class and I'll stay with SherryLynn for a few minutes, okay?"

Sara exchanged a long look with me before she grabbed her backpack and headed toward the double doors. This wasn't over. I knew Sara.

"There, now we got rid of the crowd. We'll just sit here for a few minutes until you calm down." I wanted to put her at ease as quickly as possible. Desperately, I searched my mind for past lessons about dealing with abuse victims. I could help her if I could just remember what to do.

We sat in silence. Students wandered past us without a glance. We were just two more students lingering outside the building before classes started. The splash of the fountain was mesmerizing and I stared at it lost in the rhythmic spray waiting for the girl beside me to stop shaking.

"SherryLynn, has this happened before?" I kept my voice intentionally soft and low. It made her pay attention.

She lifted her head, tears trailing down her cheeks, her blue eyes still vacant. Her tears shimmered like translucent drops. What was she thinking?

"He loves me, ya know … my husband Ray." She spoke with a thick southern accent. She must be a native Floridian – a rare breed. She clasped her hands tightly in her lap.

"Does he show you he loves you like this a lot?"

"He's letting me take these classes here so I can get me a better job."

"SherryLynn, look at me, honey." I took her cold hands in mine. "Has your husband hit you before?"

A tiny spark of recognition flickered in her eyes. The dark shadows already appearing. She was going to have one heck of a black eye.

"He hits me all the time." She whispered with quivering lips.

"Do you want him to stop?"

"I want him to—" She darted a look over my shoulder.

"SherryLynn! Git your ass in this car, right now."

"Ray wants me. I gotta go." She patted the concrete bench checking for anything she may have left behind.

"SherryLynn, wait, I can help you." I wanted her to stay away from this man. He meant nothing but trouble for her; I knew it. I wanted to help her.

"SherryLynn, don't make me come and git you." Ray's voice growled as he made his threat.

SherryLynn hurried to her feet and looked back over her shoulder at me as she walked away. "You can't help me. No one can." Then, with contrite in her voice, she called out to her husband, "I'm coming, Ray."

I watched in horror as he grabbed her by the upper arm and threw her up against the car door as if he meant to throw her through it. He was at least a foot taller than SherryLynn and a good hundred pounds heavier.

I stood quickly and half-stepped toward them. SherryLynn must have seen me or sensed that I would follow. She yelled, "Charlie, don't. I'm ok. I just fell, that's all."

"That's right, leave us alone. My wife is one clumsy klutz. She's falling down, all the time." Ray yanked open the car door and tossed his wife into the front seat as if she were a package. He could have cared less if the package had 'fragile' written all over it.

I had a decision to make.

I kept my eyes on the light blue car while I ran to mine. I would follow them for a short distance; just to make sure SherryLynn was all right. If I saw any more abuse, I'd phone the police from my cell phone.

I followed the car out of the parking lot and into traffic. I doubt if they even noticed I was behind them, so intent they were in their argument. However, it looked like he was doing most of the yelling and gesturing while she merely sat, taking it all. Each time he gestured vigorously, the car weaved in its lane.

I thought about the other cars on the road, drivers oblivious to the drama going on in the light blue sedan ahead of me. He better start paying attention to his driving or else he's going to cause an accident. I felt so sorry for her. Was this what my mother went through? Was Ray a younger image of my father?

A fire ignited inside of me. I had to help her. I couldn't let her become another statistic. Hope flared when I saw the car pull into a convenience store. Ray went inside while SherryLynn sat in the car. I parked and got out of my car and knocked on her window. She jumped in fright, saw it was me, and rolled down her window.

"What are you doing here?" She kept watching the front door of the store. I knew she was watching for her husband.

"SherryLynn, I couldn't live with myself if something happened to you. Would you let me help you?

"Charlie, you don't understand. Ray's not like this all the time. Really. He just—oh, God! Here he comes. Go on now, leave before he gets here."

"SherryLynn, you can come with me. I'll take you to the police, or to a shelter. Whatever you want." I couldn't let her go. A voice inside of me pushed harder. "I don't want anything to happen to you." My voice rose as I felt the anxiety crawl inside of me.

"Hey, git away from my car!" Ray's voice boomed loudly in my ear. He stood close to me, trying to intimidate me with his size.

My heart pounded in my chest, but my blood boiled. He wouldn't dare hit me. I kept one hand on the car door and looked him straight in the eye. "Your wife is my friend. I'm trying to help her. You don't have any right to hit her." I deliberately kept my voice even; speaking each sentence clearly. I had to show him he couldn't control me.

"Look, I don't know who you are, but this is between me and my wife." He spat the last word out as if it left a bad taste in his mouth. As an afterthought, he tossed SherryLynn a small packet of frozen peas. "Put that on your face."

"Charlie, don't get involved." SherryLynn whispered from her seat in the car. She touched my hand once with her icy fingers. The other hand gently pressing the cold bag to her swollen, black eye. "I'll be all right. Honest." She attempted a smile. "Ray, here, is all calmed down. We worked things out. Right, honey?" She reached out to tentatively put her hand on his arm. I watched, thinking it was as if she were reaching her hand toward a rabid animal, scared it might bite her.

"That's right, babe." He patted her hand in what he must have thought was a loving gesture.

I tore a scrap of paper from a notebook and quickly jotted down my telephone number. I pressed the scrap into SherryLynn's hand. "Call me if you need to talk."

I gave her husband a hard, intense look and said "I'll see you on campus tomorrow, SherryLynn."

"Sure thing, Charlie. I'll be there." Her voice was too high, too forced. I stared at the spot where their car had been long after it left the convenience store. I feared that I had just seen the last of SherryLynn.

Coffee cup in hand, I stepped out into the early morning mist for the newspaper. I breathed deeply of the wet, salty air. The gulf fog hung low over the trees. Mornings like this made me feel so isolated, so alone.

I tossed the newspaper onto the table and settled into a chair. My cup stalled half-way to my lips as I read the front headlines: "Murder-Suicide ends in fiery, fatal crash."

My insides went cold. My hand shook as I placed the coffee cup back on the table, sloshing coffee onto the paper.

I read the entire article twice before calling Sara. She picked up on the first ring as if she were expecting my call.

"Sara," my voice trembled. "Did you read the paper yet?

Yeah, I did. It was her, wasn't it?"

"Yes."

"He killed her didn't he?"

"That's what the paper said. Oh God, Sara. I tried to get her to come with me. I should have tried harder!" I slammed my hand down on the paper, covering the picture of the smashed blue car, half burned wrapped around a pole.

"Charlie, you can't blame yourself."

I sobbed into the phone. "I could have helped her. I should have insisted she get in my car."

"Then he would have killed both of you."

"So, are you saying my life was worth more than hers?"

"No, not at all. Charlie, I understand you're upset. But, listen. You couldn't force her anymore than he had a right to hit her."

"But, it's not the same."

"Yes, it is. You can't help her if she doesn't want help. Besides, you had no idea that it was going to get that violent."

"Sara?"

"Yeah, hon?"

"I'm not going to let the next one go so easily."

"That's my girl."

♦♦♦♦♦♦♦♦♦♦♦♦♦

Award winning author Vicki M. Taylor writes dramatic stories with strong women as her main characters. Her novel, "Not Without Anna" won second place in the 2003 Florida Writers' Association's Royal Palm Literary Awards and was published in January 2004. She won an honorary award for her short story, "And Justice for All" in the Fire to Fly contest from Futures Mysterious Anthology Magazine. Her manuscript "Out for Justice" won first place in the Romantic Suspense category of the RWA sponsored 2007 Golden Acorn Excellence in Writing contest.

A prolific writer of both novel length and short stories, she brings her characters to life in the real world. Her memberships include the National Association of Women Writers, Short Fiction Mystery Society; Romance Writers of America, and many more. She is published in electronic and print publications. She is one of the founding members and past president of the Florida Writers Association. She gives workshops and speaks to local writing groups about writing and promotion and also maintains an internet writers' resource forum.

When she's not writing, you will find her lurking about the many writing boards and various forums while sitting at her computer in Tampa, Florida - where she lives with her husband, their dog Jack, and their parrot Bailey.

Ms. Taylor is the elected 2008 WOW President.

www.vickimtaylor.com

DESERT STRANGER

(First Place Winner of the 2007 WOW Short Story Contest)

By Barbara Leachman

Jane Knowles slid the latch aside and opened the wooden door. Its rough scrape against the wooden frame echoed against the backdrop of the Rio Grande rushing from the north down to Mexico. The young woman smiled to herself remembering how many nights she and Michael had been put to sleep by its melody.

She stepped out of the cabin, faced the mountains to the east and watched the setting sun turn them from red-orange to grey-purple then fade into blackness. The full moon's light washed across the desert floor and silver stars winked at her from the night sky.

A coyote called in the distance and another answered. Jane hugged her arms across her chest and inhaled the night air. She wished Michael was with her and was sorry she had chosen to stay behind while he took Jessie and the wagon to Santa Fe for supplies.

Arising out of the mountain shadows, a silhouette appeared in the distance. Jane moved away from the doorway and strained her eyes to peer into the darkness. Michael? It couldn't be. He had taken the mule and wagon. This was a lone rider.

She watched as the figure neared, first as small as her hand then growing larger in the moonlight against the darkened mountains. What would Michael want her to do? Be hospitable? How many homesteads had they passed along their way out here? And how many settlers had hailed them and offered a meal? But those people had been couples, and Michael had been with her.

Jane hurried back into the cabin. She took Michael's shotgun down from the wall then blew out the lamp.

The clip-clop of the mount's hooves beat a rhythm on the hard desert floor until the rider came to a stop in front of the cabin. Leather groaned as he dismounted, then the door scraped open. Heavy boot steps scuffed on the wood floor as the stranger entered their home.

Michael pulled the mule to a halt and wondered at the fresh horse droppings near the front door. Flies droned around the manure, their buzz clearly heard in the late afternoon. Why did Jane have Buck there? Michael guided Jessie farther from the mess and into the trees where the mule gratefully started munching the tender grass.

"Jane," Michael called out but received no answer. He climbed down from the wagon, walked to the side of the cabin and looked into the trees for their horse. Where Buck had been tied were dried mounds of dung telling him the horse had been gone most of the day. Had Jane gone out for a ride or had Buck gotten loose and—no! That wasn't like her or Buck. She would never have been gone all day, and their horse had never wandered away. A sliver of worry crawled into his belly.

Michael circled the cabin and looked through the open window. The fear-sliver grew into a wedge. He hurried around the cabin to the front door. If Jane was there the door would be latched, but it opened easily. The wooden shutters on the front windows stood open which wasn't unusual during the day, but when they were away or during the night, they were kept closed to keep out the wildlife. Hungry cougars or coyotes could push open the door or jump through the windows.

"Jane?"

Ruffled bed covers. Jane would never have left them like that.

Their coffee pot hung over the cold fireplace. An empty cup sat on the table. Flies droned around his head. Buck's saddle sat beside the door where he had left it. Jane wouldn't ride without it.

Michael's eyes searched the room and stopped at Jane's trunk. A piece of cloth caught in the lid hung over the side. He opened it and knew something had happened to his bride. Jane's clothes were in bunches, a China dish from her mother in pieces. Only she would know if anything was missing.

Michael stepped out into the sunshine and looked across the desert to the mountains. A few yards from the river's grassy floor rose the dry land of chamisa, sage and prickly pear. He pulled the door closed and called Jane's name. He circled the cabin again calling out to her. He ran to the river and searched the banks and swift waters—calling her name. A few birds answered.

From behind him he heard Jessie's whinee-aw-ah-aw and the clopping of hooves. He raced back to the cabin.

But it wasn't Jane. A dark-skinned man dismounted a brown stallion. He lifted a log from the wood pile near the front door and slipped the reins beneath it before turning and seeing Michael. "You need something?"

"I'm looking for someone." Michael said.

The man rested his hands near the guns that hung at his sides. "Nobody 'round here 'cept me."

"Who are you?" Michael wished he had gotten his shotgun when he was in the house.

"The question is, who are you?"

Michael lifted his hat and wiped his brow with his shirtsleeve. He put it back on carefully straightening it. "Hot day," he said.

The man took a step forward. "I ast you a question."

Michael sensed the danger. "Like I said, I'm looking for someone."

"You see anyone 'round here?" the man said, his eyes never wavering.

"No." Michael said. "This your place?"

The man nodded. "Sure is."

Michael took a step toward the wagon. "Then I'd best be going."

"No need in that," the dark man said. A grimace of a smile turned up his mouth. "Come on in. I'll build a fire and brew some coffee. It gets awful lonesome out here, and I could use some jawin' with someone 'sides my horse." His arms relaxed and his hands dropped away from his pistols.

Michael hesitated then remembered his shotgun. "Thanks," he said. "I could use a drink of water."

"Got that, too," the man said.

The two men went into the cabin. The place where the shotgun should have been was empty. Michael's mind whirled. Who had it? The dark man or Jane? Maybe she had taken the gun and Buck, and they were somewhere out in the desert waiting for him. He needed to go.

The dark man pushed his black hat to the back of his head then dipped a cup, his and Jane's metal cup, into the bucket. Their bucket. He handed it to Michael. "River's pretty clean," he said. "That's all the water around here right now."

Michael drank and handed the empty cup back to the man who then dipped it in the water and drank from it himself. "You been out here long?"

"About as long as you," the dark man said and set the cup on the table. "Sit, mister," he said. "I think we need to do some talkin'."

"I really need to be on my way. I have a ways to go before dark and my wife will be looking for me." Michael started toward the door.

The dark man blocked his way. "Not so fast. I think something's going on here that I need to know about."

Michael felt a wave of fear and knew his expression gave him away. "Nothing's going on. I just need to go." Why had he come in for a shotgun when this man was wearing two six-shooters?

"Tell me who you're lookin' fur."

Michael didn't answer.

"Not talking?"

Michael shook his head slowly and let out his breath. "Look, I don't know who you are or what you're doing in my house, but if you want it, take it. I just need to find my wife and move on."

"So," the dark man looked around the room his eyes stopping on the trunk. "This is your place, is it? Yours and your woman's."

"Did you see her?"

"Now wouldn't you just like to know?" The man crossed his arms over his chest and grinned showing uneven yellowed teeth. "I can tell you this. She had a nice fire goin' for me when I come in."

Anger replaced the fear. Michael knew he wasn't as strong as the muscular stranger but he was taller and hoped he was quicker. He braced himself and ran toward the man. Arms outstretched in front of him, he hit the stranger in the chest and knocked him backwards. The man stumbled against the table. Before he could regain his balance Michael was out of the cabin and running.

He heard the shots behind him and saw their misses hitting the ground around his feet. He crashed through the trees and followed the river to the north. He ran until his breath came in gasps. After the first shots he heard no more. When he finally stopped, he looked back but saw nothing except trees and water.

For the first time in his life he felt a desire rise up he didn't know resided in him. He wanted to kill.

He slipped to the edge of the trees.

In the distance was his cabin. Jessie, still hitched to the wagon, dropped her head and pulled at the grass. Michael knew the mule wouldn't move unless the grass gave out or he himself climbed back into the wagon and urged her to go.

Michael's fear was for his wife. He needed to find out what the stranger had done with her if—and it was only a hope—if she hadn't run away before the stranger came. But this interloper had been in their cabin, had taken it for his own. Jane wasn't able to bring much with her to the desert and her most prized possessions were in her trunk. This man had touched them. He had lain on their bed.

The lust for the blood of the dark man boiled hotter in Michael's gut. He decided to go back the way he came. He would stay along the bank hidden in the trees, and he would find a way to kill the stranger.

Michael watched the dark man unload the wagon and carry the supplies inside. His supplies and Jane's. He imagined the stranger going through what he had bought in Santa Fe; the food, grain for planting, the Navajo rug and most of all, the silver and turquoise bracelet he'd chosen for his wife.

He looked near the river for a stone, a large one he could use to bash in the man's head while he slept. But Michael knew he wouldn't be able to take the man unaware in the cabin. The dark man would have the door latched and his pistols at his side.

The moon rose full and bright. The stallion moved into the trees to find more grass, dragging his reins with him. Jessie slept in front of the empty wagon.

Michael's stomach rumbled from hunger and he remembered the jerky he'd bought in town. He'd chewed on it as he drove back and had left some under the seat. He moved quietly to the far side of the wagon. He slid his hand under the seat and found the cloth bag. Jessie turned her head and watched, ready to move at her master's command.

"Sorry, Jess," Michael whispered and rubbed the mule's nose. He hated seeing the animal still harnessed. He moved back among the trees and devoured the jerky. The river water quenched his thirst, and he realized how tired he was. He moved farther to the south and found a place where he could watch the cabin but not be seen. He leaned against a cottonwood trunk and took off his hat. His eyelids drooped and sleep overtook him.

The scrape of the wooden door woke him. Michael crouched low and watched. The dark man stretched and unbuttoned his pants then urinated at the front door into the pile of horse droppings. Flies rose in the yellow stream, and Mike wanted to vomit at the sight. The dark man waved his hand to drive them from his body. He looked to the west and saw his horse in the trees. Michael watched him to go to his stallion. He tied the reins to a tree then lifted the saddle from the animal's back and carried it back to the cabin leaving the door open behind him.

A thin band of smoke rose from the chimney and Michael knew he was making coffee using their pot and their coffee grounds, and he had slept on their bed another night. The thought brought more fierce hatred to the surface, and under his breath, Michael cursed the dark man. He promised himself this day wouldn't end before the stranger died.

How would he do it? Michael grasped the stone he had chosen. One strike at the right time and the man's skull would be crushed. But how to get close to him, to take him by surprise? Michael moved toward the cabin, the trees hiding him.

He was close enough now to smell the bacon frying. The pork he'd bought for their breakfast. Soon the man would emerge and Michael could carry out his plan.

An hour passed that seemed like a day. He knew what the other man would do. It was natural, and when he did, Michael was ready.

The dark man left the cabin and walked to the edge of the trees. He wore no hat, his shirt open, its tail flapped around his hips, a gun held loosely in one hand. Michael watched him unbutton his pants and drop them around his ankles. He squatted.

Michael crept toward the man's back, his hand tightening around the stone. His boot sank into a soft hole in the ground. He flailed his arms trying to right himself and heard his ankle snap. Pain pushed him down, and he fell onto his back.

The stranger heard, twisted his body, and when he saw Michael, he raised his gun. From where he lay Michael sailed the stone toward the man. It struck the stranger's forehead and left a red mark. The dark man rubbed his head then reached for his trousers with his free hand but only getting them to his knees, they tripped him and he cursed. In a kneeling position he raised his weapon.

Michael struggled to rise but the movement sent crushing pain through his ankle. He heard the click and closed his eyes.

A deafening boom split the air and birds scattered from the treetops.

I'm dead.

Then he heard the oomph, like someone whose breath has been knocked out. He touched his own stomach, his chest, his head and opened his eyes. No blood on his hands. He lifted himself to one elbow. Just beyond his feet the dark man was lying, purple blood oozing from his chest. The silence was broken by a horse's whinny coming from the river.

Michael looked behind him.

Jane stepped out, smoking shotgun at her side, and smiled.

♦♦♦♦♦♦♦♦♦♦♦♦

Barbara Leachman is a transplanted Texan, born in Amarillo. She was in education for 23 years as a speech pathologist and middle school teacher. She taught everything, except math, including drama and yearbook. While teaching drama she wrote several plays for her students to perform.

She loved doing the school yearbook because she was able to create and write text and see it all in print.

From the time she could pick up a pencil, Barbara loved writing, even when the scribbles had no meaning. She has always been an avid reader, beginning when she sat on her father's lap and he read the Sunday funnies to her. In grade school, middle school and high school, she wrote short stories and poems for her friends to read. She was on the school newspaper and won a feature story award.

When Barbara retired from teaching, and never content to "do nothing", she became a certified health-care counselor, Doctor of Naturopathy and worked as a chiropractic assistant and wrote the doctor's reports. She has always kept a journal and has boxes of them in a closet.

Her husband passed away in 1997 and she began write in earnest.

She joined Tulsa Christian Writers and was awarded second place in a poetry contest. Then "The Demise of Bobby Mac" began to formulate in her mind, first as a short story then lengthening into a novel.

In 2003, she and an old grade school/junior high/high school friend began talking on the phone and emailing. Reid Leachman was a widower and by May of that year the two of them married in Santa Fe, New Mexico, and Barbara now lives in Albuquerque, New Mexico. Together they have six children and twelve grandchildren (several grand-dogs, a grand-cat and some grand-horses.) Her husband, a retired orthopedic surgeon, loves to travel and they have been to Hawaii, England, France, Italy and places in the U.S.

Today Barbara belongs to the Croak and Dagger chapter of Sisters in Crime, New Mexico Book Coop, Wizards of Words and South West Writers. She meets with three critique groups and attends various writing conferences. In 2006 she was named one of the Stand-Out short story writers at the Tony Hillerman Mystery Conference. In 2007 she won first and second prizes in Wizard of Words short story contest.

Her book, The Demise of Bobby Mac was published in June of 2006. She is working on a detective series and is nearing completion of "Penny's Worth of Murder."

Barbara is available for book signings and book club talks. Contact her at Leachman@comcast.net.

PICTURES

By Ray Myers

He'd been at it for three months, twenty-one days and nine hours; his second tour, hopefully his last. Another gig like this and Monty Groves was sure they'd have to clamp him in a strait jacket, feed him pablum and strained fruit and water through a straw.

The first one lasted more than five months. Odd that it left a taste for more. Why? Why a second time around? Was it the need to do his part, patriotism? To bolster his ego? The urge to satisfy a need, to do a better job, to be recognized?

His wife Nancy had tried to talk him out of it, but failed. Like a man unfulfilled, it was something he had to do. He had to go. Was he testing himself? Never before did he have the courage, the guts to prove his manliness. Sure the first tour had given him a buzz, as hyper a trip as any addict would take. He had wanted it again. But could it happen again? The excitement? The rush? No, this tour had proven to him that war was wrong. It was death, destruction, extinction, not an act to satisfy his needs nor staged for his entertainment. Damn his personal feelings, his involvement.

How much more of the slaughter could he take? How much could a body withstand? This was war, cut and dried. This was Iraq, the desert, hot and dry during the day, cold at night, never-ceasing winds and sandstorms that blotted out the sun and had you donning masks, handkerchiefs, crawling under blankets - anything to allow you to breathe. Misery!

Even more dreadful was the enemy, the danger, the fear that lay waiting around the next bombed out building, the next bridge, the next sand dune, the next bush. He felt for himself and sympathized with these kids playing their soldier games, some of them still in their teens and early twenties. But this was no game, this was the real thing. They had the same fears. They too had experienced the shellings, the infernal sounds of terror, the close calls. Like them, there were times he couldn't keep his food down, couldn't sleep, and suffered the nightmares. Yes, the nightmares of blood, lifeless bodies, frozen faces of the innocent, the victims, bloodied, torn and broken; so much wasted humanity.

Was it worth it? The high? Was it worth the recognition? The call to fame? Hah! What a joke. This tour had given him doubts. Would those be his reward, or would they be his regret?

His attention was diverted by the hulking figure of Gunnery Sergeant Gus Sims.

Strolling among them, Sims, a bear of a man, halted. "Ladies and gents," he announced in his steady, gravelly voice. "Last call for the latrines. Save some of your toilet paper."

A few feet away, Groves was listening to the gab, the voices of the frightened, trying to get a feel for the iron entering their souls and the fear gripping their minds. It was always the same, masks they wore to fend off the dread.

"What's 'at mean?" Pfc. Tim Harris asked the question of no one in particular. Harris was a recent replacement on his third day with the platoon. A rookie just out of rifleman's school.

"Ya don't wanna know," uttered Cpl. Jimmy Hester, pulling his boonie cover over his eyes. Hester chewed tobacco and had a psychotic penchant for washing his socks.

"No, damn it, I do wanna know," Harris went on. "What's he talkin' about, 'save some of your–"

"Well, if ya don't know now, you're gonna find out real soon," interjected Pfc. Freddie Brown, sitting up, dusting himself off. Brownie was a country boy, the comic and clown of the platoon. Every group had one. Oftentimes his humorous pranks and jokes were pointed; not cruel, but harmless in a way that gained acceptance from the others. Maybe that was what he sought, acceptance.

Within minutes, the voice of Captain Jess Craven, an up-through-the-ranks vet on his third rotation, late-thirties, tall and slender; a recipient of the Distinguished Service Cross and a chest full of combat ribbons, declared loudly as he stepped over reclining bodies, "Play time, girls and boys. Off your asses and on your feet! Check pieces and ammo." Craven was a good leader, well respected by his people; a man easy to follow. He was counting the days, and at last count he had 143 before handing in his bars and boots. He was ready for it. He and his son had invested in an upholstery shop back in Bloomington, Indiana.

Cigarettes ground into the sand. Voices of grumbling, snorting solders were heard as the rattling of gear settled on dusty uniformed shoulders. Grinding pebbles gave way to heavy boots.

Cpl. Calvin Denton stuck his gum behind his ear.

Pfc. Eulala "Lalaland" Covington stomped dust from her boots and fell in formation.

Pvt. Eldon Pryce licked his lips and followed suit.

Some stretched, some had their heads down and some crossed themselves in silent prayer.

Again the familiar voice of Sims sounded, "Let's move out, kiddies! Gonzalez, take point. Pudge, rear." He paused as he looked around, "Phillips, fer crissakes, tie those damned laces!"

"Where to this time, Cap? Gay Paree? Rio? Mebbe even Vegas, huh?" The questions came from someone in the middle of the formation.

"Knock it off, Brownie," Sgt. Sims ordered. "You'll know when we get there." Sims, himself, had a collection of medals and ribbons that would give a pack mule a hernia. He was an eighteen-year veteran who knew the ropes, Semper Fi to the bone. On and off, he and Craven had served together since the comedic exhibition the bureaucrats labeled the Gulf War.

"Yeah, Brownie," chimed in Pfc. Jeanie Samples, five-feet, five-inches, 128 pounds, as she popped him across his helmet. "What the hell diff does it make? This is Iraq. You're not bird huntin' back in 'Bama."

"Aw, d'ja hafta do that?" Brownie frowned as he straightened his helmet.

"Yeah Samples, pick on someone your own size," added a voice behind them.

Muffled laughter.

"I said, knock it off back there," growled Sims.

What was left of the platoon—fourteen men, three women—began another sortie, another stroll into hell. Not a soul would bet they'd make it back. How many would sleep under blankets tonight? How many dreams? How many nightmares? How many would wake up screaming? It would be a wild guess none would gamble on.

Groves knew them all; their names, hometowns, hobbies, most of their peculiarities, their strengths and weaknesses, frailties. Fresh in his mind were the two they'd lost: Second Lt. Ron Strumpf, Boston College, class of '05. Strumpf's fiancée was named Rachel, a dental technician from Lexington. Then there was Cpl. Arty Boyd, former Eagle Scout from Fort Collins, Colorado. A pitcher on his high school baseball team; could toss a grenade 40 yards and hit a dime.

Groves was 31 years old with a degree in journalism. He was a photo jockey - nickname for photo-journalist, the epithet was fine with him. He had worked for the *Charlotte Enterprise*. His wife's name was Nancy, one of two people he cared for the most. The other was their only child, Annie - eight years old, smart kid, hyperactive, a swimmer who hated boys especially Robbie Pierce who teased her too much. Groves longed to see them both, hold them, and tell them how much he loved them.

He, too, checked his gear: cameras (latest model Nikons on the market), 4-gig SD cards, three sets of lenses and film packs. He went over the mental list. Satisfied, he grunted, tossed the back pack over his shoulder and joined Craven at the front of the column.

Craven second-guessed him. "A palm grove three clicks northwest of Al Hillah. Insurgents dug in. There's gonna be action. And, Monty, don't want you up front, understand? As always I'll give ya the thumbs up. Till then, find ya a hole and stay put."

"Roger, Cap, thumbs up," Groves replied.

On they walked. Talking meaningless chit chat, trying to put their minds on other matters. The inevitable was a certainty filled with the fear of injured men and women, maimed or dying. Think about anything but that, anything.

Temptation was overbearing. Pvt. Donnie Brasher broke the silence, "Seventeen of us. Hey, Perfesser, what're the odds?"

"Depends," Cpl. Jason Northcutt replied. "We've been pretty lucky to this point." Northcutt had a degree from Ol' Miss; could've gone to OCS, but opted for front line action , wanted to experience the real thing. He was even tempered, articulate, scholarly, reader of classical mythology. Kept a diary.

"Depends on what?" came another voice.

"Well, the strength of the enemy, their armament, equipment, terrain, numbers. You say there are seventeen of us? They could be as many as fifty, sixty."

"Got it all figured out, eh, Perfesser?" Brasher snickered.

Northcutt let it slide. "Tell me Brasher, how many've you been on?"

"Oh, I don't know. Nine, ten. Who the hell's countin'?"

"Then wouldn't you agree that one's enough? You say nine or ten. If that's so, then I'd say your odds are getting slimmer."

Brasher's face became blank, uncaring. After all, it was just small-talk. Like most of them, he believed he was invincible. All those within earshot became silent, trudging onward, each wondering what their own odds might be.

Groves clocked it at two hours and twelve minutes, a lifetime. And for some, it had been. Another ear-splitting interval in hell, palls of agony and hideous, painful screams. Prayer. Sand spraying; ricocheting missiles of death; cries of the injured; gasping moans of the dying. His palms were sweating before they reached the culvert.

The fight began long before that. Five rag-heads were firing long range from a battered, stunted grove of palms and overgrown weeds, their shots falling short by yards. Two others with Russian AK47s were firing from behind what appeared to be the mangled walls of a nearby mud hut.

Slowly the platoon advanced - crouching, crawling, and creeping, sliding from one small hillock, dune and trench to another. First 500 yards, then 250 yards. Ever closer they came.

At 200 yards, Sgt. Sims took out the hut with one shot, a rocket launcher. Closer still, 100 yards. Two turban-twisters were brought down on a dead run for the hut; their bodies twisting eerily in mid air like puppets on twisted strings. Finally, 50 yards. The three remaining hostiles lay crumpled in grotesque, lifeless postures, gaping holes in their heads from short range snipers.

Groves got the pics. That's what he was good at, anticipating the live action shots, another reason he was there.

Finally the calm, the suffocating silence. It was over.

Craven stood, "Gonzalez, Ritter, check out the perimeter. Go!"

Two figures ran low, running fast for the cover of the far ditch. Ever wary, two Garand subs at the ready.

Once more Craven called out, "Who's down? Anybody get it?"

A voice yelled back, "Phillips. Yeah, Phillips."

"How bad," came the reply.

"Corpsman's got him, Cap." Then a hushed appeal, "Oh God, no. Looks like he triggered a mine. Oh Jesus!" The rookie Tim Harris bent over and threw up his breakfast.

"Anybody else?"

Sims, from across the road, leaning over a figure called out, "Reggie. Yeah, Washington's took it in the neck."

A bitter silence.

"Status? Gimme the goddamned status. Is he dead?" yelled Craven.

"Roger that."

"'S'that it? Headcount, Sparks get me a headcount."

"Oh Jesus! Corpsman!" screamed Jeanie Samples. "My leg, my arm! Oh sweet Mary, mother of God! Corp–"

"Hang in there, Samples," Corpsman Olin Schmidt called out. "I'm comin', jist hang tight!"

During a lull, Groves found a downed tree trunk, situated himself and began jotting down the vitals:

(1) Phillips, Eugene, age 24; Cpl.; Oswego, NY; land mine. Then he thought to himself, *poor kid; won't be tying any more bootlaces.*

(2) Washington, Reggie, age 19; Pfc.; Midland, TX; *ex All-State wide receiver, turned down Angelo State scholarship to follow dad's footsteps;* throat shot, KIA (killed in action)*; a talent wasted.*

(3) Samples, Jean Marie, "Jeanie," age 21; Pfc.; Modesto, CA; *JC*

grad fed up with school; never said much; bullet wounds left shoulder and bicep, broken left fibula from fall in culvert; profuse bleeding; latest prognosis--not good.

He replaced the notepad in his pocket. *Kids! All kids. A voluntary army of kids. Kids who deserve more. Lousy-assed war!* He got his pictures, as gory as they were. That was his job—get the damned pics.

“Show America exactly what they don't want to see,” his editor Spike Welborn had said. "If we get enough of the grotesqueness, the reality of blood and guts, maybe somebody will step forward and stop the insanity."

Around dusk they returned to base camp. Groves typed up the message identifying the dead and injured. In short snips he wrote of the event giving the when, what, where, the gaudy record of events in step by step, minute by minute sequence. Then he slipped the SD card in the lap top and sent it out. *Cyberspace, a whole new world, a whole new war.*

Shortly before noon on the next day, Groves received his mailed copy, turned to the page, and found the story and pictures. No effort, no reason to search, there they were, boldly staring back at him.

He froze. "What the–" He shook his head. "This can't be!" He couldn't believe what his eyes were telling him, the shock invaded his mind. It had to be some sort of a joke.

He threw the paper on his bunk and picked up the laptop. Quickly, he typed the IM message: "Good one, Spike. Real funny. Now fax me the real thing." He pressed the key and looked back at the article.

The answer came across in seconds, "The real what? Heat gotcha, pal?"

"The real story, authentic pics. The ones I sent you."

"Hey Mont, you got it. What you see is what you get. What’s the problem, anyway?"

He had no answer. Spike wasn't one to pull pranks. He closed the laptop, re-read the article and burned the picture into his mind. Awful mistake! This was an unconscionable mistake. He couldn't fathom what he was seeing.

The face of Gene Washington was not Gene’s face. What was going on? He looked closer, carefully focusing, studying each of the three. The faces of Phillips and Samples were there.

Upon further examination of the space where Washington was supposed to be, a familiar face began to take shape - features well known to Groves. A face from his past. *Marvin? M&M? Marvin Matson, my college roommate?* He felt dizzy, nauseated. *Ridiculous! Ludicrous! What the hell is this, Twilight Zone?* What was happening to him?

The docs had a name for it, BF, battlefield fatigue. No! No way. He was no soldier. He was a photographer, recording battles with a camera, not a rifle. But then, did it make a lot of difference? It was still blood and bodies that once were. He was a willing witness. In this hell anybody's mind could fail, go berserk.

He fell back on the bunk, racking his brain, trying to make sense of it. Peering around, he folded the section, placed it under his pillow and fought sleep.

Three weeks passed. He was back in Charlotte. Back on the job, back at the eight-to-five. The article he'd written had contained the original pictures of the soldiers: one, a black American with a hole in his neck the size of a golf ball; another, a kid not yet twenty-five with bloody stumps where healthy, attached legs used to be; and a third, a twenty-one year old blonde "valley girl" on a gurney, bleeding from gruesome wounds. It still haunted him.

Spike passed by his desk and stopped. "Hey Mont, you went to Cap State, didn't you?"

Groves nodded.

"Did you know this guy?" He held the paper up for a closer look.

"Name's Matson. You happen to know him? Went to Cap State. A drive-by shooting. Got it right through the neck."

Groves slumped, legs weak. He gasped for breath. How? How could this happen.

He reached for the briefcase, opened it to the page and glared. Eugene Washington's face was back in its proper place. Unbelievable! He gazed in awe for several minutes. Folding it, he sat back, heart pounding, fingers twitching nervously. Washington? Matson? Shot through the neck? Nah! A coincidence. He unfolded the page for another look. Indeed, Washington's face was there, not Matson's.

His eyes moved to Phillips face, looking closer. "God, no! Impossible!" He was staring at the face of his uncle Chuck on Phillips' body. Thoughts came fast, crashing, dizzying. Crazyiness! It was maddening. Hallucinations? Yeah, that's what it is. Maybe if he took a long walk? Got drunk? Then maybe things would come out right. Or, maybe if he talked to somebody about it. Friends. No, he knew what they'd say, "Whacha smoking, man? What you need is a shrink." Yeah, a shrink. No, they'd stash him away in a kook clinic; he wasn't crazy. What about Nancy, his wife? No, too practical, she'd never understand. Don't involve her.

An idea! He dialed a number.

She answered on the fourth ring.

"Aunt Grace? This is Monty."

"Oh my, Monty, it's been so long. How are you?"

"Aunt Grace, this is important. Can I speak with Uncle Chuck?"

"Chuck?" An odd silence. "You haven't heard? Why, of course not, you've been away."

"Heard what?"

"Monty, your uncle Chuck's in the hospital."

"Hospital?"

"Yes. You know, his diabetes. One thing led to another, Gangrene set in. They're amputating his left leg this afternoon. They took the right one two months ago."

He dropped the phone, feeling it bounce against his knee. This cannot be. It's mad! The similarities, were they forewarnings? Premonitions? Omens? He didn't believe in omens, ghosts, and haunted houses. But it was happening, right in front of him. First there was Washington and Matson, both shot through the neck. Now, Phillips and his uncle, one dead, one alive, both without legs.

That left the picture of Jeanie Samples.

His inner voice challenged him, *Do you dare? Go ahead, take a look, what do you see?*

Frantic and shaken, with trembling fingers he reopened the paper one last time. His eyes wandered, unsteady, trying desperately to focus on the shadowy figure on the gurney. At first he saw the hair. It wasn't blonde like Jeanie Samples, it was darker. No. It's not possible. The face, he had to focus on the face. Second by second it came more clearly into view.

He stared for a moment in horror, dropped the paper and screamed, "NO! Dear God, NO!" *NANCY!*

♦♦♦♦♦♦♦♦♦♦♦♦

Ray makes his home in Sun City, Arizona and is a retired specifications and documents editor. With him golf is not just a hobby, it's an addiction. Other hobbies are reading, watching sports on television, and working as a 'sometimes' writer. He's authored three mysteries - a trilogy involving a top secret agent: "The Saturn Profile," "Twist the Wind," "And Janus Wept." His fourth book, "Once Yer Ded, Asprin Don't Help None" is available through Amazon.com, Barnes & Noble and Borders Bookstores.

Presently, he's laboring over his fifth book and expects to complete it within, oh let's say within the next two years or so (it was mentioned that he's a 'sometime,' writer, remember?)

If you'd like to contact him about his books, or shoot the bull ...

rskuter3@cox.net.

STORM

(Placed in the 2006 WOW Short Story Contest)

By Cecelia S. Davis

Mrs. Jenkins took off her apron and lifted her sweater from a hook on the screened-in back porch. “Kenny!” she called from the window. “Come to the house for a minute and don’t let the screen door slam.”

“Yes ma’am,” Kenny said, brushing hay and dirt from his overalls before going into the house. “Do you need me to get something for you?”

“No, son,” she said. “I wanted to let you know your cousin is coming to spend the weekend and I want you to be nice to her.”

“Oh Ma, she’s just a dumb old city girl.” Kenny started to protest even more, but his mother held up her hand.

Melissa is 10 years old now, so she shouldn’t be too much trouble. Anyway, your pa and I are putting you in charge of the farm while we drive into town for a few things. There are sandwiches in the refrigerator in case you get hungry.”

Kenny Jenkins had lived all of his 13 years on a farm in Kansas. There were things a city girl just didn’t know and that frustrated him. Besides, the last thing he wanted to do was to be left with his female cousin. He still remembered her as being a bratty little kid who Uncle Simon and Aunt Jenny dropped off once in a while so they could run errands. When she came for a visit two years ago, she kept jumping from one thing to another. First, it was “Kenny, I want to see the cow.” So he took her to the barn to see the cow. Then she wanted to hold a chicken. So he had to catch a chicken to let her hold it. He had work he was supposed to be doing, but he couldn’t do it because he had to keep chasing after her.

After his parents left for the 50-mile stretch to town, he watched his uncle’s 1965 Pontiac pull into the drive.

“Hi, son. Where’s your pa?” his uncle asked, getting out of the car.

“Hi, Uncle Simon. He and Ma had to drive to town. They’ll be gone for a while.”

It made Kenny cringe when Uncle Simon called him "son". Every time he and Aunt Jenny visited, they always wanted money or to dump off one of the kids. Well, Pa wasn't home and Uncle Simon wouldn't get any money from him even if he did have a savings. It wasn't his fault his aunt and uncle spent their money on what he considered foolish things. Ma had told him not to be too hard on Uncle Simon. They were just having trouble making ends meet for now.

"Okay, now," said Uncle Simon as he set Melissa's suitcase on the ground. "You two go on and play. We'll see you later."

"Play," Kenny muttered under his breath. "He must think that's all I do, that and takin' care of a dumb ol' city girl."

Melissa kissed her parents goodbye and waved as they backed out of the gravel drive that led to Highway 53. Kenny looked at her and noticed that somehow, Melissa looked different. She wasn't as skinny as she was the last time he saw her. Her clothes fit tighter. But he made up his mind she still wasn't going to hang on him while she was there. He had promised to be nice to her and that was as far as it was going.

Kenny frowned. "Well, Lissa, what do you want to do?"

"Can we go bike riding?" Melissa asked.

"Sure," he replied half-heartedly.

Kenny took Melissa's suitcase to the spare bedroom. "Let me get you a pair of overalls so you don't tear your skirt," he told her.

After he left, Melissa sat on the edge of the bed, frowning. "He probably doesn't want to be bothered with me," she whispered to herself.

Kenny knocked on the door, making her jump. "Here. I hope these will fit you." She took them, and he closed the door and waited in the kitchen for her.

It wasn't long before Melissa joined him wearing the old shirt and overalls he had given her.

"Do you want a sandwich or anything?"

"No thank you," she said.

The two of them went to the shed and got out the bicycles. A tire on one of the bikes was almost flat. Kenny thought about giving that one to Melissa, but for some reason, he decided not to and gave her the better one. He used the generator to put air in the low tire.

After riding for a couple of hours, Kenny noticed thick, black clouds starting to form in the darkening sky.

"Let's head back," Kenny yelled, pointing at the sky.

When they reached the farmhouse, they put the bikes back into the shed.

"Melissa, you get the chickens into the barn. I'll lead Old Bessie to her stall."

"What?" shouted Melissa. "I can hardly hear you above the wind."

Kenny motioned to the chickens. Melissa understood and she began shooing them into the barn. With chickens going everywhere, it was harder than it had looked.

"Come on!" Kenny called to her. Kenny, Melissa, Shep the collie, and Freckles the cat ran into the barn. "Down in the cellar, hurry!" Kenny lifted the trapdoor. "It looks like this is going to be a big one."

Kenny grabbed a kerosene lantern on the way down the steps. He took a match from the matchbox on the shelf and lit it. "Might as well have a seat," Kenny said, putting the lantern on a crate.

Melissa looked around at the boxes of canned food and blankets on the shelves. Outside, the wind howled and moaned.

"Kenny—" She could hardly speak. "I'm … s-scared."

"I know, Lissa. So am I." Kenny would rather do anything than to admit he was scared, but he could remember the last storm that came through, swallowing up everything in its path and then spitting the objects out miles down the road.

"Come here, Shep," Kenny said. The four of them sat on the floor next to an apple crate - Melissa with the cat and he with the dog.

Kenny couldn't stop shaking as he reached for an apple and wiped it on his shirt before taking a bite. He and Melissa looked at each other, too scared to say a word.

CRASH! Something heavy fell on top of the barn.

"Kenny!" Melissa screamed as she grabbed her cousin, nearly squeezing the life out of him. The cat jumped from Melissa's lap and hid behind a box.

He thought about pushing Melissa aside and telling her to grow up, but since he was just as scared, he said nothing. Shep whined again and Kenny buried his face in the animal's fur. All three huddled together.

Everything was quiet. Kenny wondered if the storm was getting ready to hit the barn again or if it was over.

"Lissa, you stay here till I tell you it's okay to come up," he told her. He took the lamp up the steps with him and lifted the door. The storm appeared to be over. "Okay, it's over," he called to her, motioning for her to come up.

When she reached the top step where he was waiting, Kenny blew out the lamp and placed it back on the small shelf. Even though Kenny had been through several storms, nothing could have prepared him for what he saw when he stepped up on solid ground.

"Oh no! Bessie!" he gasped as he ran to her. He knelt down and touched the gentle animal he had fed and milked from the time he had been old enough to help with the chores. Tears came to his eyes and he brushed them away quickly.

"Kenny?" Melissa stepped cautiously near him.

"Don't get too close, Lissa," he told her. He didn't want her to see the cow under all the rubble. He had hoped she hadn't seen his tears.

"Maaaa! Maaaa!"

The two of them furiously dug under the roofing, trying to get to the animal that was making the sounds.

"Well, would you look at that?"

"A baby cow," Melissa said in wonder. "He's so small."

Kenny helped the calf to its feet.

"Kenny! Look!" Melissa said, beginning to cry. She reached down and touched Old Bessie.

"Lissa, I told you not to get so close!" His tone made Melissa cry even more.

"I'm sorry, Lissa," Kenny said. "There isn't anything we can do for her now. But we do have a newborn calf to take care of."

Melissa knelt down and petted the wet, curly fur on the calf.

"Is he going to make it?" she asked.

"We have to get some milk into him somehow," Kenny told her. "I'll get the animal bottle Pa keeps in the shed. You stay with the calf."

Before she could protest about being left alone, Kenny was gone. He returned shortly with some milk he had gotten from the house and a small animal bottle. He forced the bottle into the calf's mouth, but it wouldn't suck.

"Looks like a stubborn one. I'll have to try something else," Kenny told her, looking around at what was left of the barn. He couldn't stop the tear that trickled down his cheek. He and Pa and some friends from another farm had built this barn, now it was reduced to almost nothing. Now he understood what it meant to have good friends and neighbors. They would help build another barn. He spied a bucket still hanging on a partial wall. "Will you get that bucket over there, please?" he asked.

Melissa stepped carefully over debris and got the bucket. She watched as Kenny poured the milk into it and then he dipped his fingers into the milk. Kenny laughed as the calf sucked the milk from his fingers.

"Here, Lissa. You give it a try," Kenny offered.

"Are you sure a dumb old city girl can manage?" she asked.

"Oh," Kenny said, almost ashamed. "Look, I've been thinking. I want us to be friends; not just cousins. Okay?" He stuck out his hand. Where in the world did those words come from? Oh well, he had said them and Pa always said if you say something, own up to it.

Melissa looked at his hand for a second and slowly reached for it. "Okay. Friend."

"How about it, Lissa? Do you want to try feeding him?"

"Okay," she said. She dipped her fingers and they both laughed as the calf started sucking the milk from them.

After a few minutes Kenny said, "I'll put some milk back into the bottle. I think he's got the idea now."

"May I feed it to him, please?" Melissa asked.

"Sure," he told her. "You can do that while I take care of Bessie. I can't just leave her lying there." He showed her how to hold the bottle up so the calf could suck and then let her take it. He watched her as she held the bottle and put her arm around the calf. When he was certain she was doing it right, he turned back to Bessie.

He didn't know how he was going to handle such a large animal, but he started removing the pieces of rubble that had buried her. "Maybe she isn't such a dumb old city girl after all," he said just a bit too loudly. Just as he picked up the last piece that had fallen on the cow, the red pickup turned off Highway 53 and pulled into the drive.

"Kenny! Melissa!" Mrs. Jenkins shouted as she jumped from the truck. She saw Kenny where the barn was and ran towards him. "We were so worried when we heard about the storm that passed through. The police wouldn't let us leave town until the storm had passed. We got here as soon as we could. Are you all right?"

Kenny told her about Old Bessie and the calf and how Melissa had helped with everything. "You know, Ma. Lissa isn't half bad," he added.

"I knew she wouldn't be, hon. We are so glad you kids are all right."

Kenny's pa went to get the tractor and flat board trailer for Bessie. "I'm really proud of you son," he said.

"Hey, Kenny!" Melissa shouted. "I know what we can name the calf."

"What's that?" he asked.

"Storm."

"That's a great name." Kenny grinned and added, "Friend."

Melissa smiled broadly. She liked the name "friend" better than "dumb old city girl."

♦♦♦♦♦♦♦♦♦♦♦♦

Cecelia Davis lives in south Kansas City with her husband Paul of 40 years. She and Paul are the Children's Directors at First A/G in Raytown, MO. They also work with 5-6 year old boys on Wednesday nights in a program called Royal Rangers. They have 2 grown children, a son and daughter, and three granddaughters.

Cecelia enjoys watching animals in her backyard as they commune with each other in a way that most animals do not. Ground hogs go nose to nose with the squirrels and rabbits. A red cardinal feeds a bird that is much larger than itself and of a different species. A raccoon the size of a dog wanders through the back yard. A squirrel comes up to the back door begging for food, sometimes accompanied by Mr. Ground Hog. In the front yard a deer nuzzles a cat or nibbles a rose.

At present, Ms. Davis is compiling a book of devotions titled "Notes From Johnny." It is being written by Johnny Windsor - a fictional character in "Heaven's Mission", one of her inspirational novels. In "Heaven's Mission for a New Generation," Johnny is portrayed as an associate pastor. In her third novel of the series "Love Turns Lethal: Heaven Prevails," he is a senior pastor.

There will also be "Memoirs of J. T. Windsor" revealing Jonathan Thomas Windsor's innermost thoughts - Johnny's life, as though written by the character himself.

www.freewebs.com/acdavis

ON THE EVE OF CHRISTMAS

By Anne Lebrecht

Watching the snow falling while looking out of the window I am amazed at the beauty of every tiny flake. Each flake is different and unique as it falls to the ground. I smile as I realize that we will have a beautiful white Christmas after all. The doubters and weather predictions were wrong. My heart skips a beat in anticipation of the day ahead of me. My favorite time of the year.

My mother and father will spend the day with their best friends Toni and Tom Nicholas, helping them in their restaurant. Christmas Eve is a busy time and each and every year they have been there to help. When they close the restaurant, they will spend the rest of the evening at Toni and Tom's home with all of the children.

I am now at the Nicholas home with their daughter Katherine and her two older brothers. My parents dropped me off this morning. My mother gave me a lecture on how to behave and how not to get into trouble, the same lecture I receive every year. Katherine is a few years older than I. Her brothers are teenagers and they will spend the rest of the day tormenting us both. No adult supervision gives them the right. They will chase us up and down the stairs, lock the door to the cellar when we run away from them to hide, and grab whatever food we find to eat. Happy is the name of their dog and as usual he will run with us and desperately try to defend us. Yelping and barking he puts on a good show, but the reality is that he adores the boys as much as Katherine and only pretends to be our savior. If and when they bribe him with a cookie he will leave us on our own and help the boys chase us. Loyalty to only one is Happy's motto, and that one is the cookie.

My entire body throbs, my adrenaline flows as my heart beats quickly with all the excitement. These two days are pure pleasure and a time I dream about and look forward to every year.

The rest of the year, I spend in a boarding school. Sent there several years ago, I now assume I will be there until I graduate from school. My summers are spent in a summer camp and that leaves only these two days to share with my parents. Weekends at the school are for visiting and/or going home, however this has not been the case for me. I remain at school and rely on a part time staff to care for me. From time to time, a friend's parents will invite me to spend a weekend in their home. However, most of the time I am at the boarding school.

Questions about this remain unanswered; my mother it seems does not want a child in her life and certainly not at home. I have often wondered why they did not put me up for adoption, rather than leave me at school alone and feeling rejected and depressed most of the time.

The snow seems to have stopped. I press my face to the frosted window and gaze outside. The sun is starting to peak through and now the snowflakes look like tiny crystals dancing with the reflection from the light of the sun. One cannot feel sad with the sight of such beauty.

The door bursts open and I hear the two boys yelling as the chase begins. The eldest boy is George; the younger one by a year is Bob.

"I'm going to get you, Maryann, run or I'll catch you. Heaven help you if you're caught," Bob screams.

"We've got her," George yells.

"That's not fair," I say pouting. "You trapped me and never gave me a chance. I had no idea the chase had begun."

"Okay, you're right. I'll count to five, then it begins." George says.

I pass in front of them and run for my life down the stairs with Katherine yelling behind me and Happy barking loudly as we all try to hide.

Hidden out of view and feeling bold I yell, "Georgie Porgie you can't catch us. Bubbins Pubbins you'll never find us."

Just as soon as I finish yelling, the door to the closet in which we're hiding springs open. George and Bob grab us and start to tickle us as we all laugh and run to the living room. Exhausted from play we plop down on the sofa and pant from exhaustion. I feel exhilarated and happier than I have felt all year.

Minutes later, we all go to the kitchen to scrounge for food. Peanut butter and jelly seems to be the choice of the day. Sitting around the table with a sandwich in one hand and a glass of milk in the other, I wonder how life could get any better. Then I remember that all this ends tomorrow night when I will go back to the boarding school and wait another year. I feel a moment of sadness as I gulp the last of the milk, stuff the rest of my sandwich in my mouth and walk towards the living room.

The house is small, a cheap one built on a small budget. But to the family it is a haven and one they have lived in since the children were born. The carpets are worn, the furniture is old and the walls are chipped and in need of fresh paint. The entrance hallway is so tiny only one person can comfortably be in it at a time. This leads to the living room, small but cozy. In front of the window stands a huge Christmas tree. The room contains a couch and two large easy chairs. There is a bookcase with books and records and a record player on the top. An old upright piano stands against one wall. Various belongings are scattered on a small coffee table - a pair of dirty socks, some shoes, a belt and an undershirt. On the floor, some other clothing is strewn across the room. There is a single shoe that Happy is now chewing.

George hollers, "Happy! Drop that shoe! Bad dog, bad dog! Drop it now!"

Happy ignores him and scampers up the stairs with the shoe in his mouth.

Bob is in pursuit of the dog and shoe, his footsteps echo as he runs up the stairs. His screams permeate the walls throughout the house.

Katherine joins the chase trying to catch the dog and the house once again pulsates, a bedlam of commotion.

I watch and listen to the commotion as I think how wonderful it would be to be a member of this household. Every day filled with fun and games. This is so unlike my life at school. There the rules are strict and disciplined. There is not much time to run or play and laughter is not the usual. Bells sound for meals, school, to play outside and to come in. A bell wakes us up in the morning. How I wish my life was different.

The living room is quiet now and I sit listening as I hear the loud thumping of the feet and voices above. I rise from the sofa and start to pick up the clothing. I know that the house must be clean and in order when our parents come home and I feel obligated to help. Soon everyone returns and we all start to tidy the house. We wash the dishes from lunch and prepare for our parents homecoming and the celebration of Christmas Eve.

The aroma of a turkey baking in the oven now fills the entire house. The chattering of voices fills the rooms as everyone talks at once. The serious business at hand is the preparation of a late dinner meal. Pies are cooling on the kitchen table. Tom is basting the turkey and Toni is mashing the potatoes, peas and carrots are simmering on the stove. My parents are sitting in the kitchen talking to their friends as they cook dinner.

Silently I sit in the living room and watch the lights blink on the brightly lit Christmas tree. The radio is softly playing Christmas carols in the background. I notice this year there is a new string of lights that has fluid in glass stems and the fluid seems to rise and bubble. The sight of this fascinates me. I smell the scent of the pine and also the peppermint from the candy canes hanging on the tree. So much beauty before me I feel overwhelmed. I truly love Christmas and wish I could celebrate it more often throughout the year.

Walking back to the window, I peer out and can see the barren tree outside illuminated by the streetlights. The sky is dark and the world seems so peaceful and quiet on the outside. The tree branches are heavy with the new fallen snow and are bending from the weight. A pure white blanket of freshly fallen snow covers the sidewalks. All is at peace.

After dinner, we all go into the living room. Katherine plays the piano as we gather behind her and sing Christmas Carols. Some of the keys stick and will not play, but we pay little attention to that as we overpower the piano with our hearty singing. My stomach feels full with food, I am warm and comfy, and the joy of the moment brings tears to my eyes. Life can never feel better than this.

Presents sit under the tree and soon we will all gather and open them as we do every year before we go to bed. Hot rum toddies will soon be served to the adults and warmed eggnog drinks to us children. My presents are just a few, but when I open the largest box, it contains a doll I have wanted so badly, a baby doll. Her eyes close and her body feels soft. Her legs and hands feel like real flesh. She is dressed in a pink satin coat, a pink matching bonnet and under the coat a white dress with lace panties underneath. Her feet have white socks and shoes on. I gather her in my arms, holding her tightly. I cry for joy. I whisper her name in her ears. "Linda."

I hear the loud bell and feel confused. Where is the sound coming from? I open my eyes and realize the bell is the wake up bell. Slowly I rise and run to the window, my dream has vanished, but the snow is real. I press my head to the windowpane and feel the cold frost against my skin.

Shivering I return to my bed. The other five beds are empty. My roommates are home for Christmas and once again I will remain at boarding school. I go to the bathroom and wash, brush my teeth, dress, then join two other children that have remained as well. They told me they are orphans.

We now sit in front of a huge Christmas tree in the main hallway. The tree is enormous and reaches to the ceiling of the next floor. This massive hall, more of a huge room, is what separates the two stairways. One leads to the floor that houses the girls and the other goes upstairs to the bedrooms of the boys. Each floor has several bathrooms and all of the rooms have six beds in each. There are no private rooms, with the exception of the head mistress who lives on the girl's floor and resides in a suite with two bedrooms, a sitting room, bathroom, and a huge balcony overlooking the gardens. The view from her balcony is of the St. Lawrence River.

Seated on a chair is the head mistress, she smiles as we join her. We have all done this before every year, so there is no need to address us, or guide us. She wishes each of us a merry Christmas as she hands us each a stocking filled with an orange that fills the toe, a few walnuts in their shells, a firecracker this year in red, last year it was green and a pair of barrettes for our hair. Each of us curtsies as we thank her for our gifts, and then we all follow her downstairs and into the dining room for our Christmas breakfast.

The massive dining room that normally serves fifty children now appears empty as the four of us sit down at the main dining table. Because today is a special day, our breakfast consists of sausages with scrambled eggs instead of the usual porridge. Our bread is covered with marmalade, another special treat. This year has an extra and unexpected surprise when we see our glass now filled with chocolate milk. I eat all that is in front of me, for this again is the rule. I now feel so sad it is difficult for me to swallow. My tears withheld for fear of punishment.

After breakfast, I return to my room and again go to the window. Looking outside I see the grey sky and the snow covering the gardens below. A deep feeling of gloom overwhelms me. Then I remember my lessons and stories taught to me by the nuns, and that God makes all the beauty I see each day. He is our Father, and we are told to pray to him for forgiveness and for help in all things. I kneel down, and with folded hands held under my chin, I pray to the Lord to make the dream I had come true. I tell the Lord I can wait, but caution Him, I cannot wait too long. I hope he hears my pleas. I rise and again go to the window.

Looking up to the sky, I see the sun peek through the grayness. I watch it as it brightens and grows stronger. I watch the sudden change as my room fills with the sunshine. Golden rays stretch across the room and enhance every corner. I smile as I feel the warmth on my skin. I touch my arm and know that God has heard my prayer and that one day, I will have children, a home, a dog and every Christmas will be as joyful as my dream. I know that very soon my life will change. I dance and whirl in circles in the sunlight, bathed in its warmth. I can wait. I got His message. I now know that the best of times is yet to come.

♦♦♦♦♦♦♦♦♦♦♦♦

Anne Lebrecht writes novels, poetry and short stories. Available through Amazon, Barnes & Noble and other online bookstores are "Memories of a Forgotten Past", "Discoveries of a Hidden Past", "The Daughters of Nora Crawford" and "Simply Poetry".

Born in Montreal Canada, she now resides with her husband in Southern California. She has two married daughters and two grandchildren.

www.annelebrecht.com

THE GHOST AND MRS. GATH

By Ina Goodling

"In here. This is where it moans the loudest." The old woman clutched a skeletal hand to her shawl while waving the other toward the drawing room.

I entered without hesitation. Lace doilies of various shapes and sizes adorned nearly every surface of the room, along with a fine layer of dust. Though sunlight streamed in through the curtains, the mahogany paneling on the walls made the room seem dark. I chose a corner near the window to set up my equipment. The old woman eyed the camera and audio recorders suspiciously.

"What're those for?" she snarled.

"I like to document my sessions," I told her, quite frankly.

Once everything was in place, I turned on every piece of equipment I had brought and told her to be seated.

Hobbling over to the elegant oak table in the center of the room, the grizzled granny took a seat on one of the two-cushioned oak chairs. As I sat across from her, she lit a candle and placed it on a lacy cloth in the center of the table, then closed her eyes and held out her hands as though expecting a hug or a gift.

"Well, aren't you going to take my hands?" she demanded, cracking an eye open to glare at me.

"Excuse me?"

"Don't you know anything about conducting a proper séance?" she barked. "All the other mediums told me to do this, so what are you waiting for?"

"I can assure you, Mrs. Gath, there is no need for us to hold hands in order to make contact with the deceased. I have conducted many successful sessions without having to lay so much as a finger on my clients. Just put your hands in your lap and close your eyes and we can begin."

Despite my reassuring tone, the old coot grumbled vehemently under her breath before lowering her head and closing her eyes.

"Now then, what did you say his name was?" I asked her. She ignored me. I cleared my throat. "Mrs. Gath?"

"What?" she roared, eyes flashing dangerously, as though she had nearly achieved nirvana and I had interrupted her.

"What is the name of your spirit?"

"I don't know," she growled.

If not for the dim light I could have sworn she was starting to foam at the mouth. Perhaps it was a symptom of Alzheimer's. If that was the case, and I was very worried that it might be, then the whole idea of a haunt may just be a product of her deteriorating mind.

"I don't know what his real name is, but I'm sure it's a he. I call him Biminy Benson, but he'll answer just as quickly to Bim." There was an almost-tenderness in her voice just then, as though the ghost with which she had expressed so much annoyance over the phone was really her only friend in the world.

Probably the only person, living or dead, who can stand her. "Okay then, let us begin," I suggested.

Mrs. Gath nodded and closed her eyes. "'Bout time," she grumbled.

I closed my own eyes then and focused on the spiritual realm. I took several deep, calming breaths while attempting to clear my mind. Before I could open my mouth to speak, a sudden chill washed over me and I could hear the curtains fluttering as though in a light wind. I knew the window was closed, but a ghostly breeze was definitely moving about the room. Light flickered before my closed eyelids as the candle in front of me was snuffed out. That was when I heard the moan, very faint at first, echoing slightly and sounding as though it was coming from somewhere far away. Slowly it grew louder, and as it did, I lifted up my own voice and spoke. "Bim, is that you?"

"Of course that's him!" spat the wicked witch sitting across from me, making me jump. "I told you that already! He's the only ghoul around here sick enough to moan like he's being gutted and tortured to death. I wouldn't be surprised if that's how he—"

"Please, Mrs. Gath. Do you want me to conduct this séance or not? Now please, keep quiet and pay attention." I cleared my throat and continued. "Bim? Are you still here?"

"Oh, he's here all right. That's the problem," the witch muttered under her breath.

Ignoring her, I called again. On my third try, the wind whipped into a frenzy and nearly blew the scarf off my head.

Mrs. Gath was shouting hysterically, "Damn you old fool! You're going to wreck something valuable! Why do you always have to show off like that?"

The wind ceased then, quite suddenly, and instead of moaning I could hear, faintly and still far away, the sound of a grown man sobbing.

"Bim," I cried. "You sound so sad. What bereaves you? Can you not rest peacefully?"

"Rest peacefully my eye!" Mrs. Gath barked. "That old bugger won't give me a moment's peace, and you're asking *him?* He's dead and rotting, and he's got an eternity of peace to look forward to, so who cares why he's upset?"

"Mrs. Gath, be quiet." I was seriously starting to lose my cool with the wretched old woman, and I was nearly ready to walk out on this whole thing. The only thing holding me back was Bim and my desire to communicate with the spirit world. Bim definitely had something to say.

Then, with icy breath, a low voice whispered in my ear: "Let us speak in private."

Silent, I nodded agreement. With that shriveled old prune in the room, I knew that poor Bim would never be able to get a word in edgewise. I barely rose from my chair when I was suddenly and very roughly thrust back down into it. Waves of electrifying coldness washed over and through me, holding me fast to the chair. Then darkness. Complete, utter and absolute darkness.

The voice of Biminy Benson sounded somewhere in the back of my brain. "I have possessed you, Madam Carmen. It is the only way I can speak to you clearly, without interference. You are the only medium who has been truly receptive to my presence, and I have seen many mediums pass through this house."

I tried to say something then, but I had no mouth to say it.

"Amelia Gath moved into my house over thirty years ago and has caused me nothing but agitation and heartache since. I cannot leave this house, and I cannot get her to budge, either. I was here first, and here I shall remain. I am not a malevolent spirit; I mean no harm. Yet I fear being exorcised. It will mean an eternity in hell for me if she decides to bring in a priest. Please, please help me to drive this demon out. Exorcise this ghoul who haunts me and let me rest in peace!" And with a final shriek, the spirit ascended, leaving me alone in the drawing room with the old woman who had called upon my services as a medium.

As soon as my vision cleared, I looked across the table at Mrs. Gath. She was staring back at me out of wide, glassy eyes. Her pupils were fixed and dilated. I reached across the table and felt her wrist. No pulse.

I watched in silence as the ambulance bearing Mrs. Gath's corpse faded into the twilit distance. As I carried out the last piece of equipment and walked down the front steps of the old Victorian, a gentle wind swept over me, carrying with it a sound so faint that I was scarcely sure I could hear it at all. It was a man's voice, of that I am sure, but whether it was sobbing pitifully or laughing heartily I could not say.

Once I returned home, I wasted no time in playing back all the recordings made during the séance. I watched myself, sitting in a trancelike state while Mrs. Gath leaned across the table, spittle flying as she yelled and shook a gnarled fist in my face. What happened next defies explanation. I watched, engrossed, as the spirit of Biminy Benson rose out of me in a smoky silver wisp that flew straight into Mrs. Gath's livid face. Then it was gone.

Mrs. Gath fell back into her chair, clutching her heart, a short spasm contorting her face before she finally relaxed. She had died instantly.

Years later I found myself once again climbing the front steps of the old Victorian formerly known as the Gath House. Finding themselves at odds with the former residents, the current owners had called upon my services.

"The howling is enough to wake the dead!" exclaimed the husband over the phone.

"But the man is nice," said the wife when I arrived. "I certainly wouldn't mind keeping him around. It's that wretched woman that's driving us insane!"

I nodded knowingly and began setting up.

"You said you came to this house before?" the husband asked, eyeing my equipment warily.

"That's right," I told him. "Years ago, back when Mrs. Gath owned it. Marvelous woman. Delightful. Shame she passed on, though. Did you know her?"

They shook their heads.

We sat down at the drawing room table and held hands. It was a séance, after all. And it wasn't long before we were greeted by a rumble of laughter and a low growl from above.

"Hello, Bim," I said, biting my lip to ward off the contagious laughter. "And hello, Mrs. Gath. How's the afterlife treating you?"

♦♦♦♦♦♦♦♦♦♦♦♦

Ina Goodling was born in San Luis Obispo CA. She is the author of "Emoceans", "The Forgotten Fairy Tales","Nevuela" and "The Party Pups" (a comic book series). To see her cover artwork – go to:

www.wizardsofwords.org/goodling.html

GOOD 'OL BOYS ~ CATFISHIN'

By Phil Whitley

"Wooo-hoo, Look at this `un," Brother Hollis said as he pulled what must have been a three-pounder onto the bank. "Big ol' catfish, ain't it?"

The four old friends were lined along the bank of the Haney's five-acre pond, and having a great afternoon of beer drinking and fishing.

"That's a keeper alright, Preacherman," Big Tim agreed.

Big Tim was Small Tim's son; but because he was so huge, and Small Tim was so small, they had been stuck with the nicknames "Big" Tim and "Small" Tim. Big Tim's name was actually Timothy Jehu Haney, Junior, but both he and his father hated to be called Jehu, both preferring "Tim".

Brother Hollis carefully worked the hook free from the catfish's mouth, tossed it into the cooler and re-baited. Preacher Hollis was the idea man of the group—always looking for ways to make enough money to build a real church.

He looked into the cooler containing their catch so far and said, "You know, if we could get us a really big mess of these by Saturday, we could have us a catfish fry. What do you think about that, Small Tim?"

"Well, Preacher, this here's already Thursday. It `ud take us a week t' catch enough fish fer what I thank you got in mind, but I shore wish we could get rid of most o' th' catfish in hyer. They's too many, and th' bass an' bluegills er suffrin' fer it." Small Tim was referring to Brother Hollis' idea of a catfish fry. He knew that the preacher meant a catfish fry for the entire community, and using the event as a means of attracting a congregation for him to preach to. He didn't have a church of his own, but he had a huge army surplus tent that he set up frequently, much to the dismay of his immediate family. They usually made up his entire congregation, unless he could come up with ideas to draw a crowd. His previous brainstorm hadn't worked out as well as he had planned. It wasn't that it was that bad of an idea. It was just that there wasn't enough people in the community willing to pay five dollars a plate for a "Soul Food" dinner of turnip greens and cornbread—and then having to listen to him preach for two hours.

Brother Hollis had never attended a seminary, but had transformed himself into his ideal of preaching perfection by studying, then adopting the preaching style of the more successful radio and television evangelists. More specifically, it was the ones that when 'preaching in the Spirit' altered their voices into that particularly annoying habit of adding several extra syllables to one and two syllable words.

In everyday conversation, Brother Hollis spoke in a normal voice, even having done away with his southern drawl. But when he got worked up behind the pulpit, he would begin jumping up and down, waving his lanky arms, and most annoying of all, begin adding those extra syllables to certain words. 'God' for example, became 'GAW-ud-ah. 'Jesus' became 'Jah-EE-zus-ah'. "GAW-ud-ah, sent His Son, Jah-EE-zus-ah, into the WO-ald-ah, to save MAY-un-ah from his SINS-ah." Some people really like that kind of preaching, but unfortunately, not that many lived in this particular community.

The fourth man of the group, "Red" Crawford, pulled another fish from the pond and brought it up to the cooler. "Sounds lak a good idee t' me, Preacherman, but Tim's right. We cain't ketch enough `fore Saredy t' feed evvabody, but I know how we kin do it," he said, looking around the group as if he was about to tell a secret. "We'd kill two birds at th' same time, too—have that fish fry an' relieve Tim's pond o' soma these her catfish!"

"What is it, Brother Crawford? What do you have in mind?" Brother Hollis asked with growing interest.

"Hit ain't `sickly legal, though, but Dubya an' me did it lass' summer jus' t' see if hit `ud work, an' hit did!" Red said, still looking like he wasn't sure if he should tell.

Brother Hollis was already planning his sermon for the fish fry, and wasn't about to pass up a chance to make it happen. "Just what do you mean by 'Not 'zackly legal, Brother Red?"

Red, seeing that he now had everyone's attention, prolonged the suspense by pulling out a pouch of Bull Durham tobacco from his top overall pocket, carefully folding a paper and rolling a cigarette. "Well, Dubya's got one of those ringer thangs from outta his grandmaw's old telephone. We run some wars from it into th' creek behind his house an' cranked on it," he said, pausing to light his cigarette. "Seems them catfish don't lak 'lec-tristy an' come a'swimmin' to th' top. We jes' scooped `em out with a net."

I've heerd `bout that, Red," Small Tim said. "Pap called hit 'callin' catfish, er sompin' lak that."

"That doesn't sound all that illegal to me, Brother Red, and if Brother Haney wants the catfish out of his pond… and it IS his pond…" Brother Hollis said, looking from one man to another.

Small Tim pushed a couple of catfish aside to pull another Bud from the cooler and popped it open. "When Dubya gets hyer we'll ask him `bout it. Catfish fry soun's perdy good t' me!"

"Speak o' th' devil, hyer he comes now," Big Tim said as Dubya's old army jeep appeared over the hill behind them.

Dubya's real name was simply the letter "W" Jones, which had caused him a lot of grief during his military service. They wanted to know what the "W" stood for, and didn't like his answer. He tried to explain that his mother wanted to name him Wilbur and his father wanted it to be William, after him. They finally compromised on just the letter "W". He began spelling it "Dubya" on his military records and it stuck.

He climbed out of his jeep and gave them a "Hey y'all" and went straight to the cooler for a beer. "Y'all done got a few cats, I see." Then he realized that everyone was staring at him. "Whut? Y'all been a'talkin' `bout me?"

"Naw, Dubya. Well, yeah, matter o' fact we were," Red admitted. "I wuz jus' tellin' `em `bout you an' me shockin' them catfish with that telephone thang you got. You still got it, dontcha?"

"Yep. I got it, Red." Dubya said, looking around the group suspiciously. "Why?"

"Well, Small Tim needs t' get rid o' some of the catfish in his pond, an' th' preacherman wants to have a big catfish fry. I—we figgered that wuz a good way t' get `em."

Dubya reached behind the seat of his jeep and took out a six-pack of tall-boy Buds, pushed a few catfish aside and dropped it into the cooler. "Tomorrow be soon `nuff?"

"Preacher wants t' have his fish fry on Sunday, so we need t' get `em caught least by Saturday night, so I guess we best get started early tomorrow, Dubya. What all we need?"

"Just th' magneto, some dip nets, an' a boat `ud be handy," Dubya said, reaching for another brew.

"Ain't got a boat no more. Bottom rotted out," Small Tim said. "Kin we make do without it?"

"Long as y'all don't mind a'wadin'. How deep is it?" Dubya asked while he lit a Camel and squinted at Tim over the smoke.

"Hit's mostly no more`n waist deep. Maybe ten feet at the deepest near th' dam," Big Tim said. "Thank we kin do it? We kin use long hannels on th' nets fer th' deep parts."

"Sho, it'll work. I'll brang th' ringer over tomorrow mornin' an' get us an early start. Now let's fish," Dubya said as he baited up his hook. Dubya was a man of few words, but he hadn't always been that way. Throughout his school years he was the class clown, and almost daily in trouble for talking and disrupting the class. Then, immediately after his high school graduation, he joined the Army. Within six months, he was in the jungles of Viet Nam. He returned a different man. He wasn't especially moody, or depressed—he just didn't talk much anymore. He had always been an outdoorsman like his father, fishing, hunting, and trapping—but since his military service he became obsessed with it and spent most of his time doing those things.

The five friends continued fishing and depleting the beer from the cooler until nearly midnight. Then they cleaned the nearly twenty pounds of catfish and iced them down. They had one more beer apiece, then left for their homes.

At dawn the next morning, Dubya was already at the pond when Brother Hollis showed up. "We the first ones here, Brother Jones?"

"Yep, but I reckon th' others be hyer directly."

Brother Hollis picked up the magneto and examined it closely. "I remember my mother talking about using these things on the old telephones. She said that you cranked on it to ring the operator. So it really does kill the fish?"

"Hit don't kill `em, hit jus' stuns `em an' they come up t' th' top. Don't work on nuthin' but catfish," Dubya explained. He had attached a metal ring to the end of a long wire, and was now taping the ring to a doughnut-shaped piece of styrofoam. "That oughtta float," he said as he finished the taping. He carried it to the edge of the water and tossed it in. "Yep. Floats good."

Brother Hollis was anxious to get started. There was a second wire running from the magneto and he asked about it.

"Ground war," said Dubya as he pushed a metal rod into the soft mud at the edge of the water. He wound a few turns of exposed wire around the rod and taped it into place. "An' that's all there is to it. Hit's ready!"

"I think I understand now, Brother Dubya. Any catfish between the end that floats and this here ground wire will get shocked, right?"

"Yep, you got it, Preacher."

"So why don't I get a dip net and carry this end out as far as I can wade? We may as well get started now!" Brother Hollis really wanted to have that fish fry!

"Ready when you are, Preacher," Dubya grunted.

Brother Hollis put the coil of wire over one arm and put his other arm through the floating metal ring. He began wading out into the pond, playing the wire out behind him.

While Dubya was pushing the ground rod deeper into the mud, Big Tim, Small Tim and Red walked up behind him.

"Y'all getting' an early start, Dubya?"Red asked.

"Yep. Preacherman wants that fish fry!" Dubya said, still not satisfied with the ground rod.

He was distracted by a loud, high-pitched "Yeeeeeeeeeeeeee" that seemed to be coming from the middle of the pond. The sound was coming from Brother Hollis, who was standing waist-deep in the water—arms upraised—with the metal ring around one of them. He appeared to be dancing, making ripples in the water.

From behind Dubya, Big Tim said, "This thang really work?" He was cranking away on the magneto.

"Stop cranking, Tim," Dubya shouted.

Big Tim looked puzzled, but stopped cranking. The yeeeeee sound from the pond stopped at the same time. "What's Preacherman doing out thar?" Big Tim asked, giving the magneto a couple more turns.

"Yeeeeee," said Brother Hollis, waving his arms again, but not nearly as long as before.

"You `lectrocutin' the Preacher evva time you crank that thang, Tim. Put it down!" Dubya said.

They all looked at Brother Hollis to see if he was all right. He was still shaking and trying to get the ring off his arm. Several catfish were floating around his waist but he didn't seem to be interested in them.

"Anybody - so - much - as - touch - that – thing," the preacher said between breaths, "... before I get out of this water," now catching his breath, "...I will call down the Wrath of GAW-ud-ah upon him!" he finished as he stepped onto the bank. "DAMN!" he said for the first time in over fifty years.

Big Tim set the magneto down gently and said, "Don't guess I need me no God wrath this mornin'."

Brother Hollis, who appeared quite shaken, pulled himself out of the pond and sat down on the bank. The other men gathered around him, concerned for his well being, but trying hard not to laugh.

"Are you alright, Preacher?" Red asked, barely able to conceal a grin.

"I think I'm going to survive, Brother Red, but I can see your amusement. Anybody laugh right now and I will wrap that wire around his private parts and crank on that Instrument of Satan until I get tired!"

"`Twern't funny, Preacher. We jus' happy hit din't kill you," Big Tim said. "An' I really din't know you wuz on th' other end when I cranked it."

"Well, I'll be the one on the cranking end next time, if that's agreeable to the rest of you," Brother Hollis said, looking around the group defiantly. He had left the floating ring well out in the pond, so Small Tim handed him the magneto.

"May as well give `er a shot, Preacher!"

Brother Hollis seemed a little reluctant to even touch it, but soon he was cranking away. Catfish were coming to the surface almost faster than the other men could net them and dump them into the cooler; but the floating ring was drifting closer and closer to the bank.

"Big Tim, why don't you wade out and take that ring out as far as you can?" Brother Hollis suggested.

Big Tim was already standing in the water with his net, so he obliged. "This far enough, Preacher?"

"That's about as far as the wire allows, Tim," Brother Hollis said with an evil gleam in his eyes.

"Yeeeeeeeeeeeeeeeeeeee," Big Tim screamed from the middle of the pond, in an almost perfect imitation of the preacher. "Son of a BITCH!" he added as he threw the ring down. "Guess I deserved that."

Now everyone laughed, even Big Tim, after he had caught his breath.

"I don't suppose I could ever convince you that that was an accident, could I?" Brother Hollis asked innocently, then burst out laughing again.

By noon, the first cooler was completely full of dressed fish, and they had begun another one. Allowing enough room for ice, they figured there were two coolers full. Dubya volunteered to drive to the nearest store to get ice and enough beer for the remainder of the day. On the way back, he had an idea. He went by his brother-in-law's house and borrowed his aluminum canoe. "All we got t' do is connect the war t' th' canoe," he explained. "That way, we won't be a'wadin' an' getting' 'lectrocuted with that thang."

By nightfall they had filled two more coolers with dressed catfish and even had a few beers left. They decided to quit fishing for the night and build a fire to dry their clothes, and just sit and talk.

"Pretty slim catchin' when we stopped this evenin'," Dubya said, poking at the fire with a stick. "Reckon we `bout got `em all?"

"They's more in thar," Small Tim said. "We jus' got t' keep tryin', I figger."

Dubya threw the stick into the fire and opened another beer. "Member when we usta throw Cherry Bombs into th' creek? Sometimes they `ud brang up a few fish."

"Yeah, I remember, Dubya. We taped `em to rocks t' sink `em. I always wondered how them fuses stayed lit," Big Tim said. "What you thankin' `bout, Dubya?"

"I got somma Daddy's dynamite left from when we wuz a'blowin' up stumps," Dubya said, still poking at the fire.

"Dynamite, Dubya?" Small Tim said. "Cherry Bombs `er one thang, but you talking' `bout some serious stuff now!"

"Jus' a thought, Tim," Dubya said, squinting over a fresh-lit Camel.

Red was rolling a Bull Durham and balancing a beer between his knees at the same time, but paused long enough to ask, "Reckon how many Cherry Bombs hit take t' make a stick of dynamite?"

Several beers later they had estimated the equivalent ratio. Dubya said that they were both about the same diameter, and that about fifteen Cherry Bombs placed end-to-end would be about the same length. According to Big Tim, the Cherry Bombs they used in the creek brought up about three fish each.

"An' that means that one stick of dynamite ought t' brang up `bout forty-five fish," Big Tim said. After all, he was the youngest of the group, with the most recent education.

"An' I got `bout ten sticks left," Dubya said.

"An' ten times forty-five'll get us four hundred an' fifty fish!" Big Tim said with authority. You just can't argue with a good education!

"Dang, we gonna have us a BIG fish fry, Preacher!" Red said. "You lettin' everybody know `bout it ain'tcha?"

"I've put posters all over the community, Red, and my wife has been calling all the ladies, letting them know about it. With all our wives making slaw and hushpuppies, we should be all set," Brother Hollis said.

With that settled, Dubya offered the first part of the plan. They would take all the entrails and heads from the catfish they had already cleaned, put them in a burlap bag, and sink it in the middle of the pond.

"By tomorrow, ever' catfish in thar'll be gathered `roun' hit. Daddy called hit 'baitin' a hole'," Dubya said.

Dubya was already at the pond the next morning when Brother Hollis arrived. He was taping the sticks of dynamite together and setting the fuse.

"Good morning, Brother Dubya," the preacher said.

"Mornin', Preacher. You ready to blow this pond up?"

"I'm not so sure after sleeping on it. Is this safe? I mean to us and Brother Haney's pond."

"Yeah, it'll be alright. Dynamite underwater ain't all that dangerous. Hit don't even make much noise," Dubya said with confidence.

"I just don't want anyone to get hurt, Dubya… and should you be smoking while you're doing that?"

Probly not, Preacher. Thanks," Dubya said, flicking his Camel into the pond.

The two Tims joined them, each carrying two large Styrofoam coolers.

"Thought we might need these," Small Tim said.

"Those an' mebbe more, if this works, Tim," Dubya said. "Those catfish probly done foun' that bag of guts by now."

Big Tim saw the long fuse coming out of the bundle of dynamite and asked, "That fuse burn underwater, Dubya?"

"You cain't hardly put hit out once hit's lit. I got `er cut to `bout a minute, give 'er take a few seconds, I figger."

They were all set when Red appeared. His old pickup truck rattled to a stop and Red slammed the door twice before it closed. "Dang ol' Ford," he said grumpily, but everyone knew how much he loved that old truck. He had a practically new one at home, but preferred rattling around in this one.

"Y'all ain't done blowed th' pond up yet, didja?"

"Naw, we wuz a'waitin' on you," Small Tim said. "An' hit looks like Dubya's got evvathang ready."

"Then let us do this thing," Brother Hollis said. He wanted to go with Dubya in the canoe, and they had decided that only two of them would be on the water when they blew it.

Dubya sat in the bow with his dynamite bundle, and Brother Hollis took the stern and paddled. The other men watched from the bank as the two made their way out to the middle of the pond. Dubya was watching the water intently, looking for the cork bobber they had attached to the bag of entrails.

"Hyer it is," he said, reaching over the side for the attached line.

"Hold `er right hyer, Preacher, whilst I get this ready. Soon as I light th' fuse and drop th' charge over th' side, paddle like hell!"

Dubya balanced the taped dynamite bundle on the side of the canoe while he fumbled for his lighter.

Brother Hollis was getting increasingly nervous as he watched Dubya light his Zippo, then hold it to the fuse. There was a sudden hiss and sparkle as the fuse ignited. Dubya waited a moment to make sure it was going good, then pushed the charge over the side. It was sinking slowly as he hollered, "Paddle, Preacher, paddle!"

Brother Hollis paddled so hard on his very first stroke, the paddle broke, leaving him holding only the upper half.

"Uh-oh," the preacher said.

"Uh-oh, hell! Use yore hands!" Dubya said as he frantically demonstrated from the bow as the canoe drifted directly over "Pond Zero".

Just as he had said, it didn't make an awfully loud noise. There was a hollow sounding "WHUMP" that the men on shore felt more than heard.

Then, a moment later, a ten-foot diameter column of water rose up from beneath the canoe, lifting it and its occupants twenty feet into the air. It seemed to the others as if it all happened in slow motion—the canoe rode up on a giant tower of water, with the preacher and Dubya still seated, their arms over the sides paddling away at empty air.

The top of the water column then exploded and collapsed on itself, leaving the canoe momentarily suspended in empty space, but not for long. It tipped to one side, obeying the Law of Gravity and fell, along with Dubya and the preacher, into the pond.

Small Tim, Big Tim and Red never had time to run as the resulting tsunami wave hit them. One moment they were watching the explosion, and the next they were being carried nearly twenty feet from where they had been standing. Then the receding water swept them into the pond.

No one spoke for several minutes as they re-grouped on the bank and checked for injuries. Brother Hollis and Dubya were the last to crawl out of the pond—the surface of which was covered with dead and dying fish. There were even fish flopping around on the ground around them.

"Well, that worked," Dubya said solemnly, trying to conceal his shaking hands.

Brother Hollis, who in one twenty-four hour period had nearly been electrocuted, then nearly blown up, just stood there, staring into the sky.

After a moment he said, "If you men will begin cleaning the fish on the bank here, I will get the net and gather the ones in the pond." He had the beginnings of a brand-new sermon for the meeting tomorrow and needed the time alone to think. It was going to be about the disciples of Jesus who were fishermen. They had used nets. He wasn't planning on mentioning magnetos or dynamite, but he figured that they would have used them—had they been available.

Their wives had been preparing all the other food to go along with the catfish while the men were cleaning the fish. There were gallons of cole slaw, and the batter for the fish and the special mix for the hushpuppies were ready.

Brother Hollis had his huge Army-surplus tent set up in the large community picnic area that was located beside the creek that ran from the Haney's pond— the dam of which was about two hundred yards upstream. The fires were ready to light beneath the two huge iron pots of peanut oil.

Now all that was necessary was for people to show up. Brother Hollis had paid for an ad at a local AM radio station that specialized in

Christian programming, and the ad had been repeated every hour for the past two days.

Realizing his mistakes from his earlier 'Soul Food' event, he had decided to offer a free dinner to those who attended his sermon. Those who came only to eat would be charged five dollars, but that was for 'All You Can Eat' as the ad had promised. Southern dining at its finest.

They lit the fires at dawn on Sunday morning. The folding chairs were set up in neat rows beneath the tent. Outside, the picnic tables and benches were cleaned and ready. Brother Hollis was pacing nervously between the tent and the picnic area, watching the drive for cars, and praying that they would come.

The sermon was to begin promptly at 10 a.m., but by 9 a.m. the first people began arriving. They continued to arrive until the parking area was full and the drive was lined with vehicles along both sides. The preacher's fears subsided as the grounds filled with people.

The kids were playing in the creek and running wild, and the atmosphere was one of a joyous family reunion, even though very few were related.

Brother Hollis then gave what was the best sermon of his life. He was inspired and eloquent in his delivery, and the 'Amens' and the 'Preach it, brothers' from the congregation inspired him even further. Even those in the crowd who weren't seen inside a church except for their own funeral were impressed.

Even more amazing was that at the 'Alter Call", old J.D. Scroggs, moonshiner and chief partaker of his own product, asked to be baptized.

Brother Hollis, who had never been asked to baptize anyone in his entire career, was near tears of joy when he led J.D. down to the creek after the service. Just as he and J.D. waded into the creek, there was a distant rumbling sound and people looked up, expecting to see rain clouds, but it was a clear, sunny day.

The preacher placed his hands on J.D. as he prepared him for a good old-fashioned creekdipping and said "I baptize you in the name of the—GOOD GOD ALMIGHTY!" as a ten foot wall of water surged toward them from upstream.

Apparently the dam had been more affected by the dynamite blast than they realized; or maybe God, in His Infinite Wisdom, figured that old J.D. needed more than just a dipping to wash away a lifetime of sins.

Whatever the cause, Brother Hollis and J.D., together with a few kids who were playing in the creek, were swept nearly a hundred yards downstream. The two men were still clinging to one another when the wave passed. Standing up in the now knee-deep water, Brother Hollis completed the ceremony by adding, "… Father, Son and Holy Ghost."

Fortunately, the fish, already fried and piled on the tables on platters with the rest of the food, was safe. The fires were extinguished, the tent was gone, and people's shoes were soaked. The kids made a game of throwing the few stranded fish into the creek. They seemed to think that the whole thing had been part of the planned entertainment, and the ones who had not been in the creek wanted to know, "When is it going to do it again?"

A wet and bedraggled Brother Hollis stood in the ankle deep water and said Grace over the food.

There were over three hundred people served that day, and not a single one complained or thought of it as a bad experience. Most of them had heard a superb sermon, enjoyed a wonderful meal and above all, had gained a memorable story to pass on to future generations.

The Federal Flood Relief Program received word of the tragedy. They sent funds sufficient to not only repair the Haney's dam and re-stock the pond, but enough to "rebuild the little country church that was swept away", the accompanying official report read. Someone had failed to mention in the initial report that it had been an Army-surplus tent.

Brother Hollis considered the omission as an Act of God. His dream of having a real church with a returning congregation that loved him was fulfilled. He even had a creek-dipped deacon who idolized him. It turned out that old J.D. had a magnificent baritone singing voice and doubled as the song leader. But most of all, he still had his four Good Ol' Boys who listened to his ideas—the latest of which was presented to them one afternoon on the bank of the newly-stocked pond. "You know, deer season is almost here. Reckon we could have us a big ol' venison barbecue?"

♦♦♦♦♦♦♦♦♦♦♦♦

Phil Whitley was born on January 1st, 1943 in the rural community of Pine Mountain Valley, Georgia, and now resides in Riverdale, Georgia with his wife and daughter. Recently retired after thirty years as a hospital Biomedical Equipment Technician, he now spends his time researching and writing.

Keechie was his first full-length novel of historical fiction, based loosely on his childhood in the 1950s south. His love of southern humor led him to write several short stories based on characters from that time period, capturing the southern dialect as it was and still is spoken.

www.philwhitley.com

BLUE PAINT

By Jean Limongello

My brother Jack tells me my eight year old daughter resembles me as a child. Same hair and slight build, except that her eyes when you can see them are oversized and blue. He says mine were always small and the color of mud. I have no photographs of my childhood.

"Kel-ly," I crooned as I tried for eye contact.

My daughter didn't answer; she looked at her lunch box instead of me. I wanted to scream, but the counselor said not to push. She said Kelly talks to her sometimes. The word bullshit formed in my brain, but didn't get past my tongue.

I handed her the lunch box and walked ahead of her to the front door. As I opened it, the warm, very warm, Florida breeze rushed at me undeterred by our central air conditioning. I could hear the school bus. At least she was going to school again.

After Kelly stepped on the bus, my husband John came up behind me and slipped his hands around my waist. I stiffened and then forced my torso to relax as I turned to him. "Did she talk to you this morning?"

He dropped his hands and ran them along the sides of his thighs. "No, but I heard her crying in her room again last night."

"Then why didn't you wake me up, or at least go to her?" I stomped back into the kitchen, plopped two pieces of toast into the toaster and poured him a cup of coffee. When the toast popped I slapped it on his plate. "You just don't seem to care." I couldn't keep the whine from my voice. Then I began to giggle, a knee jerk reaction I often had when stressed or nervous.

"Teresa," he said. "Please. Everything is Kelly, Kelly, Kelly. The doctors say there's nothing wrong. Just leave her alone and she'll come out of it when she's ready. Can't you see I'm trying to be patient?"

"Ha," I said, pouring him more coffee. "I wrack my brain trying to figure this out. What happened that weekend? When I left to go out with my friend Sally she was fine. When I came back the next day Kelly was . . . silent. No more smiles or laughs – no more joy. You were here, John. Can't you think of anything that could have caused this change in our daughter?"

"No, Teresa, I can't." His voice was hoarse. He wrapped his uneaten toast in a napkin, took a swallow of coffee, and left for work without saying anything more. Not even goodbye.

I sat with my coffee and turned on the TV for noise. My head was throbbing. I had one of those crazy black and white tiles, faucet-dripping dreams in the middle of the night. Until this happened I had been faucet-dripping dream-free since high school. I know something happened, but what? My mind hasn't gone in circles like this since I was a child, and Marty.

"Marty! Yes!" I shouted out loud. Why hadn't I thought of Marty? I reached for the phone and called him.

"It's been a long time, girl," Marty said. "Of course I'd like you to visit. But, listen, I don't know if I can help your Kelly. Maybe you need a professional. I'm just an old man-"

"It's okay for us come then?" I interrupted. "It's okay that you try? You helped me, remember?"

"Yes, I remember," he said.

He didn't sound like the same Marty. I knew I should ask him what was wrong. But instead I blurted, "We'll fly out tomorrow morning. We'll see you sometime in the afternoon."

"You're making too much of this, Teresa," John said when I called him at work.

"It's something I have to do, John. Give Kelly a chance with Marty, you know? He might be able to open her up."

Thirty years ago Marty came to live next to my family in our Forest Street house in New Jersey. He seemed old, but we were children so he might have been in his thirties. On weekends we would sneak into his back yard and be kings and princesses, toads and snakes, very good or very bad, but never just Jack, Jane, and Teresa. We loved him and trusted him. I know he saved my childhood, and now I needed him to save my daughter's.

I had three hours before Kelly came home from school, so I made a mental to-do list to relax and keep myself going: pay the bills that were due, make airline reservations for the next morning, pack clothes for both of us. The Florida sun made it feel like June instead of April. April in New Jersey would still be cool. I left a space in Kelly's suitcase in the event she wanted to take anything special. She was so passive now, I doubted she would object to the trip or to anything I packed.

She didn't. She just sat in front of the TV after I told her we were going, and turned up the sound.

John came home early and sat next to Kelly on the couch. I watched them as I prepared dinner. I couldn't hear what he was saying because the TV was too loud, but I could see she wasn't answering. After a few minutes she got up and smoothed the couch cushion before she sat on the chair furthest from him.

He sighed and joined me in the kitchen. We kept our voices low and talked as he made the salad. He made no more objections about Kelly seeing Marty.

"But when you get back we have to talk," he said, clearly, in a monotone that dripped with exasperation.

I chose the Howard Franklin Bridge to drive over Tampa Bay to the airport. Kelly used to love to see the bay from the bridge. She'd say the water looked "sparkly", like a fairyland. Today the sky was clear, bright, and a deeper blue than the water. We were driving east so the sun seemed to shine through, missing the clouds and lighting up the white-capped water. It did look magical.

"Hey, Kelly," I said. "Look at the water. It's fairyland again." She shaded her eyes with her hand and said nothing.

I cleared the constriction in my throat. I was tired of thinking of all the ways she had changed. Every time I thought of her former excitement when driving over the bay, the contrast between then and now would hit me hard. I missed my Kelly.

Once on the plane I pulled a Curious George book from my carry-on and started reading to her. I got to the part where George was trying on costumes from the upstairs trunk when I noticed Kelly was asleep. I looked at my beautiful daughter. Her curly hair fell over one eye as her head tilted toward me. She was so petite and fragile, and so very sad.

While she slept, I thought of that summer during my own childhood. Marty had been in a motorcycle accident. His knee was strained, one arm in a cast, and he was home every day. I pictured him in his baseball cap, tattered jeans, and a plaid flannel shirt sitting on his back porch asking us what we would like to pretend that day. And I could see us laughing, pretending to be such wonderful things, brave, happy things, acting out solutions to our problems with Marty waving his good arm, laughing and pretending with us, and then sitting us down to rest. We could talk about anything then.

One special day we painted on the outside of the old garage in his back yard. We were helping him, he said. It was white, and he had wanted to paint it dark blue. He had said we could paint anything we wanted and then fill it in to erase it before we went home.

My sister Jane painted a girl crying, and Jack painted a boy with his arm around a woman. I knew it was our mom; he tried so hard to be her protector. I painted our father beating on my mother. I remember it so clearly. Then Marty and I had a talk about our life and survival. Marty's back yard – our safe place. I prayed it would be Kelly's.

Driving the rental car to Lynwood I was amazed at all the changes. Forest Street changes were for the better. Most of the narrow two story homes had received face lifts: aluminum siding, brick fronts, paved driveways, new attached garages. Others had the old clapboard siding I remembered, gravel driveways, and back yard garages. It was familiar, and yet somehow frightening. Change does that to me. I giggled.

Thirty years ago, towards the end of that summer, we moved away when my mother scooped us up and dropped us off at Aunt Jo's, and we never saw her or my father again. I shook my head to stop that memory, and focused on the trees grown so tall they formed a canopy over the street.

"Another half a block and we'll be at Marty's," I said. I was flooded with memories, good, and bad.

Marty's house still had the garage in the back of his yard, but the yard was now fenced. An iron gate closed off the driveway just before the back porch. The garage and the house were painted dull beige. Not colorful like Marty, but then he must be very old now. Do heroes ever get old? I glanced at my house as I pulled into Marty's driveway. It was one of the ones with a face-lift. Goodness knows it needed it, poor sad thing!

Marty and his wife Georgia both had white hair and looked aged until you looked into their eyes. I guess when someone is at least thirty years older than you, no matter how old you are, they look old. But Marty's eyes were young, clear, hazel happy-to-see-you eyes; his gray hair curled around his ears. The shining dome of his head was hairless except for a wisp of gray fuzz right at the top. I fell into his arms.

"Sweet girl," he said. "Georgia, remember the good times I told you I had with the Walsh kids?"

When Georgia smiled, deep wrinkles lined her cheeks. "Come, honey," she said taking Kelly's hand. "I made cookies. We can have them on the porch while these two catch up."

And we were alone. I had so much to tell Marty, yet I was afraid to start. I wanted to find my old safe place and hide for a while.

He put on his jacket and said, "Let's go out to the back yard. I'm sure you'll find some changes."

No more changes, I thought as I followed him. The backyard was beautiful – changed, yet still safe. "Oh, Marty," I said.

The old willow tree was greening up. A new dogwood not quite in bloom grew next to it with a table and chairs placed between the two trees. Pansies and petunias bloomed around their trunks. The lawn was still brown in spots. And the side of the garage had two child-like figures painted on it – in blue.

"My grandchild," he explained. "No neighborhood kids come into the yard to see me anymore. Nowadays the parents around here, and maybe everywhere, keep their children close."

"No more magic?" I asked. I started crying and babbling at the same time. "I don't know what happened to her, Marty, and John doesn't care. He didn't even drive us to the airport."

He took my hand. "Okay, sweet girl, let's sit under our willow tree. Tell me when this started with your girl."

"Three months ago. She had a normal week. She seemed like the same happy Kelly. She went to school on the bus, and played with her friends on the block in their yards or ours after school. There are two boys about ten years old and a girl about nine in her group. Kelly is the youngest. She's eight. I didn't notice any change in her. On the Sunday she rode her bike with the same children on the trail."

"A trail?" Marty asked.

"It's a wide cement path created after removing track from an old railroad line. We live a block away from it. It covers half the county."

"Okay, go on."

"I didn't see her that Saturday night. I visited a friend of mine and stayed over, so I didn't come home until noon on Sunday. John watched her. Every other month my friend Sally and I used to meet, go out to dinner, and to the movies, and stay over at her house or mine."

"Used to?"

"We stopped after Kelly changed."

"Go on."

"When I got home that Sunday, Kelly was on a bike ride with her friends. When she got home she went right to her room. I heard her climb the stairs and called after her. Then I heard her door close, so I didn't bother her until it was time for dinner. When she came downstairs to eat she was as she seems now. No joy, so very quiet."

"Is that all?" His eyes continued the question.

"I've asked her what's wrong, what happened, and I've gotten nowhere. I don't nag. I have tried to stay gentle, and patient like the pediatrician and counselor suggested. But it's hard." The tears were flowing again.

"OK, now about John. How does she act around him?"

"She acts the same as with me. At first I thought he might have done something to her, but the doctor said there was no physical sign of abuse. I still wonder, sometimes, because he was alone with her Saturday night and Sunday morning. But I try not to think about that. I don't want to." I opened my mouth, but no more words came out.

"Have you accused him?"

"No. But I think he must know how I feel. He changed towards me not long after Kelly changed."

He looked hard at me. "Has there been any abuse to you?"

"No, Marty. None."

"Okay Teresa, now you listen to me. I'm just an old man. That summer, when you started sharing what it was like for you at home I just listened. Then we listened to each other about what we thought life should be, and what we wanted it to be. Do you remember?"

"Yes, Marty. That's why I'm here. You helped me to survive. Even after my mother and father died I would picture this yard and you, and it helped."

"Oh, Teresa," he hesitated. "If you want me to try to find out what happened with Kelly, I will." Pausing again he started walking toward the back porch. "But not tonight. Tonight you'll eat here and sleep in our spare room. We'll start tomorrow. You can both stay as long as you like. Okay?"

"Thank you, Marty."

Later that night Kelly turned her face away as she lay next to me on the double bed in Marty's spare room. This was more intimacy than she had allowed in the past three months. So far, taking her away from home seemed good for her. I could sleep.

Nothing happened the first day, or the second. It rained. Marty played games with Kelly. She seemed to like "Go Fish". Before bed she surprised me by saying, "Marty's nice." How I treasured those words.

A ceiling of gray New Jersey clouds hovered overhead the third morning, but there was no rain. Marty, Kelly, and I went out to the back porch.

Marty stepped in front of us and said, "Kelly, you're unhappy, and so is your Mom. When she was your age we played a game. After a few games her sadness left, and she could smile again. Has she told you about that?"

Kelly nodded.

"Would you like to smile again?"

Another nod.

Oh, God, is it going to work?

"Alright then, what do you want to be today? Teresa you go first."

"A wise woman."

"Kelly?"

"A brave power ranger," she whispered.

"Hmm," said Marty stifling a laugh. "What's a power ranger, girl?"

Kelly was silent.

"A power ranger is an action toy," I said. "There are lots of them. Different kinds."

He lifted Kelly's chin and looked into her eyes. "Are they all brave, Kelly?"

"Yes, brave," she whispered.

"Then I'll be the power ranger's assistant." He rubbed his chin with his thumb and forefinger. "Do we need the wise woman, Chief Power Ranger?"

Kelly looked over at me with a shy please mom smile and shook her head no.

"Okay wise woman, you go inside until we call you."

I left, shocked, not hurt. Marty knew best. I could see them through the window in the door, but he swept his head to the side in a clear, go away motion.

I grabbed the last cup of coffee. You're a mess, Teresa. You're going to need patience to give this a chance.

Georgia and I ate lunch together after she gave some to Marty and Kelly.

"Marty told me about that summer," she said. "I'm so sorry, Teresa."

I heard laughter outside. "Marty made the summer good," I said.

"How could it be good when both your parents died?"

"But we weren't there. We were at Aunt Jo's," I said quickly.

Georgia stared at me, eyes hooded. A new set of wrinkles made her resemble a bulldog.

"You're right, of course," I said breaking the silence. "I don't let myself think about that part."

"Did your aunt tell you how they died?"

"Car accident. I don't remember the details. I was only nine. We didn't talk about it. Our Aunt Jo loved us, but she didn't like to talk about our parents."

Georgia nodded, and said, "Shall we play cards?" And we played Rummy silently.

I concentrated on bringing my mind back to the present. I was just about there, enjoying the bursts of laughter I heard from the yard, when Georgia said, "It's good to see Marty playing with children again. It's been a while."

"Really? Why?" I asked.

"He plays with our granddaughter, that's all. When our children were young they brought neighborhood children over. Marty was often between jobs so he would be here watching them, and more often than not, playing with them."

I smiled remembering how he played with us.

"But then some of the neighbors tried to have him arrested. They accused him of being inappropriate with their children. Of course he wasn't. He was just being Marty. The only thing he did was hug them when he thought they needed it." She took a deep breath and continued. "Our son Marc was embarrassed and so angry, even after the police found no truth to the charges. Marty stopped all backyard play then, and Marc never got past that anger. I find myself wishing he was back there working things out like Kelly is." Frowning again, she drew a card and put one down. "I was worried about you coming here, Teresa." She glanced at me. "I didn't know Marty when you were living here. But he told me how much your parent's death affected him. He felt responsible."

"Responsible?" I didn't want to hear this.

"Yes, you see, he told his mother what you shared with him. Then she told your mother."

"How could telling that my father beat my mother make him responsible? I don't understand."

Georgia closed her mouth in a slit and said, "Rummy," as she laid all her cards down. She looked at me and said, "Ask Marty."

I shuffled the cards, and it felt like I was shuffling my insides. My mind flipped questions and facts into strange places, poking them where they didn't fit. Marty told what? Ask Marty. The words kept rhythm with the shuffle and the deal.

At 4:30 Marty and Kelly came in from the backyard. Kelly had a glow about her. She smiled at me before she ran up to our room.

"We didn't need you today, Teresa. Maybe we will tomorrow." He was smiling.

I wasn't. "Georgia told me that you felt responsible when we moved in with my aunt. Why, Marty?"

He answered by holding his index finger in front of his lips and tipping his head toward where Kelly was skipping down the stairs.

I had those strange dreams during the night. Black and white tile and a faucet dripping in time with my heart beat. I was stuck, unable to get out of the bathroom or the dream.

"Okay, Kelly girl," Marty said after breakfast. "The sun's out. It's time to be power rangers. Maybe we'll paint later today."

Georgia brought us coffee, and we watched them from the back porch windows.

Kelly and Marty zoomed around the yard, and sat and talked for a while. Then Marty brought out the blue paint and Kelly painted blue over beige as I had once painted blue over white. She finished one picture and then painted a second that contained three or four stick figures. I couldn't make out the details. After they finished they sat at the table and talked. It was thirty years ago, all over again in my mind.

Sometime later they walked back over to the wall. Kelly looked up at Marty. He nodded his head. She dipped the brush in the blue paint and painted over the last picture with quick deliberate strokes. I remembered doing that.

She called me and ran toward the back porch door. The brush dripped bright blue paint. Marty was waiting in the back yard.

"Okay, Kelly girl," Marty said. "Tell your mother what we just did."

"I put what was hurting me on the wall," she said proudly, "and then I erased it with the blue paint. Because Marty says sometimes we just have to start over. It's okay to start over. See? It's all gone!" She jumped up and down.

My heart was full. "What do you need from me?"

"To keep it gone," she said, making eye contact. "I'm going to paint a happy sun," she shouted over her shoulder as she ran back to the wall.

Marty could still smile like I remembered. When he was happy he had the kind of smile that lit up everything, including your heart. "Let's go inside," he said.

"Well?" I needed to know.

"I told your Kelly I'd explain to you, and she said okay," he said. "When they went on that bicycle ride, she and the other children stopped at a woman's house on the trail. They stopped there several times before. They were playing in her yard when one of the boys pulled down Kelly's shorts and under pants. Everyone laughed at her."

Marty paused and I giggled in the silence. I clapped my hand over my mouth. "I'm sorry, Marty. Nerves, I guess."

"Mrs. Lacy, I think she called her, came out on her porch and yelled at her. She called Kelly some nasty names. Bad and dirty were the words Kelly used. Anyway the woman told her she should never let a boy pull down her pants, only very bad girls did that. And she threatened to tell you how dirty and bad she was." He paused.

And I giggled again.

"This is not a small thing to her, Teresa. She was too ashamed to tell you, and too sure she was a bad girl. She needs to know you still love her." He gave me a Marty hug. "Ahhh," he sighed. "So she wasn't abused like you were." He squeezed me tight. "I'm so thankful, girl."

I froze. "Not me, Marty. My mother was abused. Not me." I pounded my fists on his chest as he hugged me tighter.

"Oh, my dear Teresa," he said, not letting me go. "You told me what your father did to you, don't you remember?"

"No," I shouted. "I told you what he did to my mother."

"Yes," he said softly, "And what he did to you. You asked why I felt responsible for you moving. After I told my mother that your father had started to abuse you sexually, she told your mother. And before I knew what had happened, your mother took all three of you to your aunt's house."

"My mom said she'd be back soon," I said. "And Aunt Jo said she'd be back to get us before we knew it. And then my mother died. She and my father died and couldn't come back. That's all I remember."

"You erased the rest."

"I erased the rest." I looked back at the garage wall. "But Kelly's safe, isn't she?" I pushed out of his arms.

"Yes, I'm so very thankful for that." His body trembled.

"I came so she'd be safe, and you fixed her. That is what's important," I hugged myself. "I don't have to remember anything else, do I Marty?" My head was spinning.

He reached out to me, lifted my chin, and wiped my tears with his thumb. "You're important, Teresa. You're important to me, to Kelly, to your husband, to yourself. You don't have to remember, but you might want to know."

"The dreams, something happened in the bathroom, didn't it?"

"Yes, Teresa," he said.

I leaned back to look in his eyes. "Did my mother know?"

"Not until my mother told her," he said, closing his eyes. "Then she packed up you kids and took you to your aunt."

Such a dread in my heart. "And?"

"She drove right back and confronted your father in the bar, there were witnesses. He was drunk and he hit her. One of the men got him into her car. She said she was going to drive him home, but—"

"She crashed the car. She was protecting me, wasn't she?" All the air seemed to leave as I struggled to breathe. Years of fuzziness scrunched making room for just an ounce of clarity.

Marty was crying, but my tears had dried. "And you felt responsible." I touched his cheek. "I remember feeling guilty that they died. But I didn't know why."

"You were just a child. I should have told the police instead of my mother. I have always wanted to tell you how sorry I was. I should have—"

"Stop," I said holding up my hand. My knees were shaking. I was crashing, but he looked so old, so weak, so lost. I clenched my jaw. I wanted to shake him back into the happy magical Marty that knew all the answers. His eyes seemed to be pleading, and that little wisp of gray on the top of his head looked so precious. "It's okay," I said. "I forgive you. But it wasn't your fault. You did what you thought was right." I patted his back. "Oh, Marty, I've missed you and your backyard. My safe place."

He sighed. "Not all backyards are safe, Teresa. Not even this one."

I thought of how I had blamed John, poor John, and I wanted to ask Marty what I should do. I could see Kelly through the window painting a huge blue sun high over several flowers. Her mouth was moving rapidly, talking or singing as she painted. I excused myself and went for a walk alone.

Standing in front of my old house I spoke to my mother. I told her that I remembered how she used to brush the tangles from my hair and kiss me goodnight. I imagined her kissing my cheek and closed my hand over the spot. A familiar song was playing in my head. The one about sugar helping the medicine go down. I remembered how she used to sing it to me when she disguised my medicine with honey, and I thought of how she disguised her bruises with makeup, dark glasses and scarves.

"But sometimes you have to taste it, Mom," I said out loud. I thanked her for saving me, and I let myself miss her. I couldn't talk to my father. Marty's words - you might want to know - echoed, and looking up at the house, I did know. As I let the dark facts settle, images of my father touching me, whispering to me not to tell, came into focus then fled. I shuddered.

When I turned away from the house a bunch of reasons circled my thoughts – reasons for the bathroom dream and reasons why I never entirely trusted my husband or any other man. Reasons why I still didn't want to remember – totally. I vowed to get help. I knew I needed it.

Walking back to Marty's I felt exhausted, yet lighter. I wanted to sleep and I wanted to sing. I wanted to hug Kelly, needed to hug Kelly and Marty and, yes, John.

I started making a to-do list in my head to focus. Paint the garage blue with Kelly and Marty, and call John. Tell them I love them. Make airline reservations for tomorrow and plan a visit to Mrs. Lacey. Somehow, deal with all this. Could I know and yet let go?

I looked up in the direction of the stars. None were visible. Then I turned my mind back to making my list. I would buy some blue paint when I got home. I stood still in front of Marty's house wondering if there was enough blue paint, or paint remover, to get Kelly through her childhood, and me past mine?

The lightness left. I heard no music as deep tears, a torrent of tears, escaped. I sat on the curb and let them flow.

♦♦♦♦♦♦♦♦♦♦♦♦

Jean Limongello, formerly from New Jersey, lives in New Port Richey, Florida. She enjoyed a long career as a Registered Nurse - the last 20 years of which she spent happily managing a team of Hospice clinicians, and facilitating creation of software designed to document that unique form of care.

Jean fell in love with reading and writing as a child. Besides writing short stories and poetry for her own enjoyment, and writing for her agency, she once wrote publicity for a singer.

After the deaths of her husband and son in 2003 she turned to writing as an outlet. In 2005 she took online courses at Gotham Writer's Workshop to improve her craft and decided to get serious. Besides writing short stories and flash fiction she has completed "Apples Fall", a mystery/suspense novel which she hopes to get published, and is busily writing a sequel. In March of 2007 she traded her career as a nurse for that of a full time writer.

Jean is also a chapter leader for The Compassionate Friends of Pasco County, Florida. She has written articles and poetry for the chapter newsletter she also co-edits. She finds her volunteer activities for The Compassionate Friends healing, challenging and worthwhile.

These days you will find Jean pounding her laptop keyboard with her cat GrayC snoozing at her feet, or she may be swimming in her pool or in the Gulf. She also loves spending time with her daughter, grand-daughter and friends. Her life is full, memories dear, and her future will be a writing adventure to work at and enjoy.

PAINTED LADY

By Anne Elwick

Sylvia stepped out of her car and sucked in the fresh air that carried a hint of Jasmine from the untrimmed hedges lining the walkway to the house and clustered at the front corner of the unkempt lawn. After leaving the confines of the city with its sprawling acres of concrete and towering glass and steel trophies, her whole being screamed with relief, accompanied by anticipation of a little suburban tranquility.

She looked up at the house with its ornamentation and remembered the photograph that had attracted her attention in the newspaper's real estate section. The photograph had been black and white, yet had beckoned to her, holding her attention and piquing her interest. She wanted out of the hectic city. The house in the photo seemed to call out "Come to me! Let me give you the peace of mind you crave." She couldn't resist the invitation.

Now that she stood before it, she was amazed at the subtle hues to the chipped and peeling paint. The Victorian colors of cream, green and burgundy were appropriate for a regal painted lady. And, even in its weathered and faded condition, this house just oozed with genteel charm.

A quick glance at her watch told her that the realtor was running late. Their appointment was for two o'clock, and it was already ten after. Sylvia glanced around and noted that no neighbors were outdoors that she could see, no people strolling down the generous sidewalks in the neighborhood, and no cars moving along the narrow streets. An eerie shiver went down her spine, as she suddenly felt quite alone. Only the sound of a motorized machine, perhaps a hedge trimmer or an electric lawnmower, hummed from a lawn much further down the block.

The other houses in the neighborhood also possessed the charm of a bygone era of gentility and grace. All of them looked to be lovingly cared for, and meticulously restored, whereas this house needed some work. Just a cursory examination of its facade revealed some sagging trim, a few warped boards, and more than a hint of weather damage here and there.

After pacing back and forth on the public walkway several times, Sylvia decided to go ahead and wander around the grounds. The realtor had mentioned that the house was vacant. The owners had been transferred out of state and were already gone. She followed a narrow bricked path that led around the house. Every few steps she would pause and look up to admire the scrollwork and carvings that decorated the lovely old home.

She thought about the workers who must have climbed rickety ladders almost a century ago to work on the beautiful trim. She imagined the owners having a lengthy discussion about just which colors would compliment each other and add charm. She could almost hear the soft voice of a lady cajoling her stubborn husband into permitting the use of bright colors instead of leaving everything whitewashed and plain.

As she rounded the corner toward the back yard, she thought she heard giggling voices. Looking through a ragged hedgerow she noticed a decrepit swing set. The breeze rocked the empty swings gently to and fro. She smiled as she remembered happy moments from her childhood spent swinging on a similar set. She could almost feel the wind on her face as she recalled how she had stretched her toes toward the sky and swung as high as the ropes would reach.

She thought about the last time that she sat in a swing. It was early in summer when she was eleven years old, and Richard Butler had asked her if she wanted a push. She had gladly accepted his offer. She could still feel the heat of his hands on her back as he pressed against her to push her gently forward. Then he had pushed harder until she thought she might be flying. It was exhilarating. They had spent the afternoon taking turns on the swing.

After she grew tired of swinging, Richard had walked her home from the park. They held hands, and just before they reached the sidewalk to her front door she turned to him and said, "I have a secret to tell you." His twelve-year-old eyes flashed with interest as he leaned over toward her. She placed her hands on his shoulders and pulled herself up until her lips were next to his ear.

"I love you." Her whisper was followed by a quick peck on his cheek before she turned and rushed indoors. He lingered near the sidewalk for several minutes; gazing toward the house. Sylvia had returned to the park almost every afternoon that summer, watching for him to return, but he never did. Then, when school started in September, she discovered that his family had moved away to another state. *God, what a crush I had on him! Puppy love.*

A short distance away there was a rusty tricycle from a bygone era. It had a tall front wheel and two small back wheels joined with a graceful arch topped by a worn wooden seat. Sylvia had seen similar tricycles in antique shops.

"That will be wonderful when I restore it and display it on the front lawn."

A shiver ran down her spine as the words echoed in the stillness. *Where did that thought come from?*

The walkway was in bad shape in several places. Bricks were missing or jutting upward at odd angles. She thought about how much work had gone into laying that lengthy walkway, and how sad it was to see that former owners had let it get in such terrible condition. *Well, a strong will and a strong back can fix that.*

"A strong will and a strong back." Those words had meaning. Her thoughts wandered back to her college years. It had always been her dream to be a doctor, and when she was accepted at Johns-Hopkins for her internship, she had thought that all her dreams were coming true. She had always learned quickly and proficiently, finishing each semester at the top of her class.

Then she met Joe.

He worked for the hospital in the maintenance department. "I'm the heating and air-conditioning medic." He laughed, and it was a robust rumble that filled the room. He had deep-set blue eyes and wild light brown hair. There was a small patch of hair at his right temple that was blonde, almost white.

Sylvia wanted to reach up and touch it.

He entered her room and looked at the thermostat on the wall. Setting his tool chest down in the floor, he had crossed the room to look over her shoulder at the pages in the book she was intently studying. "So. You a doctor, or what?"

Sylvia sighed, "I'm an intern. I've got two years before I become a doctor, and then will have to serve a residency before I'm independent."

"Wow. Takes a long time, don't it?"

Sylvia cringed at the bad grammar, but the conversation continued for only a brief moment before he returned to his work. As he repaired the broken thermostat, she watched him work. His movements were quick, precise, and efficient. "You're almost a surgeon at what you do," she said.

"I'm good at what I do," he responded, matter-of-factly. "But, don't take much education to do what I do. Mostly a strong will and a strong back."

A few days later Sylvia had bumped into Joe at the campus coffee shop.

When he saw Sylvia his blue eyes sparkled and he came to greet her. "Hiya, Doc! That AC working okay for you?"

She laughed, "Too good. I had to put a blanket on the bed." She noticed the only unoccupied table in the room and nodded toward it. "Care to join me? Seems like the only vacant spot in the house."

They were so comfortable with each other and the afternoon drifted away while they each talked about where they had grown up, and their aspirations. Sylvia had led a blessed, though sheltered life in an upper middle-class family. Joe had grown up in a very similar home, but his father had been killed in Vietnam, leaving his mother to provide for the family. Times were rough and they moved to a different, less affluent neighborhood. Even though he excelled in school, he knew that his mother couldn't afford to send him to college, so he didn't even think about what options lay in his future. He knew that he would have to learn a trade, and make a living.

Their friendship blossomed, and they eased into an intimate relationship as comfortable as a warm sweater on a chilly morning. Sylvia was light-hearted and jolly. Her co-workers at the hospital couldn't help but smile as they watched her walking down the halls and giving gentle pats of encouragement to the patients she encountered.

Two years later, when Sylvia was offered a residency at Sloan Kettering in Houston, Joe patted her reassuringly. "Go. Do what you're meant to do. Become a wonderful heart surgeon, and save lives. You'll be fine. I'll be fine."

"I don't want to leave you," she hesitated. She knew that there had never been any promises, and neither had seemed to seek a commitment. But, after almost two years as friends and lovers, she thought that their relationship had more substance than a simple short-term romance.

Joe placed his hands on her shoulders and looked into her eyes. "I love you. I want you to be happy, and successful, and have everything you've ever dreamed of. I've never seen myself in that picture with you. I've always known that your life would really begin after you leave me."

He loved her. Why hadn't he ever uttered those words before? Why did he wait until he was telling her goodbye to say the thing she had wanted to hear so desperately? But, what if he had said it sooner? Would she have changed her plans? Would she have begged him to go with her? Would she have begged him to let her stay?

Sylvia ached with loneliness for a while, but soon her new responsibilities and the demands of her career filled her days. And her nights. She followed her career opportunities to some of the finest hospitals in the country. She broadened her skills. She was published in medical journals. Her life was more than she had imagined it could ever be. And less. She only dated occasionally, and no other romantic relationships had ever developed. "You're an old maid," she often remarked to her image in the mirror.

Now, she was at a point in her career, and her life, where she wanted peace. She had given up a successful Seattle practice to become a teacher at Johns Hopkins where her career had begun. She was significantly more wealthy, secure and confident. But, she was right back where she started, almost.

"Funny, to think of life like that. Full circle. Back where I started. Who ever said 'You can't go home again'?" She shuddered when she realized she had spoken out loud once more and shook her head as if trying to shake off the unwelcome memories. She wasn't accustomed to talking to herself. Sylvia straightened her back and stiffened her shoulders before walking further along the path.

A gate sagged from its hinges where the fence opened into the back yard from the walkway. Two enormous Oak trees flanked it, and Sylvia noted a large heart with other inscriptions carved into the bark of one of the trees. She moved closer and stood on tiptoe to peer at the faded markings. "Joseph loves Sylvia." *What an odd coincidence.* Another Sylvia had once lived here, or perhaps Joseph had been the resident and Sylvia had been his sweetheart. Then she noticed shallow lines had been scratched across Joseph's name. *What does that mean?*

After she had completely circled the house and returned to the front walkway, she went up the steps and sat down on the top one. She gave another glance at the wristwatch.

Still there was no realtor in sight. "Hmmmm. Twenty minutes late. No cell phone? Should I call her? It's her place to call me to say she'll be late, right? Surely she must be almost here." Sylvia didn't even realize she was speaking out loud.

As she perched on the steps her mind wandered back over who might have sat where she was sitting now. A young girl named Sylvia might have sat here watching for her sweetheart to come for a visit. Perhaps the original owner had spent some time sitting here, watching the neighborhood blossom a hundred years ago. The trees must have been very small then; maybe some of them had not even been planted in those early years. And, as the years went by, other homes began to fill the lots across the streets. Trees were planted and flowers blossomed. The laughter of children playing filled the air.

She looked around at the curved porch. *How many people had sat out here to sip tea, or read the newspaper and enjoy the wonderful fresh air and fragrance of the blossoms?* She could already imagine herself living here and doing just that. She was also considering how many of the neighbors had lived in their homes for long periods of time and could help fill in the blanks about the people that had lived here before. Somehow she knew that there was an interesting history to be learned. She knew that she wanted to know all about it. She wanted to become part of it.

A quick walk out to the curb was fruitless. No traffic to indicate that the realtor was coming down the street. She leaned against the side of the car and looked up at the house. She loved it already. It felt like home. She smiled as she spoke to the house. "You're an old maid, like me." She felt welcome here, and couldn't wait to see the inside. It might be old and a little worn around the edges. So what if she had to spend a little extra money to freshen it up? *Old girls need a little extra makeup to look their best.*

"Gee, I'm getting a bit senile, I thought that shutter was sagging when I drove up." A brisk breeze that blew her hair around and into her mouth stifled her remark. Shaking the hair away from her face she looked up at the side of the house and noticed that the peeling paint appeared smoother, too. "What's this?"

Some magnetic pull drew her toward the house and she walked up the steps and laid her hand against the coolness of the ornate brass knocker on the beautifully carved door. She gave a gentle tap. After a moment the door swung slowly inward, and she stepped inside. As the door closed silently behind her, the breeze picked up again and the scent of Jasmine wafted through the air. Blossoms opened on the neatly trimmed hedges, and the young trees swayed in the gentle spring wind. The sun glistened on the freshly painted house, and the regal lady seemed to look toward the clear blue sky and smile.

♦♦♦♦♦♦♦♦♦♦♦♦

Award-winning author Anne Elwick was born in East Texas. She began writing poetry and short stories as a teenager, and also became a talented artist. She won several art competitions and at the age of thirteen was commissioned to do a painting for the Gregg County Courthouse. She studied Journalism and Creative Writing in Texas and Arkansas while raising a family and pursuing a career in office management.

She has written numerous poems and short stories that have been published, as well as articles and columns that have appeared in Texas and Arkansas newspapers. Involved in several community and social organizations, she has served as President of two writing groups - River Valley Writers and Wizards of Words. She is also a member of Romance

Writers of America, Oklahoma Writers Federation, Inc. and Mid-America Authors.

Her debut novel "We Don't Say Goodbye" was released in 2006. A chapbook titled "Jonquils in January" was released In December 2007, and a new novel, "Bawdy Old Broads" will be released in 2008.

Now retired, she travels extensively to give presentations and informative workshops to aspiring authors. Anne resides with her husband Arthur in western Arkansas, near the foothills of the Ozarks where she is currently at work on her next novel.

www.anneelwick.com

THE GHOST OF HI JOLLY

By Edd Voss

Throwing a cell phone across the room just didn't have the same therapeutic effect as slamming down a telephone receiver. Even though the person on the other end only heard a click when the call was ended the person doing the slamming was afforded some release of anger. Dave Kennedy was angry partially because he couldn't slam down the receiver in frustration; the client had called him on his cell phone.

Now his plans were screwed. Instead of getting out of the office by noon and enjoying a leisurely drive to Phoenix, he wouldn't be able to leave till around three that afternoon. It wasn't like he could just blow this client off either because he just happened to be one of the hottest producers in Hollywood.

If he wasn't working so hard to get the screenwriting gig it would have been different. He groaned at the idea of fighting traffic from his office in L. A. out to at least Palm Desert. It wasn't that he didn't like flying it was that he had just bought a new Mercedes convertible and really wanted to get it out on the open road. Besides the fact that it was too late to make other plans, and the client in Phoenix was a very influential director who had an idea for a screenplay he wanted Dave to write.

By the time he got out of the office it was three-thirty in the afternoon and traffic was at its worst. It was stop and go from the moment he pulled onto Interstate10 until he was rolling through the town of Banning four hours later. It was only eighty-five miles but the traffic was bumper to bumper all the way. Even at that point traffic was still heavy, but not as bad as it had been.

He pulled into a small truck stop in Cabazon to grab a cup of coffee and a couple of energy drinks. The evening was warm but not stifling hot like it could be during the day, so he took the time to put the convertible top down.

"I might as well make the best of it, I guess," he said to himself as he drove past two full-scale concrete dinosaurs on his way back onto the interstate. He chuckled to himself as he thought about how the concrete monsters served to entice tourists to stop. Good thing that the food was even better than the dinosaurs at getting the trucks to stop, or the casino next door would take away all of their business.

He took out a disc he had recorded just for long drives with the top down and popped it into the CD player as he accelerated to just above the speed limit. He let the music wash over him. Jan and Dean sang "Dead Man's Curve," followed by the Beach Boys, then The Mamas and Papas, along with Three Dog Night and other groups from the sixties and seventies. It was what he called his cruising music. Occasionally the Rock and Roll would be interrupted by a trucking song by someone like Red Simpson, Dave Dudley, C. W. McCall, or Del Reeves. Music soothed the anger that had plagued him all afternoon. He was still angry that he had been delayed, but he did enjoy driving with the top down and the music playing loud enough to be heard over the road noise.

He passed through what he called the "Valley of Don Quixotic" as the last light of day was fading. For miles in every direction nothing could be seen but windmills. Not the quaint little windmills from storybooks, but towering structures reaching high into the sky. Many of them had blades that were over a hundred feet long. The blades moved slowly through the air as they made their rotations generating electricity with each sweep. In his mind's eye he could see the errant Spanish knight tilting with the monsters. Sometimes he felt that he was tilting with them.

One of his favorite songs began to play so he sang along as he drove on into the night before him. Mile after mile passed as he rolled on towards the Arizona border town of Ehrenberg. Seeing a rest area just past Desert Center he stopped to stretch his legs and use the men's room. When he walked out of the facility, he was stopped dead in his tracks.

Standing next to his car was a camel. The animal was nosing around the front seat as if looking for some tasty morsel of whatever it is that camels eat.

In shock he stood there trying to make sense of what he was seeing. A camel, in the middle of the California desert, what a ridiculous idea! Was this a caffeine induced hallucination? How many cups of coffee had he consumed?

He finally found the courage to approach the car and the animal. For the first time he noticed that the rest area was deserted. The interstate seemed to be unnaturally empty also. There wasn't a single car or truck in sight. It was just him and the camel. As he got closer, the animal raised its head and stared at him. The large brown eyes appeared to be sizing him up as the mouth just kept chewing.

Do camels chew their cud like a cow, he wondered, and continued to walk closer.

"He will not bite you but he does drool a bit sometimes," a voice called to him out of the dark.

Dave spun around looking for the source of the voice.

A man walked out of the darkness dressed in long flowing robes, wearing a burnoose like something out of an Arabian Nights movie.

"Where did he come from?" Dave asked the man.

"His ancestors were brought here and abandoned in the desert." The man patted the camel affectionately. "It is my job to look after them and care for them."

"I've never heard of such a thing. Why would anyone bring these animals over here?"

"Your Army thought that they would be of use in these deserts, and they were till the war in the east took everyone's attention away from them. Now they have only me to care for them." The man used a switch to prod the camel away from the car and back out into the darkness of the desert night.

Standing there watching them go, Dave was not sure how to react. The sound of a semi truck pulling into the parking area roused him from his reverie. He looked up and saw that the sky was filled with more stars than he could count. He had made this drive many times before, so why hadn't he ever seen this man or the camels?

Shaking his head to try and clear it, Dave opened the car door and got behind the wheel. He took one last look in the direction the man and camel had gone and then put the car in gear and started east once more.

It was after ten when he stopped at a large truck stop in Ehrenberg. Thinking that maybe he was just so hungry that his mind had played a trick on him, he went into the café and sat down at the counter.

An old man was sitting across the U-shaped counter from him. His skin looked like tanned leather, creased by wrinkles that resembled the dry, rolling desert. Snow white hair poked out from under a battered old cowboy hat. Dave figured he was an old desert rat, one of the people who lived in the desert who were known to scratch out a living any way they could. He just sat there drinking his coffee and gazing at a place far away in both distance and time.

"Have you lived out here long," Dave asked the man after giving his food order to the waitress.

"Ever since I was just a whippersnapper," the old man said in a voice as dry as the desert wind.

"Can I ask you a question?" Dave asked him.

"What would you like to know?"

"I don't know exactly how to say this," Dave hesitated.

"Well the best way is to just spit it out, son."

"Have you ever seen . . . I can't believe that I'm about to ask this . . . have you ever seen any camels out here?"

The old man took a long time to answer while he searched Dave's face for some sign of mockery. "Why do you ask?" he finally asked his voice very soft.

"I think that I saw one in the rest area west of here."

"Was it alone?" the voice held no sign of doubt.

"No, there was a man with him dressed like a Bedouin."

"Hi Jolly," was the only response.

"Hi Jolly?" Dave asked.

"My father used to talk about him a lot when I was a kid." The old man looked off in the distance again. "He came over here when the Army experimented, used camels before the Civil War." Taking a sip of his coffee the man pushed his hat back on his head before continuing. "When the war started, the Army gave up on it and just turned the animals loose in the desert over near Gila Bend. Instead of going back to the Middle East, Hi Jolly stayed on here for the camels. Eventually he worked for the Army as a scout and lived over in Quartzite. He is buried there."

"But who was that I saw tonight?"

"There are those who say that the ghost of Hi Jolly roams these deserts looking for his beloved camels so that he can care for them."

"You're telling me that what I saw was a ghost? What about the Camel was it a ghost too? If so it was a very fragrant one."

"No," the old man laughed, "it was very real. Probably one of the descendants of those original animals brought over in the late eighteen-fifties."

They talked about the camels and their ghostly driver while Dave ate his meal. For the next hundred miles Dave couldn't get the thoughts of Hi Jolly and the camels out of his mind. When he finally fell asleep in his motel room bed his dreams were of caravans of camels crossing the Arizona desert.

The director wanted to remake a western, and Dave suggested making a whole new one. They bantered back and forth over the idea of adapting one of the newer writer's books into a screenplay versus writing a whole new idea. After the meeting Dave decided to do some research in Phoenix before driving back to L A. He spent the day looking for anything he could find about the U.S. Army Camel Corps, including the legends that had grown up around them. He was especially intrigued by the story of the Greek Syrian camel driver known as Hi Jolly. The thought that Hi Jolly was buried in the tiny town of Quartzite kept popping up. Visiting the grave of this unusual man became a must. After checking the internet for hotels in Quartzite he finally found one and booked reservations online.

The sun was sinking in the west as he drove out of Phoenix heading into the sunset. Heat waves shimmered off the asphalt in the distance making it seem as if the road ahead was wet. Dry hot wind blew through Dave's hair as he relished the joy of driving with the top down.

Songs about cowboys, gunfighters, and the west in general poured out of the CD player. Since the idea of writing a western had come up, he recorded a collection of music that would help put him in the right mood to write about the west. He had searched the internet and downloaded songs by Chris LeDoux, Ian Tyson, Red Stegal and others who helped get his mind focused on the west and the early cowboy culture.

Darkness was settling in as he took the exit for Quartzite. It was situated in the middle of a desert mountain range where the temperature during the summer could reach well over the hundred degree mark. Even the nights could be almost unbearable.

Quartzite becomes one large flea market and haven for rock hounds beginning in late November and continuing through December and January. People flock from all over the country to enjoy the weather when it is at its coolest. Many flea marketers are modern-day gypsies living in RVs as they travel from one flea market to the next all year long, others are retirees supplementing their incomes. The year round residents are the hardcore desert dwellers who relish the harsh environment and the challenges that living there presents. Some came just as Dave had, to see the grave and monument raised to a simple camel driver, known as Hi Jolly.

He toyed with the idea of driving out to the grave in the dark but decided to wait and check it out first in the daylight. After he checked into the hotel and paid for two nights, he thought it might be a good idea to see the grave both in the daylight and after dark.

He awoke early, found a small café, and had breakfast before going out to the grave. He parked on the main road, walked down the dusty side road that led to the town cemetery and the Hi Jolly monument. Wind blew dust across his path as he approached the pyramid with a sheet metal camel on top of it. On the face of the tomb was a plaque telling the story of Hadji Ali better known around this desert town as Hi Jolly. Standing there, letting the wind blow around him, Dave took his time reading the story spelled out on the plaque. The seed of an idea took hold and a story began to take root.

The rest of the day was spent exploring the town talking to the year-round residents about the tales of their famous camel driver. It would take a long time to sift through the tall tales to get to the truth. Most places were closed by the time the sun had set. Only the few fast food places and the twenty-four hour truck stop remained open as he again walked the dusty road towards the cemetery.

A full moon let him see his way and let him identify the tumble weeds for what they were. As he approached the pyramid once more he could see a lone figure standing there watching him approach. The watcher was dressed in the long flowing robes of the eastern desert but they didn't move in the night breeze.

David knew instantly who was waiting for him. He was frightened and excited at the same time. There stood the ghost of Hi Jolly.

He played the movie in his mind. It was exactly what the producer had been looking for and what the director had wanted. Here was the story, a story of adventure, exploration, and humor.

Author's note: The use of camels in the southwest is real, so is the basic story of Hi Jolly. Are there still descendants of those original animals roaming the deserts of Arizona and California? Some say that they were sold off, others say that they were turned lose near Gila Bend, Arizona. While I doubt the ghost of Hi Jolly roams the area, you can find his grave on the west side of Quartzite, Arizona.

♦♦♦♦♦♦♦♦♦♦♦♦

Edd lives with his wife near Springdale, Washington. Having grown up in Colorado he has always loved the west and especially the mountains. While Edd pulls oversized loads all over America, Polly his wife takes care of things on the ranch and helps with their photography business. They soon hope to start breeding Paint Horses. Over the last 15 years Edd has driven truck across all of the lower 48 states and most of Southern Canada pulling vans, refrigerated, flatbed, and a variety of specialized trailers.

His love of photography began during a trip to visit his older brother Bill who was living in New York City during the late 60's.

In high school Gordon Parks' book "A Choice of Weapons" had a profound effect on Edd. He took advantage of an Army program to reenlist for a change of specialty to attend the U.S. Army Still Photography Course at Ft. Monmouth, New Jersey. He went on to serve as a Photographer at Ft. Knox, Kentucky, Seoul, Korea, Ft Rucker Alabama, and Bad Toelz, Germany before leaving active duty in 1980.

After struggling to make a living in his beloved Colorado he moved to Washington State in 1986. He first resided in the Seattle area then moved south to Tacoma after meeting his wife Polly. Later they left the hustle and bustle of the city behind and moved east to the mountains north of Spokane.

Since beginning his driving career in January of 1990, Edd has logged well over a million miles.

You will find many of his short stories published by Amazon.com included in the Amazon Shorts Program. "A Tree for America" was published as his first novella, and he has written a sequel that has been published by Amazon Shorts.

http://eddvoss.com/

COMING HOME

By Tory Lynn

For Tricia Conway, coming home was a relative term. She didn't consider the lonely apartment where she lived in New York City a home, not at all. After she graduated from high school in New Jersey, she had moved to NYC with her mother. Since they'd been there, Tricia had taken odd jobs to help make ends meet until she finally found one she enjoyed at The Pastry Pub, a very popular deli that provided a catering service as well as serving the public directly. The only problem was she didn't like her boss—an impersonal, grumpy man. But since her paycheck kept their heads above water most of the time and she'd promised to stay and help till her mother had the job she was striving for, Tricia had no choice.

All the while Tricia knew in her heart that there was something better for her in Small Town U.S.A. where people were friendly and would make her laugh, people who would love and respect her. She hadn't found that in the city and she wanted to break away in the worst way to find her dream life. In spite of it all, she had learned a valuable lesson from her mother that to have anything worth having, one must be patient and persistent.

One night Tricia awakened to a feeling of despair beyond anything she had ever felt before. Something was wrong, she felt it. She listened but heard nothing in the quiet night. Suddenly the doorbell rang. Even before she opened the door and saw the police standing there, Tricia knew something terrible had happened.

Her mother had been killed in a car crash.

The night of her mother's funeral, after scant sleep, Tricia woke up to the scent of jasmine in the air. It was soothing, gave her comfort, although a bittersweet comfort. With tears in her eyes she lay awake thinking of her mother, wishing she could hold her one more time.

She was 18 years old when she lost her mother and didn't know how she was going to live without her. As far as she knew she didn't have family anywhere, she was alone in the world. There was a small insurance settlement that had paid the funeral costs and would pay most of the debt her mother had incurred, with a little left over, but not much.

An older couple, Ted and Rita Kurn, who had befriended her mother during her last days, had offered to help Tricia, to help put her affairs in order. Tricia was so grief stricken and vulnerable, she was glad of the offer from the kind couple.

Her boss had been his usual unsympathetic self. He had expected Tricia to be at work the very day after the funeral. No extra days off, he told her. He said he couldn't afford to have her on the schedule if she wasn't going to work it. Said he would hire someone else if she didn't show up. But Tricia needed her job, so she worked while grieving.

A week later a woman came into the shop out of the blue and offered her condolences. The woman hurried back toward the door before Tricia could ask her any questions. She suddenly turned, and with a look that frightened Tricia, she told her not to trust the Kurns – then she disappeared.

At that very moment the scent of Jasmine surrounded Tricia and a feeling of forebodance overcame Tricia. The feeling was so powerful she began shaking. When she asked her boss if she could leave, he became angry. She promised to finish the order she was working on, first, and also promised to work an extra shift for him if he'd let her go home for the day. Told him that there was something urgent she needed to address. She knew that without her paycheck she'd be out on the streets, so she had to be careful and bargain with him. He relented. After she finished the order, she smiled at the old man, said thank you, and took off.

When Tricia opened the door to the small apartment she found the Kurns going through her things. She didn't even know they had a key. They were surprised at her sudden appearance.

She looked down at the scattered papers on the table and saw that they had written her bank account numbers on a sheet of paper and that they had also forged her name on a check drawn from the insurance money account.

They attempted to convince her it would make it easier for them to pay things off for her, if the money was in their account, that way she wouldn't have to worry about anything. They would manage her money for her.

Tricia wasn't that gullible, however, and became livid. She had trusted them.

They glared at her with harsh mean stares.

It frightened her.

The door was open and the neighboring couple, who lived down the hall, stopped in the doorway when they saw her in the apartment. It wasn't usual for Tricia to leave her door wide open, and the two men knew it.

They looked in. "Are you alright, Tricia?" one of them asked.

They were the only neighbors she knew, and they had been kind to her and had always engaged her in light conversation whenever they saw her. They had even shared a few meals together when her mother was alive.

The Kurns pushed past them and left in a huff.

At the insistence of her neighbors, Tricia called the police and reported what had happened. She was told that the man and wife were fugitives and wanted by the F.B.I. They were scam artists and had a history of violence. The agents told her she had been lucky to get away unharmed and unscathed. They had stolen thousands of dollars from the elderly during the past few years, and now they had a vulnerable 18-year-old to add to the list. With this fresh lead, law enforcement was able to arrest them as they attempted to leave the city.

Tricia felt lucky to have escaped their greedy hands, but in the process she lost trust in everybody. She couldn't help it. She felt that the people in a big city didn't exude trust, and when her gay friends moved out of state soon after, there was nobody left who she could trust.

She continued working at the bakery/deli, but she wasn't happy. She knew she had to make a change soon, for if she stayed, her spirit would die. She knew her mother would not have wanted that for her.

The holidays were arriving in full force. Tricia couldn't bear the thought of another Christmas in the lonely city.

One night she woke up after a dream. She couldn't remember anything about it other than it left her feeling safe and secure and the smell of jasmine was in the air once again. Words kept echoing in her mind as she lay there, *it's time, it's time, it's time ...*

She got up and packed her belongings. That morning she called her boss and quit her job. She picked up her final paycheck, then bought a one-way bus ticket heading west. Nothing in the apartment was worth taking so she left it behind.

Leaving with only two large suitcases and her backpack, Tricia felt free for the first time in her life. She watched the city disappear behind her and looked forward to a new beginning somewhere else. She didn't care where she ended up. She just wanted out.

An older lady sat next to her on the bus. "Where are you headed, dear?"

Tricia smiled sweetly, "I haven't decided." It was the first kind face she had seen in a long time. The woman looked vaguely familiar, but Tricia couldn't place her.

The old woman pulled out a bottle of perfume and dabbed some on her wrists and a little under her ears.

Tricia felt emotion rise within her. It was that unmistakable smell of Jasmine again.

The woman smiled broadly. "This is my favorite. It is a special blend and is made by my sister."

"I love that smell. Where are you headed?" Tricia didn't know what else to say to the woman.

"I'm going to Montana. To a little mountain community in the Bitterroot Mountain range where I grew up. I'm on my way home."

"So you have family there?"

"Oh yes, most of my family is there. A few have moved on to other parts of the world, but this particular town is where I'll always call home." The woman looked at her with a big grin as if she had a secret and couldn't wait to tell her. "You know when I first went there I was alone. I was young just like you and I was looking for a place to call home, too."

A warm shiver run through Tricia's body. It was as if this woman knew all about her.

The woman pulled out photographs of her family and some of the small town. She held out a photo of an old storefront window and one of a small house, quaint and very homelike. "You keep these dear, to remember our conversation. You'll find your place in this big world, I promise."

Tricia looked at the old woman in wonderment and reached for the photos. "Thank you," she said, looking down at the pictures. "You never told me your name."

The woman had fallen asleep.

Tricia leaned her head back and closed her eyes as well. She'd find out her name later. But when she woke up the woman was gone. The small perfume bottle was the only thing that was on the seat. She picked it up. She looked around the bus at the other passengers to see if the woman had moved to another seat. She thought maybe she had gone to the restroom.

The bus stopped for a break at a rest stop and the woman was still nowhere in sight.

Tricia boarded the bus again after the stop and took her seat. She was thinking about how strange it was that the woman had disappeared.

A young mother sitting in the seat across from her, smiled. "Excuse me, I wonder if you'll let my son sit next to you. It is getting cramped in these seats and my daughter is getting cranky."

"Sure, I don't mind. I guess the woman who was sitting here earlier has left."

"What woman? You've had the seat to yourself the whole time." The young girl looked at Tricia suspiciously and then changed her mind about letting her son sit there.

Tricia reached into her bag for the photos. Yes, she still had them. Why would the young woman say she had the seat all to herself when she hadn't? Then she reached into her pocket and pulled out the perfume bottle. She placed it in her purse with the pictures.

Two days later, when the bus pulled into a little town in Montana, a strange feeling came over Tricia. She got out of the bus and shivered in the cold. Everyone seemed to want to rush into the restaurant, but Tricia stood and breathed in the fresh air.

She looked around, the place was beautiful. Rich green forest was all around, smattered with recent snow. The town was small, but busy. The first thought that came to her mind was that she was home.

She went into the diner and sat in a booth. When the waitress came to her she ordered a coffee and a sandwich. Tricia was looking at the photos again when the waitress came back with her order. "Do these pictures look familiar to you?"

The girl stared at them for a moment then answered, "Sure, those buildings are in the old part of town, down on Main Street."

"Is it far from here?"

"No not really, less than a mile down that road."

Tricia looked out of the window to the two lane street where the waitress was pointing.

"I'm almost off work. I can take you if you want. I noticed that you got off the bus, are you here to visit someone?"

"No, I don't know anybody here, but I'd sure like to see Main Street." Tricia looked at the young girl who was just a little younger than her. "I'm Tricia Conway."

"Mary Stuart," the waitress replied. "Give me about thirty minutes and we'll go."

Tricia knew she was not going to get back on the bus, and after she finished eating she asked the driver to unload her two suitcases. Mary met her in the parking lot in front of the diner. They loaded up her luggage into Mary's four-wheel-drive jeep.

"How long have you lived here, Mary?"

"My whole life. I suppose one day I'll venture away from here to see what is in this big world of ours, but I love it here. I'm going to get married soon," she said with a smile. "Where are you from?"

"New York." Tricia answered. "Jersey, before that."

When they got to Main Street, Tricia felt a deep sense of belonging and a feeling that she was being guided. It gave her courage and a renewed sense of hope. Tears filled her eyes.

Mary saw Tricia's tears, but didn't say anything. From the moment she had met the girl she had felt a connection. She pulled to a curb across the street from one of the buildings that had appeared in the photos.

Tricia couldn't believe it, and the strangeness of how she came to be in that small town was overwhelming. She got out of Mary's car without a word and crossed the street and went into the large country store.

Christmas music was playing softly in the background. The smell of cinnamon and ginger lingered in the air creating a homey feeling. The store had a variety of merchandise: books, greeting cards, candles, vintage and Victorian items. There were specialty items and what appeared to be one-of-a-kind dresses. They were beautiful. She let her fingers slide along the soft material as she passed. She took the stairs up to another floor. At the top of the stairs was an open area with tables and chairs. It was a coffee bar with a variety of pastries, and they had soup and sandwiches. A man and a young woman were talking and she couldn't help but overhear them.

"Please don't quit on me, Sarah. I need to find someone to replace you first. Not many people here can cook the way you do."

"You knew it was temporary, Mr. Carson. Billy and I are getting married. He wants to leave tonight to head for California. He told me he was leaving town with or without me. So I'm going with him." The young girl was determined as she took off her apron. She accidentally brushed against Tricia on her way out and said sorry as she hurried down the stairs.

"We're closed." The man said irritably, and then took a second look at Tricia. When their eyes met a spark of attraction shot between them. He was older than her, but that didn't seem to matter.

Suddenly three women came up the stairs, interrupting them. They went to the counter and began ordering pastries as they chattered about what they were doing for the holidays. Tricia watched as the man turned his attention to the women, but glanced back at her a few times. When one woman ordered a coffee that had to be specially made, he told her that he didn't know how to work the machine and that Sarah had just quit.

Tricia couldn't stand it any longer. He looked helpless behind the counter and was trying so hard to please the older ladies. She could see he didn't have the heart to turn them away. She went behind the counter, surprising them all, took off her jacket and washed her hands. She sized up the equipment and knew she could work the machine.

The man was dumfounded.

She smiled at him again and felt awareness flow between them. "I'll make the coffee and you get whatever else they want," she instructed. "I'm Tricia, what's your name?"

"Brad Carson."

The women looked from Brad to Tricia with raised brows. One of them said, "You'd better do as the lady says, Brad, she may quit on you, too, if you don't. You may be the sheriff of this town, but you definitely need help behind the counter." They laughed.

Brad took the teasing with a blush and a grin and tore his eyes from Tricia. He concentrated on all the customers that now seemed to be coming out of the woodwork and made conversation with everyone who entered.

Tricia guessed that it was busier than normal because of the holidays. She hadn't had this much fun in a long time. The customer aspect of it never seemed to change, but she noticed how these people were kind and personable and seemed to be genuinely curious about her.

She and Brad were working well together, as if they had for years. There was no time to talk, and Tricia could see the curiosity in his eyes as well when she caught him looking at her periodically. She found herself blushing at one of his smiling glances.

Finally there were no more customers. Brad turned to her with a no nonsense look and his eyes belayed a warmth that touched her heart. "Okay, Tricia, where did you come from? I know everyone in town and I don't know you. Are you visiting someone here?"

"I brought her," Mary said as she made her presence known. She had been sitting in the corner, unobserved, watching the obvious attraction that had transpired between the two. "Tricia got off the Greyhound when it stopped in town and came in the diner with everybody else from the bus. She ordered her food and showed me some pictures of your place. She wanted to come and see for herself that this place was for real."

"What pictures?" Brad asked through squinted eyes, looking at Tricia as if she were a suspect in a crime. He never did like being thrown off balance - something this new girl was doing to him without even trying.

Tricia took her purse from beneath the counter where she had put it earlier. She pulled out the photographs and handed them to him.

"Where did you get these?"

"A woman who sat next to me on the bus gave them to me. She said she was going home, then she fell asleep before I could get her name and so did I. When I woke up she was gone. The strange part was there was another passenger across from me with her kids who said that I had been sitting there by myself the whole time, that there was no woman sitting next to me. I know that makes me sound crazy, but it is the honest to God truth, she was sitting there. So when we stopped here for lunch at the diner I just knew I was in that woman's town. That's when I asked Mary if the pictures looked familiar to her."

"Let me get this straight. You got off the bus and stayed in town for no better reason than to find this particular place because of some pictures a stranger gives you? You say you got the pictures from a woman who sat with you, but no one else saw her?"

"I know that makes me sound crazy, but it is true." Tricia grabbed the pictures from Brad. She was feeling self conscious and put on the spot and wanted to get out of there. She picked up her jacket and headed for her suitcases that Mary had set at the top of the stairs.

Brad seemed to have other ideas about her leaving so quickly. "Wait!"

At the same moment Tricia saw a framed photo on the wall of the old woman on the bus. "That's her! She's the one who gave me the pictures."

Both Mary and Brad came to her side and stared at the photo on the wall.

"That isn't possible. It's Angelina Sinclair," Mary said.

Brad added, "We used to call her Angel when we were kids."

"Why isn't it possible?" Tricia asked, feeling puzzled. The whole thing was all so weird.

Brad lowered his eyes, "She died about twenty years ago, traveling from New York to here. She was on her way home when the bus crashed. She was my aunt."

"Why was she in New York?" Tricia whispered, feeling her heart fall. This was not what she had expected to hear.

"A dear friend of hers had died and she went to help with the arrangements. Aunt Angelina was always like a guardian angel to anyone who knew her." The silence that ensued after Brad's statement was heavy.

Suddenly the scent of Jasmine was strong. Tricia couldn't stop the tears that rolled down her cheeks.

"I smell Jasmine. It seems Angelina is making her presence known again," an older woman said as she came up the stairs.

Tricia turned to see a woman who resembled Aunt Angelina.

"Mom, what are you doing here? I didn't expect to see you today." Brad looked a little irritated. "You're sick, you should be in bed."

Mary smiled at his mother and hugged her. "I'm glad to see you up and about, Mrs. Carson."

"Quit calling me that," she said sternly, but with love. "You're going to marry my son and I would like for you to call me mom."

"Yes, ma'am," she smiled. "I mean, mom. Mom, this is Tricia Conway, Tricia this is Annette Carson."

Annette looked at Tricia and her son Brad as if they were under a microscope. Brad seemed uncomfortable and flushed.

"I had a strange feeling I needed to come in today. Who can stay in bed anyway? What is going on here?"

Mary was the one who filled her in what was going on and how Tricia came to be there. When she finished with the mysterious tale they all just stood and looked at each other. No one knew what to say.

Tricia handed the pictures to Mrs. Carson.

Annette looked at them closely, and then looked at her son.

Brad shrugged his shoulders.

"Whose house is that in the other picture?" Tricia pointed.

"It is a cottage that I own. What kind of work do you do, Tricia?" Annette asked out of the blue.

"I'm a pastry chef. Well, that was what I did in New York."

"A pastry chef?" Annette looked wide-eyed at her son who was looking at Tricia in surprise. "Well, it seems we are definitely in need of one around here, doesn't it? You're hired if you want the job. I take it you don't have a place to stay?"

Tricia shook her head.

"You can stay in my cottage, the one in the picture. It is just down the street, has a full kitchen. Rent is free if you take the job and of course you'll get a fair wage. If you don't want the job I'll have to charge you rent."

She didn't hesitate, "I'll take it. The job and the place." She looked at Brad who was grinning at her. With him being the sheriff in town, she knew he would grill her later, she could see it in his eyes. And she had nothing to hide, so there was nothing to worry about. She looked forward to getting to know him. She suddenly felt guilty about her thoughts. Her new friend Mary was going to marry him. But in her heart she knew that everything would be alright now.

"I'm glad," Annette said with a nod of approval. "With Sarah quitting on us before the holidays, it would have been very difficult finding good help. This is one of our busiest times of the year."

Tricia suddenly remembered the bottle of perfume in her purse and took it out. She handed it to Annette. "I found this on the seat where Angelina was sitting when I woke up. I think it belongs to you."

Annette reached for the bottle as tears filled her eyes. "I gave her a bottle like this at Christmas the last time I saw her, before she died. I had these bottles made especially for this perfume." Quickly she wiped her eyes and became very business-like. "My dear, you'll be expected to make all the pastries, muffins, soup and sandwiches and have everything ready before we open in the morning. All of the ingredients and supplies you need to make the goodies we serve are bought from our local store. We have an account there. I'll let Brenda know you have authorization to use the account. Brad, you take Tricia to the cottage and help get her settled. She doesn't have a car, so help her with the supplies and make sure she has everything she needs for tomorrow. Now, Mary, you can tell me more about what you and Tyson are planning for that wedding? After you two are married, that leaves Brad to find a bride." She winked at Mary as they gave each other a knowing look.

Brad made it his business to find out everything there was to know about Tricia Conway. He never before believed as his mother did that his aunt Angelina was watching over the family. He couldn't explain the things that brought Tricia to his town or how she ended up with photos and his aunt's perfume bottle. But it seemed that his aunt Angelina had known his heart better than he did. Brad and Tricia soon became the most important people in each other's lives.

Tricia would forever be grateful to Angelina - her guardian angel. She believed she had been at her side all along and had helped her during the most difficult times in her life. She had led Tricia to this small mountain community where she at last found the love, acceptance, friendship and future that would give her the happiest most meaningful and fulfilling times ever.

♦♦♦♦♦♦♦♦♦♦♦♦

Tory Lynn's love of writing began when she was a child, expressing herself in poetry and short stories. Her inspiration came from reading the classics like "Little Women" and "Anne of Green Gables". She was also influenced by works of Hans Christian Andersen, and was especially fond of stories that had happily-ever-after endings.

Tory and her family moved from California to Utah at the end of 2005 and has had a diversified employment history, including being a long haul truck driver with her husband. She spent eight years working with troubled teens and now works with the mentally disabled. Seeing how others have learned to cope with the odds against them has made Tory resilient and has instilled in her the drive to win despite all odds.

Working with many diverse types of people has given Tory the ability to be patient and has shown her that she can achieve goals by motivating people. Tory says, "everything that I have accomplished along with every new experience, negative and positive, has led me to where I am today. I have a better understanding of the world around me, and as a result I am able to write with my heart, and I feel my readers can identify with my stories.

www.freewebs.com/torylynn/

COONSKIN CZARDAS

By David S. Rosenberg

Many things happened just right for my parents to provide the world with two children. I'm not talking about the chance happening between a woman and a man and the subsequent miracle that occurs from the romantic coupling of two consenting adults. I'm talking about big picture items like my mom daring to leave her home in Knoxville, Tennessee for the big city of Cleveland, Ohio and my father miraculously having an American citizenship because my grandfather had lived in the United States for only a brief time. This permitted my father to leave Hungary just before the extermination madness in the late 1930s.

Picture how difficult it was for these two people to communicate. Although my father spoke five languages, he knew only a few words of English and I'm sure my mother's southern accent threw a curveball in his ability to learn the language of his new homeland. With all these hurdles and difficulties cast aside, a common bond existed and they married and I was born in 1946 and my sister, Betty, was born in 1951. It was a unique household to be sure.

There was a lot my father would never talk about, such as the loss of his parents, sister, and former obstinate wife, who had refused to leave Hungary even though the dangers were more evident every day. My father loved America enough to join the army to help defeat Hitler and his band of lunatics that dominated Europe in those days. Illness forced him out of service minus one kidney, and he found work in a defense plant where he met the pretty woman who became my mother. She was a riveter, he was a welder and together they built B-29s and a family.

Years later, when I was almost ten, my father's homesickness for his native country surfaced. I remember the family going out to the movies. In those days, there was a cartoon, a newsreel, and often a double feature - good value for a seventy-five cent adult ticket and twenty-five cent child's ticket. One of the stories on the newsreel showed Hungarian freedom fighters attacking Soviet tanks in Budapest as the proud and rebellious populace tried to regain their independence. President Eisenhower appeared on the screen and proclaimed to the world that the United States could not support any country born out of violence. My father took it personally and stood up in the middle of the theater and shouted at the projected Eisenhower image, "that was how this country was born." He was right of course, but also wrong because the President and the country feared the Soviets at that time. He left the auditorium to vent his anger and returned after a few minutes.

As a child, I didn’t realize that his Jekyll and Hyde personality, his vast temper, and his romantic nature are not present in all male parents. Surviving meant loving him and fearing him at the same time.

It took more years on the planet for me to understand the sadness I often saw in his eyes, but I knew his passion for Hungary was sincere, repressed, and deep-seated. He filled the house with classical music and flowers, and we ate fresh fruits and vegetables. Years later, when I visited Budapest, I knew these were common among Hungarians and existed in our home to make a little Hungary in our small East Cleveland apartment.

On looking back, I'm not surprised that my mother yanked me away from the daily neighborhood baseball wars to scrape the dirt off so that I matched my sister in cleanliness for a special event. Bathed, inspected, rejected, and bathed again I was prepared for the event and dressed in a freshly ironed shirt and dress pants that weren't shiny at the knees.

Because our family didn't have a car, on rare occasions we traveled by cab. Soon one came and tooted its horn in front of our building. Feeling special, I waved to my dirty-faced pals as we drove away headed to an unknown and distant section of town. A thirty-minute taxicab ride was an extravagance for a factory worker in the mid-fifties. When we arrived, I noticed the shop windows displayed signs in English and some unknown cryptic language that I deduced was Hungarian. The driver stopped in front of a large restaurant and we piled out of the car. A pleasant and unique fragrance met us at the door and moments later, we followed a waiter to our table.

Since this happened fifty years ago when I was ten and my sister was five, I don't remember much of the restaurant decor or service, but I do know that it must have been good, because my father's temper remained in remission. I remember him speaking that strange language with several restaurant employees. Here he felt like a king and no doubt, the Hungarian conversations improved the cuisine in quantity if not in quality. I noticed the glow on his face as the waiter opened a bottle of Egri Bikaver (translated as 'Bull's Blood' - a blended red Hungarian wine).

Again, I really don't remember precisely what I had for dinner, but for those who have never had Hungarian food I'll tell you it is generally delicious and heavy. Typically, Hungarian restaurants prepare food such as toltott kaposzta (stuffed cabbage) and paprikas csirke (paprika chicken in a green and red pepper cream sauce) served with potatoes or dumplings.

Pushing a dessert down the hatch on top of these main courses felt like stuffing an anvil on top of an elephant, but no child could resist a slice of Dobostorta (a seven-layer torte with light chocolate between the layers, dark chocolate on the outside, glazed with caramel and topped with a candied cherry). After a meal like this, you needed to do one of two things: Take a four-hour nap or burn off the consumed calories by cutting a cord of firewood with a dull axe.

When my parents finished the last sip of their coffee, my father paid the equally hefty bill without the slightest complaint. We trundled our way to the front door and back to the sidewalk. I thought we would soon jump back in a taxicab and return home, but what did I know of the neighborhood or the true romantic nature of an impassioned Hungarian. Across the street, there was a neighborhood tavern and I could hear the strange music that came from within.

The music tickled my father's soul and sensibility and we dodged a few cars to cross the street and entered the tavern that rarely had children cross its threshold. After a little negotiation, we sat at one of the tavern's small square tables on bent wood saloon chairs. I noticed a large bar in one corner that kept the patrons separated from rows of liquor bottles and several ceiling fans that labored endlessly to homogenize the air with the fumes from others who enjoyed smoking while consuming their alcoholic drinks.

About twenty feet away from our table on a raised platform above a small dance floor, six musicians cranked out strange melodies. For those who are unfamiliar with Hungarian style music, realize that Hungarians feel cheated when blank spaces separate musical notes. As a result, composers of this music place as many quick notes as they possibly can in each measure and the ear barely resets from one tone before the next arrives. My father told us that they were playing a type of music called a Czardas that is also the national dance of Hungary.

The musicians dressed in flashy multicolored gypsy-style clothing and they labored in the production of this music. The violinist's bow moved at sonic speed across his instrument's four strings, but the violinist was a shirker, an orchestral slug in music production compared to the Cimbalom player.

If you've never heard of a cimbalom, I'm not surprised. The Cimbalom is the great-grandfather of the American Hammer Dulcimer. It is a set of various length wire strings, tuned to perfection and set in an ornate wooden case. The musician strikes the individual strings with small mallets (called shoes) perched on the end of sticks. If anything on planet earth approaches the speed of light, it has to be Cimbalom mallets in the hands of a Hungarian musician. The musician, playing this instrument at lightning speed, causes the mallets to move so fast they become a mesmerizing blur to the eye.

After several melodies, containing several trillion notes each, a male singer appeared and several couples danced to a slow romantic song. The singer looked in our direction and a smile appeared in his eyes.

If that night my father became the self-appointed king of Buckeye Avenue in the old Hungarian neighborhood, the locals instantly elevated little Betty to princess status. Betty oblivious to her effect on others, sat there awestruck by the entire experience sipping her Shirley Temple.

After the singer completed his song, he pulled the microphone from its stand. My sister in her frilly dress, with two little ponytails jutting from the back of her head, and her dark brown eyes with long eyelashes enchanted the singer. Suddenly, he walked toward our table. My parents sat noticeably lower in their seats, not knowing what was about to happen. (I've admitted to failing memory in parts of this story, but if I live to be nine hundred and sixty nine years old, the lifespan of Methuselah, I will never forget the dialogue or the event that followed.)

Bending low with the microphone hidden, the singer asked my sister, "Sweetheart, do you like the music?"

My sister nodded and whispered, "Yes."

"You'll have to speak a little louder, I don't hear so well."

"Yes," she repeated, this time louder.

"The boys and I would like to play a song for you. Is there something that you would like to hear?"

She sat there thinking while there were a few titters and giggles from other tavern patrons as she captivated them with her natural charm and innocence.

"Just pick a song that you like," the singer said to encourage her to name a song.

"Davy Crockett," she said proudly, creating overt laughter from all those in the tavern.

"I'm not sure the boys know this tune. Maybe, if you could sing it for us, you could teach us the song and we could play it for you."

My parents wished they could hide under the table while Betty sang Davy Crockett a cappella batting her long eyelashes until the musicians accompanied her with a few notes.

While Betty's career as a Hungarian nightclub singer didn't last very long, those that attended that evening will never forget the night they heard the Coonskin Czardas and the little girl whose sweetness touched them all.

Often I return to the Cleveland area to visit my mother. Once, I drove to Buckeye Avenue and the old neighborhood. Alas, things change. The Hungarian neighborhood, restaurant, and tavern exist no more, but by telling my heart's story, I've kept alive my fondest recollection of my sister, who is no longer with us.

♦♦♦♦♦♦♦♦♦♦♦♦

Author David S. Rosenberg, a native of Cleveland, Ohio, served as a reactor operator aboard a U.S. nuclear submarine where he became an avid reader. Later, he served as a utility industry business consultant for twenty years. His fertile imagination blends his vast engineering and travel experience with his passion for creative writing.

To date, he has published three books: "No Shortage of Evil" and "Extension of Evil" are political thrillers and "Infusion of Evil" is a techno-thriller.

"Infusion of Evil"/won the Wizards of Words Book-of-the-Year award for 2007. "

The Hungry Dragon" his next political thriller is scheduled for release in mid-2008, and his work in progress, "The Obvious Answer" will be released in 2009.

While he claims to be a perpetual student, he shares his passion for creative writing by lecturing at writers' conferences. His non-fiction e-book, "The Compact Guide for Creative Writers" provides guidance designed to enhance and encourage skill-building to those writers seeking to advance their craft.

Mr. Rosenberg lives with his wife in central New York where he claims that 'every day is a day for writing.'

www.drosenbergsbooks.com

THE LIST

By Larry L. Evans

The place had a bohemian flair about it, something I just couldn't put my finger on. Maybe it was the darkness, maybe not, but it was there.

She sat in a far corner, her back to the wall, looking every bit as much as a seductress from a Fitzgerald novel. The closer I got, though, I could see that her yellow hair came from a cheap bottle and her cheeks were hollow from worry and age. An ersatz fur stole around her shoulders made her seem less nefarious the closer I got. I stood by the table and muttered.

"The midnight train runs only east."

"The green goose follows," she replied.

According to plan, she held out a cigarette. With the blue flame of a kitchen match I lit it for her. She stood and walked out of the darkened room with me in quickstep right behind. The red orange of the sun was her backdrop now and it did wonders for her appearance. The dark room held her features sharp with shadows, but the setting sun softened them pleasantly.

I started to speak, but she shook her head and motioned for me to follow her up the street. I complied, and from five or six paces behind her I watched a once beautiful woman.

An alley ran perpendicular to the street and suddenly she was jerked into it by someone unseen.

I drew my pistol, but held it close so as not to attract attention. I carefully approached the alleyway and peered around the corner. My lady fair was on the ground in a heap, blood had pooled beneath her wide-open throat. I slipped the rod back in its place, walked out of the alley and headed for the train station and the next name on the list.

The trip to the station went as expected, nobody knew of my meeting with the woman. I told the Jake at the counter I needed a ticket on the next train out. I bought the ticket and found a seat in the middle coach.

The train heaved and with a slow and deliberate tug pulled away from the platform. I guess I should have looked to see where it was going, not that it mattered. I only needed space between me and here, or there now, I suppose.

The car was almost empty at that time of night, so finding a secluded spot was easy. I did a check of all my belongings, just to make sure I hadn't left anything behind. Nope, all was in place. I always kept a careful eye on everything I carried, whether it was a book of matches or my I.D.

I took the list out of my pocket and perused it for the next in line. Another woman. Not that I have anything against killing women - a job's a job. I sat back, closed my eyes and drifted off to a dreamless place.

I woke as the train jolted to a stop. I sat up and looked at my watch - two and a half hours had passed. The train had stopped at a busy station, lots of people on the move. I stood, making sure I had everything with me and departed the coach.

I glanced at the name of the town as I left the station. I needed to check in, so I drifted towards the center of town looking for an all night diner for a coffee, a smoke and a phone.

The place was all silver and looked like an old club car. I went in, found a booth and ordered a cup of Joe and a piece of pie, Dutch Apple. The waitress was an old pro wearing worn-out shoes that once were white, rolled down stockings, and a rather comically short skirt trying to hide her ample thighs. She pitched an ashtray on the booth top along with change and pointed to the phone on the back wall when asked.

I put a nickel in the phone and dialed a number I had called more times than I care to remember. I didn't say a word at first; I listened and then spoke the right numbers into the phone giving the information needed to terminate the last contract. The Jane on the other end gave me a number to call in four days. I memorized it and hung up, killing the connection. I went back to the booth and *short skirt* brought my pie over and refilled my cup.

Four days to kill, and this burg was as good a place to be as any, I supposed.

On the third day while I was eating breakfast, *short skirt* laid an envelope on the table. She immediately retreated back behind the counter and busied herself with the coffee. I wanted to ask her about the envelope, but knew better.

I opened it up, knowing what was inside, a new list. It always amazed me how they knew where to find me. The list was always different, but the assignment the same, wet work for reasons unknown to me. The big difference this time was that along with the list were two tickets. Tickets for a steam ship out of New York in two days and a new number to call. One ticket had my current moniker, Gerald Bascome, on it and the other was for a woman named Amelia Bascome. I read the name out loud and much to my surprise a woman answered.

"Yes?"

I looked up and saw a skirt sitting across from me in the booth. "Amelia Bascome," she said extending a well-kept hand across the table.

I told her the name I was using, not knowing just how much she knew of the operation. Then I slid out from the booth and went to the phone on the back wall and dropped a nickel. He answered on the first ring.

I asked, "What's with the skirt?"

"You got a partner working with you on this one," he said.

"I work alone, see," I told him.

"Not this time Mike, you have a partner, end of discussion."

"Danny!" I yelled into the phone and was answered with a bang and a tone. The son-of-a-bitch hung up on me.

I went back to the booth, no longer interested in breakfast.

Amelia Bascome sat there, stirring a cup of Joe, looking at me.

"He give you the scoop?" she asked as I scooted in across from her.

I just shook my head no.

"That's okay, I got the dope, so listen up, Bub," She said.

I eyeballed the skirt and from what I could see from the tabletop up wasn't half bad. She filled the white blouse nicely and was a looker of sorts. Dark hair in a Vicky Lake style - you know, kind of covering one eye. The one eye I could see was cold, like the ones reflecting in the mirror every morning while I shave.

"Look sister, let's get one thing straight, I run the show, got it?"

She kept looking at me while stirring her coffee. The spoon chiming off the china mug sounded as loud as the bells of St. Mary.

The trip to New York was uneventful; she brought me up to speed as we sped down the road in her coupe, a yellow Ford that rode like a hay wagon. She turned out to be a wealth of knowledge. Mrs. Amelia Bascome, my new wife, had all the poop. Her list had four names on it, four with photographs to go with each one and they were to be on the boat, two men and two women. We were to ice them all. We were to board the ship in New York as husband and wife. We had a first class stateroom to share on the upper deck; this didn't seem to bother Amelia one iota.

One of the things Amelia supplied was a bundle of cash, about five-grand worth. We were to board as society slugs from the northwest, unknown to the local gentry. Why we were on the east coast was something for us to work out.

Our luggage was waiting for us in our stateroom when we got there. As we unpacked, I found a couple of monkey suits and other dressy duds that I would have never bought in a million years. Amelia had a trunk full of slinky gowns and a whole box with nothing but shoes.

"Maybe she's a real society dame," I thought.

"Get dressed, Gerry; we have to be on deck waving to the dockside crowd." She told me in a sweet sing-song tone.

"Yeah, yeah, keep your pants on, sister," I told her. I had a feeling this was going to be a long trip.

I chose a white jacket to wear on deck, but my new wife told me that it was a dinner jacket and was unacceptable. She picked out a brown corduroy thing with patches on the elbows. A shooting jacket she called it. Yeah, I could tell this Jane was real society.

We went out on deck and stood by the rail like the other stiffs and waved to nobody. Amelia moved away from me for just a minute and in a heartbeat was back by my side. The crowd was starting to disperse when a scream erupted just down the railing. A woman was slumped over the rail with a red stain creeping down the back of her dress. The ship's crew scurried about and the ship's doctor appeared.

"She's been shot." He announced. "She's dead," he said to another officer as he placed a finger to her throat.

Amelia clutched my arm and swooned with an "Oh, my Goodness!" and collapsed in my arms. I helped her from the deck back to our stateroom.

Once the door was closed, she pitched her clutch bag on the bed and said with a smile, "Then there were three." Her eyes were like ice cubes and her tone just as frigid.

This skirt is one scary dame, I thought, she reminded me of me.

On the third day of our ten day trip to Lisbon we were strolling on the deck, the Lido, I think she called it. Hell, I didn't know one deck from the other and didn't really care. On about our second trip around, I was getting ready to hit the chairs because this was way more walking than I wanted to do.

Amelia nudged me. "There's one, the guy in the striped coat and boater."

"Yeah, so what, there's too many peepers out here to do anything," I told her.

"No, just follow my lead, Gerry, that sap won't know what hit him, come on."

It seems this was only a game to my newly acquired wife, not business.

The sap was a real ladies' man; a wolf that liked the ladies and knew the ladies liked him. When Amelia hoisted her skirt up above her knee and rubbed her thigh, complaining about a pulled muscle, she immediately caught his eye. I couldn't blame him though; her gams were all right.

Just as he was passing and eyeballing her, she lost her balance and fell into him. When he reached out to help her she leaned back pulling him towards the rail then pushed him over it and watched as he fell fifty feet into the ocean.

With an ear-piercing scream, Amelia brought dozens of people to the rail to watch as the sap was drug under by the prop wash. Again she collapsed into my arms saying just loud enough for me to hear, "Serves the pig right, looking at me like that."

Yeah this was one cold-hearted Sheba, I thought.

Later that afternoon in our stateroom she smiled that evil smile and with a glint in her eye and a laugh she said, "Number two down the drain, literally."

The next few days rushed by without any chance of getting to the others on the list. Amelia shared my bed in the most complete way, telling me we had to put on a convincing portrayal of a married couple on their honeymoon. That was how we had explained our being on the east coast, Niagara Falls and all that malarkey.

Four days out of Lisbon, I encountered the second guy on the list in the men's sauna. I was sitting there by myself when he entered. He waved at me and without a word started to climb the seats to the top tier. On the second tier I grabbed his arm and jerked him down hard and slammed him into the wooden bench, snapping his neck. I immediately called the Steward to report the man had fallen in the sauna, and had hit his head. The steward got the Doctor and the rube was pronounced dead at the scene. They said he had apparently slipped on the wet wood and had fallen, breaking his neck.

The news of his demise excited Amelia and that night she was a wildcat in the sack.

Three deaths in less than two weeks on the ship caused rumors to abound. A killer was loose onboard, or the ship was jinxed or it had something to do with Voodoo.

One night, two days before making port, as we sat at the captain's table, my new wife and I encountered the last name on her list. The woman was introduced as Marion Dushawn, the captain's niece. She was in her mid twenties, pleasantly apportioned and well-educated. She was short, not quite five foot, a blonde with a bob and blue eyes. What she had done to warrant the wrath of the company was beyond me, but that wasn't my problem, business was business.

The two women were the same age and hit it off. Amelia invited Marion for a stroll around the deck after dinner, without me. I didn't mind though, two weeks with my new bride had me longing for some alone time.

Amelia came in late that night and while preparing for bed talked about how she had gotten so close to the mark and about the things she could do to her. I fell asleep with Amelia still yapping about it.

The next day, the day before we were to make port, Amelia asked Marion to show her the workings of the great ship, mentioning that being the captain's niece she must have access to spaces us regular Joes didn't get to see. As arranged the night before, I followed the two women into the recesses of the ship and in a far boiler room amid all the noise I shot the Dushawn dame in the back of the head. Amelia spun around with a big grin on her face and I plugged her right between the peepers.

Checking to make sure I left nothing, I slipped the roscoe in my pocket and returned to the main deck where I dropped that hot piece of iron into the cold blue Atlantic.

The next morning as the ship made port, I heard the crew was forming a search party to look for the captain's niece.

I walked down the gangplank leaving Mr. and Mrs. Gerald Bascome behind forever. Heading into the city I couldn't help but think that Amelia never suspected I had five names on my list.

♦♦♦♦♦♦♦♦♦♦♦♦

Larry is a retired manufacturing engineer who grew up in the Happy Days era in the blue-collar town of Pontiac, MI.

In the mid sixties he was drafted into the Army and spent two tours in Viet Nam. A few years after getting out of the Army he met his wife Jann, raised two kids and they were very happy.

Now a recent widower, Larry lost the love of his life after thirty-two wonderful years together. He is currently living in Waterford, Michigan with his little buddy, Herbie the pooch.

Larry was elected 2007 WOW Secretary and has been appointed to the Board of Directors for the 2008/2009 term. One of his short stories placed in the 2006 WOW Short Story Contest.

www.freewebs.com/larryjann

/

THE FORGOTTEN SOLDIER

by A.J. Rodriquez

The hands of time move swiftly through the ages and years are but a flicker of time in eternity. Every person's life is entwined with many and fate always has the last laugh, for each and every man must one day face his greatest fears.

The misty rain fell gently upon the parched earth. The sweet smell of the falling rain added a new aroma to the drying grass and rotting leaves. It was a typical summer day in the small town of LaPlace, LA - a town of less than 10,000, a town where everyone knows everyone, or do they?

Audrey loved the town. She was a transplant from a small town in Pennsylvania. She and her husband David had decided to make LaPlace their home and they lived the typical retirees' life. Audrey volunteered at the local VA home. David spent his leisure time puttering around the yard.

Since she and David had both spent 21 years in the military, Audrey enjoyed her volunteer work at the local Veterans home. She felt close to the soldiers that lived there. She loved to read stories to the patients and listened to their tales of military adventures.

One day, as Audrey's volunteer hours at the VA home ended, Nurse Jones stopped her. She asked her if she would be willing to read to a new veteran soldier - Sgt. Jacobs - who had just arrived. He had been in various rehab homes over the past forty years and according to his records he had never had a single visitor. He had never received any letters or packages. Nurse Jones said she felt sorry for the soldier. Said that he was a bitter and angry man, and that most of the staff avoided any contact with him. She felt that since Audrey was from Pennsylvania and so was Sgt. Jacobs, perhaps he might be willing to speak to someone from his own state.

Audrey agreed to meet the man.

She entered his room and saw him sitting in a wheelchair, staring at the wall. She noticed that there was not one picture on the walls, not one personal item of any kind within view. The room had a few cast-off pieces of furniture and it was the saddest sight Audrey had ever seen.

The soldier quickly turned when he heard her presence. At first, Sgt. Jacobs just stared at her. Then he said, “Who are you, what do you want? I didn’t ask for visitors.”

She was a little taken back with his bitterness. “My name is Audrey and I hear that you are from Pennsylvania. I am too. I was born in a small steel town called Ambridge. Where are you from?”

A brief hint of a smile came across Sgt. Jacobs’ face as he continued to stare at her. *This has to be some sort of a trick. The doctors told her, that’s how she knows. She’s making this up to get close to me. She can’t be from Ambridge. Ambridge is a town where everybody knows everybody. If what she is saying is true, then we should know each other.* “You say you are from Ambridge, so tell me, where did you go to school?”

“I went to Ambridge High School, of course. Didn’t everyone go there?”

Now that was a stupid answer. All small towns name their high schools after their towns. “What is your name, again?”

Audrey quickly replied, “Audrey Cymbalak.”

Audrey Cymbalak? No, no. It cannot be. I have been trying to forget that name for more than forty years. Fate cannot be so cruel as to bring her back into my life. I have spent every waking moment of every day trying to forget her. She filled my dreams and my nightmares. This is not possible; it must be the cancer drugs I’m taking. I’m having hallucinations. He squinted his eyes at Audrey as she came closer, thinking maybe she would go away since she was only a figment of his imagination. But no, now he could see the young girl he had once loved so many years before. Her hair was gray now but her eyes were still the same hazel color that he had dreamed about for years. How was this possible? He had given up hope of ever seeing her again and here she was. “You do not remember me, do you? My name is Michael Jacobs.”

Audrey looked hard at the soldier. *Michael Jacobs? Oh my gosh! Is it possible that he is alive and right here in LaPlace?* “Mickey, is it really you? My God, after all of these years. Where have you been? Why didn’t you come home?” Michael had been her best friend in high school. He had gone off to the Viet Nam War and after a few months he had stopped writing to her and they had lost touch. Audrey moved closer and looked even harder at his scarred and disfigured face.

Michael smiled, yes, this had to be Audrey, no one else had ever called him Mickey. People had called him Mike, never Mickey. It was Audrey’s nickname for him. The girl that had broken his heart and had doomed him to this solitary life was standing right in front of him. Michael looked up at her and said only one word, "Why?"

Audrey was confused. "Why, why what, Mickey? What is it? Talk to me."

Mickey looked at her and said, "Get out of here. You ruined my life once; you will not have the chance to do it again. You have made me what you see before you: a broken bitter man. I will never forgive you for this. Get out and don't come back. You were not there when I needed you and I do not need you now. I never want to see you again." He spun his wheelchair around and faced the wall again.

Audrey could see that he was upset and didn't want to upset him even more. So she turned to leave. Just as she reached the door she said, "Mickey, when you are ready to talk just ask Nurse Jones to call me and I will come. I am here for you, if you need me."

Later that evening, obviously troubled, Audrey told David all that had happened that day. He assured her that she had done the right thing and that when Mickey was ready he would call for her. She just had to give him some time. After all it had been forty years since they had seen each other and many things had changed. Mickey was surely not the same man he had been back then just as she was not the same woman.

Months passed and Audrey continued to visit the VA home. She would ask Nurse Jones about Mickey and the answer was always the same. "He is doing as well as can be expected under the circumstances."

Audrey wanted so much to speak with Mickey again and to clear the bad air between them, but at the same time she wanted to respect his need for privacy. Each time she passed his room she just shook her head and walked on.

Finally in May, Nurse Jones called Audrey and asked her to come quickly. Sgt. Jacobs had taken a turn for the worse and was asking to speak to her. Audrey immediately went to the facility.

When she entered Mickey's room, she found him sitting in his wheelchair, this time staring at the door. As she entered, she could see that his shaking hands held a yellow piece of paper and some photos. Audrey sat down across from him.

"Why did you call me, Mickey?" she asked.

"I need to get my life in order. I want someone to understand, someone to remember me when I am gone. Over the years I let my hatred take over. I have no friends, no family, no one that cares. I need to share my story with you."

Audrey stared at Mickey. "I would have been here for you all along if you just had let me. What happened, Mickey? Why did you shut me out? What happened so many years ago that you never came back home? Mickey, you must know that I cared for you and when you did not return home we were worried about you. No one seemed to know anything about what had happened. We all assumed that you had died in the jungles of Viet Nam."

Mickey looked straight into Audrey's eyes and began his tale. "Remember our prom night and how we danced until midnight? Then later we went to the beach. That was my last happy memory. The next day I received my draft notice and had to report for my physical. After that I was off to basic training. I hardly remember the next few months of training.

"You wrote to me every single day. After basic training, I received my orders for Viet Nam. It was a very sad time for me. I had to leave everything that I had ever loved and known behind me. I had never before been out of State and now I was going to fight a war in a country that I had never even heard of. The one thing that kept me going was knowing that you were back home waiting for me. You were my one true friend, my one true love. I knew that I could count on you no matter what happened. You were my anchor, my strength, my link to home."

Audrey was moved by his heart rendering story. She had never realized that Mickey loved her. She considered him her best friend, yes. Sure they had always done things together, but she hadn't loved him like that. It was true that at first she had written him faithfully every day, but with college and work her letters became fewer and fewer. She thought he understood that they were just friends, but apparently he did not.

Mickey continued, "The war was so terrible. I saw horrible things that are best forgotten. My life was a total mess. Then I received this letter from you with a very moving poem." Mickey handed the yellowed letter to her that he had been holding in his hand.

She had written it to him those many years ago. In the letter was a poem that she had written just for him. She was surprised that he had kept it.

"Read the poem to me, Audrey. This poem kept me alive in those jungles, it gave me a reason to fight, a reason to live."

Audrey began to read.

"What are we fighting for? I've heard people say
If it weren't for war, we wouldn't be free today
Our fathers fought in the First World War
Never once asking 'what am I fighting for'

Now people who will never fight

Shout out with all their might
'What are we fighting for?'
The only answer to their plea
They are fighting for you,
they are fighting for me

How many more tears would be shed
If not for these brave men, we all would be dead
So let us, Americans, as we say we are,
Stand behind our brave men whether near or far
For peace cannot come without war
And this, my friends, is what we are fighting for.

Tears filled Audrey's eyes as finished reading the poem aloud. She remembered the times well. It had been a hard time for America. Many young men had gone to fight a battle in a far-off land. So many had died, and many had been lost forever. Our country had been divided over the war and there were many protests. Our soldiers returning from the war were treated badly. Unlike the hero's welcome given to the soldiers of other wars, most were shunned by their own people. It was a hard time for all.

Mickey continued, "I fought hard for this country. I did everything that I was asked to do. Many things that I did not want to do, but felt it was my duty. I lost many of my friends in the rice fields of Viet Nam. I stood there with their blood on my hands and watched them die. Many were boys like me. We'd had our whole lives ahead of us. The only thing that kept me going was knowing that you were waiting for me, that you were my one true love.

"Your poem kept me alive. I read it every night. The guys would laugh at me, but the poem became my anchor. It was the one sane thing in an insane war. It helped me through the darkest days, and it gave me hope. But it ended the day that your letters stopped. It seemed that your attitude toward me and the war had changed. The very thing that had held me together during those horrible months disappeared with your last letter. I thought that you had given up on me, too. I truly believed that you, too, had come to hate the war and all that it stood for.

"I was lost, devastated. It seemed that in a matter of months everything that I had known and believed was gone. The war had taken away my innocence, my childhood. I was lost. It felt like my whole world, the neat little world that I had known all my life had been taken away from me. It was not long after that when I stepped on the landmine that took my legs. I was too ashamed to return home half a man, and with you gone, I had nothing.

"I asked the military to send me as far away from Pennsylvania as they could and they sent me to a hospital in Mississippi. Over the years I have moved time and time again. I finally arrived here. It was like fate had planned for us to meet again."

"I have never shared this story with anyone. Now my time is short. I wanted to share it with you: my one true love. I am so sorry that I never came home. I heard that you had married a soldier and got on with your life. I am sorry that I missed out on everything. Please grant me one request. Dance with me, dance as we did on that last happy day of my life."

Mickey wheeled to a table and put on an old record.

Audrey laughed through her tears. It was the song they had danced to at the prom so many years before. She placed her hands on the wheelchair and tenderly moved it around the room in time with the music. It was as if time had stopped. The music took them back to a different time and place. A place of peaceful existence, a place full of young hopes and dreams and for just a few minutes, Mickey was whole again.

Slowly, his eyes began to close.

Audrey thought he was asleep, but when she tried to wake him, she found he had passed on. Mickey had gone to join his fellow soldiers in a sacred place. He had finished his journey on earth. Poor, sad Mickey had led such a lonely life.

Audrey and David attended Mickey's funeral in Pennsylvania. As the misty rain fell upon the almost deserted graveyard, Mickey was laid to rest beside his ancestors in the cemetery at the top of the hill. As the lonely sounds of Taps filled the air, a single white dove flew by. Audrey knew that Mickey had finally found his peace. He was finally home. The lonely forgotten soldier had come home to stay.

♦♦♦♦♦♦♦♦♦♦♦♦

Louisiana motivational storyteller and author A.J. Rodriguez currently resides in LaPlace, Louisiana. A.J. is the author of the "Theodore Da Baer" series of books for children of all ages. When not writing, she and her husband David travel to schools around the country and share stories from her books and Ms. Rodriguez has dedicated herself to bringing children back to the art of reading.

A.J.'s literacy program, "One Angel at a Time", is spreading throughout the South. In the past year A.J. has entertained thousands of children in six different states and is slated to appear in three additional states in 2008. Her message of Teddy Baer Hugs and Magical Wishes is making its way around the world, one child at a time.

www.theodoredabaer.com

HIJACKED!

By Astor Lane

Excerpt from "Sell Out"
an unpublished novel by Astor Lane

Todd and Jane Whitmore sat in Row 7 on American Airlines Flight 1535 from Boston to Miami. They were on their way to visit their parents to announce that their prayers were answered; Jane was finally pregnant.

"My parents will go crazy," said Jane. "I can't wait to tell them. They'll be waiting at the airport, just like they always do, but wait till I tell them!"

"I know, and make sure they don't call my mom and dad before we get to their house tomorrow. Your mom's gonna be out of control."

"This is one of the happiest days of my life. We're finally gonna have a baby."

"And you're glowing, my darling." He raised the armrest so that they could snuggle together. Soon after takeoff they were both asleep with smiles of contentment on their faces.

Air Marshal Judy Thornton sat in her usual aisle seat in Row 20. From there she could observe everything that took place at the front of the plane. Her rookie sidekick, Jarvis Baxter, sat further back, but he wouldn't take any action unless he got orders from her, or she was incapacitated. She had accumulated enough air miles to provide worldwide trips for several lifetimes, but her preference was to chill at the family lakeside cabin, just an hour's drive from her Boston home. Although her job was mostly uneventful, she had to stay alert and make mental notes of the most insignificant details, just in case a pattern emerged that might mean danger. In her three years of duty, however, her professional services were required only once when a drunken bum had threatened a flight attendant who had refused to serve him more booze. She was trained for so much more.

Chief Flight Attendant Margie Sanchez was in her fifties and planned to take early retirement the following year. The date was set to coincide with the retirement of Captain James Paxton. The two were divorcees and had been a couple for almost ten years, working the system so that they could fly together as often as possible. Margie and James were best friends and devoted lovers. During their flights together, Margie would elect to serve meals to the crew so that she could add a couple of Hershey's Kisses to James' tray and he would arrange for flowers to be waiting in her hotel room. This day, they were looking forward to a two-day layover in Miami. Maybe they would rest on the beach or maybe they would visit the Everglades; neither cared as long as they were together.

As soon as the plane was stable, Margie took up her usual station in the front galley and began preparing coffee and soft drinks for the first-class passengers. She sang quietly to herself as she worked. Meanwhile, James was settling back after takeoff and following instructions from the air traffic controllers as he negotiated the busy air traffic routes on the East Coast. The co-pilot was new to him.

Israel Rebarak was in his thirties. He had worked for the airline for almost three years and had quickly moved up from narrow body jets by pursuing aggressive training at every opportunity. Six years in the Israeli Air Force with the highest commendations for skill, bravery, and loyalty all spoke of a burning desire to be the best in everything he did. After the Air Force, he moved to the United States and took a job with the airline.

James had learned Israel's history at their first meeting in the airline's Flight Planning and Weather Room, just an hour before the flight. The two had hit it off immediately and James hoped that they would become friends.

Twenty minutes into the flight, Judy saw a man move from his seat in first class to the restroom at the front of the plane. She took note of the time, 2:30 p.m., E.T. He returned to his seat five minutes later. Then another man approached the front galley from first class. Judy's anxiety doubled, and then tripled, as she saw the man go behind the screen into the galley area. She pressed the button on her wrist microphone and alerted Jarvis, "Check the front galley. A man just went in there."

As soon as the plane had reached cruising altitude and had left the Boston area controllers, Captain Paxton set the plane's automatic pilot, and pulled the foil wrapper from his first Hershey's Kiss. He smiled, thinking of Margie, just a few feet away, and how happy it made her to do these little things for him. She would love the three dozen long-stemmed roses waiting in her hotel room and he hoped that their romantic dinner together would be perfect in every way. His last thoughts were of Margie, the love of his life.

Israel's knife slid effortlessly across James' throat and then plunged deep into his heart.

Jarvis walked past Judy, brushing her shoulder with his hand. He walked swiftly to the front galley and then suddenly turned back with a look of terror on his face. He began to run, but someone in the second row tripped him and he slammed into the aisle floor. Judy watched as an arm stretched out and plunged a knife into his back. He tried to move, but soon collapsed, motionless, onto the cabin floor.

This time Judy hit her microphone button twice and was immediately connected to her head office in Washington. She bent down as if to retrieve something from her carryon bag and softly spoke the words, "Judy T, trouble, flight AA 1535. Jarvis down."

She heard her boss' voice in her tiny wireless earpiece, no mistaking Tom's somber tone, "You know what to do. Birds will be there in a few minutes. You're in charge. Don't be caught, you're it."

She sat up to the noise of screams and confusion as the story of what had happened spread back through the plane. The man appeared from the galley, dragging the dead body of Chief Flight Attendant Margie Sanchez with him. Four men stood up in first class and others began walking down the aisle from behind. The man at the front dropped the body and picked up the flight attendant's phone, "Do not be alarmed. We are taking a small diversion. We will get you there safely if you sit quietly and cooperate."

The door to the cockpit opened and a package was handed out to the terrorist leader. Judy reasoned that the cockpit was compromised and that the package contained weapons. How the weapons got onto the plane was a mystery, but that was for later. She whispered a brief prayer and sat quietly waiting and hoping that she would not be discovered.

Where were they going? It didn't take long for her to find out. The plane took a left turn and dropped altitude fast. 'Washington,' she said to herself. Ten minutes later, two F16s joined them, one on each side of the wide body. The pilots would demand that the plane turn and land at the nearest airport but she knew that the terrorists wouldn't obey. With their missiles armed and locked on the wide body, the F16 pilots would threaten to shoot the plane down and then wait for the final order to be given.

But would it be given? Ever since 9-11, philosophers and experts in ethics had wrangled with this problem. The public knew they all took this risk every time they boarded a plane, but three hundred civilian lives lost to deliberate action by American military was a disaster almost too horrific to comprehend. How would the public react to such an act? Surely they would say that there should have been better alternatives.

An elaborate set of top secret conditions had been prescribed by the experts to guide those charged with making the final decision. The message promulgated by the government was that any hostile plane would be shot down before it entered an imaginary ring, one hundred miles in diameter, centered on the White House. A much more complicated set of scenarios had been documented for negotiations with the terrorists and a set of locations had been chosen to bring down a hostile aircraft; one that could be controlled, one where the press and the public could be managed, and one where there would be the fewest casualties.

The ruckus aroused Todd and Jane; they tried to make out what was happening over the screams of the passengers and someone bellowing into the plane's intercom for everyone to stay calm. Their hearts sank as they heard what had happened. This was supposed to be the best time of their lives. Jane was carrying their firstborn, the one to continue the family line, the perfect baby, the perfect scholar, and the perfect athlete but, most of all, the child who would love them as they loved each other. This baby would complete their family and they had waited so long. Todd tried to placate his wife, "Don't worry, look, planes are escorting us. They'll make this thing land. We'll be safe." Jane looked into his eyes, but she said nothing.

Judy listened to mile markers in her earphone, 800, 750, 700. She waited for instructions and reviewed the protocol she had practiced and perfected in her training. They were on their way to Washington and Judy surmised that the target must be the Year of Peace Rally on the Mall. She looked down at her carryon bag under the seat in front of her.

Three college students in Row 25 were on their way to watch the Browns play the Dolphins that evening. Matt and Jason had been best friends since high school and Jake had joined them during their freshman year at college. They had all played football in high school, but now they were pursuing business degrees at Northeastern. When Jake saw the terrorists and heard their threats over the intercom, he decided on a plan of action, "We can take these bastards. Let's rush them." The plan was revised a few times and there was a great deal of nervous shoulder punching before the three agreed.

Matt was shaking with fear, "I don't know if I can do this, I'm really scared."

Jason tried to help him, "I'm scared too. Look, we're all going down. Let's do it our way. If we're lucky, we'll get these punks."

Jake added, "He's right, no one else is doing anything but saying prayers and crying. Let's do it. If I'm gonna die, I wanna die a hero."

Matt's face was covered with sweat and tears, "Sorry, I'd do anything for you guys. But you'll have to push me out of the seat."

The three shared nervous grins and punched knuckles. They waited until the terrorist leader was distracted, then they charged. They kept as quiet as they could, save for their heavy footsteps as they raced down the aisle. Jake was first, fully charged now with clenched fists and head bowed, ready to hit someone very hard.

Judy heard their advance. She saw football players charging after a punt. Their intent was clear, but she could do nothing but watch helplessly, her heart racing and hoping and praying that they would succeed. They didn't make it past the sixth row. There was a burst of fire from an Uzi and then silence and smoke. Three bodies lie writhing in agony for a few seconds and then there was nothing but screams from passengers. Judy reported in, "Three civilians rushed forward, all down, machine gun." She felt the pain of knowing that three wonderful young heroes had died trying to save everyone on that plane. A lump welled up in her throat and she had to struggle to compose herself.

In the White House, President Avery was being briefed on the findings of the Secret Service investigation. "Sir, we think we have the Mall covered. We'll have almost one-thousand foot soldiers there, cameras looking at faces, and lots of uniforms. Everyone will know that we're ready for anything."

"So what do you expect," asked the President, "another aircraft attack, missiles, drones, anthrax, smallpox?"

Head of the Secret Service, Victoria Cobrander took over, "Mr. President let me congratulate you on your fine mind. You've just mentioned most of the ideas that we've been working on and we've covered them as best we can. We still can't cover for a few suicide bombers, but we don't think those ideas have much merit."

"Because they can't get close enough to me?"

Vickie bowed her head, "Yes sir, you've hit the nail on the head again."

"Vickie, you look tired. Thank you for all your hard work over the past few days. Did you ever reel in that CIA officer, the one that started all this, what was his name?"

Vickie completed the President's thought, "Don Marshal. No sir, he managed to stay loose."

"What's he up to?"

"He's pursuing his own investigation. We lost touch with him yesterday. He was in Omaha at that time."

"Do you trust him, this, Don Marshal? I gather he has a 'kill on sight' classification."

She stood tall and said, “I’d trust him with my own life. He’s on the team and we’re staying in touch. I know Don, he’ll be here. We go way back.”

“But would you trust him with the lives of 250,000 Americans and their president?” He just looked at her for the longest time.

She nodded. The President turned to an aide, who was tugging at his sleeve. He listened to the aide’s whispers, swore under his breath, and then turned sternly to the assembled group. “Listen up. I want those of you with level-four clearance in the Situation Room pronto. Vickie, walk with me.”

“Sir, I’ve got Tom Barton in my ear. He’s got an air marshal on a rogue flight heading this way.”

“I know, that’s what I just heard. Keep him talking. We need all channels.”

Vickie turned and said to her wrist microphone, “Tom, my folks will relay all we know to you right away, principally a list of suspects. We need to know who we’re dealing with. Stay in my ear.” She turned back to the President and said, “Sir, the intel from Don Marshal may have given us a break. Excuse me, I’ve got to call my staff.”

It was 2:45 p.m. and the President was due to leave for the Mall any minute. They took the elevators down to the Situation Room, fifty feet below ground level, and settled into chairs around a long table that was equipped with phones and computers. On the walls were huge TV screens, some bearing images of a wide body passenger aircraft and one showing a map of the Washington D.C. area, embellished by two concentric circles, one at fifty miles and another at fifteen miles from the White House. A trace line on the map came in from the west and ended abruptly two hundred miles out. The symbol of the hostile plane slowly advanced toward the center of the map.

“I’ve given orders to evacuate the White House and all government buildings nearby,” said the President. “Is this your bird Vickie?”

She looked shocked, “Sir, I’d give anything to say no, but we can’t take chances. We’ll have to shoot it down.”

The President looked calm, “As you know, that decision usually falls to others but, because of the security scare today, I’ve taken it back. It’s my call. Experts are talking in my left ear, covering the scenarios.” He pointed to a small earpiece. “There are three-hundred people on board. Give me your opinions quickly, I only have five minutes.” Everyone agreed that the President had no choice but to order the plane’s destruction. “Will you share the heat? It’ll be pretty intense.”

“We’re on record Mr. President,” said Vickie, and the others nodded, one by one, sternly, some wondering if their careers in government were over.

There was deathly silence on Flight AA 1535. Jane was quietly sobbing, thinking of her unborn child and the sacrifice of the three young men, and of their mothers. The terrorist leader had explained that he intended to crash the plane into the Washington Mall where 250,000 people were attending a peace rally. He allowed the passengers to use their cell phones to give last words to their loved ones, saying, "Your salvation is at hand, you and your loved ones, if you give praise to Allah."

Judy pretended to call her husband, but connected instead, to Tom, who now had an open line to everything the leader of the terrorist group was saying. She was hoping for a voice-identification. Tom soon came back with a ninety-percent probability that the speaker was Imran, a well known terrorist leader. The CIA agent who had uncovered the evidence of a planned terrorist attack on the Mall, Don Marshal, had sent strong evidence to Vickie Cobrander that Imran was involved.

Judy received the 200-mile marker, plus the warning, "Ready yourself; let your training take over."

Two passengers had apparently fallen unconscious. A medical student was pumping the chest of one elderly woman who was stretched out across two seats. A terrorist stood guard over them, making abusive remarks. "Don't waste your time, you'll all rot until you stand before Allah on Judgment Day and he will send you to hell. Turn to Allah before it's too late, and you will be with him in heaven this very day."

"You're wrong about that," said a Baptist preacher seated nearby. "Hundreds of Muslim clerics have denounced that doctrine. Murder is a dreadful crime in the eyes of Allah." The preacher stood and raised his voice to get the attention of the terrorists at the front of the plane. "Islam is a religion of peace, and those 72 virgins that you all hope for, well, that's a mistranslation. It's 72 pearls, not virgins—"

The fist of the terrorist sent the preacher back into his seat unconscious. "Are there any more intellectuals?"

There was silence.

Amy Johnson sat next to her six-year-old daughter, Molly. Amy started picking up toys and putting them into her carryon bag. She had already stowed her magazine and folded Molly's coat across her knees. Her hand went to her face often to conceal her tears from Molly, who was kneeling on the floor, reading a comic that lay on her seat. Amy picked her up and buckled her into her seat. Molly didn't understand what was happening, although she had seen her mother crying many times. The marriage had been a terrible mistake and ended soon after Amy became pregnant. He wanted a life of travel and sports and he saw children as an impediment, a drain on his time and his money. She refused an abortion; she had already fallen in love with the child she carried. Now Molly was more important than anything else in the world.

Amy was a nervous tidy freak who kept folding and unfolding the coat in her lap. All she could do now was to wait and pray. Molly turned to her and said, "Mommy, where is my dolly, I need my dolly." She began to cry. In that moment, Amy fell apart. She wrenched Molly's seat belt undone, grabbing the doll from her bag and thrusting it into Molly's arms. Then she gathered both up and hugged them to her chest with all her might. "Mommy, you're hurting me."

She relaxed her hug and looked Molly in the eyes. "Molly, you're the most wonderful gift. I love you with all my heart."

Molly looked confused; she said, "I love you too mommy, why are you crying?"

Amy's tears began to flow freely now, "Because I never want to be without you my darling, let's hold each other for a while and I'll tell you a story." Amy began to tell the story of how Jesus had asked his disciples to let the children come to him. She said that Jesus waited in Heaven for everyone who died. He loved everyone, especially little children.

"Are we going to heaven mommy?" Amy just hugged her and began to tell her about her own parents who had died and were in heaven with Jesus. Molly remembered her grandmother, who had died just last year. Someone released a balloon at the graveside to symbolize the rising spirit of the deceased on its way to heaven. She said, "Mommy, don't be afraid. I'm with you."

Todd and Jane hugged each other. They had called their parents and said that they loved them before pretending that the calls had been dropped. Prayers were heard throughout the plane in several different languages. No others were willing to risk their lives; everyone was becoming numb.

In the Situation Room at the White House, everyone sat waiting for the President's decision. No one spoke. As the trace on the screen approached the 50-mile circle, the door opened and a young man walked in. The President recognized him immediately, "Dr. Preston, please come and join us. What do you have to say?"

Bob and Cathy Traxley sat in row seven. They had witnessed everything that had happened at the front of the plane. The bodies of the three heroes had been dragged forward and stuffed into the galley area. Scarlet bloodstains showed where the three heroes had fallen. Bob and Cathy were on their way to the Miami area to buy a house for the winter months. They were in their seventies and in good health and they were still very much in love with each other. Bob had thought of trying to rush the terrorist leader, but Cathy had begged him not to, "If you die, I'll be left on my own. If we are going, let's go together. I know we'll meet on the other side. We'll be together forever."

They held hands and tried to keep each other as positive as they could. Cathy's tissue was at her nose constantly and Bob's voice had become broken and frail, "You know I've always loved you?"

"Yes, my dear, and I've always loved you."

"There's never been anyone else. I've never wanted anyone but you."

"I know that my dear, you've kept me quite busy all these years with your affection, I don't know how you could've had energy left for anyone else."

"You've been an angel to me. I'm so sorry that I planned this trip. How could I ever do such a stupid thing? We should have driven."

"Be still Bob, I wanted this trip as much as you. You mustn't blame yourself. We've been together for almost fifty years and I want to keep it that way."

He squeezed her hand and strained awkwardly against his seatbelt to kiss her gently on the cheek. Cathy responded, "You know, we've had a wonderful life, children grown, grandchildren in college, everyone a success, what more could we want?"

Bob looked at her tenderly, "One more day together, just one more day."

Craig Hudson sat alone at the back of the plane. He was a salesman who traveled the East Coast selling computer equipment to engineering companies. He had been married for a year, although Freda and he had dated for much longer. He searched for his cell phone in a small carryon bag and tried to call her again. She had not answered so far and he was getting frantic. There, in the bag, was a bar of his favorite dark chocolate with a bow tied around it and a little note tucked under the bow. He nervously opened the note. It read, "My darling Craig, don't be gone long, I love you and I want you always. I'll love you forever."

Craig was stunned. Her love for him and her enthusiastic participation in their lovemaking were never in doubt, but she had never given him a note like this. Could she have sensed something? Once before, she had spoken of a premonition of danger that turned out to be accurate. They had joked about her being psychic, but Craig didn't have much faith in such matters. Freda believed in her premonitions and Craig didn't openly doubt her. He dialed the number and waited. It rang three times before she picked up, "Hello, is that you Craig? You've been trying to call. What's happened? Was your flight delayed?"

What could he say? He had rehearsed it, but the script seemed futile now, "I just found your note." His voice was breaking up, but he tried to carry on. "You know how much I love you and how much I'll always love you my darling Freda."

"Craig, I think I know what you're trying to tell me. I didn't want you to go today, remember I said that? You're on that plane, aren't you?"

He replied with just one word, "Yes."

"And it's going to crash, isn't it?"

He couldn't hold back the tears any longer, "I'm so sorry, I don't know what to say."

Freda was crying too, "Craig, I won't give up on you. You're going to make it through this. I can feel it strong in my heart. I want you to sit back and don't try to do anything brave. Please will you eat the chocolate, it would mean a lot to me? I know it's silly, but please eat it."

"Yes, I'll do anything. I love you completely."

"And I love—"

Her reply was cut short; the call had been dropped. Craig just sat staring at the phone as the display showed the message, 'Searching for service.'

Across the aisle from Craig, were Jack and Zena Arnesto and Pete, their autistic son. Pete lived in a world of his own, one that was filled with literature. He read everything that Jack and Zena put in front of him but, although it was clear that he remembered the stories vividly, he never spoke of them. Whenever he watched a movie version of a book he had read, however, he would get agitated each time the screenplay departed from the book.

Pete had been watching Craig. "Are you scared?" he asked.

Craig was a little shocked. He didn't know what to say to a twelve-year-old kid, "Yes, a little, but I'm eating my favorite chocolate bar. Want some?"

Pete looked back and said, "Don't be scared, we aren't going to die."

Craig glanced at Zena, who had been listening in. She just smiled back. Craig broke off half of the chocolate bar and offered it to Pete, "Here, you'll like it."

Pete took it, saying, "I know for sure we'll be okay. Believe me?"

Craig was completely transfixed by the boy's confident words. Pete just swung his legs back and forth while his gaze was fixed on Craig's eyes. After a while, Craig said, "You know, I think I do believe you." The boy nodded back at Pete. Craig yelled out so that half the plane could hear, "We're going to make it, we're going to live!"

Within seconds a knife was at Craig's throat. He took the warning and sat back in his seat, glancing at Pete, who just calmly continued to swing his legs.

Don had been on the Mall since late Saturday night. His CIA flight from Cheyenne was filled with brass on their way to take part in the events of Veteran's Day. No one bothered him while he slept, probably assuming from his street clothes that he was a member of one of the secret services. Once on the Mall, he looked for a homeless person wearing a long overcoat. Don hated to give up his favorite ski jacket, but the man was more than happy to swap coats and threw in his hat. An extra $50 made sure that the man talked to no one about the deal, at least until after the ensuing drunken haze wore off. Don scuffed his shoes against a curb and rubbed dirt onto them. He massaged dirt into his hands, hair and face and scratched his nose and cheeks with a rock until they bled.

No one paid any attention to another unkempt bum standing to attention and shedding a few tears in front of the Vietnam Veterans' Memorial, where the names of several of Don's CIA fallen colleagues would never appear. Neither would they appear in the Book of Honor in the CIA Headquarters in Langley, Virginia. Less than half of the CIA dead have been so honored, the circumstances of their deaths remaining top secret.

The Mall was already occupied with thousands sleeping on the ground, in sleeping bags, and on lawn chairs transformed into makeshift cots. Conversations were underway on every topic imaginable as various groups were meeting up, and making ready for whatever cause they wished to promote. It seemed the perfect location and setting for a terrorist attack and, once he saw the scope of the place, and the thousands already there, he was overwhelmed by the numerous possibilities for a terrorist attack. Don shuffled around the perimeter, looking at faces and listening in on conversations, but nothing useful was seen or heard.

Apart from stopping for hotdogs and coffee, he continued his slow, aimless shuffle. By the time the music began at 10:00 a.m., there were so many people on the Mall that it was getting difficult just to move around. People occasionally offered him money and he accepted with the panhandlers' catch-phase, "God bless you." He kept checking his watch, getting more and more desperate. Vickie's team had done a thorough job. They had saturated the site with agents, but was it enough?

He was tired, frustrated, and making no progress with his private deliberations on the mechanics of the attack. It was already 2:50 p.m. on a perfect sunny seventy-six degree day, and the crowds were enjoying the poetry and music of some of the country's favorite entertainers. The Marine Band was stationed near the stage, making preparations for the arrival of President Avery. No one would have thought credible the images of terror and destruction that haunted the shoddily dressed bum as he shuffled by.

Don called Vickie Cobrander, concealing the cell phone inside his collar and hat, "Vickie, tell me what do we know now?"

"A wide body's on its way in, fully loaded. Imran is in charge. Your intel nailed it."

"A wide body? But that can't be it, can it? It's not big enough."

"Think about it, if the plane skids down the mall spewing ignited fuel—"

"It doesn't fit Vickie, you'll shoot it down before it gets there."

"We've got it covered. Now, call me if you get anything. I assume your somewhere on the Mall. I'm with The President." With that, she hung up.

Back in the Situation Room at the White House, the air was tense and everyone was silently watching the President. He said, "Dr. Preston, Is this plane covered?"

The doctor stopped before reaching the President and said, "Yes sir, but remember it's experimental. We'll know by the trace behind you. Do I have your go-ahead?"

The President sighed with obvious relief, "Yes sir, you do."

"Excuse me sir, I must make the call."

He picked up one of the phones and dialed, "Preston here, code Pigeon, we are go." Then he sat down.

Marty Taylor, head of the NSA, was the first to speak, "Can you tell us, sir, what in hell's name you're up to?"

The President gave her one of those 'be quiet' looks, and told everyone to watch the screens. His right hand was trembling a little on the phone in front of him.

Judy received the 50-mile marker together with the command, "Go, God speed." Her training took over. She kicked the end of her bag, waited three seconds and kicked it again. She repeated the procedure, taking a deep breath before that last kick. Two seconds later, the plane instantly depressurized to 12psi and oxygen masks fell from the cabin ceiling. The passengers and terrorists scrambled to put on the masks, and breathe the precious oxygen. Judy took her time, fighting the urge to empty her lungs. She watched the commotion at the front of the plane. Terrorists were ripping oxygen masks from the passengers. Within seconds nerve gas began to flow through the plane's oxygen system that rendered everyone, except Judy, unconscious.

There was a short burst of machine gun fire from Imran's Uzi machine pistol as he fell to the aisle floor. Bullets ripped through the upper fuselage, but the plane was flying so low that the extra cabin depressurization was minimal. As soon as the terrorists were down, she pulled her personal oxygen mask and tank from her bag and took a long deep breath. She had held her breath for the full minute. Her training had paid off. For the first time, she was grateful for the fifty painful daily repetitions of the procedure that she had endured during training and during recertification.

With her weapon drawn, she searched among the piles of bodies lying in all kinds of distorted positions, looking for the terrorists, and handcuffing each one that she recognized to any available metal structure with plastic ties from her carryon bag. Then she secured their visible weapons and deposited them through a hatchway into the baggage compartment. There was no way to know if she had identified all the terrorists or secured all of their weapons. She had to rely on the nerve gas to keep everyone down until the plane landed and more help arrived. The scene was chaotic, but her orders were strict. Security was top priority and there had never been a trial of the nerve gas with a full plane of passengers. She wedged herself with her back to the cockpit door, facing toward the rear of the plane, so that she could observe any movement in the aisles of the passenger cabin, still breathing from her own oxygen tank and holding her pistol in both hands, ready to fire.

The plane lost altitude for a few seconds and then pulled up, banked gently to the north and headed sedately toward a military base just outside of Washington, flanked by the F16s, all the way to a perfect landing. A row of ambulances waited at the end of the runway with doctors masked and gloved, ready to jump into action. Portable stairways were connected to the plane and, within seconds, soldiers were opening the plane doors and emergency exits.

By now, the nerve gas had been flushed out of the plane but, just in case, everyone wore oxygen tanks and masks. The military carried guns cocked and ready to fire. After a few minutes, they dragged out the unconscious bodies of the suspected terrorists. Those first boarding the plane were warned to watch for Judy. When they entered, she sat in her assigned seat in row twenty, wearing her oxygen mask and holding her air marshal's badge above her head with both hands. For the next day or so, everyone that was onboard the plane, except Judy, would be a suspect.

Doctors began bringing passengers out on stretchers. Most were rousing and disoriented, having received injections of an antidote. Some were slow to come round, and three elderly passengers and two others were dead. Bob and Cathy made it alive, although both would stay in the hospital for a couple of days. Amy and Molly were shaken but very relieved to be back on the ground. Todd and Jane just stood and hugged each other, not quite believing that they had survived. Craig kissed the ground and then called his wife and promised to take her premonitions seriously in future.

Pete waved at Craig in the crowd and walked over casually. They shook hands, rather formally, and Pete said, "I told you we would be fine."

Craig just replied, "Yes you did Pete, thanks for the tip," still shaking hands.

"Thanks for the chocolate."

"I'll send you a case of that stuff."

"No, I'm going to eat a hamburger now," and with that Pete turned and walked back to his waiting parents.

Judy was in great spirits, but beginning to feel a sense of complete exhaustion. She reported in to her boss that everything was normalized and then she clipped on her air marshal's badge and helped get the remaining passengers off the plane.

A captain, a flight attendant, an air marshal and three college students would receive posthumous medals for bravery. Five others would be buried by their families, victims of collateral damage in the ongoing war on terror. Ten terrorists would be tried for acts of terrorism, murder, and conspiracy to murder thousands. Judy would receive a small raise and a couple of day's leave for successfully deploying a highly secret research weapon that, when perfected, would be used to thwart terrorist attacks on commercial aircraft. No one on the plane ever knew who Judy was or what she had done to save their lives. She was pleased.

In the Situation Room, everyone watched aghast as the plane turned north. The images from the cameras onboard the F16s showed the plane making a perfect approach and landing. Those lucky enough to be in the Situation Room all cheered and applauded their President.

"Gentlemen, you're sworn to secrecy. You've just witnessed the first live deployment of Project Pigeon. The idea was to put everyone to sleep and then fly the plane under remote control to a military base, like a pigeon flying home. We'll have to wait for the casualty figures, but we believe the losses should be restricted to the elderly or infirm, those with a severe heart conditions mainly. There'll be some pretty severe headaches but, overall, it seems the experiment was a resounding success."

Everyone applauded the President again, but he held up his hand to stop them, "Give your thanks to Dr. Preston here from NASA. He's had a team working on this since 9-11. Let's keep the lid on it. We're late for the party across the street."

With that, he shook hands with Dr. Preston, who was getting backslaps from others in the room. They all followed their President to the elevators and up to the ground level. He caught Vickie's arm, "Is that it?"

"Yes sir, I hope so."

"Good work. Let's get moving, we're late."

The President was due to speak in less than fifteen minutes at the Year of Peace Rally on the Mall. Secret Service agents boarded the President into his limo and the entourage headed for the Mall. Escort cars and motorcycles led, flanked and followed the President's car. Family members and other dignitaries came behind.

Vickie Cobrander's car was immediately behind the one carrying the President. Her phone rang and she noticed that it was Don Marshal again. She said, rather dismissively, "The plane's on the ground. It's all covered. Stand down, it's over—"

No one took any notice of the homeless bum, running at full speed through the crowd on the Mall, shouting into a cell phone, "No Vickie no! It's much bigger! I'm on the mall. Alert every agent within range . . ."

TO BE CONTINUED . . .

♦♦♦♦♦♦♦♦♦♦♦♦♦

Astor Lane has lived in Dallas, Texas, for the last two decades and writes poetry and mystery novels. Astor has worked mainly in university settings, teaching and advising students. Inspiration comes from music, nature, Douglas Adams and John Le Carré.

MAMA'S DIARIES

She handed the faded, pink floral fabric-covered, lace-edged diary to me; two satin ribbons were dangling from its spine.

"Open to where the ribbons are, Honey. Read it aloud to me."

Not a nickname, Honey really is my name. Honey Ray Howard, initials H.R.H. Since I was a child I've been teased and called H.R.H. - Her Royal Highness - but Mama always called me Honey, the name she gave me at birth, her only child.

I never knew my father. Mama had never mentioned his name and had never told me anything about him. I questioned, but there weren't any answers. A shrug of the shoulders was the most I ever got out of her and no one else seemed to know either. I didn't look like my mother, I had dark hair and green eyes, and she was blond with blue eyes. She was small; I was taller than Mama by the time I was 13 years old.

When I got older and learned more about getting pregnant, I figured maybe she didn't know who my father was, so I quit asking out of respect. I didn't need to know, anyway. I had my mother and that's all I needed. And she didn't need to know about the nights I cried myself to sleep because the kids at school had taunted me about not having a father.

Now Mama was dying. For 32 years we had lived together in loving harmony. Her life revolved around me, mine around her. She was there for me on my first day of school right on up through high school. She was there for me when I graduated from Harvard. She was there for me through a relationship that went south, deep south. And she was there with me when my first novel became a best-seller, the novel that changed our lives, made it much easier for us.

Mother had worked her way up in the school system from teaching at high school level to becoming a principal of a middle school that served the small communities of Los Osos, Baywood, and Morro Bay on the Central Coast of California. All three towns snuggled the coastline halfway between Los Angeles and San Francisco. I grew up in those communities, but was born in San Luis Obispo, a college town twelve miles inland. The only time I lived away from the Central Coast was while I was at Harvard. My mother had wanted me to become an attorney. Well, I got the degree from Harvard for mama, but I had no intention of becoming an attorney. I had wanted to write since I was a little girl nestling in our worn, overstuffed chair, reading my mother's books and literature that she taught in her high school English classes. Luckily the local newspaper hired me after college and I was there until I began making money freelancing - writing articles for every magazine that would publish me - while I was writing that first novel. This week my tenth book was released.

"Go on, read it, Honey."

"Which page, Mama?"

"Start from where I drew the star. There on the right." She began coughing.

I panicked. "Should I get the nurse, Mama?"

"No, no. I'll be alright. Read."

I began, "*Today, my dearest, darling child was born.*"

I stopped and looked at mama, tears already forming in my eyes.

"Go on. Don't stop. " She coughed again. She was suffering from inoperable lung cancer.

I read on. "*I have wanted a child of my own for as long as I can remember. I've wanted to know how it would feel to give birth to a baby. I could have done without the pain, though – ha ha.*"

I smiled and reached over and stroked Mama's arm, then continued, "*I wanted to feel her tiny fingers gripping mine and wanted to rock her in a rocking chair and sing to her like mothers do in the movies. I have always wanted a little girl to dress up in frilly, lacy dresses that I never wore as a child. I have always wanted my own dear, dear daughter in the worst way, and now I have her.*"

I stopped to wipe my eyes and covered my mouth and chin that were trembling. It was difficult to read about the love my mother felt for me. I had always felt it from her, had never doubted it, and now that she was leaving me, I couldn't bear the thought of being without her and I wasn't ready. We'd always been together. The pain of loss was already stabbing me through the heart. How could I live without this loving creature who had been my entire life?

When my first novel made the New York Times list, we built mama's dream house on the side of a hill overlooking the sea. We bought her dream car. We took a summer vacation to Canada like she'd always wanted to do, a cruise to Alaska included. I wanted her to have all she'd ever wanted. Everything I did was for her.

"Keep reading, Honey." Mama turned over on her side and closed her eyes.

"You want me to fix your pillow?"

"No, just keep reading, dear."

I took a deep breath and continued to read, "*I had prayed long and hard to have a baby. I believed in the Mary and Joseph story about Jesus, even though there were those who said it wasn't true, that the story had been concocted by religion, that there was no immaculate conception. And no matter how hard I prayed, nothing happened – no repeat immaculate conception.*"

I chuckled and continued reading, "*So I thought I had better take the matter into my own hands if I were to ever have a precious wee one to cuddle and raise as my own. Adoption agencies wouldn't accept a single mother, so that left me with only one choice.*"

I darted a look at Mama, she appeared to be asleep.

"I'm listening, go ahead," she said without opening her eyes.

"Is this going to tell me who my father is, Mama?" My heart was pounding, blood pressure rising. I could feel it. My face was hot. "Is it?"

"Read on."

I wasn't sure I wanted it to happen like this, after all these years, with Mama on her deathbed. It frightened me for some reason, but I did as she said, I read on. "*The best candidate to make a baby was one of the teachers I worked with who I had been attracted to and was always after me. But that was too close to home and I didn't want marriage. And besides, I wanted a handsome man as well as an intellectual, so that left him out. He was intellectual, but was a little twerp.*"

I laughed out loud. Mama could be funny when she wanted to be. I loved that about her. Her sense of humor was always an unexpected surprise.

"*The good looking men I knew were either married or gay, so I began thinking about going on holiday to another country and having a fling. No ties and far from home. Yes, that would work.*"

Mama was smiling; her graying blond curls nestled in the pillow, her eyes still closed.

"Mama! You didn't?"

"Yes, I did. And he was fabulous. Your father was the most fabulous man I ever knew. Go on."

I was feeling excitement now. The fear of finding out was dissipating. Now I was eager to know.

I began reading on the opposite page. "*I met Gregory in a little fishing village in Cornwall called Weymouth. Weymouth is more of a working man's village, or town, actually. Not as upscale and touristy as Bournemouth and Southampton. As a matter of fact, Weymouth was larger than a village, had a shopping mall and all that - not like our shopping malls, but called that all the same. It was a town, actually; villages only have a few shops and a grocer, a pub and a post office. So, Weymouth was a fishing town, and Gregory was a fisherman. I used to walk along the quay and breathe in the marvelous sea air and watch the fishing boats unload their daily catches and would most times sit on the wall and have a crab sandwich. One day Gregory came out of The George Inn across from where I was sitting, carrying two beer steins filled to the brim, and he asked me if he could join me. Said he'd be honored if I would relieve him of one of the drinks he was carrying. Of course, he wasn't really a two-fisted drinker; he had brought the drink to me purposefully. He'd been watching me every day that first week. Going to the George at lunch for a sandwich had become a habit.*"

Mama was looking at me, grinning widely. "He was a charming man, Honey. A good man. Gregory Raymond Sinclair. I named you Ray after him."

"Oh, Mama," I said as I gently grasped her hand. "Why didn't you tell me about him before?"

"I didn't want you to know because I didn't want him to know. I wanted you all to myself."

"But, it would have helped me to know who my father was. I needed to know that."

"You haven't suffered. You're more perfect than any other girl I know and were as you were growing up, too. You didn't need to know, you didn't need him. But now—" She turned her head and coughed hard into the pillow.

I laid my hand on her back and could feel the wrenching gasps between the croaking coughs.

Finally she turned and looked up at me again and said, "Take the diary with you, Honey. I won't be here much longer." She coughed again. "He's your father . . . we were in love . . . didn't want to fall in love . . . but I did." She was struggling to breathe. "Desire to have my own child . . . stronger than love . . . maybe did the wrong thing . . . don't think so."

"It's alright, Mama. At least you've told me and that's enough," I lied. I thought of all the times how much easier it would have been to have had a father to talk to, to go to. Mama was definitely Superwoman, but she was limited in her thinking. I had needed more than a mother.

"I never contacted Gregory after I returned from that wonderful summer on the south coast of England. I told him when we first met that I lived in New York and didn't tell him any different. Will you forgive me?"

"Of course, Mama. It's alright, don't worry about me. I'm just grateful you have at last told me the truth. You don't know how it makes me feel. I feel- I feel complete, now. Do you understand what I mean? Now I feel normal, I know who my father is. It's a huge relief, it really is."

"Take the diary home with you, Honey . . . read the rest of the others in my closet . . . my gift to you . . . I'm getting tired . . . need to sleep now . . . love you . . ." Her voice trailed as she dropped into a fast slumber.

That night mama died. That night she came to me in a dream that I was having about her precious diary, she stood beside my bed and reached over and closed the book. She looked down at me with those kind blue eyes and broad smile and said, "Don't read about him, go find him."

After mama's funeral I booked a flight on Virgin Airlines from Los Angeles to London Heathrow. The 11- hour flight gave me ample time to read more of the diary and prepare myself to meet my father, if he was still alive, he just had to be.

Gregory and I have seen each other every day for two weeks. Only during lunchtime, though. We sit in front of the George every day, sometimes having sandwiches, sometimes having fish and chips – his favorite. Fish and chips wrapped in newspaper, with vinegar sprinkled on the chips. And beer. He loves his beer. He says his dream is to own a pub or a tea and sandwich shop in Abbotsbury, which is a quaint little village just a short distance from Weymouth. He's going to take me there today. I think he just might be the man I'm looking for to father my child. He seems to be interested enough in me. We need to be having some night dates together, though. I don't know why he doesn't asked me out at night. I'm going to ask him today when he picks me up to go to Abbotsbury.

My first thought was that Gregory was married. When a man doesn't ask a woman out to dinner, only has lunch with her, he's usually married. Two weeks? They'd been seeing each other every day at lunch for two weeks? He's married.

I stuck the diary in the pocket of the chair in front of me and unfastened the seat belt. Time for a pit stop. As I walked back to the toilet compartments I couldn't help but notice loving couples to the right and left down the aisle. They were either sipping wine together, most likely on a holiday, leaning on the other's shoulder or holding hands or kissing or whatever. It was reminding me just how single I was, and that I was almost forty without a man in my life and now, no family. The few friends I had were either married or paired off. I was always the fifth wheel at any gathering, the odd man out. It was times like this that it seemed to hit me the most, when I traveled. And it wasn't like I sat around pinning away for some dreamboat to come into my life because I was usually too busy spending my time writing about romance in my fictitious characters lives. Writing about it seemed to take up the slack somewhat, but not at times like this. No. Romance was all around me.

When I returned to my seat, I decided to watch a movie and have a glass of champagne. I wasn't ready to read what was going to happen next in the diary. So I decided to put it off till later. But then I fell asleep after the movie and slept soundly for two hours. By the time I woke up we'd been in flight for five hours, only six more to go. I picked up the diary again.

Well, we're going out to dinner tomorrow night. I asked him why he hadn't taken me out to dinner and he said he was afraid to. Said he couldn't trust himself with the moon and the sounds of the seas, it would be too romantic and more difficult for him to keep his hands off me. I smiled at the sincerity in his face and told him not to worry. That we wouldn't do anything either of us didn't want to do. So he said he'd pick me up at eight and we'd go to a pub for steak and ale near the docks. Abbotsbury was absolutely beautiful today. We went to the swannery and the Abbotsbury Gardens. I see why he wants to live there. It's a quiet little village, but very touristy, for they come through to the swannery and the gardens by the busloads. But the village people and the tea rooms are lovely. He said he'd like to take me to Dorchester next weekend, it's just a few miles from Weymouth, too. That's where the writer Thomas Hardy lived and wrote. I hope Gregory's dream comes true and he gets his pub. Right now he works on one of the fishing boats, though. Says they go out very early in the morning which is why he isn't out late at night. But he doesn't have to work this weekend, so we'll have our first evening date tomorrow. I like Gregory and I wouldn't mind living over here. But no, I can't be doing that. I came after my baby. That's all.

Well, so maybe he wasn't married. Maybe.

"Excuse me, may I borrow the airline magazine, I didn't get one."

I leaned forward, retrieved it and handed it to the woman next to me. "There you go."

"Thank you. Are you from the States?"

"Yes, I am. Going to Dorset for a holiday. You?"

"I'm going back to England after vacationing in California." She was a chubby, older woman, about the age of my mother.

"Where do you live in the UK?"

"In Bournemouth."

"Oh, yes. That's not far from Weymouth, where I'll be staying."

"Oh, so you're off to Weymouth, are you?"

"Yes, I am."

"You're taking the train from Heathrow?"

"Yes."

"We'll be on the same train, then."

I wasn't sure if I wanted to strike up a friendship with this woman and be talking to her all the way to Bournemouth, so I did some quick thinking. "Well, actually, I'm staying in London for a few days before I go to Weymouth." I wasn't.

"Oh that's too bad; I could have used the company, it's such a long trip."

"Oh, I'm sorry. Uh, will you excuse me?" I unbuckled my belt, grabbed my purse, and thought I might stretch my legs a bit to avoid any further conversation. My legs were beginning to feel as if the circulation was slowing anyway. While I was walking up and down the aisle, I spied a seat back a few rows without anyone sitting on either side. So I returned to my seat, leaned in and grabbed the diary. The woman's eyes were closed as the music played in her ear phones, so she didn't even know that I had moved to another seat. Something about airplanes, I prefer not to talk. I guess I'm just not a friendly sort. I either read or watch movies or sleep. Now in a bar or a restaurant or club, I'll talk to anyone. I guess it's because I can walk away or leave when I want. On a plane, you're stuck.

I opened the diary to where I had left off.

I'm waiting for Gregory, it's nearly seven forty-five. I've been ready since seven. This B&B is really comfy, I'm right on the seafront. I can hear the waves. The couple who owns it is such a delight and has made me feel at home. There's a Chinese restaurant on the beach down to the right. I wonder if Gregory has been there. I think if this room were larger, I could live here. I wonder if Gregory has a house or lives in an apartment. I'm wearing a new gray outfit that I bought today at Marks & Spencer's, downtown, an ultra-conservative department store - one of the oldest in England. Oh, here he is!

It was time to close my eyes for awhile; I felt a headache coming on. I slept for another hour until the sound of the food and beverage carts awakened me. I had lasagna and another glass of champagne. As I ate I thought of mother and wondered how she had kept the secret of my birth from her friends. Surely they must have known she was pregnant. And how had she explained my sudden appearance to everybody?

My thoughts wandered to Weymouth. I was going to go to the pub at the quay first to find out if anyone knew the whereabouts of Gregory Raymond Sinclair. He was probably retired by now, too old to be a fisherman. Or maybe 60-year old fishermen don't retire; age probably doesn't matter in that line of work, although he had wanted his own pub according to the diary. I just hoped he was still in the area. Most likely he had married and had a family, though. If not before he met my mother, at least afterwards. What would I say to him if I found him? I hadn't really thought about that. What if he didn't remember my mother? Now that would be a hardy blow.

The hostess picked up my tray and refuse. I asked for coffee and reached for the diary, again.

I am in love. I don't want to go back to the U.S. Gregory wants me to stay here and marry him. Says he can't live without me. I don't know what to do. It's been two weeks since I've written in this diary. We have been together almost every day and night he's been home. He has a lovely house just outside of town on the road to Abbotsbury with a rose garden near the front gate. A farmhouse made of grey stone; walls are at least two-feet thick. His front door is painted Red, a dark beet red. He calls it royal red. The house belonged to his parents and he was an only child, he's never married. How can I do this? How can I stay here? If I marry him I can stay, I think. I can still be an American citizen and be married to a Brit. I can go back and forth. Stay here six months at a time and make quick trips back to the U.S. to satisfy immigration. Or maybe I can get a permanent visa. Oh, I don't know what to do. When we make love it is heaven, it is all I ever dreamed it would be. He does nothing wrong. I have never felt this way before. He is the most romantic man I've ever known, a fisherman in Dorset, who would've known. What a surprise!

"Here's your coffee, Miss." The hostess handed a napkin and the cup to me.

"Thank you." I set the diary aside and sipped my coffee. I couldn't help but feel sorry for mother. All those years living for me, all those years teaching school, all those years being where she didn't want to be when all she wanted was to be with him in England. I wondered why she didn't stay. She had never loved anyone else. I had never seen her with a man, she never dated. She wasn't interested, she'd say, when I asked her why she hadn't dated or married. Why hadn't she told my father where she lived? She loved him that much, why didn't she contact him? I couldn't read any further. It was too much to take in. No wonder I had a headache.

I didn't pick up the diary again until I was on the train to Weymouth. The English countryside was something to behold. I had never seen such rolling green hills and stone houses dotting the landscape. Clusters of cottages and farmhouses nestled into crevices formed the myriad of villages along the way. Each village had its historic church with steeple rising above all else. Country roads were dotted with people walking their dogs, for it's a canine country, and I'd heard that regardless of the size of the dogs, most live indoors. I'd never been to that part of the world. I'd been to France, Italy, Belgium and Switzerland, but never to England. So I was enjoying the ride to Weymouth. And I hadn't run into the chubby woman from the plane, of that I was thankful.

Something is wrong. Gregory was different last night. He hardly talked to me and didn't laugh at all. That's not like him. We've had such laughter bouts in the past few days. I'm worried. I'm feeling he's changed his mind, that he doesn't want to get married. I haven't said I would marry him, but I've hinted at the possibility. We've talked about me coming back at Christmas. My plane leaves for the U.S. tomorrow, school starts in two weeks. I have to leave on the train for London today to make the connection tomorrow. I have been here for two months. Two wonderful months I'll never forget, regardless. Gregory is taking me to the train station; he should be here any minute.

We were making a stop in Southampton, I had to change trains. I gathered up my belongings and went to the baggage rack near the door where I would exit. I'd brought one roller bag and a shoulder valise. So maneuvering was relatively easy. I'd learned that on other trips I'd made to Europe when doing research for my books. If I could eliminate the shoulder bag, I would, but I found it just couldn't be done. At least I couldn't do it. The train I was to take to Weymouth would be on another platform upstairs in ten minutes, so I had to hurry. That was cutting it pretty close, and I barely made it. I didn't read the diary because the view from the train was so intriguing the rest of the way.

I hadn't made room reservations in Weymouth because I wanted to check out the vicinity of the quay first. I'd done an Internet search and came up empty-handed. Sometimes British pubs or inns rent out rooms above their restaurants, I'd heard. Surely there were accommodations near the docks. So I hired a cab to drive me to the quay, I saw the George Inn, but we found that there weren't any hotel rooms. We were directed to a large hotel down across from the beach and were also told about a row of B & B's further down the Esplanade. I selected the Prince Regent Hotel. It was Victorian and elegant, had a restaurant and bar. Perfect. I checked in.

It was late by the time I unpacked, so I decided to grab a bite to eat and go to bed. I'd set out on my quest the next day. Besides, the time change was eight hours ahead and it was a day later for me. I'd left California at noon the day before and had only the few naps on the plane. So it was 8:00 p.m. the next day already, by the time I showered and freshened up before going downstairs for a quick meal. I needed something substantial other than plane and train food. I was thinking fresh fish and salad.

That night I slept twelve hours. I couldn't believe it. I didn't wake up till eleven the next morning. It's always hard to acclimate going to Europe from the USA, the return trip is much easier. So I took a quick shower and donned a pair of jeans and a sweater and took off towards the boat docks. It was a lovely day, crisp, cool, just the kind of weather that I love. Walking along the Esplanade, which was a sidewalk bordering the pebbled beach with concrete flower boxes along the center, felt good to me. I could understand already why mother had wanted to live here. It's unfortunate she didn't return. I was carrying her diary in my shoulder bag, hoping to find out why she hadn't returned as I read it during lunch.

I'd decided to go the George Inn for a crab sandwich, just as mother had done all those years before. The walk along the beachfront all the way to the boat channel and the George Inn was stimulating.

I had read on the Internet that the original George Inn was known to have existed on the same site since before 1665 when its owner, Sir Samuel Mico bequeathed it to the Corporation of

Weymouth and Melcombe Regis (the opposite bank of the channel). The profits from it were to apprentice three poor children amongst other things and the charity continues even today. I had wondered whether or not the George Inn would still be there. In the U.S. there aren't many businesses that last 20 years much less 220 years. So I was happy to know that this was the very site my mother met my father.

I stepped through the door into a darkened pub area. It smelled of sea water and was cool and comfortable. The aged wooden timbers and walls gave it a waterfront ambiance and added to its quaintness. There were quite a few patrons scattered throughout, some at the tables, some at the bar. All eyes were upon me as I entered, it seemed.

I moved to the bar and sat on a barstool. I had found over the years that I could learn more about the people and the town by sitting at the bars instead of the tables. Conversation ran rampant, if not with the patrons sitting there, always with the barkeep.

"What would you like, darlin'?"

"Do you serve wine?"

"Red or white?"

"White, please. Oh, wait. Do you have Champagne?"

"Yes, I do."

"By the glass?"

"Yes, is that what you want?"

"Yes. And one of your famous crab sandwiches, please."

"Would you like chips or salad with that?"

"Salad, please."

I turned on the bar stool to take in the view of the room. I was sitting at the end near a wall, the seat of choice wherever I went, and I leaned back against the wall, somewhat. Three rough-skinned sunburned men, rugged types dressed in sweatshirts and jeans, were sitting towards the other end of the bar. They were drinking beer and laughing loudly, all three with thick British accents, some words undecipherable to my ears. One was older than the other two who were in their 40s most likely. There were other groups of men around the room, some at tables, and some in the adjoining room where the bar continued to run the length of that room, too. There were men sitting outside the door, smoking and drinking. And there were a few women situated here and there. Two were between me and the three men.

They all seemed to know each other. This had to be a locals' pub which is the best kind to frequent if you're a traveler. I'd learned to do that wherever I went – find the local haunts, my first rule.

"Here you go, your champagne. The sandwich is coming up. You from the States?"

"Yes, I am. Taking a holiday away from it all."

"I just got back from Florida, go there every year."

"You do? That's great. Have you ever been to California? That's where I live."

"No, but I am thinking about it. The owners went there this year. After they went to New Orleans. See the photo up there? That's them in New Orleans." He walked over to the three men and poured more beer for them.

The photo drew my attention to all the post cards and other photos that were tacked on the wall behind the bar. Post cards from travelers and friends, from far away places, and quite a few from the States.

"Do you know Gregory Ray Sinclair? He was a fisherman around here 40 years ago."

The older man at the bar turned his head towards me. "You asking about Greg Sinclair?"

"Yes, do you know him?"

"Haven't seen him in about five years. He retired from fishing. Doesn't come around here anymore."

"Do you know if he's still in the area?" I was getting excited and I'm sure it was showing.

"So why you looking for him?" The man lifted his pint of beer and sipped, squinting at me over the top of the mug.

Everyone sitting at the bar including the bartender waited for my answer. I wasn't sure I should divulge the reason of my quest at that moment, didn't feel it was something I felt they all should know. I felt it was private information only for my father's ears, if he was still living.

"I'm a distant cousin, have only just found out that his branch of the family was from Dorset and I've traced some of them to Weymouth. You know us Americans; we love to claim our British heritage. I'm just hoping I can find him or any of his family still living in this area."

Another man from one of the tables stepped up to the bar, "As a matter of fact, I was his brother-in-law."

"You say 'was'. You mean he's dead?"

"No it was me sister. His wife. She died ten years ago. I haven't seen him for five now, but then he wasn't much of a socializer with our family. After me sister died we didn't hear much from him."

"Are there any children?"

"No. They had one way back, but it was stillborn. They didn't try for any more after that."

My heart was racing, *no children, he was still alive five years ago.* I took a deep breath and then took a sip of my drink as I quickly organized my thoughts.

One of the young men sitting at the bar added, "I saw him a couple weeks ago at in the Cove , you know. On Chesil Beach. He'd been out fishing with his mates, they were having lunch. I overheard him say he was glad to have a day off from working his pub in Abbotsbury."

"Didn't know he had a pub in Abbotsbury," the older man said.

"I was with Kathy's family, so I didn't go over and talk to him. We were getting ready to leave."

I was taking it all in and getting more excited by the moment. The bartender brought the crab sandwich to me.

"Do you mind if I take my lunch outside and watch the boats?"

"Not at all, here let me help you carry it." He came from around the bar and carried the food outdoors, while I carried the drink.

"Thank you so much. I'll bring the plate and glass back in when I finish."

"No problem, take your time."

He went back into the pub. I could see through the open door and could hear the laughter and the conversation that would switch back and forth between loud and a constant hum.

The sandwich was still as good as my mother had said it was. I closed my eyes and tried to visualize the day my father met my mother, probably in that very spot where I was sitting.

"Excuse me, Miss. The birds are eating your food."

I opened my eyes to see a man lifting my plate and shooing the birds away.

"If it's your plan to feed the birds your sandwich, then that's all right, but I don't think that is the plan, am I right?" He set the plate on the bench and sat down next to it. Then he stretched his arms out across the back of the bench, staring at me and grinning widely.

I was speechless.

"Are you all right? I didn't mean to startle you."

"Uh, yes. I'm okay. I mean, well, I was just somewhere else, that's all. Sorry. Thank you. I didn't see the birds."

"Seagulls love crab meat. You're eating their favorite meal, you know."

"Oh, I didn't know that. I didn't know." I couldn't believe I was looking into the face of the most rugged, handsome man I'd ever seen. He was dark brown from the sun; at least it appeared to be a suntan. Either from working outdoors, or maybe he was a sailor, a fisherman. My mind ran wild with assumptions. He didn't appear to be of a darker race. His features weren't giving that away, if he was. His accent was British.

"So, are you American?"

"Yes, I am. You?"

"French, but have lived in England all my life. I was born in St. Malo, across the channel. My father brought us across on his fishing boat when I was a baby. Actually, I'm French and Portuguese, my mother was from Portugal, her father was a fisherman. I'm from a long line of fisherman."

"Oh, then you might know my cousin, Greg Sinclair. He was a fisherman here in Weymouth, I'm told. I've come to find him. Do you know him?"

"Well, I didn't live here. Went to school in London, started my own business there, and only come here to visit my parents. So no, I don't know him, but my father might."

"That's okay, I think I can find him. One of the guys in the pub said he thinks he runs a pub in Abbotsbury."

"Have you been to Abbotsbury?"

"No, I haven't. My name is Honey, by the way, what's yours?"

"Honey?" He laughed. "Are you kidding me?"

"No, I'm not kidding you. That's what my mother named me. You can imagine all the teasing I've been subjected to and worse yet, my full name is Honey Ray Howard. HRH the kids called me all through school. The nickname still sticks. So please don't call me HRH. Honey is fine."

The man displayed the widest grin and the whitest teeth I'd ever seen.

"I am Jean Vincent Doucet. And I will not make fun of your name. It is a beautiful name and eliminates the difficulty of remembering. I would imagine your husband finds it very easy—"

"Oh no, I'm not married. Never have been. And yes, the boyfriends, few that there were, found it easy to remember, too." I took a bite of my sandwich as he drank his beer. I could feel his eyes on me as I watched a fishing boat attempt to maneuver broadside to the pilings.

Finally Jean broke the silence and stood, "Would you like me to take you to Abbotsbury after you have your lunch? My car is near."

I looked up at him, "Well, I don't know—"

"Everyone in the pub will vouch for me, they all know me. You will be safe with me. I would be happy to do this for you."

He was such a handsome figure standing there warming me all over with his penetrating gaze. I felt helpless all of a sudden. I felt feminine for the first time in years. I felt tingly and giddy. It was ridiculous. I had to get control of myself.

"No, that's all right. Thank you, but I've some other things I must do before I go to Abbotsbury. Thank you. You're most gracious."

I could see the disappointment on his face, but it would be frivolous for me to accept a stranger's offer to cart me around the countryside. I didn't know the man, and who's to say the men in the pub didn't know his innermost secrets. He could be a serial killer, he could be a rapist. It would be foolish for me to accept his offer. No. I couldn't do that.

"If you change your mind, I'll be back here around six this evening. That should give you time to take care of your errands. And it it will take about an hour to get to the pub in Abbotsbury, so we can have a meal there, if you want."

Why was I hesitating? It would be madness to take off with a stranger, especially at night.

"Would you let me do that for you? Show you some local courtesy?"

"All right. Yes. I'll be back at six. Thank you." I must be crazy.

"Then I will be off to take care of a few jobs myself. Honey, it's been a pleasure talking to you and I'll see you at six, right?"

"Yes, at six." I couldn't believe myself. Pure craziness!

It was five o'clock and I was taking a last look at myself in the mirror before setting out through town and down to the quay and the pub where I was to meet Jean. My plan was to get there before him and have a glass to relax a bit.

Earlier in the afternoon after lunch, I had walked further down towards the mouth of the channel and had watched passengers disembark the gigantic watercraft that had just arrived from St. Malo. I made a mental note to do an Internet search on St. Malo, to see what kind of seaport it was and learn more about the birthplace of Jean Vincent.

I found myself thinking of him off and on all afternoon. Thoughts of him crept into my mind at every turn I made, in every shop I browsed. I even thought of him as I dressed, wondering if he would like this or that sweater, this or that pair of pants, this or that pair of boots. I settled on all black that was my norm and grabbed my black wool pea coat and off I went.

It was a cool evening, nippy, but not freezing. The sea breeze against my face felt good. I loved the smell of the environment in Weymouth. It was a clean and natural town, no foul smells, no garbage littered streets as in New York City. The last time I had been to NYC, as exciting as it was, the smells were horrific. I imagine one gets used to it when one lives in it, but I had difficulty not putting my hand over my nose to prevent breathing in the stench.

Weymouth smelled good. Even as I reached the bridge that crossed the channel, the docks smelled heavenly – a refreshing sea and fish smell, not stale. I walked down the stone steps to the quay and breathed in more invigorating sea air. Wonderful!

Inside the pub I seated myself at the bar on the same stool I'd occupied at noon. The bartender was preparing to leave, a shift change. He recognized me and gave me a cheerful greeting. I ordered a white Zinfandel and relaxed as I sipped and absorbed the local color.

A hand touched my shoulder and I turned to face Jean Vincent. He didn't look like the same man I'd met that day. His black hair was slicked back which made his dark eyes even more dominant and sparkly, his clean-shaven face softened his tanned skin, and his attire was entirely unexpected – a black leather flight jacket and a gray turtle-necked cashmere sweater with matching wool flannel slacks, black Italian loafers shined to perfection. I was taken aback and he saw my surprise.

"Oh? You expecting someone else?"

"No, no," I laughed. "I just didn't expect you to look like you do. You were a bit more rugged before."

"That was my daytime look; this is my nighttime look. You like?"

"Oh yes, I like. You're very handsome. I suppose everyone tells you that, though, so I take it back."

He laughed heartily. "I suppose I shouldn't tell you how beautiful you are, because everyone tells you that, right?"

"As a matter of fact, only my mother told me that. So you're quite safe, it won't go to my head. Thank you."

"And is your mother waiting for you back in the States?"

The question startled me. "Well, no. She died two weeks ago."

"I'm so sorry. I didn't mean to be flippant, I didn't know."

"It's okay. Really. She'd been sick for quite some time. She's peaceful now. It's okay."

"I'll have a pint, John," he called out to the bartender. "Do you mind if I have a drink before we go?"

"Of course not. I'm having one. In fact I think I'll have one more."

"Bring the lady another, John, while you're at it." He sat on the stool next to me. "Why are you looking for Sinclair? To tell him about your mother? "

"Yes, that too, but mainly because I want to meet him . . . and meet my other British relatives."

"I made a few calls this afternoon to see if he is indeed in Abbotsbury, and was told he does own a pub there, but couldn't find out anything more about him. So I know where it's located."

Goosebumps popped up on my arms and my hair felt as if it were standing straight up. *I am so close to meeting my father. I don't know how I feel about it. What if he rejects me? What if he says' so what?' I don't know what I want from him.*

"Are you all right?" Jean put his hand on my arm where I had pushed up my sleeve. "You have goosebumps, are you cold?"

"No, I'm fine, really."

We were entering Abbotsbury along the main street that was lined with thatched roofed cottages. It was just as mother had written in her diary and it was beautiful, even at night. The cozy lamps shone through the cottage windows and gave off a luminescent, inviting feeling. It felt as if it would be alright to walk up to any door and no doubt being welcomed by friendly inhabitants – strangers or not. What a lovely village! No wonder my mother loved this place.

"This is beautiful, Jean!" My neck felt strained from looking back and forth from one side of the street to the other. "Just like my mother said."

"Your mother was here?"

"Yes, she was." Oh no, I didn't intend to let it slip out. "Years ago."

"There it is, up ahead. I'll park the car here, we can walk since it appears this is as close as we're going to get to the pub. Looks busy tonight."

Suddenly I was frightened. I recalled the portion of Mama's diary I had read that afternoon.

I was dumbfounded when Gregory told me at the train station he was getting married in two months, that it had been planned long before he knew me and that it wouldn't be appropriate for me to come back at Christmas. He had tears in his eyes when he said he loved me and that he meant it when he asked me to marry him. But the families had always expected him to marry Louise Becker. He and Louise had grown up together and had always been an item. She'd been in the States for the past two years at university and had suddenly returned the day before, unannounced. He said he was sad and heartbroken, said he'd hoped Louise wouldn't come back at all and had been trying to figure out how to tell her and her family. He held me and said he would always love me, but he just couldn't tell Louise he didn't love her anymore. He was fond of her, he said, and didn't want to hurt her. He told me he would never love her as he did me, and that he felt confused, but if I'd please stay in contact with him he'd try to find a way that we could be together. Maybe he could come to the States to visit me, he said.

I felt as if a knife had stabbed me in the heart and its serrated edges were twisting and turning. I felt as if an iron-clad fist had plunged into my belly and struck my back bone. I felt as if a rope had tightened around my throat and was squeezing the life out of me. I couldn't breathe, I couldn't think, I couldn't bear the thought of living without him. I reached into my pocket and squeezed a piece of paper into a tight wad. I had written my real address and phone number on it to give to him. The tears blurred my vision as I turned and ran to board the train without looking back. I never looked back.

I wondered what might have happened if she had given him her real address and phone number. I can't imagine anyone rejecting my mother and I felt she should have tried to work out something with him. That had explained her whole life as I knew it. I couldn't imagine how she managed to overcome her broken heart and raise me as she did, seeing my father in me every single minute of every single day. Maybe that was how she coped, knowing she had a part of him with her. I don't know. I can only guess.

The pub was a charming one. Very homey and very friendly. The patrons were mostly locals with a few tourists that were staying at nearby B & B accommodations.

Behind the bar was a strapping man, ruddy complexioned, happy eyes and countenance. Beside him was a younger woman, although older than me, serving up drinks at one end of the bar. And there was a cook in the kitchen and a food server. Only four people manned the busy establishment. The laughter and loud voices made it even more hospitable and fun loving. I felt very comfortable, especially with Jean's arm around me as we stood there taking it all in.

"Shall we find a place at the bar?" he asked as he headed me in that direction.

"Sure. I prefer sitting at the bar. I'd rather eat there, too, if you don't mind."

"That's exactly what I had in mind."

We found two seats at the far end. It was the perfect spot, we could see all that was going on and I could watch the man behind the bar who I was hoping was my father.

"Good evening to you both, and what would you like to drink on this festive occasion?" The bartender asked. He was grinning from ear to ear.

"The lady will have a White Zinfandel and I'll have a pint of the dark, thank you."

"All right." He walked away.

I couldn't help but feel a connection to him, he's got to be my father. We had the same color hair and eyes. I was tall like him. We were both left-handed, I noticed. Both have dimples in our chins.

"Here you go. Are you going to be dining with us tonight?"

"Yes, we are," I responded. "What do you suggest?"

"Roast Lamb for the gentleman, yes? And we've a delicious poached salmon for the lady, both served with steamed vegetables and potatoes."

"Sounds yummy to me. What do you think, Jean?"

"Sounds great. We'll have just what you suggested, but let's wait a while, shall we? Say in about thirty minutes or so put in the order? And we'll dine right here, if we may."

"Enjoy your drinks, and relax right where you are. Are you from around here, lassie?" He was looking curiously at me.

"No, I'm not. I'm from America. Just here to visit my relatives."

"What is the name of your relatives, maybe I know them."

His eyes were searching mine. I honestly felt like he knew.

"She thinks you might be her relative, as a matter of fact. You're Gregory Sinclair aren't you?

"That I am, yes. And who might you be, young lady? I didn't know I had any relatives in the U.S."

"My mother was Lydia Howard. Do you remember her?"

He blinked his eyes and gasped as he moved his hands from the bar and put them on his hips. He stared at me for a few moments then turned in a circle, rubbing his hands through his hair. When he looked at me again he had tears in his eyes.

"I'm your daughter, Honey Ray Howard. She named me after you, my middle name."

He was flabbergasted and was finding it difficult to speak. He took a handkerchief from his pocket and wiped his eyes. He looked as if he was going to cry.

"Are you all right? I didn't mean to be so abrupt, but I've been so eager to meet you and to get to know you. Too much time has been wasted and I just had to blurt it out. I'm sorry, I hope you're all right."

"Oh yes, yes. I'm perfectly all right. I just never dreamed—how is she? How is Lydia? Did she come with you?"

"She passed away two weeks ago."

"Oh no! Lydia!" He buried his face into his handkerchief and wept, turned towards the wall trying to control his crying.

"I didn't know about you till just before she died when she told me about you and wanted me to find you. She said I looked like you and I think that made her feel close to you through the years. She never married, raised me alone. She was a wonderful, loving mother."

Sean was taking it all in, hadn't said a word since I began talking. He tightened his grip on me as I continued.

"I don't want anything from you, I just want to have a chance to get to know you. I've not had a father in my life. And well, I guess it's better late than never. You know?"

Gregory blew his nose and looked at me again. "You're right about that, Lassie." He quickly lifted the bar gate and came right for me. "Let me hug my daughter, Laddie. This is my daughter."

He lifted me off the bar stool and held me so tight I couldn't breathe. But it felt better than any hug I'd ever had. I couldn't believe my father was holding me. I couldn't hold back the tears that had been stored inside me since I was a little girl when I first asked my mother who my daddy was and then through all the years of wondering.

"This is my daughter, everybody! I have a girl I didn't know I had!" He stood beside me and held up my hand in his. "She's come to meet me! This is my Honey Ray!"

Two days later this is what I wrote after mama's last entry in her diary.

Mama, I have met my daddy. He is everything you said he was. He said he never got over losing you and his childless marriage was an unhappy one. He really loved you, Mama. And I understand why you loved him and wanted to live here.

Dorset is absolutely beautiful. And Mama, you aren't going to believe this, I met a lovely man in the very same spot you met daddy. I was eating a crab sandwich just like you were, when Jean came out of the George Inn and sat by me. He's fabulous. I've never met a man as charming and kind.

I'm meeting daddy in the morning and I think I'm going to stay for awhile to get to know him and maybe help him out in his pub, if he'll let me. Yes, he bought a pub in Abbotsbury several years ago and has beautiful living quarters upstairs. You would love it, Mama. I know you would.

I love you and I miss you.

The next day I packed my bags and rented a car for the drive to Abbotsbury. Daddy had invited me to stay with him, said there was plenty of room, I'd have my own bedroom, sitting room and bath. The upstairs quarters were set up to be four ensuite tourist accommodations, which he used instead as his own living space. He said once in a while he would rent a room out if necessary to a patron who couldn't make it home after a night of heavy drinking, but usually no.

As I drove the short distance through the hilly countryside, I thought of my life as it was and how it might be if I were to stay in England. I imagined my mother must have gone through the same mental process when she was faced with the decision.

I rounded the corner and saw a commotion outside my dad's pub. People were standing around, some were going in and out of the pub in a frantic-like manner. Luckily there was a parking space opposite the pub and I grabbed it before anyone else could. There was a line of cars behind me.

I left the luggage in the car and hurried to see what was going on. Since I didn't recognize anyone, I went through the door and saw the barmaid. "Hannah, what's going on?"

"Oh, Missy. Your father's been taken to hospital in Weymouth. He's had a heart attack, Missy. They just pulled off no more than ten minutes ago."

"Where is the hospital?"

I drove as fast as I could and still be able to control the car. The hospital was easy to find with Hannah's directions. He'd been there 30 minutes by the time I was ushered to the area where they were working on him. I was crying before I saw him, and cried even harder when I did see him.

His eyes were closed, he was ashen, tubes were running all over the place, monitors beeping. He was hooked up to a ventilator . . . it was a replay of my mother. I felt devastated and helpless.

I caressed his big, rough hand, squeezed it, kissed it, laid my hand on his brow, talked to him. “Daddy, please don’t go. Please don’t leave me now. I just found you. I need you.”

He opened his eyes and looked directly at me, tears ran from the corners, and he squeezed my hand. He couldn’t talk because of the tube down his throat, but his eyes told me that he loved me.

“I love you, too, Daddy. Mama loved you and I love you.”

The corners of his mouth formed a smile and he took his last breath.

Mama, I’m sure you already know this; Daddy died three days ago, the service was today. I was there when he took his last breath, Mama. I told him you loved him, and I hope that he has found you by now. I’ve put aside my grief and am replacing it with the romantic notion that he just couldn’t bear to live without you any longer, he’s in search of you, Mama. He left this world three weeks to the day you left.

The day before his heart attack, he drew up a will with his solicitor leaving me the business in Abbotsbury and the house outside Weymouth. He still owned that house, Mama, the one with the royal red door.

Abbotsbury is a lovely village and I do feel like I’m home. I feel like this is where I should have been born, with you and daddy in Dorset. I can write anywhere, so it doesn’t matter where I live, we both know that. And Jean Vincent is loving and comforting to me. I don’t know what I would’ve done without him. We’ve become even closer through all this. We’ve been intimate, Mama, and I’m feeling as if it’s a replay of how it was for you when you were here with daddy. The only difference this time, however, is that I’m going to stay – for you and for me.

♦♦♦♦♦♦♦♦♦♦♦♦

When asked at what age she began writing, Rebecca Buckley replied, "I have always been a writer."

From acting out stories with paper dolls as a child to writing and directing her first stageplay at the age of nine which was performed by neighborhood kids on a dirt floor of a dilapidated garage in the farming community of Wasco CA , Rebecca has gone on to travel the world and write about her life experiences. She's written stageplays, screenplays, short stories, and novels. And has most recently entered the world of "How To" non-fiction with her "Write it Right" series of books.

Even though the first third of her life was focused on schooling, followed by marriage and giving birth to four children, she continued to write stories that were filed away in boxes.

The second third of her life was spent in corporate America - writing policy & procedure manuals, editing/writing presentations, creating forms, editing/writing newsletters, etc.

She enrolled in a Film & Television Screenwriting program at UCLA, worked days, went to school at night, and plotted to leave corporate America to make a living writing screenplays. That ambition was short lived since every other person in Los Angeles is a screenwriter and has the same plan. She switched to writing stageplays and several were produced at community theatre level, but in 2005 she completed and published her first novel "Midnight at Trafalgar Square". In 2006 she published a collection of short stories "Love Has a Price Tag" which also includes two stageplays and one screenplay. In 2007 her second novel "Midnight at the Eiffel" was published. Her goal to publish at least one book a year is right on the mark. She just recently published her second collection of short stories called "Bits & Pieces of Me" and is on Blog Talk Radio.

The Amazon Shorts Program has published several of her short stories, and Ms. Buckley is also Founder and CEO of Wizards of Words.

www.rebeccabuckley.com

ODD JOB

By Woodrow W. Walker

Norman Beal was a typical unassuming businessman. He had met his supportive wife Linda, five years his junior, in college. They had married after graduation. Against his better judgment he had taken a job in his father-in-law's company, as an accountant. He had tried sales, that was where the money was, but he had sucked at it.

Now twenty years later Norman at forty-five felt trapped. He had not risen in the company because his father-in-law believed that promoting his son-in-law would not look good to his other employees. On his accountant's salary, he could barely keep his wife in the style in which she was accustomed. The house that they lived in had been a wedding present from her father. They would be living in a small apartment otherwise, something he could afford.

Linda did not understand why she needed to live on a budget. Every month Norman cringed at the pile of bills that he had to figure out how to pay. He always managed, but there was never enough leftover. Their bank account never had more than a few hundred in it. His car was a decade old that he had bought from a used car lot. His wife Linda drove a new car that had been a birthday present from her father. Norman felt that the one bright spot was they were not burdened with children.

Then in an unexpected move, his father-in-law, in a cost cutting measure, decreed that all employees not essential to the day-to-day operation of the company would be allowed to work at home.

The accounting department was the first to be shut down. Norman hated the idea at first, but his wife Linda embraced it whole-heartedly. She designed his home office, making sure that it had everything a home office should have.

So Norman settled into his home office, and Linda did whatever it was that wives do while their husbands are working. Linda had many interests and was often away from home as her husband toiled.

One day while pouring over a mound of statements, Norman groaned, "However hard I work, I can never catch up on these bills."

Linda gave him a bored, but sympathetic look. "Why don't you ask father for a rise?"

Norman laughed. "I have asked. Several times in fact. His answer is always the same. No. What I need is a part-time job, one that wouldn't interfere with my work for your father's company."

Linda smiled. "I'm sure you will manage. Daddy can sometimes be an ass, but he did give us this house. And he would never fire you."

Norman nodded. "Yes, as he has often reminded me."

A month later, on a Sunday, the one day that Norman could relax, he was taking a nap.

Linda awakened him, holding the classified section of the newspaper. "Honey, look at this advertisement. I think it might interest you."

"Let me see." Norman took the paper and put on his eyeglasses. He found the item that Linda had circled in the employment section.

PART-TIME WORK
Four hours a week
Saturdays, good pay
(555) 193-7000

"What do you think? You did say that you needed a part-time job."

"Yes, but I don't think I'd have much chance. It's probably already been filled."

"Why don't you call and see? You will have as much chance as anyone else."

Unable to think of a reason not to at least try for a job he knew he needed, Norman reached for the telephone. He figured he wouldn't reach anyone on a Sunday, so he dialed the number. It rang four times, before someone came on the line.

"Hello." It was a man's voice.

"Oh, hello. My name is Norman Beal and I wish to inquire about the part-time job that you have advertised in today's newspaper."

"Do you wish to apply?"

"Well, yes. That is, if it is still available."

"We've received calls, but the requirements have turned off most. The job still needs to be filled."

"What kind of requirements? Is the work dangerous?"

"No, no, nothing such as that, Mr. Beal. To tell you the truth it's a bit boring."

Norman laughed. "Is that all? Well, I am an accountant, how boring can that be? I didn't get your name?"

"Oh, I'm sorry Mr. Beal. It's Blake, George Blake. Would you like to come down for an interview? I can tell you about the job and the requirements then."

"Yes, I think I would. Where are you?"

There was a pause. "I think it best, if we meet at the office where you will be working, that is, if you accept the job. Do you know where the Ashcroft building is?"

"Yes, I do," Norman said.

"I can meet you there at your convenience."

Norman looked at Linda who was holding her breath. "I suppose today is out of the question, after all it is Sunday?"

"No, in fact it might be best. You see, I must fill this position, before next Saturday. It's two o'clock, say in an hour, at the Ashcroft building?"

"Yes, I'll be there," Norman said.

Norman replaced the telephone receiver. Linda could not contain herself any longer. "Well?"

"I am to meet him downtown in an hour," he said.

Norman changed into his best suit and drove downtown. He was not sure about the job that no one else wanted. Norman reached the Ashcroft building at two-forty-five. Because it was Sunday, he managed to park in front of the seven-story building. As Norman got out of his car, he was met by a man about ten years younger than himself.

"Mr. Beal, I'm George Blake."

Norman took the offered hand.

"Shall we go in? Our office is on the sixth floor and that's where you will be working, if you take the job."

Norman nodded, but said nothing. As he followed the younger man into the building and then into a prewar elevator, he had a brief but fleeting feeling that he had seen him before. On the sixth floor they turned to the right and stopped before a frosted glass door. There was no name on the door, just the number 604. George unlocked the door and they stepped into a single room office. There was a desk with a telephone, a small table with an electric coffee pot, a tattered plastic plant, and on the wall next to the door was a time clock.

George grinned as if he were presenting the Taj Mahal. "Well, here is the office where you will be working."

"What, am I suppose to do here, George?"

"First, I should tell you the requirements. If you take the job, you must clock in when you arrive and clock out when you leave. By the way, do you want to come in the morning or the afternoon?"

"What would be the times?" Norman asked.

"You can come, eight to twelve or one to five, but it must be consistent."

"The mornings would be best, I think," he said

"One thing, I must make clear, you must clock four hours in this office without fail. If I call and that phone is not answered promptly, you will be fired."

Norman nodded. "I understand, but what is the work?"

"On Saturday, when you arrive and clock in at eight o'clock, you will find a cardboard box here. You will follow the instructions that will be in the box until twelve o'clock when you will close the office and leave."

Norman looked perplexed "Is that all?"

"We will pay you twenty-dollars an hour and if you clock a full four hours, not a minute less, you will get another twenty-dollar bonus."

"Sounds good," Norman said.

"One last thing, if you should ever clock in and there is no box. Do not clock out for four hours."

"But if there is no work?"

George frowned. "You must be here to answer the telephone, if it should ring. Don't worry you will be paid, even if all you do is stare at the walls for four hours. I told you it would be boring work. You indicated that you could accept boredom."

"Oh, the boredom part doesn't bother me," Norman said. "But how do I know that this business is legitimate?"

"Well, if you should find anything unlawful in the box, I suggest that you call the police. Otherwise, do as I have said and collect your pay."

"How do I get paid?"

"When you come in on your second Saturday and every Saturday after that until you quit, your pay will be in the center draw of the desk."

Norman smiled. "I'm your man then."

"I'm glad to hear it. Here are the keys. You won't see me again, but I might call anytime, to make sure you are here."

The week passed slowly for Norman Beal. He did his normal work for his father-in-law, but he could not help thinking of his new part-time job. What would be waiting for him on Saturday?

On Saturday morning, Norman rose at six o'clock. He showered, shaved and dressed before going downstairs and preparing his breakfast. He started a pot of coffee and as it brewed he collected the morning paper from the yard. At precisely, seven o'clock, Norman Beal left the house.

His wife Linda was still asleep in their upstairs bedroom.

Norman drove downtown and once more arrived at the Ashcroft Building. He parked his car at seven forty-five. At five minutes to eight, he unlocked the door to room 604. Everything was the same as he had first seen it. There was a cardboard box on the desk. Norman clocked in just as the time clock clicked over to eight o'clock.

Norman dubiously eyed the box. He took off his jacket and prepared the coffee pot. He knew that he was delaying the inevitable, but he was reluctant to open the box and face whatever was inside. What, if it were drugs that he was to bag or maybe it was pornography? Could he, a law-abiding citizen, force himself to do the work anyway? That was the question and he did not know that he could.

He poured himself a cup of the fresh brewed coffee, added Equal and powdered creamer and stirred it with a wooden coffee stirrer. *I must stop my ridiculous delays. George said that it would not be anything illegal. I must get over this paranoia and open the damn box.* Norman emptied his cup and set it on the coffee table. He then went to the desk and looked over the mystery box. It was a twelve-inch by twelve-inch by eight-inch cardboard box that was taped shut. He found a box cutter in the desk and slit the tape. Taking a deep breath Norman opened the box.

Inside were hundreds of coupons. Norman was flabbergasted. He read the instruction sheet aloud that was on top of the coupons.

"Please sort by type and amount. Use the rubber bands that you will find in the desk to bind them. Put the bound coupons back in box and leave it on the desk."

Despite his surprise at so mundane a task, he set to work. He soon found that many coupons were the same and could therefore be bundled quickly. Others were more difficult to sort.

Norman bundled, the last batch of coupons, and saw that it was five minutes to noon. He gathered the bound coupons and stacked them in the box. As the time clock clicked over to twelve o'clock, Norman clocked out.

On the drive home he could not believe that he had found such a simple part-time job and would get an extra one hundred dollars a week for it.

His wife Linda was in the kitchen preparing lunch when he arrived home.

As he ate the chicken salad sandwiches that she had made, Norman told her about the job. "I sorted coupons into little bundles."

"What does it matter if you get paid for it?"

"Don't get me wrong. It's alright. I'm just surprised, that's all."

Norman and Linda enjoyed their Sunday together before he once more became an accountant for his father-in-law on Monday.

Accounting wasn't really boring to Norman; he had always had a head for figures. The numbers told a story to him, just as words could be made to tell a story to a reader. Profit and loss was something that he could get his teeth into. Nothing bothered him more than numbers that did not add up correctly, however.

On Saturday, Norman once again drove into the city to his new part-time job. He could not help wondering if his pay from last Saturday would be there as promised, or had the entire episode been a dream? Maybe, he had blacked out and it had never happened. Who in their right mind would pay a hundred dollars to someone who bundled coupons for them? It was insane. But he had been brought up to believe that once he began a job, he must finish it.

Norman entered the office at ten minutes to eight o'clock. He at once saw the box on the desk. It looked the same as the first box. Was it possible that no one had collected the coupons? What if his pay was not there?

He avoided the box as he pulled open the center desk drawer. Lying there was a white envelope with his name on it. He picked it up and opened it. Inside was a crisp one hundred-dollar bill. He put the bill in his wallet, clocked in, made coffee, and then with coffee in hand, he was ready to face another mystery box.

Inside the box, he found hundreds of old faded black-and-white photographs. They were the kind that you find in thrift stores for ten cents each. None were newer than the fifties, judging by the automobiles and clothes. Norman read the instruction sheet.

Please sort by type. Use the rubber bands that you will find in the desk to bind them. Put the bound pictures back in box and leave it on the desk.

Norman frowned. What lunatic would pay to have someone do such trivial work? The man he had met, George Blake, had not appeared to be crazy. But then how would he know? Even if George might be crazy, he had paid for the coupons to be sorted. So Norman set to work sorting the photographs into groups. Some were on old postcards. He finished by eleven o'clock, but knew he could not clock out until noon.

As he drove home, Norman reviewed what he knew about the man he was working for. He realized that he knew nothing about George Blake. *If that is his name*. He did remember the uneasy feeling he had on first meeting the man. The feeling, that he had seen him before. But he could not put his finger on how or where.

Norman was a fan of Sherlock Holmes and had read all the stories countless times. As he pondered his problem, he remembered a story called the "Redheaded League." In that story a gang of crooks hired redheaded men to cover up their crooked scheme.

When he reached home, he declined the lunch that Linda had prepared for him and went to his home office. He knew that he was not doing anything illegal, but something was not right with the job either. If he were not involved in some crime, then the other reason someone would pay for him to be in that office during those four hours on Saturday was to keep him away from home. But that made no sense because since he had been working at home, he had spent every Saturday there, just as he did every other day. Suddenly, Norman knew. He felt sick to his stomach. Why? was the question he could not answer, but his gut told him his hunch was right.

The following Saturday, Norman left the house at seven o'clock, his wife Linda was still in bed. He drove to a nearby diner and had coffee as he planned his day. If he had guessed right, the action would start about eight o'clock.

At eight-fifteen, Norman drank the last of his coffee at the diner, paid his bill and left. Once in his car, he opened the glove compartment and removed a small black case and placed it on the seat beside him. He had a knot in his chest and hoped he was wrong, but knew he wasn't.

When he reached his house, he parked on the street. There was another car in his driveway beside his wife's. Norman wiped his brow. The street was deserted as he slid out of the car, easing the door shut, but stopped it before it closed to retrieve the black case. He let himself into the house and climbed the stairs, lured by the sounds coming from the bedroom. Norman saw what he had dreaded through the half-open door. George Blake and his wife Linda were both naked. He had caught them screwing in his bed.

Norman opened the black case and removed a thirty-eight revolver. He pushed open the door and stepped into the room. "Is this what you were paying me for?"

Blake rolled off Linda and both stared at the figure in the doorway.

"Norman, please I-" she said.

George held up his hand, "Put down the gun. We can talk this out-"

BANG. BANG.

The gun smoke burned his eyes and prevented him from seeing what he had done. As it cleared he saw the two dead bodies.

Norman walked out of the bedroom. He would need to report it to the police, but he had one phone call to make first. Downstairs he poured himself a drink. He could not understand why his wife would do such a thing. Any more than he could understand what he had just done. He downed the raw whiskey and relished the fire as it burned his insides. He poured himself another and then picked up the telephone. He dialed his father-in-law's number and sipped at his drink while listening to the ringing.

"Hello?"

"Is this Sam Simons?" Norman asked in a slurred voice.

"Yes, is that you, Norman? Have you been drinking?"

Norman laughed. "That is not the worst of my sins."

"Well then, what do you want? I am busy and don't have the time to chitchat."

Norman took a deep breath. "I caught Linda in bed with another man."

"What? Let me speak to her."

"I don't think they have phones in hell, Sam. That's where I sent her and her lover."

"You aren't making any sense, Norman."

"Let me say it so you will understand. I just shot the whore and her lover. The bitch is dead, just as I will be," he said.

Norman replaced the receiver before his father-in-law could respond. He downed the last of his drink and while laughing, he placed the gun to the side of his head.

BANG.

Darkness, absolute everlasting darkness, enveloped Norman Beal.

♦♦♦♦♦♦♦♦♦♦♦♦♦

Woodrow W. Walker was born in Columbus, Georgia in 1942 and was raised in a foster home. His foster mother became a widow when Woodrow was five.

He grew up doing the things that all boys do, both good and bad. When he lost his mother in 1966, he found himself on his own for the first time. In 1990 he went to Las Vegas, NV and became a convention security guard. It was there he met the woman who would become his wife.

In 2002 at the age of 60, nearing retirement, he turned to writing. He wrote his first book "Murder at Republic" because he had always loved the

B-westerns and movie serials and thought that a murder in a movie studio would be a good plot device. He followed up that book with another "Murder at Columbia." Both books are about private detective Buck Ames, a former movie stuntman, and are set in the 1940s.

Vampires have always intrigued Woodrow, and they had always been portrayed as totally evil or as romance figures. In search of a different kind of vampire, he wrote "Legacy of Adrian Blackthorn, Vampire".

Next Woodrow wrote a western "Wolf Johnson Mountainman."

His books can be purchased online or ordered in bookstores.

He has quite a number of short stories in the Amazon Shorts Program, too. You can buy them at Amazon and on wizardsofwords.com.

Now retired, Walker writes full time. He and his wife live in Tucson, AZ. Woodrow is a charter member of Wizards of Words.

http://woodrow-w-walker.tripod.com

TO SLEEP PERCHANCE TO DREAM

By E. Robert Orn

That damn idiot, Slick Starkweather thought. *That brainless, stubborn misbegotten son of a filthy whore. Everything would have been just hunky-dory, but that silly sonofabitch had to go and play at being the star of his own raw remake of "Reservoir Dogs."*

Starkweather hunched over the steering wheel, looking hard through the cracked windshield as he sped down the narrow street. Agonized moans rose up from behind him, echoing the wail of approaching sirens.

Blood and panic filled the backseat where his brother Jason lay dying. Tears streaked Jason's face as he beat at the air with bloody hands. In the rearview mirror, it looked like he was trying to push death away, but Starkweather could smell the ozone reek of it crowding into the car like an unwanted passenger.

They had walked into the Korean grocery easy enough. Jason had been popping his gum, sauntering like a teenager, as cool as silk in summer. The fat old man stood behind the counter, jabbering meaninglessly to some ugly crone buying rice and noodles and pulling singles out of her bag like they were delicate little hankies. He looked up at them as the bell jingled over the door. Besides Jason and Starkweather, they were the only people in the little family-owned establishment.

Jason walked down the candy aisle. He was picking up bags of cream-filled oatmeal cookies, *Little Debbie Zebra Cakes*, *Twinkies*. Junk food fuel. Cellophane wrappers crackled in his hand like charged electricity. The old woman turned to look at him and Starkweather saw her lip rise with a contemptuous sneer.

The owner just looked bored. Unconcerned. He bagged the hag's groceries while she continued to peel wrinkled ones out of her little black purse.

Jason ambled up next to her and dropped his armful of goodies onto the counter. An oatmeal pie slid to the floor and he accidentally stepped on it. “Hey, Benny-Hanna, how much is all of this?”

“I be wit you one moment,” the owner held up a chubby finger and scowled. “And you pay for one you step on.”

“I ain’t paying for nothin,’” Jason howled. He pulled the broom-handled Mauser from beneath his jacket and pointed it at the Korean’s face. “And you gonna be wit me now!” he screamed, doing a fair impression of the porker’s thick accent. “Gimme the money! Gimme the money!”

They had scoped the market out a couple of times. For a small convenience store, the place generated mad cheddar. It was located in a low-rent district, sort of a no man’s land for decent people, almost a demilitarized zone as far as the police were concerned. And the Starkweather boys were far from home. No one would know them here.

The old lady screamed and dropped her purse when she saw the Mauser. A bag of noodles followed her purse to the floor with a muffled whap. Jason slammed the butt of his gun against her head. “Shut-up!” She flopped against a rack of magazines, knocking it over.

“Empty the register! Don't make me ask you again. I'll blow your fat ass back across the 38th parallel.”

The Korean pulled rumpled bills out of the register and slammed them on the counter. “You take, then get out!”

“All of it! I want all of it!”

“That all, damn you! Now you go!”

“You don’t tell me what to do. I want the money that’s in the safe. Now!”

Jason was funning with him. They both knew there was no safe. Starkweather laughed. God, his brother was funny.

The Korean turned purple. “No safe, no safe. You have all. Just go now.”

Jason grabbed the cash and stuffed it into his pockets; less than two hundred in small bills. It wasn’t much, but it would be enough to keep them in booze and hookers for the long night ahead.

The woman was still screaming. She lay on the floor next to the overturned magazine rack and shrieked at the blood oozing down her forehead. Jason kicked her in the back. “I told you to shut-up!” She wailed louder and he kicked her again. “Shut-up, shut-up, shut-up!” She began crawling across the floor trying to get away from him, but he just kept kicking her.

“Damn, Slick,” Jason called back to his brother who was standing guard at the front door. “I thought soccer was a sport for losers. But this is fun!” He kept kicking her. Starkweather could do nothing but stand next to the door and giggle. His brother was a total riot.

That was when the Korean pulled the sawed-off from underneath the counter.

"You stop kicking now! I kill you."

Jason turned, his eyes huge, and raised the Mauser. Both guns went off at the same time. Rolls of toilet tissue and paper towels exploded over Jason's head. Strips of confetti rained through the store like a ticker tape parade. The shelf of cigarettes crashed behind the Korean. Jason was funny, but he couldn't hit water shooting out of a boat.

Starkweather screamed a warning, jumped away from the door with both hands on his .38. His first shot hit the Korean in the left shoulder, knocking him back against the broken shelf. Cartons of cigarettes hit the floor along with a display of colorful cigarette lighters. The Korean dropped his right hand and the shotgun went off again. The old lady had scrambled to her feet to make a run for it out the back door. She was hit in the back. She fell against Jason, knocking the gun from his hand. The Korean fired again. Dish washing liquid containers burst apart, filling the aisle with soapy bubbles.

Starkweather heard the door jangle behind him as someone entered. Two oriental kids, maybe seventeen years old, rushed in. One male, one female. The girl had cute pigtails that flapped behind her like black streamers. The boy wore a red head band and a street-gang expression. They both had guns.

Starkweather spun toward the street punk and shot him in the chest. Blood splattered against a cardboard cutout of a pretty model hawking beer as the kid dropped to his knees, firing with a vengeance. Bullets ripped past Starkweather's head. They punched through bags of flour, shattered jars of pickles, shredded boxes of dry cereal. A gumball machine fell over. Bright colored gumballs careened everywhere. It looked like a sledgehammer break in a game of nine-ball.

A bullet grazed Starkweather's thigh. He screamed and fired again. The kid dropped dead at his girlfriend's feet. She shrieked animated curses as she sighted down the bore of her weapon from a traditional shooter's stance.

Starkweather noted absently that she was a pretty little thing, with long legs, a short skirt, and a black tank top which read *Nobody Screws Karma* in garish purple letters. He aimed carefully and put two bullets in her chest. The glass door had swung closed behind her. The concussive force of his slugs knocked her back, and she smashed through it and fell into the sunlight. Broken shards skittered across the sidewalk, winked beneath the blood and her bouncing pigtails.

"I screw Karma every day, tramp," he screamed after her.

The Korean had regained his balance. Jason struggled beneath the body of the blubbering hag squirming on top of him. He pitched her into the aisle, reached for his gun, and slipped in a blue puddle of dishing washing liquid. The Korean shot him right in the gut. Jason squealed as his hand closed on the haft of his weapon. He raised it, finger tight on the trigger, and tore the top of the Korean's head off. The shotgun went off in his hands again as he fell, blowing a big hole through the cash register in front of him. Metal shrieked, loose change flew; shredded checks and food stamps filled the air. The crumpled register flipped off the counter and landed on Jason's head. Starkweather heard the vicious crunch from the other side of the store. Blood rolled down his brother's face as the thick man fell on top of a glass case full of lottery tickets. It shattered beneath him with a loud crash.

Starkweather ran through the hailstorm of rolling change and the tissues floating through the air on swirls of gun smoke. As he bent down to help his brother he could hear the rising wail of approaching sirens. *Damn!* The owner must have released some sort of silent alarm. No way the cops could be here this fast. Not to some corner-store-grocery-trap in a run-down neighborhood like this.

Damn it all to hell!

His brother moaned. He had tattered pieces of toilette paper caught in his hair, plastered to his red spattered face. Blood drooled over his chin, pooled beneath his pants. Starkweather helped him up and the poor kid screamed.

"Easy does it, bro," Starkweather whispered. "Got to get you out of here. Work with me, now. Cops are on the way."

"That bastard!" Jason wailed through the blood and the tears. "Damn bastard shot me. What kind of bullshit is that, man?"

"Well, bro, we were trying to rob his store," Starkweather answered emotionlessly.

He dragged his limping brother down the aisle. Soap bubbles floated in the air in front of him, gum balls rolled beneath his feet. A child's wonderland of candy-coated dreams. Vinegar and smoke filled his nose. Blood shimmered on broken glass beneath their feet as they staggered outside.

An old woman screamed vile curses from the Laundromat across the street. Evil-looking street kids watched curiously from behind a row of sun-mottled cars. The heat beat down on Starkweather's neck, and a mongrel dog barked angrily from behind a rusty fence half a block away.

The first cop car on the scene squealed to a halt in the middle of the intersection. Jason gripped the Mauser tightly and fired with a low moan. The windshield exploded. Bloody hands flopped against the dashboard as a blue shadow slumped against the steering wheel.

The slaughtered pig's partner, a woman with short red hair beneath her crisp, navy blue uniform cap, jumped from the passenger seat with her county issued .40 caliber Glock 22 gripped with both hands. She crouched behind the open door of the cruiser and fired. Bullets whined off brickwork behind them. The large window came down, crashing at their feet, nearly knocking them off balance. Starkweather felt the bite of glass on the back of his legs.

He was holding his brother in front of him, unintentionally using him as a shield. The cop hit Jason in the leg, then again in the shoulder. Starkweather felt Jason take the hits, feeling the concussive force of the bullets punching into his brother's flesh. The impact tremors knocked them both back a step. Jason screamed and dropped his weapon.

Cursing a Viking blue streak of warrior rage, Starkweather emptied the .38 at the red-haired Valkyrie blocking his way to freedom. Glass broke. Metal screamed. A bullet shattered the center of her pretty face and teeth hit the street like hailstones as she fell nervelessly against the car and flopped against the hot pavement.

The blare of sirens sounded over the screams of the old woman in front of the Laundromat, but the other cars were still a way off.

"Shut up!" He dropped the .38 in the street. It was empty and cold. Untraceable. Just like the .9mm he pulled from a holster sown into the inside of his jeans vest. He shot the old woman and her screams ended on a choking gurgle. Her fat body went down, knocking over a beat up trash can. She lay quiet and still beneath a shroud of stinking garbage. "That's what you get! Next time I say shut up, you shut-up!"

Starkweather dragged his wailing brother toward their yellow Dodge Charger. Someone shot at them. Not the cops. A bullet tore into the street near his brother's feet. Then another. Starkweather looked around. There was a kid in a black leather jacket on the fire exit of an old building. He had a gun in each hand. He didn't know how to use either of them. The kid fired another volley. Starkweather snarled animal hatred and fired back. The kid was thrown against the chipped brick, bounced off the wall and sailed over the railing on a red contrail of blood. He dropped three stories and bounced on the hard sidewalk.

Starkweather threw open the back door and pushed his brother inside. He jumped into the front of the car and jammed the keys into the ignition. The engine rumbled to mad life, roaring like a wild behemoth. Starkweather popped the car in gear and squealed through the intersection. He had to swerve to avoid the police cruiser decorated with the bodies of two dead cops, and tore away from the approaching sirens. A young punk swung past him on a souped up Kawasaki Ninja 750cc. On impulse Starkweather turned the wheel and forced the motorcycle off the road. The kid plowed into a parked car and launched himself, shiny helmet over scuffed boots, through the window of a noodle shop that reeked of fried pork and garlic.

People screamed at him from the sidewalk. One man ran out of the restaurant and threw his food at the car. Thick soup and fried chicken wings slapped against the glass. A mad chorus of epithets followed him down the street as he roared away on a smoking thunderbolt. Blood bubbled in his wake.

His brother was screaming in the back seat. In the rearview mirror, Starkweather could still see bloody hands flailing at the air. He wanted to reach back and hold him, to comfort him, but he needed both hands on the steering wheel. He didn't know what he was going to do with him. He thought about pulling over somewhere and just pushing him out of the car. They would find him and get him to a hospital. But for what? They'd save his life so he could spend the rest of it in prison.

Jason wouldn't want that.

Starkweather wondered if it wouldn't be better if he just let his little brother die.

His thoughts were interrupted when he pulled up behind a large gray van. It had the flashers on. It was double-parked. A small, elderly man in a grocer's smock was unloading produce into a corner supermarket. Starkweather slammed on his brakes, unable to get around the van because of oncoming traffic.

Sirens wailed behind him and Starkweather glanced into his rearview mirror. Flashing lights strobed behind him. He had to move.

Starkweather jammed his foot on the accelerator and pulled into oncoming traffic. Horns blared and tires screeched as cars came to sudden, shuddering stops. He sped across the lane onto the far sidewalk. He hit a newspaper vending machine as pedestrians scrambled to get out of his way. Crates of tomatoes and cabbages crashed over the top of his vehicle as he smashed through a sidewalk vegetable stand.

He careened over the sidewalk and into another intersection. More cars slammed on their brakes as he pulled out in front of them. He caused half a dozen fender-benders as he plowed back onto the street. Newspapers and tomatoes flew from the top of his car, wet, shiny cabbages rolled beneath his squealing tires.

He swerved to avoid a yellow taxi-cab. The block-faced, bald-headed driver waved a sweaty fist and shouted at him in gutter Cyrillic as he streaked down the street, his Dodge dodging through the crawling traffic. He took a left out of Little Korea; the pagodas of Chinatown rose up in front of him like alien flowers.

He took the next left on two wheels, his souped-up engine screaming an ozone banshee cry of heavy metal octane fury. Faces passed by in a blur; his windows framed a surreal painting of constant confusion and panic. People were screaming at him as he thundered past. He wondered if they could see the smear of blood on the back of his car; if they could see his brother dying inside, wrapped in a cocoon of twisted teenaged-angst and blood.

His heart pounded a Keith Moon solo in his chest, and adrenaline thrummed like a Steve Vie riff through his veins. He had never felt so alive. He checked the rearview again. There was one police car behind him. It was losing ground.

"Hang on, bro," he screamed. "We're going to make it. We're going to make it, dawg, and then I'll get you some help. You'll be all right. You'll see."

He veered hard into another turn, weaved through the traffic stopped at a red light, and spun his squealing tires between two cars skidding to avoid him in the middle of the intersection. He pulled back into the oncoming lane. A woman in a red Toyota was driving her kids home from school. He grinned defiantly, honking his horn, roaring toward her on a wave of fire and smoke.

She turned her car into the sidewalk and slammed into the middle of an outdoor café. Wooden chairs and tables went flying. A table umbrella crashed through a plate glass window with a sound like the devil's choir striking up the band.

He roared past the tumult, a yellow, mechanized demon of wind and fury, and entered another intersection. A cop on a motorcycle screamed into his path. Starkweather hit the Harley doing an even seventy. Pieces of the hot bike flew in every direction as the rider flailed through the air. A teenaged girl behind the wheel of a green Camry swerved to avoid him, but his helmeted head cracked hard against the corner of her car as he fell, destroying her headlights and shattering his neck.

The Charger rattled over what was left of the bike. Sparks danced in gouts of gray smoke as something popped loose from the bottom of the car and sailed across the street in a sheath of black oil.

He took a sharp right, then the next left, dragging part of the motorcycle beneath his car as he went. A fender had crumpled into the front right tire, making the steering sluggish. He was losing speed as well as control.

Another Electra Glide in blue appeared on his right. He saw the flashing red lights of an approaching siren two blocks away. More lights in his rearview mirror.

Damn, damn, damn! The pigs were everywhere!

He passed a small park on his left. Civilians were walking their dogs. Pushing their babies. Leading their quiet, hopeless little lives. Starkweather hated them without knowing why. He careened around the park, narrowly missing a black girl on a pink bicycle. He was tempted to back up and try again, but the police were closing in. He saw more flashing red lights. A shot rang out and a hole appeared in his cracked windshield. Another shot. Pain, an explosive red bomb in his left shoulder set off a spinning Catherine Wheel in his head.

He skewed onto the sidewalk, struggling with the steering. He drove past a jewelry store and a donut shop, knocking a mailbox off the curb and into the back of a parked car. There were flashing red and blue lights all around him. He took the next right on smoking tires. Two police cars pulled together half a block ahead creating an effective roadblock. Enraged civil-servant wage slaves armed with guns and self-righteous bravado leapt behind the barrier. Grim faces and silent bores stared unblinkingly in the bright sunlight.

He tried to turn away from them when the police sharpshooters opened up on him. The windshield exploded in a bright raindrop configuration of shiny pieces of flying glass. . .

There was a bright flash of light. . .

Starkweather saw himself as a mangy cattle rustler gunning down an unarmed man in the middle of a dusty street …

… he had the impression of a dozen hornets flying at him at the speed of light …

... he was suddenly a painted cannibal ripping savagely at a handful of raw flesh over a pile of human bones …

Bullets whacked into his body. Blood spurted. Impact tremors shook the core of his soul, and he felt something give, a broken part of him, deep in the recesses of his flesh.

The smoking car swerved, a wounded predator searching for escape, and lurched across the street on steaming tires. Starkweather saw the corner bank in front of him. A two story plain brick structure with large, sparkling windows. It rose in front of him like a tomb. A woman pushing a pink baby carriage stood frozen on the sidewalk. The yellow Dodge scraped past a parked car. Starkweather hit the curb. The car bounced high in the air, like it was launched from a short ramp, and broke a single parking meter. The metal pole flipped toward the woman with a loud whooshing sound …

Starkweather saw himself as a laughing Roman soldier butchering Christians with a bloody short sword …

… and slammed into the center of her bright dress, knocking her across the sidewalk and into the wall like a broken toy. The car plowed into the baby carriage …

Starkweather saw himself standing before a fire dressed in a black cowl as he gleefully mutilated a young girl accused of being a witch …

… sending it over the top of the Dodge with a vicious crack. Starkweather saw the small baby, a helpless angel caught in a firestorm, smack against what was left of the windshield, and then it was gone.

The car was still in the air. Flying. The wall of the bank loomed in front of him, filling his vision. In crazy slow-motion, like some cool Hollywood special effect, he could see people in the bank scurrying to get out of his way through the large window. They looked like peasants running from the torches of the conquering hordes.

The two front tires spun through space, the engine roared on wings of air and shooting sparks. The car headed for the bank, a two-ton missile of twisted metal and human desperation, steel and plastic and the raw bitter stuff of psychotic rage.

Starkweather heard a terrific crash, like the sound the end of the world might make, and the wall of the bank folded around him as the car rammed through it. He felt himself lifted from the seat. Ribs splintered, his chest collapsed. The steering broke away.

For a brief second he was a desperate country boy shooting it out in the dark woods with prohibition revenuers …

A tower of flame shot out of the front end of the car. Flying bricks and broken glass swirled everywhere. Starkweather hit the windshield with his head, knocking it out, and flew into the heart of that maelstrom.

Lightning flashed. A red pulse of pain and red tinted light. Starkweather blinked.

… he was a swarthy buccaneer on the deck of a reeling ship, chopping the hands off a screaming cabin boy caught filching his rum …

The mangled Dodge came down on its side, halfway through the wall, knocking a wooden counter full of white deposit slips and pink withdrawal slips across the bank lobby.

… he was a battle scarred cavalryman disemboweling an Indian brave with a notched saber …

Blood filled his vision as he sailed across the room, a mote in the dark fury of an erupting volcano.

In the new thunderclap of raw pain Starkweather saw a drunken gangster with a lockjaw grin strangle a delicate flapper with her own silk scarf. He could not understand the visions quick-flashing through his head.

Nature's last joke on him. He was about to die, and the wrong lives were flashing before his eyes.

Starkweather hit the marble tiled floor in a wet sprawl and rolled against the far wall, forty feet from his smoking car. He lay there twitching. Blood filled his mouth. Blood filled his eyes. Far, far away, he could still hear people screaming.

He stared up at the ceiling, where dust and smoke cavorted with crackling red flames, and stared, and stared …

… he was dreaming. In his dreams the smoke from his burning car transformed into broken clouds drifting lazily over a quiet cemetery huddled beneath the cold stars. The clouds flowed into and away from one another, coming together, breaking apart, slowly forming and reforming phantom shapes that boiled above him. At first it appeared that long, white-cowled figures seemed to ponder his unseemly predicament. The clouds swirled some more, and became bleached, toothless skulls that mocked his twisted body with silent screams. Then these, too, faded as the clouds merged into the vision of a milky angel on the back of a flying horse. The angel's delicate lips formed his name, and he could hear …

… his mother sobbed. She sat in a small chair outside the emergency room crying into an old shawl as doctors and nurses operated frantically on his brother, attempting to save him for a life in prison. She was shaking her head. "Why, why, why," she sobbed. "I told you to stay away from him, that he was no good, that he would only get you into trouble. Why didn't you listen to me? Why didn't you listen to …

… the steady pounding of Starkweather's heart was slowing down, like a high performance race car running out of gas. He could feel his body growing cold, yearning once more for the feel of the earth from which it had been formed. Darkness, soft and warm, tugged at the root of his soul still entwined with a protoplasmic umbilical tentacle around the base of his spine. Slowly, implacably, he could feel it letting go, drifting like a haunted spirit swimming …

… in the darkness were the shapes of his past. He could see them, as insubstantial as dreams, cold and deathless phantasms plodding through the dizzy mists of time. Golden spires pierced the clouds, rich castles in the sky, like Eden and Elysium beckoning them onward with the promise of heaven. The dark shapes strained to reach the clouds, shrieking in silent suffering like Dante's demons as they fell short time after time …

… to go, he thought. He could feel shapes moving about him, his old enemies closing in. The bald Korean store owner was there, looking down at him, his face a gruesome ruin of muscle and tissue. The young Korean girl was there too, her jet black hair swirling above her like the wings of a raven. Ana Ruben was there as well, the girl who had overdosed in her apartment the day he had raped her. She was ghostly pale. The rubber hose was still tied around her arm, distending the veins like thick worms in her flesh. Paco Jurado was there, the wild Mexican wetback he had handcuffed to a car before he drove it into a black lake, as was the dead baby who had fallen out of the stroller. The baby looked down at him with an expression of pity. She looked like an angel …

… on horseback rode down on wings of mist, hovered over him. Her lips formed his name again, and this time, he could hear her talking to him. She had a voice like liquid gold spilling into a magical grotto, a pied piper of the dead singing to him, a naked Godiva of silk and foam beckoning him out of this cold world of savage cruelty and violent death. He knew he loved her. He would have followed her anywhere …

… he did.

A pressure grew around him. He sensed a warmth and brightness full of the ephemeral stuff of clouds and dreams. He could feel his soul being pushed out of the darkness and into the warmth of a glowing light. It was a little like being born, he imagined.

On the marble floor, Starkweather's eyes slowly glazed over, unblinking, unseeing, as he lay on his back, his warm blood cooling, his moist flesh drying, his hot body growing stiff and cold. He stared up at the ceiling, at a heaven he could not see, and stared …

… and stared … and stared …

The ground beneath his blood-spattered boots was spongy soft, like star-flecked foam, and his footsteps made a silky murmur as he walked. The naked Godiva was there with him. She floated beside him with enigmatic grace. Starkweather could feel the faintest tug of gravity exerting itself upon his limbs, but the woman seemed to float beside him, shifting fluidly in a way no human could. The Pegasus pranced behind her, a silent dervish of vapor and fancy, and then with a whispery tread of smoky hooves it sailed into the air, as light as a feather in the wind, and was gone in a blink.

He knew that he was dead; he didn't know why, but he felt certain he was no longer dreaming. He had never believed in heaven or hell, except for the woman-given heaven of sexual release or the man-made hell of violence and anger. He had always thought that once you died, that was the end of the story. There were too many religious wars. If there really was a God, why were so many people killing each other in His name? If there really was a God, why were there so many Godless people like him running around in the world? There were too many different religions. They couldn't all be right. Starkweather figured they were all wrong.

He had always thought that death was an interminable nothing. Existence was finite, like a spark in the cosmos.

He looked around. Horses of mist floated over golden spires of sparkling castles that rose through dreamy clouds. Like Horatio, there seemed to be more to heaven and hell than he had ever dreamt of in his twisted philosophy.

"Mr. Starkweather, you have made quite a trip."

He wasn't sure if her lips had moved, but he heard her voice deep in the center of his heart.

She had hair as red as passion, and eyes as bright as hope. He was in the presence of beauty, and although he recognized it, it was still as alien to him as the existence of life on other worlds.

"You're telling me," he blinked at the magic around him. "That was some car chase."

The clouds parted beneath his feet to reveal bright rolling pastures. The thick sward was spongy soft, as green and bright as sparkling emeralds in the golden glow of the sun. Groves of susurrant trees stretched around them. Exotic blossoms dotted the landscape and the sky was filled with gaily plumaged birds. The pure air stirred softly, caressing the tiny hairs on his skin like a loving mother's gentle touch. He could smell peace in heaven's flowing breezes.

If this is heaven, then what am I *doing here?*

"I didn't just mean that," she said. This time he thought he saw her lips move, but he couldn't be sure. She was no longer made of clouds, but appeared to be formed of flesh. She was so beautiful. Glowing and ethereal. Her skin was unblemished, bronzed by the sun, shiny and radiant. She had donned a rich full gown which flowed around her, as translucent as a mystic's eyes. The diaphanous material seemed as fragile as butterfly wings. It was gilt with gold and was as green as the sparkling sward that stretched before them.

"I meant all of it cumulatively," she continued. "Your whole life. Your past lives. I was remarking upon all of your reckless incarnations and impetuous embodiments, all of your madcap substantiations and your unscrupulous corporealities. Mr. Starkweather, I was referring to all of the virulent and ungovernable avatars that have been you through the ages, from now back to the very dawn of life, and even before then, back through the dark realm of possibility."

"I'm sorry?" He didn't understand.

"Yes, Mr. Starkweather," she nodded and blinked her eyes, "you should be."

He could see the ocean in her eyes, as deep and unfathomable as time itself. "My brother," he swallowed. He could taste magic on the back of his throat. The glory of heaven, like slanting sunbeams, washed deep into him, filling him with raw wonder. "What happened to him? Where is he?"

"He didn't make the trip, Mr. Starkweather."

"What do you mean? Why isn't he here?" *Hell, hell, his brother went to hell!* "He should be here!" He reached out and grabbed her then. His fingers closed on the folds of her robe, and her skin warmed the dark cuts on his hands. She felt like soothing music.

She turned and looked at him. She didn't scowl, she didn't glare; her expression didn't seem to change at all. She remained bright and angelic, but something in him turned. He released her and stepped away, more afraid of her than he had been of anything before in his life.

"I'm sorry, I—." He looked down at his hands as if they had betrayed him.

"Your brother is not in hell, Mr. Starkweather," she smiled. She was more gorgeous than a swimsuit model. But looking at her, he couldn't think of sex. All he could think of was love. Love in its purest form. Like the love of a sweet mother for her beautifully perfect child. "He's still alive. He's in a hospital. A woman of a gentle spirit is praying for him. She has the heart of an angel."

He knew she was talking about their mother.

"Is he going to be … okay?"

"Eventually," she replied evenly. "His soul is coming along. But it may take a few more … incarnations."

He still didn't understand what she was talking about.

"Besides, Mr. Starkweather …"

"Please, call me Slick."

"Besides, Mr. Starkweather," her lips curled enigmatically, indicating that she wasn't going to refer to him as anything but Mr. Starkweather, "there is no hell. Souls who have not evolved to a high enough level of purity or consciousness are simply sent back."

He looked at her curiously. Her noble, feminine visage embodied the wisdom of the ages. Her lustrous mane of red hair looked as soft as a warm thought.

"You mean, like starting over?"

"Yes."

"Like reincarnation?"

"Yes."

He had seen the glory of heaven, the path to truth, the ray of enlightenment. For the first time in his life he could see happiness. He could taste contentment. The air brushed against his skin. It felt like joy. Starkweather did not understand the concept of synesthesia, but he knew intuitively that his primary senses were sharing abilities. In heaven it was possible to hear colors, to see the aroma of fresh orchids, to taste emotions. He was absorbing sensory input in new and invigorating ways. It was all very weird and wonderful.

"Some people look at life as a gift from God, Mr. Starkweather. A miracle."

He nodded, his brow furrowed in thought.

"Life is not a gift. It is a test. A series of tests, really. In order to progress, to evolve, you have to pass a final exam. You have to overcome specific challenges laid out before you begin each new incarnation."

She bent easily, like a flow of water changing direction, and casually brushed her fingertips across the petals of tiny purple flowers. They turned toward her as if she were the light of the sun. Rosy pink buds opened and spread. He could taste them growing beneath her silky touch.

"The world is very old. You measure significant events in your life in hours. Maybe days. You think of your life in terms of decades, your lineage in terms of centuries, and perhaps, if you ever bothered to think of it at all, the whole of recorded history in terms of millennia. But you, too, are old. Older than you can contemplate. Almost as old as the earth itself."

Starkweather had never bothered to think of it. He didn't really care to now, either.

"Eukaryotes were the first cells with nuclei to flourish out of the milky swirl of protoplasm," she told him. "The earth was so young then." She sighed wistfully, and zephyrs of breath danced across the treetops.

Starkweather imagined himself as a eukaryote floating in a great black vastness, hunting the cells around him like a predator. He could feel himself absorbing other cells. Breaking them down. Ingesting them. Feeding on them like a vampire.

Maybe he was still dreaming.

"Amebas evolved," she continued, "ingesting nutrients through fusion. Nature's first hunters. Cellular organization took eons, but then came colonial protozoa. Cells learned to split, to reproduce, by binary fission. Now cells could work together, sometimes symbiotically, toward a common goal. Even still, there were maverick cells, working against the host, sowing discord. Reveling in chaos. There was algae, paramecia, bacteria. Today, antibiotics have been produced from molds and soil bacteria. But some forms are harmful. Even as an evolved thallophyte you were always pathogenic. We thought it was just a phase you were going through. That you would outgrow it." She spoke like a parent to a petulant child.

"The first worms evolved during the Precambrian period. After that came the invertebrates, plankton, trilobites. During the Ordovician period the first fish learned to swim next to the first vertebrates. And then came the Silurian period. Vascular plants were learning how to colonize the land."

He listened to her. He could feel himself writhing like a worm, feeding off the decaying matter of dead things, while all around him other creatures struggled to learn and grow. Where they found joy in exploration, mutation, and evolution, he found glorification in the corruption of life.

More dreams, he thought. Heaven was a theater of mad dreams.

"Some fish formed legs, and at some point during the Devonian period, the first amphibians crawled out of the sea and walked on dry land. There were reptiles, then mammals, then dinosaurs."

He remembered then, stalking through the steamy jungles, tearing savagely at small warm-blooded things with sharp teeth. How much better it was to devour hot, moist flesh than it was to feed off cold, decaying matter. No longer a worm now, he let the worms feed off his mangled leavings.

"Primates formed, and modern man's oldest qualified prehensile ancestor took to the trees to escape the jaws of hungry beasts that still haunted the primeval forests."

He saw an image of himself squatting amidst the thick fronds of a huge tree. He pushed a small monkey thing off the swaying branch and watched gleefully as it plummeted squealing to the ground. Broken and helpless, it lay there crying as a tiger the size of a behemoth mauled it like a cat with a mouse before biting its head off. The Starkweather-tarsier munched on juicy grubs while he watched the saber-tooth devour his dead comate.

"The tarsier was the precursor to the hominoid. During the Miocene period, old world primates known as Limnopithecus and Dryopithecus set course on a new wave of evolutionary growth. From Proconsul to Australopithecus, to Pithecanthropus to the Swanscombe Man to the Neanderthal, hominoids continued to evolve. They developed through the pre-glacial period of the Cro-Magnon into the Pleistocene age of the erect Sinanthropus. Over time they learned to use tools. They developed language and art, created a complex social organization based on a set of widely recognized moral and ethical precepts. They learned to view the world through various philosophical and religious perspectives."

Starkweather listened to her and remembered himself in various forms. In one vision he cracked open an anthropoid's skull with a stone cudgel, in another he was lumbering through a tropical landscape after some nubile female ape he would later rape and strangle just for the animal thrill of it.

He came to realize that these weren't just dreams. He was remembering past lives that stretched back to the very dawn of time.

"But there were still those among them who clung to the old ways, who could not or would not rise above the base instincts of the simplest creature or the most savage hunter. You are such a person, Mr. Starkweather. Putting your own needs above the needs of all others. You do not care about anyone but yourself. As far as morals are concerned, you are no higher on the scale of evolution than the first oceanic Trilobites. Violence and anger regenerates in you. You are unable to move past the chaos that was the nucleus of all creation. You seem comprised almost solely of turbulence cells. Have you ever been in love, Mr. Starkweather? Have you ever felt remorse?"

"Yes," he answered. "I feel both of those things right now. Right here."

"No, Mr. Starkweather. Those are not your feelings. They are mine. I am projecting them to you. As I have done countless times before. I have brought you here at the conclusion of many lives, and I have shown you the glory of heaven, and each time you have sworn to change, and each time you have failed to do so. You have come close a couple of times, but you always revert. To bloodshed. To violence. You give in to anger, and bring hell to earth. I have to send you back. You have to start over again."

Now that he had seen heaven, he knew he did not want to leave.

"Just give me one more chance. That's all I want. Just one more chance. I know I have made a mess of things, but don't make me start over again. As a baby. Listen, you're an angel right, of course you are, you can just wave your hand or something such and put me back in my old body, right? Make it so I survive that crash. I go back to earth as my old self, act like a good boy, and help you get your wings. That's got to be easier than sending me back as a new baby. What can I do as a baby? Let me go back as my old self. Right as many of the wrongs as I can. I'll do it. I swear I can do it. Just don't make me go back as a baby. I can't do that again."

"Mr. Starkweather, you don't understand."

"Then please explain it to me," he said, hoping somehow to get out of this with a fresh start on his old life.

"Your social pathology is partly our fault. So we are going to try to rebuild you from scratch. Cell by pulsing cell. We are going to take you *all* the way back. To begin life anew from the very beginning."

Starkweather screamed.

He felt himself being flung backward, through the black swirling mists of time. Horrific vistas swept past in a dizzy rush. Great wars. Massive floods. Black eruptions of organic matter spewing from the protoplasmic pool that spawned all life.

He closed his eyes.

It would take 400 million years and over 973 trillion incarnations for him to evolve eyes so that he could open them again.

Nobody screws Karma.

♦♦♦♦♦♦♦♦♦♦♦♦

E. Robert Orn is the author of "Dancing With Ghosts," a terrifying morality tale of blood-soaked violence and redline passion, but maintains that he is still a nice person.

He was born in Christchurch, New Zealand, and was raised in Northern Va., not far from the looming peaks of the Shenandoah Mountains where the majority of the action in his first novel takes place.

"I love writing," he claims ruefully, "but it does not love me back. When I first started, I collected so many rejection slips I could have completely wallpapered my dining room with them. And I might have, except the pattern didn't really go with the light blue loop pile tufted carpet or the pleated drapes. After I self-published my first book, the bad reviews started to roll in. I was tempted to use those to redo the tiles on my kitchen floor, but again, there was nothing there that did not adversely clash with the rich wood-toned cabinets, the finely beveled granite countertop, or the tres cool appliances by Bosch and Dacor. So I put the rejection letters and the bad reviews in a drawer, and tried to move on. Whenever I start to feel good about myself, I take them out and go over them one by one. Like running dull knives over brittle bone. It's sort of like sentencing yourself to the eighth Bolgia of Hell, but it helps keep me centered."

When not circumnavigating the eighth Bolgia of Hell, E. R. O. likes to test the limits of his corporeal soul; he is a skydiver, a scuba diver, a spelunker, a skier, a motorcyclist, and he likes to make balloon animals. He juggles knives, knows how to make paper roses, and once smoked an entire pack of cigarettes while watching an N.F.L. playoff game. He has breathed the air of Death Valley, and has laid a pristine bottle of quality American whisky on the grave of Edgar Allen Poe. He has dated women far smarter than he is, and is not afraid to admit it. He has been a wedding coordinator, a stand-up comedian, a motorcycle courier, a banquet manager, and a bottle-flipping, joke-spitting bartender from this side of Nirvana.

What can you learn from a guy like this?

Maybe nothing.

But he rarely, if ever, suffers from 'writer's block.'

He currently lives in Kissimmee, Florida, where he is working on his next book, a case of Scotch, and a quality tan.

www.myspace.com/67471289

PASSAGEWAY TO HELL

By Barbara Watkins

I'm writing this to you my son, in hopes that you will never have to read it, but if you are, that means some time has passed and you must wonder why I've abandoned you. And although what I'm telling you will sound surreal, seek and you shall find the answers. For you to understand I need to explain how it all began.

My parents, your grandparents, James and Ester Whitmore were killed in a terrible accident when I was just an infant. With no close relatives to speak of, I was tossed around from one foster home to another.

My earliest memory was when I was about six years old. My foster mother punished me for tracking mud on her precious floor. There was a small basement that they used for storing old furniture, basically a junk room. She dragged me kicking and screaming towards the basement door, for I wasn't about to go without a fight. She opened the door and pushed me in, closing and locking the door behind me. I remember screaming and scratching at the door until my fingers bled. It was cold and dark and I remember thinking if I ever got out of there, I'd run as far away as I could. Well, I did get out and I tried to run away many times, but they would always find me and bring me back.

From the age of six to nine I learned to endure many trips to that dark cold basement. But one cold winter night, I sneaked into the kitchen and took matches from a drawer. I went into my foster parents' bedroom and set their mattress ablaze. You see, they slept quite soundly. The bottles of liquor they consumed every night saw to that.

There wasn't a question as to what happened. They were both smokers and had passed out while smoking in bed. I would like to tell you that I felt remorse, regret, or something, but I didn't.

Once again I was placed in foster care and the new couple was nothing like the others. Mr. and Mrs. Hawthorn, or mother and father as I would come to know them, were quite loving and caring towards me like true parents could be. They were older than the others and had tried for many years to have their own child, but with no success. Mother had lovely long dark hair and eyes as blue as the ocean, her porcelain skin reminded me of a delicate china doll. When she spoke it was almost in a whisper. Father was tall and lean and wore a handle bar mustache. He had a gentle presence about him, but when he spoke in his baritone voice people seemed to hang on every word.

My new parents made me feel wanted from the moment I arrived. They had one of the most beautiful homes I'd ever seen. It was a two-story Victorian home with a beautiful garden filled with roses and a play area they had provided just for me. The time I spent with them was invaluable. They taught me how to love again. Father was an engineer for the railroad so we would travel quite often. Mother would always say that riding a train was a good learning experience, a way to see beautiful countryside and meet interesting people.

On one of our trips we had to stay over a couple of days in a small town due to a mix up in our train schedule. It was a dark little town known as Hellion. I say dark because there were very few houses and all were exactly alike. Each painted black with dark heavy drapes over the windows. The women all dressed in long dark flowing—what appeared to be—robes. The men wore dark suits as well. I remember father telling mother if he had known beforehand what a strange place it was, he would have made other arrangements.

The next morning after we arrived I was awakened by a loud, almost deafening thunder. The clouds were ebony as a raven in the night. Father had gone to the train station to straighten out the schedule while Mother packed our belongings.

I stood at the window and watched the rain beat down on the windowsill outside. I began to have an uneasy feeling. I began to feel sad, then almost ill. My hands began to sweat and it felt like the floor was rolling beneath my feet. I remember wanting to call out for Mother, but the words wouldn't come.

I awoke some time later to find myself in an unfamiliar room, alone. The room was dark, no pictures on the walls, no fixtures of any kind, just the bed and me. Frightened and confused I yelled out for mother and father, but no answer would come. I tried to get up but it felt as if my legs were paralyzed. I kept telling myself, this has to be a nightmare … wake up …wake up!

I must have gone to sleep again, I'm not sure exactly how long. The door opened and what appeared to be an elderly woman in a long black dress that dragged the floor came walking towards my bed. I began to cry and plead with her to get my father and mother.

She wiped my tears away and said, "There my child you just lay back and try to rest. You have been through such an ordeal, but you are safe with us. We will take good care of you."

I knew something was terribly wrong; father and mother would never have left me alone. Still weak, but determined not to stay there another minute, I managed to get up. I pushed the woman aside and ran out of the room, only to be stopped by another dark figure - a man that stood waiting in the hallway. Tall and appearing to have a muscular build, he too was dressed in black.

He held on to me and began to speak in a firm but calm manner, "Your father and mother are gone. They boarded the train the day of the terrible storm. We found you alone, hysterical, and running a fever in the boarding house. So we took you in and gave you medicine for the fever to help you rest. That was a week ago."

"You're lying. Mother and father would never leave me. Why are you telling me such lies?"

"It's the truth my little one, but never fear, we won't let anything bad happen to you. You're safe here"

"I want to go home to my father and mother," I screamed.

"We are your parents now, so you may as well accept it. Your time here can be a happy one if you so choose, or it can be a very long and torturous one, it's your choice."

Overcome with fear, I could say nothing. I knew I had to escape this nightmare, but didn't know how. Why was this happening to me? Where were my parents? Would I ever wake up from this nightmare?

In disbelief I turned and walked back into the cold dark room. I pulled the blanket over my head and began to sob. I began to say a prayer my mother had taught me shortly after I'd arrived in their loving home. "Oh Heavenly One, help me to greet each day with love and kindness. Help me to put others' needs before my own. Give my soul strength to turn away from evil. Show me the right path to take when I'm lost, and help me to forgive my own sins as well as those of others."

The next morning I awoke to find a tray with a full-size breakfast sitting at the side of my bed, and although I was afraid to eat it, I was starving. I hadn't eaten in a week, so I began to feed my starving body. I'd finished the last bite when the old woman came in.

"I've brought you clean linens, a wash bowl, and some fresh clothing for you to wear." She then turned and walked away. At the foot of the bed lay a long black dress with matching laced up boots.

As I held it up I could see the dress was just my size. I put it on and felt as though I should be going to a wake. If I could just get out of the house I would run like hell and never look back.

I knew what I had to do. I would gain their trust so they would feel safe in leaving me alone. Then I would have a chance to get away. I got up enough courage to open the door and venture out. There sitting at a hand carved, large, wooden table that looked centuries-old was the old woman, the tall muscular man, and a young man closer to my age. He too was dressed in black, but I couldn't help notice that he wore a shiny silver chain with some sort of trinket hanging from it. When he looked up at me I got the strange feeling that I knew him, but that was impossible.

He was the first to speak. The sound of his voice put me at ease.

"Please, sit down. It pleases us to see you are feeling better. If you feel well enough, I would be delighted to show you around our little town."

We walked outside and I became aware of how everything was strangely still. There was no wind, no sound of birds, not an animal in sight. I could see the empty train station where just days earlier my father, mother, and I had arrived.

We hadn't walked far when we came upon some small children playing in a nearby walkway between two buildings. First I thought they were playing some sort of game. One child lay still on the ground while the others walked in circles around him. The closer we got I could hear him weeping, while the others seem to be amused. I suggested we go over and see what was going on. But I was told if someone needed our help they would ask for it. We walked in silence for what seemed to be an eternity until we came upon a huge three story, scary looking, run-down building.

"Why are we stopping here?" I stepped backwards.

"Inside is someone I want you to meet."

"I'm not about to step a foot inside that place," I protested. The look the young man gave me was one I wouldn't easily forget. Without another word, I put one foot in front of the other and followed closely behind him.

He opened the huge doors and I could barely see inside. Only a small glow of light came from the foyer. A masculine voice from across the room invited us to enter.

When my eyes adjusted to the dark, I could see he was a dark mysterious looking man sitting in a Victorian high-back chair covered in red velvet. I noticed right away he was wearing the same trinket around his neck as the one who brought me there.

"Welcome to my home, little one, and what might be your name?" He had a hellish grin on his face.

Nervously I replied, "Alexandria, sir."

He stood up from his chair and started towards me.

I was trying desperately to keep my legs from folding under me out of fear.

"Xavier, why have you waited so long to introduce us?"

"Alexandria, this is my father Sir Vincent Hellion and this is our home."

Trying to keep my voice from shaking I replied, "So very nice to meet you."

Sir Vincent then gestured with his hand for both of us to follow him into the next room.

"Alexandria's father and mother sadly left her here when she became ill."

"That's not true, Xavier!" I shouted back. "They would have never left me on purpose. Something horrible has happened to them. I just know it!"

"Calm down my little one, you are safe with us," Sir Vincent responded. "There is no need to be frightened. We will be your family now. And rest assured, my son and I will never leave you." The tone in his voice was firm, but not reassuring.

He told me to listen carefully, that I was too young to understand why we'd been brought together, but in time it would be revealed. "I have powers to which you cannot imagine possible. I have seen the past and what you've endured, the torture, the loneliness and desperation. I can take that all away, give you eternal strength and knowledge of what lies ahead, and in return you will in time give my son what he needs to fulfill the prophecy."

"You are not God, so who are you to say you know me? You know nothing of my life or what I need. Only God can give me what I need." I was angry and I stood up and headed for the door.

"Sit," he demanded. "You know nothing of this God of whom you speak so highly. Has he brought your father and mother back to you? Was he there when you were locked in darkness? Did he stop the hands that beat you and tormented you night after night? Where was your God then, the one you say that can give you what you need?"

I could feel my heart racing. My mind was scrambling for an answer. How did he know of my torture and abuse? And how did he know I had been confined to living in darkness night after night? There was no explanation. I was confused and tired of trying to make sense of something I had never before encountered.

My mind was frantic. Did he have special powers? Was he an angel? Why was he questioning my faith and my God? And if he were evil then why would he offer to take care of me and make sure I was never alone again?

For a child with no self worth who had lost the only people that had ever showed me the true meaning of love, I had started to think maybe he was right. Maybe he could help me. I had no one else. I began to cry uncontrollably.

Then, after hours of silence, Xavier spoke. "Father, I think the little one is exhausted. There will be plenty of time for conversation later. I will show her to her room and bid you a goodnight."

Xavier helped me from my chair, carried me up the steep and winding staircase, and led me to the master bedroom. When he opened the double doors I couldn't believe my eyes. It was the most beautiful room I had ever seen. The design of the wallpaper was a peaceful flowing cascade of flowers, vibrant in color, and the bed was dressed with beautiful soft linen. On the nightstand there was a vase of orchids and a luxurious washbowl trimmed in gold. It was as if the room had been prepared for a queen. This was the first sign of color I had seen since arriving. The whole town, all the buildings and even the people I had encountered were covered in dark drab colors. Nothing was making any sense.

"Try and get some rest, little one. My father is right, you're too young to understand now, but you will fulfill your destiny soon." Xavier closed the door behind him.

Who were they to tell me what my destiny would be? I wasn't sure how he could have known those things about me, but I was sure it had to be some sort of trickery. Why me? Why did they want me? If I had known the real horror that loomed ahead, I surely would have been mortified. Overcome with exhaustion, I lay on the bed, but rest would not come. Thoughts of father and mother and what could have happened to them haunted me. For the last six years they had been my life. They were the first people to show me kindness and what the meaning of real love and compassion was. I missed them so. They had many friends back home; surely someone would come looking for us. It was as if I was in a place and time that didn't exist. I thought if I could just play along with this frightening game of manipulation, maybe soon I could seize the opportunity to escape this hellish nightmare.

Early the next morning, Xavier came to my room. He informed me that one of my duties, now that I was the mistress of the house, was to pleasure him in whatever way he saw fit.

I had lost my innocence long ago while incarcerated in foster care and I didn't intend on being raped again.

"I'm not your mistress or anybody else's. Where I come from it's not proper for a girl of my age to act in such a manner, nor would I want to. You may have me captive here, but I will die before I let you touch me in such a manner."

With a glare cold enough to freeze ice and veins bulging from his neck he looked at me. "Where you come from? It doesn't matter where you come from. You are here now. I will not force myself on you at this moment, but there will be another. You will have my child, a son. And he will have powers that mankind has never seen. This is your destiny, my prophecy. You are not captive here. Feel free to visit our people. You'll see they will welcome you, for they too know why you have been sent here."

In shock and disbelief I stood there looking into his cold dark eyes looking for some sign of normalcy. For years I had lived with and had to tolerate abuse. Alone and frightened, locked away in darkness, and now I had to live in a psychotic nightmare with no seemingly way out. How could a whole town be so deranged? What happened here to make these people believe they had such powers, or that they could manipulate someone into believing in such nonsense? All I could hope for was to find one person in the town, someone like me, someone who didn't believe in all this craziness and who was too frightened to take a stand. I knew how to fight to stay alive. I had plenty of practice and I would do whatever it took, even if that meant giving my body at one point to this crazed deviant. He might get my body, but he would not get my soul.

Playing on his sympathy, hoping he would believe I was sincere, I made a plea. "Xavier, if it is my destiny to give you this child, then it will happen. I want to fulfill what you say is meant to be and I mean no disrespect to you or your father. I'm beginning to understand. I just want to know more about your people and this extraordinary gift that I have been chosen to birth." My plea had worked, or so I thought.

I told Xavier I would like to meet the little children I had seen playing in the courtyard. I told him not to worry I wouldn't try to run. I had nowhere to go. He didn't seem to object. I walked out of the house and down the walk. I couldn't help but be reminded of the total silence. The only thing moving about was the dark rolling clouds above. I hadn't gone far when I saw some children playing in the same courtyard as the day before. As I got closer, they began to run. I yelled for them to stop and told them not to be afraid, that I just wanted to meet them and introduce myself. Out of the four children who looked to be around eleven or twelve, there was one who looked much younger, a little girl. I proceeded to introduce myself, "I'm Alexandria, what are your names?"

"My name is Zachary."

"My name is Caleb.

"I'm Jacob."

When it was the little girl's turn to tell me her name, she hid behind the others. She reminded me so much of me at that age. She was clearly shy and somewhat suspicious of me. I told her not to be frightened, I meant her no harm, and that I was new here and wanted to make friends. She then peeked her little head out from behind the others and said, "My name is Alexandria."

"Well then, we already have something in common."

She gave me a half smile. Zachary appeared to be the oldest. He had a slender little body with long dark hair and dark sad eyes. His clothing was tattered and dirty, and it appeared that none of them had bathed for some time. Caleb was short and one side of his little mouth seemed to slant downward slightly. Jacob had blond curly locks and eyes so dark they almost appeared to be black. Then there was Alexandria. She had long dark hair with many curls and the deepest blue eyes I'd ever seen, and I noticed she had a constant habit of biting her bottom lip.

Looking into their eyes I could see sadness. With a little coaxing, trying not to ask too many questions, I found out they were all orphans. They all said the same thing. They had been told their parents abandoned them. They had been so young they didn't even remember them. They said the town had taken them in. They remembered no other existence. I asked them what kind of schooling they were getting, if any. They were clueless. I found out that they were being treated like slaves. They fed and watered the animals and did other chores Mr. Hellion saw fit. I asked them where the other children were, and if it was the same for them too. They said they were the only ones.

I was trapped in a town with very few women, just a handful of children, and the rest appeared to be nothing but crazed domineering men. How could a place like this exist? I had seen no one arrive or depart from this place since I had arrived with father and mother.

When asked how often the train stopped in the town, the look on their faces told me I wasn't going to get an answer. This town was more like a cult with Mr. Hellion as their leader.

I noticed that Zachary had been staring at me for some time. He looked as if he wanted to say something, so I asked them if they had any questions they wanted to ask me.

Zachary was the first to speak up. "How old are you," he asked nervously.

"I'm sixteen, but very soon I will have a birthday.

"Are you the chosen one? Mr. Hellion said you would be coming, and that soon there would be many changes."

Startled I asked, "How could Mr. Hellion have known I was coming? And what do you mean by being the chosen one?"

Looking as if I had just scolded him he grabbed Alexandria's hand

and yelled for the others to run.

I yelled for them to come back, but I had frightened them away with my questions. I wanted to go back to where this nightmare had started, back to the house where I had collapsed, and to the place I last remembered seeing my Mother. But every house looked the same. I walked up to the first house I came to and opened the door. It was clearly vacant and the smell of rotting meat took my breath away. I covered my face and continued on into the next room. Lying on the floor partly covered by the bedspread that hung loosely from the bed where my parents had slept that fateful night, was my mother's silver cross necklace. I had never known her to take it off. It was clear to me something horrible had happened here. About the time I reached down and picked up the necklace and stood up, I saw Xavier coming up the walk. I made it to the front door when he stopped me.

"What are you doing in this abandoned boarding house? There is nothing here you need to see,"

Ignoring his question I asked him where the horrible smell was coming from inside. He informed me it was probably a dead rat and there were many rats in the vacant houses. I had smelled dead rats before and this wasn't a dead rat. I wouldn't argue with him for now. My intentions were to come back later and look around for myself. My mother's necklace would be my secret. For now, I would go quietly.

He told me there was to be a town celebration that evening and we didn't have much time to prepare. We headed back to the cold dark place I would learn to call home. Not really my home, but a place of horror.

I got back only to find a change of clothes laid out for me on the bed. The same dreary black clothing I had become accustomed to.

Xavier came in a short time later and told me the festivities were about to begin. I couldn't have known what I was about to witness. Looking back now I don't know how I ever endured such fiendish and diabolical acts. What would happen that night would be forever burned into my soul.

In the center of town a small fire was burning. People had gathered in a circle around it and were holding hands. There seemed to be some sort of trestle with a ladder attached in the center of the fire. Xavier and his father along with the others were chanting a language I had never heard before. It was then I noticed Zachary, one of the children I had spoken to earlier. He was being escorted towards the flame. He wasn't making a sound. It was as if he was in a trance. Then, there was dead silence. Everyone had stopped chanting and Xavier's father, Sir Vincent, began to speak.

"The time has finally come. We shall wait no more. This sacrifice we give to you in return for our everlasting life and powers which no earthly man can behold. Zachary has betrayed our trust and spoke out against us. We will first drink his blood and then burn his flesh as a warning to others who shall try the same."

Horrified I screamed out, "He's an innocent child! You can't do this! He said nothing to me!"

I watched as they put the knife to his throat. Trying desperately to reach him before it was too late, I struggled to break free from the hands that held me back. I began to sob uncontrollably. What kind of monsters could do this to an innocent child? My body felt numb and I gasped for breath.

"Alexandria, Alexandria, wake up. It looks as if you had a nightmare. You've been crying in your sleep for the last thirty minutes. You mentioned Zachary's name over and over. Did he tell you something earlier to upset you?" Xavier asked in a suspicious tone.

I noticed the black dress still lay untouched on the bed.

"Maybe it would be best if you didn't talk to the children. It might hinder their chores from getting done. You wouldn't want to see them scolded for something you had caused, would you?" It sounded more like a command instead of a question.

I realized then I'd had a terrifying nightmare. I understood he was not asking me to stay away from the children; he was giving me a warning. Was the nightmare a warning? I believed it was. Was there something the children knew that I could use against Xavier and his father? Something that I could use to get out of this Hell, this nightmare I was living in? As bad as I wanted to find out, I knew I couldn't put their lives in danger. The nightmare could easily become a reality.

Xavier stressed the fact I needed to get ready for the festivities that were about to begin.

So, I slipped on the dark and dreary black dress that had been chosen for me, and still feeling groggy I told him I was ready. As we left the house, in the distance I could see what appeared to be a light. Getting closer I could tell it was a fire burning. Everything so far was just as in my dream. The trestle looked the same along with the ladder that led to the top of a platform. The people were surrounding the fire and chanting in the same foreign language. Then, like in my nightmare there was complete silence. To my horror I looked up at the platform and I could clearly see two human bodies. They had been decapitated and the smell of human flesh was sickening. Xavier's father began to speak.

"We shall burn their flesh and drink of their blood. All who are fit to kneel at my side shall come forward and drink from a cup."

I was disgusted and sickened from what I was witnessing. How could a human being do this to another? What could those two people have done to deserve such a heinous death? I couldn't bear to witness another second of this terror.

I screamed at Xavier, "Explain to me how you people can justify this horror. How could you do these things to another human being and for what reason?"

"You were brought here tonight to witness this ritual. Those people were important to us for one reason only. They possessed what we need to survive. We drink from their bodies; we have no need for their flesh, as you will soon understand."

"I could never understand something this evil. I will never be a part of this nightmare. How could you let the children witness such evilness?"

With a barbaric look on his face, he answered in a sarcastic tone, "These children you seem to be so worried about share the same need as ours. Look around you my dear. For this world is now going to be yours as well. The children are many centuries old, same as the rest of us. My father is the oldest and the wisest of us all. Their appearances will never change. They, like the rest of us, experienced the gift of immortality centuries ago. The younger ones are used to seek out what we need to survive as immortals. Pure blood is our means of existence. Your father and mother came to know that all too well."

I knew at that moment Xaviar was telling me who the bodies were. They had viciously killed my parents for their insane pleasure. They must have brainwashed the children. Nothing like this could exist. I thought about my poor parents, how they had gone through such torture. My heart was filled with such sorrow. When would my time come to be tortured and persecuted? They had kept me alive for one reason, to have this so called child of extraordinary powers. Xavier's child. In their sick demented minds this would fulfill their prophecy. They actually thought that I would do as they wanted, that I would have this prophesized child. They thought because of me, the child would have the immortal soul of his father but his mother's mortal means to reproduce. They believed this child would help them overcome the world.

Xavier told me later that I had been chosen because of the true evil that lay deep within my soul. He reminded me of the cruel torture I had endured by the hands of my so-called foster caretakers, and the devilish way I had planned and executed both of their deaths. It's true I had felt no remorse. He said the reason I felt such a connection to him was because we shared the same evils in our souls. With him I could have immortality. We could have the child that would save our existence. I thought about the little girl Alexandria, and how she reminded me so much of myself. At the time I couldn't have known her little innocent soul had been taken and replaced by evil. Before this night of terror was over Xavier would convince me this was where I belonged.

While living with father and mother I had attended St. Mary's Catholic School. They spoke of fables, witches, warlocks, vampires and demons. We were taught they were myths and that man himself made the only evil. We were told we could overcome these evils with faith. What if your faith is not strong enough, could these evils become real?

The answer is yes, my son. I had lost my faith long before I met your father. I never really believed in my soul. I had given up and evil had won. Hellion became my home. Sir Vincent became my father and Xaviar my master. I pleaded for your soul to be spared at birth. I promised them my soul and every child thereafter, if they would give you the chance that I never had. You were my firstborn. I slipped this letter into your blanket and at the time could only hope it would never have to be read. Xavier let you go. He said one day you would return. As for me my soul became immortal. The flesh never dies but the soul rots forever, and even though your soul is immortal you can choose to fight the evil that lies deep inside you. Don't let them win. Choose to turn this omen around and make it a gift. Hell is my home and I can never leave.

Your Loving Mother, Alexandria

Reading this letter many times I began to fixate on finding a clue to what had driven my poor mother insane. My adoptive parents gave me the box that held the letter years ago when I turned eighteen. They told me I was adopted at an early age from a hospital in upstate New York, and had been left there anonymously. The letter found in my blanket was the only connection to finding my mother. It was clear she had been mad. But what could have happened to drive her so far over the edge? Yet in her letter she gave great detail to the characters. She speaks of this town and the people, or monsters as she describes with such conviction. I've often thought about her and wondered if she was still alive. Could she be in a mental institution? It seems most likely. I guess I'm like most people that have been adopted; most of us at some time in our life need the answers to our questions. Grown with my own family, two beautiful daughters and a son, it's up to me to find where we came from and what we are made of.

The airplane flight has been a little turbulent, but it's almost over. I'll soon be in upstate New York at the hospital where I was born. I figured it would be the best place to start looking for clues.

Because of bad weather a few of us have taken a train to the next destination and will wait there for another flight. But wouldn't you know it the train is having problems as well. I've traveled around the world a few times in my life, my job as a salesman demands it, but this town looks quite different than any I've ever seen. Looking out the window of the train I see people passing by, quite oddly dressed I might add. All appear to be in black … looks like robes. I'm getting a very eerie feeling, déjà vu.

We're getting off the train now; I hear a man's voice. I think he's welcoming us, but I can't quite make out the words. "What exactly is the man saying?"

The woman standing next to me answered, "It sounds like he is welcoming us to their town."

"What is the name of this town?" I asked. Then I heard clearly.

"Welcome to Hellion! You'll never want to leave."

♦♦♦♦♦♦♦♦♦♦♦♦♦

Barbara Watkins is an author from Southeast Missouri. Her credits include two novellas in publication, "Behind the Red Door" and "Thorns of an Innocent Soul". She's an active member of The Heartland Writers Guild, and was voted 2008 Vice President of Wizard of Words. Her articles and short stories have appeared in online journals as well as in print. She has just completed her first full-length novel.

http://www.barbarawatkins.net/

SOON

By Ian de l'Autin

I peered out of the plate glass window of the Starbuck's Café where I sat. Patrons milled about the store—sporting recent purchases of books and magazines, some with cups of coffee and snacks in hand. Their preoccupations, much like my own, filled their faces with frowns and smiles, and even in a rare case a blank stare. A mere reflection of my own demeanor, I wondered. For a man who spent nearly every waking hour on the road somewhere, either preparing to leave, preparing to arrive, preparing for the next event, always preparing for something, I guess it was no wonder why I saw myself in them.

My journey had taken me to, of all places, Bakersfield, California. As one of the first Barnes & Noble stores to accept me as a legitimate author I felt compelled—almost duty bound—to visit whenever requested. And I had been frequently requested, the reason eluding me to this very day. Why would anyone want to hear my rants?

I had driven California's Central Valley many times and had grown quite familiar with the fine people of Kern County. In some ways they had adopted me—a loner of sorts finding home where home was not. Maybe it was my Cajun ancestry they found intriguing, or better yet the fact that I had traveled from one end of the earth to the other - searching, seeking, hoping. My yearning for truth seemed universal at some basic level. Still, my quest to find answers to questions that occupied the mind, even when seemingly empty, proved to be a journey fraught with peril.

Even the mountains of the Tehachapi range provided little respite for me. More questions than answers greeted me among the beauty of the finger-laden slopes—all but reaching from the heavens down to the earth. If the Hand of God could have been seen somewhere, this could have been the place. But, for me the Hand of God seemed to only touch me with heartache and troubles—at least that's what it felt like.

When I started this adventure the mystic Jean-Pierre de Caussade warned me, well not personally. In his Abandonment to Divine Providence he cautioned that for the spiritual novice the first encounter with God was filled with glee: a drunkenness of Spirit. In time, God would grow silent, he advised, a journey of solitude enveloping the neophyte, much like that experienced by the Hebrews when they roamed the desert for forty years. Even Jesus had experienced such—forty days in a desert filled with loneliness and temptation. And for me silence is what I got, or was it more like abandonment? Whatever it was I felt alone, even in a crowd of people.

"In deep thought?" Kyle, the CRM (Community Relations Manager to those outside of the publishing world) shared a reassuring smile with me. Resting his hand on my shoulder, the warmth from his palm eased my saddened heart. My eyes drifted across the café, searching for the strength to move me from the safety of my corner and somewhat secluded seat.

Like a movie frame set on slow speed, the activity of the café blurred into a cacophony of motion matching the stir in my bowels; that is until a woman, aged, yet still beautiful moved into my line of sight.

With no one else sitting near me, her graceful nod seemed to be directed towards me, that and a subtle smile offered through her silky smooth skin and high cheek bones. She moved with the charm of the wind under her feet, her slinky and toned body reflecting that of a woman that had aged with grace and elegance. Would she had been wine, "vintage" would have distinguished her bouquet with words like "balanced" and "full-bodied" and "complete."

"Are you ready?" Kyle offered me a hand up. He escorted me to the podium and tapped the mic. "Can I have your attention, please. If you could take your seats, we'll get started in just a moment." He perused the sprawling crowd and the rattle of the folding chairs competing with soft jazz playing in the background.

As the flock meandered between parallel rows of bookcases, the pitch of their voices muffled the store music. Within the narrow aisle two sets of metal chairs, neatly arranged into matching rows of four-set columns, pressed bodies against one another in orderly chaos.

With the last of the patrons seated, the roar of conversation settled into a dull drone - the soft vibration of the A.C. almost in harmony with the whispers of the assembled.

My stomach soured. The hot breath of acid reflux raced up my esophagus. What if they hate it? Damn, I'm no poet.

"Ladies and Gentlemen, it is my pleasure to welcome you to Barnes & Noble." Kyle's warm greeting stilled the antsy crowd. "We are fortunate to have with us, author and poet, Dr. Pierre-Paul de la Moret VI, visiting us from New Orleans, Louisiana. Dr. de la Moret, or Paul as he prefers, is well known to some of us here in Bakersfield. He has been working on a new novel, which I understand is partially set here and into the Mohave Desert. Paul prefers short introductions, as he believes long intros bore people to tears. So without further delay, please help me in welcoming Dr. Pierre-Paul de la Moret."

The applause thundered across the store, attracting customers not initially interested in my presence. The center area set-up for my talk filled to overflowing capacity, every seat and inch of standing space occupied by a body.

With my sweaty palms neatly tucked into my jacket pockets, I approached the mic—the black wire bulb reaching my forehead. I had no choice but to remove my now trembling hands to lower it. As the metal casing holding the wires screeched, the crowd silenced. The music lowered. I felt my presence shrink. Their eyes fixed upon me. Their calm unnerved me. Their focus—oh!—their intense focus was like none I had experienced before. Naked? Yeah, I felt naked!

Why me, I wondered. I had so little of worth to offer an audience of this caliber, much less this size. Yet, a hush rippled through the crowd, the lack of movement and any other such distraction drawing my mouth closer to the mic. With shortened breath and tensed frame, I forced added air into my lungs. My heart pounded, all but rattling my ear drums. My swollen tongue pressed against my dried pallet. And with one more breath I released the words through my pursed lips.

Soon, peace will be soon.
Soon, love will thrive soon.
Soon, man will care soon.
Soon, hearts will mend soon.
Soon, war will end soon.

Young men and women,
some with child
will live in peace.

Bombs no more will explode
for liberty bought with violence.
Hatred sought for religion's sake
will cease soon.

Soon grandmother's child
will see her child
running through the fields.

Landmines no more will explode
removing limbs,
crushing bones,
taking lives,
soon, no more.

Soon lives entwined
will live in calm
knowing we need each other.

Soon men of power
and of might will stop
Stop!

Stop the bombs, and the wars,
and the need, and the want
for greed, and oil, and gold,
and more.

Stop the strife,
dividing us all
no more, soon.

Soon peace will be
love will thrive
man will care
hearts will mend
war will end
forevermore
soon.

With the poem complete, not a soul moved. An advertising banner above me flapped in a stream of cool A.C. blown air, drawing my eyes to the ceiling. I lift my eyes to the heavens, from which shall come my aid. Boy, did I need aid.

My head lowered to the awaiting crowd. They remained motionless. I searched for a nod, any form of approval easing the tension gripping my frame. Sweat beaded on my upper lip and brow. They hated it. I knew it. What was I thinking? What do I know anyway? They see right through me. My shallow life exposed to all of them, my confusion and doubt, the loneliness and fears. They see. They see.

But, a young man with long blond hair and seated on the first row stood. He began to clap. Another man joined him, then a woman. With each second another person stood – clapping, clapping loudly. The crowd erupted into applause and ovation louder than when they greeted me.

My face flushed red, heat pouring through my open pores. Oh, the humility of it. How could my mere words inspire and touch others this way?

Moved, yes I was moved.

At last the crowd stilled. They sat not moving a muscle. Not even the usual cough and normal clearing of the throat.

My throat tightened into a balled knot. Tears pressed upon my open eyes. How could I speak now?

With a deep breath drawn to still my shaken nerves, I released the air once more. "I am touched, deeply touched by your outpouring of sentiment. When I undertook this assignment from Kyle, accepting to be the keynote speaker at Educator Night, it dawned on me that I had undertaken a task of incredible significance. Your time is the most precious thing you have. To invest that time in listening to the expression of another person's thoughts or ideas is the most precious of gifts you can offer him or her. For your gift tonight, I am deeply appreciative.

"Soon, as I have come to know this poem was written one night when I saw pictures of young men and women, American soldiers in foreign lands, fighting and sacrificing for what we are told is the democratic way for peace on the planet. Yet, while their sacrifice touched me, I felt angered by it. Why? I asked myself. Why was bloodshed required for peace?"

In a deepening hush, the crowd focused onto a single entity - me. As I peered into their attentive eyes, I wondered once more what right I had to speak of this. How dare I stain such patriotic actions as that of the young patriots who so selflessly lost their lives in the fight for freedom?

I folded the page with my prepared words. From the heart, just speak from your heart, I told myself.

"Ladies and gentlemen, where I stand before you as one who knows not the sacrifice borne by the young men and women I speak of this night, I would admit to you that wonder does fill my mind. We claim ourselves as 'one nation, under God, indivisible, with liberty and justice for all.' Thus I am compelled to ask of the innocence lost by the manner in which we presently strive for peace. Were the man called Jesus to walk the earth amongst us now, what would he say of this? It is to this that my questioning centers. What would Jesus do?"

Even as I stood there speechless, the words of St. Luke resonated in my head: To you who hear me, I say: Love your enemies, do good to those who hate you: bless those who curse you and pray for those who maltreat you. When someone slaps you on one cheek, turn and give him the other; when someone takes your coat, let him have your shirt as well. Give to all who beg from you. When a man takes what is yours, do not demand it back. Do to others what you would have them do to you. If you love those who love you, what credit is that to you? Even thieves love those who love them. If you do good to those who do good to you, how can you claim any credit? Sinners do as much. If you lend to those from whom you expect repayment, what merit is there in it for you? Even sinners lend to sinners, expecting to be repaid in full.

Love your enemy and do good; lend without expecting repayment. Then will your recompense be great. You will rightly be called sons of the Most High, since He Himself is good to the ungrateful and the wicked.

Be compassionate, as our Father is compassionate. Do not judge, and you will not be judged. Do not condemn, and you will not be condemned. Pardon, and you shall be pardoned. Give, and it shall be given to you. Good measure pressed down, shaken together, running over, will they pour into the fold of your garment. For the measure you measure with will be measured back to you.

My pleading eyes scanned the crowd, hoping that I might find in their reflection validation for my thoughts. The man who first applauded the poem sat motionless, focused intently upon me. His eyes did not bat, nor did his frame move in any way. A girl I had noted out of the corner of my eye did the same. Even the second man to stand in applause stared at me with blank eyes.

Over and over I perused the crowd, searching, wanting, hoping for a hint of encouragement to move forward. The silenced hum of the audience, with no sounds from the store at large, unnerved me. How could I have been so thoughtless to say what I said and in the way I said it?

But a sniffle drew my attention to the rear of the crowd. Through piercing blue eyes the elderly woman who crossed my path earlier wiped a tear away. The wrinkled tissue in her hand suggested she had used it before. Her sniffles, soft and gentle, could only be those of one who had loved and lost.

Our eyes connected once again. I left the podium and stepped down from the small stage where I stood. Through the narrow aisle separating the two columned-groupings of metal folding chairs I walked towards her, never once breaking eye contact with her, nor she with me.

My breath shallowed from my hastened pace. My arms flayed in sync with the rapid movement of my feet. For such a short distance it was as though a chasm separated us.

I approached her welcoming eyes. In her hands three photos lay cradled with care, though worn on the edges from use.

"May I," I asked, reaching for them with open hands.

She placed each into my palm, gently layering them in order. Pointing with a crocked and arthritic index finger, she said, "This is my husband. I lost him in Korea only three weeks after we were married at Annapolis."

His lean frame and full head of lightly blond hair smacked of youth and innocence. A smile filled with broad white teeth against the backdrop of a fighter jet showed no cause for alarm or concern, even with him dressed in his flight jacket and full gear.

"Then there is my son." She lifted the first photo, exposing the second. The young man standing with two other buddies was an image of the boy in the previous picture—the one exception—his green battle fatigues.

"I lost my son in Viet Nam to a landmine. He was twenty-one at the time. He graduated from West Point, and was married there. And then—" Her voice cracked, the knot in her throat certainly as large as the stranglehold now gripping my own.

She lifted the picture, glaring at it lovingly before putting it away. With the third and last picture resting in my hand, a weighted feeling seized me. I could not move a muscle, nor so much as flinch a finger.

The elderly lady's faced ashened. Her countenance seemed to drain of blood. "This was my grandson, my only son's son. He was recently killed in Iraq. He left his wife with a baby, like his father and grandfather." Her softened tone shifted to one of harsh resignation. "I've got three Purple Hearts and three Silver Crosses. Not much when you think of the cost. I'm not sure if you went to any store you could trade all six of them for one life." Her head lowered. Her eyes seemed to trace the brown and tan carpeted floor. "Sometimes, late at night, I wonder about the women on the other side. I wonder if their hearts ache like my own." With a tear drizzling down her soft, yet colorless cheeks, she wiped away the drop with her finger. "I thought after my son was killed, 'No more.' But, I wasn't done. Not yet. And for what? It is just like you've said in your poem. For oil, or greed, or whatever the excuse. None of my men have seen their children. But, I have a great-grandson on the way, and he'll never—" Her voice trailed into tearful release. She wept, silently so.

I rested my hand on her shoulder, wanting to comfort her, but unsure as to how. What words could I speak to give her solace? What action could I offer to ease her pain?

She muttered as she cradled the photographs into her soft, but wrinkled hands, "'He that lives by the sword, shall perish by the sword.' That's what we do, we all perish by the sword. My men with their lives, and we women with our hearts. But, not my great-grandson. No! He'll never fight. Never." Her chin lifted. Her tear-filled eyes met my own.

I had no more to say that could ease her pain, no more. How could God be silent now? So I stood there, motionless amongst the commotion that raged a mere three-thousand miles away, bombs exploding, lives cut short - innocent men and women, young and old, American and other, all the same, all the same - soon.

♦♦♦♦♦♦♦♦♦♦♦♦

Internationally known management consultant, speaker, and coach, Ernest de l'Autin is the author of one published novel, one short story, and over a dozen technical articles. "Reach to the Wounded Healer" has sold nearly 5000 copies in just over one year with sales growing (especially after being rated 5 of 5 in four categories at the "Writer's Digest 12th Annual International Self-Published Book Awards for Mainstream/Literary Fiction"). He has also completed a second novel "Of the Oaks" and over seven volumes of poetry.

Ean, as known by friends and family, presently resides in Texas, yet anticipates a move to New York City this year. In his research and life's work, Ean has discovered extreme hurt in the hearts of many. Their grief matched his own anguish and he (through the gift of his "woundedness") found the courage to reach to those in despair. "Reach to the Wounded Healer" was founded on his journey into healing and recovery after the loss of loved ones. As best expressed by Terry Tempest Williams, "Perhaps, I am telling this story in an attempt to heal myself, to confront what I do not know, to create a path for myself with the idea that 'memory' is the only way home."

www.ernestdelautin.com

THE CIGAR BOX

By Debra Shiveley Welch

It looked to be a long night. I had agreed to play the fiddle at a harvest dance in the next county. At first I had shilly-shallied about takin' the job. It were a tedious drive over rutted country roads, and instead of ridin' my horse Rusty, I were, perforce, obliged to hire a cheap buckboard from Silverman's livery stable, a much slower conveyance and a nuisance as well. It seems I could earn a few much needed dollars by deliverin' a hand carved chair ordered by a Mr. Riffle who lived in the county to which I'd be a travelin'. By agreein' to play at old Silverman's daughter's weddin', I had me a free rig for the night. Grumblin', I gave a slap of the reins and a giddy-up to the hired horse and set upon my way.

Normally, I enjoyed fiddlin'. I had me an old cigar box fiddle, which my daddy had made back in 1875 from a used wooden cigar box he'd found in an alleyway. I got her for Christmas, and promptly named her Bessie. She felt so good in my hands. From the moment I touched her I knowed we was meant to be together. She seemed to say to me, "I am yours!" and I fell completely in love with her.

She were a beauty, and lands sake, could my Bessie sing! She could wail like a newborn babe, and make the stubbornest foot begin to tap and stomp until the floorboards of the sturdiest barn was a thumpin' in time to my sweet Bessie's song. She were my pride and joy, and I never passed an opportunity to show off what she and me could do together. I couldn't figure out why she could wail like she did—better 'an any fiddle I'd ever heard, but I didn't care none neither. She were mine and that were all that mattered.

Many times, I would play her when we was all alone. I'd go up to the loft of our cabin, hunker down on a old tree stump I'd drug up there, and I'd just play my girl. Sometimes a feelin' of desolation and malaise would come over me, a feelin' I couldn't understand, but I figured my Bessie had her reasons, so I just kinda flowed with her.

Anways, here we was a bumpin' and a jigglin' over these dad-blasted roads, Mr. Riffle's chair a wobblin' and a bangin' in the back, when we come to the woods. I never did cottin' to this particular patch of woodland. I ain't an imagin'ful man, but on the sunniest of days it were forbiddin'. Dark trees loomed menacin'ly over the road, squelchin' the sun, makin' deep dark patches of dankness; black holes, like some'un had put a red hot poker into the night and left parts that were darker than others; black holes which had burnt away the sky to let in the cold.

It were always cold, even on the hottest days, and now, as always, the chill seemed to creep into my chest. This were the first time I'd taken my Bessie through these woods, and I were concerned lest I would have to high up the horse and make a run through its dark nothin'ness. I grit my teeth and with a somewhat nervous, "Giddy-up!" I urged my equestrian companion forward.

We finally left the forest without some kind of terrorizin' happenin', and a cloud seemed to pass beyond the sun allowin' a stream of sunlight to fill the road with relief. I felt better, and knowin' I were close to my destination, my heart lifted as I made my way to first Mr. Riffle's and then on to the dance.

Bessie had endured the ride strapped to my back by a sturdy piece of bailin' twine. I kept her there 'cause she were my girl and I didn't want nothin' to happen to her. Nary a scratch nor a dent were allowed to mar her beauty, so when I reached the barn where we was supposed to play, it were with renewed pride that I brung my Bessie with me down from the buckboard and strutted into the barn.

The barn were as festive a place as you'd ever want to see! Chinese paper lanterns was strung from front to back. Tables a groanin' with pies, cakes and donuts lined each side, and the floor had been scrubbed then sprinkled with sawdust to give each dancin' foot better purchase. It promised to be a grand night, and I could feel my Bessie a vibratin' with anticipation.

Lots of folks in their Sunday best was there: tight sack coats for the men, colorful calicos, dimities and gingham for the ladies. I seen a couple of right pertty young gals that might require my attention later on in the evenin'. Now, I don't want to say I'm a looker, but I've had my share of eyes made at me, and I've been told I cut a dashin' figure. I'm rather tall, standin' at six-two with dark hair and eyes. I prefer the Jesse James Duster to the tight fittin' sack suit of the times. The long, loose fittin' linen coat do cut a dash as I whirl with my Bessie; the ladies, I've been told, find my Western wear romantic.

I tucked my Bessie agin' my shoulder and blew upon her gently. "Play fair, my sweet Bessie," I crooned, and as I walked the length of the barn, I resined up my horse hair bow and drew it agin' my girl's strings in a long, drawn out note, leadin' into a dramatic piece that showed off what my Bessie could do. As I played, I made toward the platform at the back of the buildin', stoppin' now and then to appreciate a nubile young lady, then movin' on, gettin' in a bit of fancy foot work as I went. It were my own particular style of enterin' a dance. Folks seemed to like it, and it made me and Bessie feel right proud. I leapt upon the platform at the end of the barn, and commenced to regale the folks therein with Bessie's sweet, ulalatin' music.

The dancin' became frenzied. The floor boards thumped and bowed as the weight of hundreds of feet stomped. The air became warm and close. Bessie were outdoin' herself and the room seemed to swirl and spin about in a frenzied combination of howlin' music, swirlin' skirts and petticoats. Sweat run into my eyes, my heart raced and Bessie seemed to throb agin' my arm where she lay. Then I seen her.

The rest of the room seemed to fade into a mist except for this one gal. She would have stood out in any case. Her clothin' were rather old fashioned, it havin' no bustle nor puffy sleeves, and it were trimmed in pink lace at the neck and hem, but her eyes was what drew mine to her - burnin' green eyes like beacons, eyes that trapped me, imprisoned me in a green pool of promise. Bessie faltered in my hands. Her wailin' ceased, breakin' the spell and I, released for a second, almost fell from the platform as I leapt to the floor. Had the girl spoken to me? I could a sworn I'd heard her say, "I am yours."

Removin' my large white handkerchief from my coat pocket, I mopped my streamin' forehead and eyes. I searched the room for the girl, but she were gone. Someone shoved a cup in my hand and I swigged, then choked. Strong corn liquor burned my throat; I felt obliged for the drink. My head felt light and empty; my stomach churned and tilted.

I don't rightly remember much more of the dance. I guess maybe me and Bessie played some more, and maybe we didn't. The next time I recollected myself, I were in the rattley buckboard, headin' towards the woods. Bessie, once agin across my back, seemed to thrum as we drew nigh the woods. "Now, Bessie, it'll be all right, my girl," I crooned. We entered and blackness fell.

I heard what seemed to be a Bobcat; unnatural for these parts, but not unheard of. I heard a hiss. I looked up and there were a gruesome sight. It were a woman - gaunt, pale, with eyes like burnin' coals. I seen a fallin' shadow and it were upon me. At first I were too flummoxed to realize what were a happenin', and then I realized I were being attacked by some Thing from the trees.

I grabbed for the whip, hopin' to drive my attacker from me, when it wrapped its arms around my neck and hissed agin. It's breath were fetid, as if blowed out by a rottin' corpse. Matted, black hair blew in my face and my open, screamin' mouth. It tasted squirmy and dead, as if a decayin' animal had entered that howlin' cavity. Taloned nails begun to rake my skin, and sharp teeth dug into my neck.

I fought! I grabbed its arms and tried to release its stranglin' hold, but I were quickly weakenin' from loss of blood. I heard it screech, an eerie, manic cry, and once agin' I thought I heard, "I am yours!"

My head begun to swim. I wrastled with the fiend, tryin' to tear it from my back, and finally, leapt from the careenin' buckboard to the ground, rollin', rollin', tryin' to free myself from its deathly embrace. The last thing I remember was hearin' my Bessie crunch beneath my weight.

They never found my body. The horse and buckboard returned to the stable, and a search were commenced forthwith. All they found were my Bessie, layin' in the road in the middle of the forest. She had splintered and were now a shattered skeleton of wood shards and strings. Only one part of her remained all of a piece: the bottom of the fiddle, which had once been the lid of the cigar box. Attached to it were a scrap of pink lace, and lettered upon it were one word – *Bessie*.

♦♦♦♦♦♦♦♦♦♦♦♦♦

Best Selling Author of "Son of My Soul - The Adoption of Christopher," "A Very Special Child - An Adoption Story", co-author "Jesus Gandhi Oma Mae Adams"; scribe for "Christopher Bullfrog Catcher".

www.DebraShiveleyWelch.net

THE PROWL

By Dian Butler

No one seemed to recognize her as she walked slowly past the first table. All eyes were on the shooter—an older man with white hair and thin-rimmed glasses that spoke to his profession. She glanced back at him and thought to herself … *accountant, out on the town*. She moved to watch him from the opposite end of the table. There were all sorts of people standing around the table and most of them were men. He caught her attention because his thin face looked serious. She loved the serious ones, men that had a drive to win.

Slowly mixing into the crowd she could stare at him without him noticing her. His suit set him apart from others; it was more of a midnight blue, not black, expensive and possibly purchased in Hong Kong. It had the tell-tale silk threads. Every now and then as he moved, the top threads would shimmer ever so slightly.

She kept lowering her eyes so he would not catch her staring at him. Then she made her move as any cat in a jungle would. She had sized up the prey and it was time to move in for the kill. Still keeping her distance, she allowed her spontaneous plan to unfold.

He collected his winnings and began to walk away from the table when she deliberately bumped into him. If he had been paying more attention he might have felt the lifting of his wallet. But he was still convinced the night belonged to him and was heading for the lounge to celebrate with a non-alcoholic drink.

He wasn't drinking because he didn't want his wife to think that he was downstairs partying while she was sleeping in their hotel suite. Keeping his wife happy and content while they were away from home might help squelch the suspicions she had at home while he traveled alone. However he wasn't innocent, he was accustomed to having 'affairs of the loins' on his business trips. The many times she had phoned when he was not in his room and his refusal to have a cell-phone on his person kept her thoughts diligently skeptical about his business trips. So bringing her on this journey was not only to prove she was wrong, but also strengthened his opinion about cell phones.

He felt the need for privacy and explained to all that wished to hear, that business calls could be monitored and market deals could be swayed from the use or misuse of a cell phone. His stand on cell phone use kept his occasional trysts secret as well as supplied him with firm control of his business dealings. Appointments were normally kept because a client was unable to cancel at the last minute, knowing that contacting him was impossible. Besides it was one less item to carry on his person. But at this moment his ego was silently skewed and too mobile to think what anyone might take from him. He decided that the dimly lit cocktail lounge was the perfect location to relax and have a quiet time to reflect on the next day's business meetings.

The cocktail waitress hurried to him, looking forward to a big tip since he was a winner. The winners were easy to spot. More confident than the losers and they usually sat away from other people in the lounge. Not wanting to 'catch' a losing streak from some overly indulgent alcoholic types. He was typical in that he shied away from those who were drinking heavily.

The waitress took his order for a tall iced tea and walked away wondering if he'd tip much for an un-intoxicating drink.

The 'cheetah' woman reappeared after she had rifled through the man's wallet as fast as she could and had dropped the evidence in a toilet tank. This was something she'd done many times before and had found that a toilet tank was better than a trash receptacle in the women's room. Inside the stall she was away from curious onlookers while she gleaned the black snakeskin wallet. She wondered about the snakeskin. He didn't look the type. A cowhide man, maybe, not a snake man. He appeared to be very conservative with a small flare for gambling, not to be confused with the 'whales' she had known in most of the casinos she frequented.

The last 'whale' she accompanied gave her some of his winnings, but she found herself chip-hustling him to get the money she needed to make her necessary day's take to keep her lifestyle solvent. He kept taking her up to his room every time he dropped over $40,000 on the dice table. It was odd behavior that he wanted her body every time he lost. Not really what the casino preferred, they wanted to keep the gamblers on the floor, gambling. But he wanted her up in his room, so she went. And after a brief interlude he'd head back to the tables. That 'whale' even offered her a ticket back to his home in Chicago. He said he would put her up in an apartment and pay all expenses. Oh yes, she'd received that offer many times before. A slow road to hell, without the benefit of a marriage license and fear of answering the phone, afraid the current wife might be calling after finding out the cheating husband had set her up and was supporting her. No, she preferred to stay in Vegas and make her money with an assortment of men.

If she went back and forth to a 'whale's' hotel room, she would always manage to keep her hair in place and makeup glowing. So even if the employees knew she'd been up in his room, she didn't want to look as if they'd been away from the casino having wild sex. The Pit-Bosses allowed her to pick up the 'whales' because she was supposed to keep them at the tables, shooting.

Tonight the Pit-Boss was different. He did not flirt with her and look her up and down as usual. She thought she might be becoming too much of a fixture. It was better to be a sparkler than a burnt out firecracker. For a fleeting moment she felt old and felt that her time in Vegas was nearly over. It was time to make another plan and tonight she would be playing her own kind of game. She needed a shooter that wanted more than her body. The trips to the rooms were getting tiresome, and had been for some time. Now she wanted more; she wanted to leave Las Vegas.

Her long flowing blonde hair was sure to catch the shooter's eye when she returned to the floor, for she was not finished with him. The wallet had revealed his identity and that indeed his company was based in Hong Kong. According to a note she had found in his wallet, he was in Las Vegas for meetings and now she wanted more from him. She wanted a job and she wanted to go to Hong Kong. Maybe work for him and then move on to a better job, or maybe start a business there. Maybe, just maybe, he was her way out, her salvation in a silk suit.

He was now considered her mark and meeting him would be easy, she was an expert. She slipped the waitress a hundred dollar bill to spill the iced tea on her as she walked by. The waitress was very obliging with the man's iced tea. The accident was quick and smooth. The bottom of the 'cheetah's' dress was drenched with tea.

She asked the man if she could sit down next to him for a minute while the waitress fetched a towel to blot her dress since it was dripping all over the carpet, and then she would go to the restroom to finish cleaning it.

He said, yes, and at the same time he was thankful the drink had not splashed on him. He noticed that her hair was similar to the color and length of his wife's hair when he had first met her over 25 years ago. They hadn't had any children and he thought for a moment that this young woman could have been his child had they been fortunate enough to have a baby after the fertility treatments. The thoughts ran rampant through his brain. His first wife, too, resembled this woman, but that marriage lasted only a year and his second wife was much more attractive anyway. He realized how shallow he had become. He wanted only beautiful women to compliment his arm. A woman to show and then tell later to his priest in the confessional along with all the other women he bedded quite regularly. Yes, this one was very pretty to look at and his hands felt like reaching out to her.

All the while she was speaking softly but he could barely hear her above the noise in the casino. The lounge was a little quieter but it didn't seem to filter the noise that was blaring into the area where they sat. And softer lights, yes, but all the loud drunks seemed to congregate there. Sitting further away would not solve the problem. He was feeling that he wanted to get to know her better, but at a more romantic location and far away from the possibility that his wife might see them together.

He didn't want this woman to leave just yet.

The meeting he had to attend the next day was going to be an important one, and his wife only had been interested in shopping. He'd wanted to talk to someone about the business of the meeting, so the drink spill occurred at a time when he needed someone the most. It wasn't a habit of his to talk to strangers about personal business, but tonight was different, he needed a willing ear. He wondered if she would walk with him after her lovely black dress dried. He remarked that the naked eye could not see the tea stain easily and that he wished she would sit with him for a few minutes, she didn't have to leave to attend to it in the ladies room.

Her plan was working better than she had hoped. His eyes told the story of the usual lonely businessman out on the town. His wallet had spoken of a successful man with all the credit cards and cash and important business cards that his success warranted.

"Have you been to Las Vegas before?" she asked.

"Actually, I have been here a couple of times, but I prefer Monte Carlo. The drunks there have more money." He grinned.

She giggled as if on cue.

The waitress arrived with his iced tea and a cloth and asked if he wanted anything else.

"Would you like a drink?" He touched the woman's shoulder as she blotted her dress.

"No, thank you."

The waitress handed him the bill and he reached for his wallet. Of course it was gone and the look on his face was one of complete surprise. He told the waitress that if she would trust him, he would go to his room for the money.

But she was convinced that not only was she not getting paid, she was not going to get a tip. She was on the verge of calling her manager to the table.

The 'cheetah' immediately handed the waitress another hundred dollar bill and told her to keep the change.

The man was grateful and said he would be forever in her debt.

That was music to her ears. Forever in her debt was exactly where she wanted him. She got up to leave, but he insisted that she wait till he went up to his room to get the money to repay her. He went on to explain that he was embarrassed by his failure to know his wallet was missing.

She told him she was happy to have come to his rescue and that maybe they could meet the next day. She gave him her phone number. Now he would have to see her again to return the money. She smiled and walked away.

He looked at her card and immediately called out after her. "Your name, what is your name? It isn't on the card."

She stopped, turned and smiled as if she were 15 years old and about to make a date for the first time. "Ana, just call me Ana, and your name?" She knew his name but figured that asking him was appropriate.

"Charles Parley."

Both grinned and then she took a few steps toward the casino, looking back again to say, "Tomorrow," and gave a feminine wave. She had a strong urge to dance right back to him and take him for everything she could get out of him that night, but she knew instinctively, as any cat in the jungle, that to stalk and wait could bring more 'meat' to her bank account.

The next day the 'cheetah' was slithering around a different casino, specifically the slot machines. She again moved with the litheness of a cat in the jungle. This was her jungle so she was not aware that she was being watched. She was contemplating finding another mark in the meantime when her cell phone rang and it was Charles. He wanted to meet with her to repay his debt.

As I watched her speak on the phone I was again thankful that I had taken a lip-reading course. She's going to meet him at another hotel on the Strip, the Bellagio. From other such women I have observed, I felt she was going for the huge score this time, and after listening in on her home phone, it is obvious she wants to get out of Vegas. But I wonder.

Many girls working the strip want to leave at one time or another, but the ones making the type of money this one makes, hardly ever leave. I've counted at least $10,000 a week and on occasion that much in a day for her. Some go on to trade schools or the local colleges so they can stay in Vegas *and eventually find other employment, but very few actually leave town. They like the action and this town is their mating arena. Like the jungle, cats prefer to stay in familiar territory. Straying could mean death. Without the jungle of glittering lights, booze and cigarettes, men and crowds, they are lost. No matter what state or country they originate from, the Strip is their home, their hunting grounds. If and when they become too old to hunt, they are still drawn to the action.*

Me, I am just the detective watching. The police department allows the casinos to hire me so their clients are not bothered by the hookers and scam artists working the casinos. I don't arrest them, I only detect them. If they get out of hand, I make the phone call and quietly the perpetrator is escorted out of the casino and warned.

In the old days many were removed and taken to the 'cat houses' to work. But that was in the beginning. Now the casinos want the hookers around, but encourage them not to be so obvious. It's a fine line and they all have to walk it.

So every night I go from casino to casino watching the ladies of the night that have made it to the top of their game - the ones who are allowed next to the whales, the big spenders of Las Vegas, the gamblers that get all the services. And I get to watch, but not touch. It's eye candy for me.

The smaller hustlers go through other channels. The bellhops are now in competition with the massage services and escort services. A few pimps are still around, but it's the dedicated loners that the casinos want close to their prime clientele. Ana has been in the area for about three years and is well-liked. She prowls. She doesn't linger. Her eyes only go for the active shooter. She doesn't go for the quiet man in a card game. It's too boring for her.

Last night was different, though. She actually took a wallet and normally I'm supposed to report her. But I couldn't. I wanted to see it through. I believe that she wants out of the life. I believe she might be ready to leave Las Vegas. Maybe this mark is her way out. If she doesn't leave with him, though, I'll have to report what she did. Then her time in Vegas has ended. Either way Vegas is over for her, and whether or not she is leaving with this man, he is her last mark. She made the mistake of stealing and the casinos won't allow her on the floors when they find out.

I'll give her time to play it out and if she doesn't, well, I have no choice. I have to keep my job. My report will be filed and the call will be made.

Charles had wanted to meet her at the Bellagio, away from his wife. He rarely traveled with his wife and now he was wondering why he bothered to do it this time. The trip from Hong Kong had been uneventful, but it made him wish that he wasn't married. Their marriage wasn't working. He had contacted a lawyer in Las Vegas the first hour after arriving. His wife was American and he was a British citizen. The lawyer gave him a few details about American and Nevada law regarding divorce. But any decisions would have to be made after he returned to Hong Kong. They had been married in California and split their time between there and Hong Kong; it was complicated and he could hardly believe how many years had passed since he first met her.

I just made a phone call to find out if Charles is still in the meeting. It's over and he's on his way to the Bellagio. My credentials allow me to enter the security area where the cameras are to watch the casinos. So I'll use the cameras to document and use the recordings later, just in case she's about to do something over the top again with this client.

Ana is stunning. Her hair is flowing and she's wearing less jewelry than usual - one necklace with a silver cross just below her throat that would be nice to touch. Her dress is simple and almost sexy. It's pastel blue, matches her eyes, and her face is glowing.

He's wearing a different suit today. Not as dark as the one he wore yesterday when he met her. It's a lighter blue and coordinates well with her dress. They both look like two teenagers with all their teeth showing and their hands reaching out to hold each other. It's as though they've been friends for years.

The camera tech just moved the camera into position so I can read their lips. The focus is perfect and the angle just right. He's asking her what her job is and she's lying to him. She's saying that her administrative assistant position has ended and she's looking for new employment.

They've been chit-chatting for over an hour now and I'm getting tired. He must be biting at the bit to get to a craps table, because he just told her he wants to try his luck and of course, she's all for it. No doubt thinking if it doesn't work out as she's planned, then she can hustle him for some chips. That way the day won't be a total loss.

The camera is in position over the craps table and Ana is going to the restroom again. She keeps going back and forth. I need to get onto the floor to make sure she's not stealing again.

Here she comes out of the restroom again, and this time she's using a paper towel to wipe her face. Normally I don't make contact but I have to find out what's going on. She looks pale. Uh oh, she's leaning against the wall and definitely doesn't look right. Something is wrong. I'm going.

She's still there, her eyes are closed.

"Are you all right?"

"It must have been something I ate. I'll be okay. Thank you."

Perfect. Just perfect. I blew my cover and all she has is an upset stomach. She's heading back to the table where Charles is gambling. He's grinning and winning, loving the action, not knowing if it will all be lost in the next roll of the dice.

Now I have to decide whether I'm to return to the cameras or stay on the floor. I'll go back to the cameras.

A loud scream came from the direction of the table where Charles and Ana were. Ana was on the floor and Charles was standing over her. She wasn't moving. She wasn't breathing.

She was dead.

One could see that Charles didn't want to be there right at that moment. Sure his eyes had strayed, but gambling with a dead woman was not something he could tell his wife about, especially if he wanted to have a 'clean' divorce.

As they lifted Ana into the ambulance, I asked what had happened. The paramedic said it must have been a heart attack. I couldn't believe that one minute this beautiful woman was standing next to her future and the next minute she is on a gurney and on her way to the morgue.

My report will be filed about Ana and her apparent death due to natural causes, but I won't mention the stealing. She only did it one time that I saw, and there is no reason to mention it. Charles will never know and Ana is gone.

God, I'll miss her. I loved to watch her prowl the casinos.

The next woman on my list to spy on is someone I have watched before, and she doesn't walk like a beautiful cat, like my 'cheetah'.

♦♦♦♦♦♦♦♦♦♦♦♦

Dian Butler has been writing since she was a little girl. For twenty years after leaving the nest, she ran an escort business which led to writing a series of novels and short stories about her unusual vocation and experiences. She gives a new twist on an old topic.

Dian has held positions as an investigator, singer, model, movie extra, and mother, to name a few, and with the insights she has garnered over the years she is able to write unique and believable characters in her manuscripts.

Writing science fiction is her favorite, however, and her ability as a telepathist is used in the book she is currently writing. She is a published journalist and has written lyrics with a well-known blues singer for ISIS Music in Marin County, California.

In 2006 Dian served a partial term as the first Wizards of Words President and in 2007 she was appointed as WOW V.P. when the elected V.P. resigned. Now in semi-retirement in Arizona she is currently the elected treasurer for the Wizards of Words org.

http://www.freewebs.com/dbutler33/

REST: PERSPECTIVE

By E. Don Harpe

When Eddie Danforth heard the voices telling him to let his gleaming silver blade bring rest to the lost souls of Savannah's back streets, his mission in life became clear. He walked among the homeless and hopeless multitudes, offering them a way out of the wasteland they had made of their lives. When the first victim was discovered draped across the altar in a waterfront mission, Detective Rhonda Tucker was assigned the case. Beset with personal troubles, Rhonda took the case, not knowing that before it was solved her very foundation would be shaken to the core, not knowing that sometimes rest comes only to the soul of a true believer.

April 16, Morning, Cornerstone Mission

Savannah Detective Rhonda G. Tucker had never seen a murder victim that was quite as viciously mutilated as was Reverend Dalton Glover. The young preacher who had recently taken over the mission down on West River Street lay spread-eagle over the altar, his body already stiffening in a congealing pool of his own blood. Glover's blood had stained both the wood of the altar and the worn carpet upon which the altar rested, somehow blending in with both. The altar was old, made of beautiful polished cherry, and the new stains made it even darker. Tucker couldn't help but think that it had taken on a somewhat sinister appearance.

There were several strange things about the murder, things that made little sense. Nothing was taken from the church, so far as Tucker could tell. Money was left lying on the preacher's desk, a couple hundred dollars it looked like, and it hadn't been touched. Then there were the slashes. Tucker had seen knife victims before. In fact, she'd even seen one or two who had actually died from the cuts, but never anything like this. She had stopped counting the slashes on the preacher's body when the number reached 26. This killing went beyond simple robbery, looking more like the unbridled rage of a madman.

Perhaps the strangest thing of all that sent chills up Tucker's spine and quickened her thirst for a long drink from the flask of Black Jack that she kept in her glove compartment, was the drawing on the floor. Tucker had examined the drawing from several different angles, and each time she saw the same thing. The killer had used the preacher's blood to draw a pair of eyes on the floor, and Tucker could swear the eyes were filled with fear. Looking at them for the tenth time, she was still unsure if they were the eyes of the victim or of the killer. Whichever they were, they were like the eyes in the old cartoons, the ones that always followed you around a room. Tucker couldn't get over the idea that they were watching her. The longer she stayed in the room, the more the hair on her neck bristled. She needed some cool night air and that drink she'd been thinking about.

Rhonda Gale Tucker had only been in Savannah for a little more than a year, having re-located from Oklahoma City. Before that she was in Memphis, and before that Baton Rouge. She was accustomed to seeing the brutal side of the city, and violent death was nothing new to her. She'd worked cases where the victim was a child, and cases where the victim was elderly. She'd seen it all, or she thought she had. That had changed a few minutes ago when she'd walked down the aisle of this old mission. Long ago she'd stopped thinking of the victims as people. They were corpses, dead things, and she firmly believed that the souls had vacated the bodies at the moment of death.

Rhonda believed in God, and she knew that her faith was the only thing that got her through the nights after she'd worked a case.

She didn't know that in the next few months her faith would be stretched to its limits, and that before this summer was over she would question every belief she'd ever had.

April 19, Mid-morning, River Street

Rhonda knelt at the side of the girl and wept. This was not like Rhonda, not like the hardened detective who had worked so many of these brutal cases before. Rhonda couldn't help it. Like the preacher she'd seen three nights ago, this one was different.

The problem was that this girl reminded Rhonda of her own daughter. Not that Kristin was a junkie or a prostitute or anything like that, but for a while now she had been away from home, and Rhonda worried. Especially when she saw something like this.

It was a combination of the needle tracks that dotted the girl's arm, the black circles under her eyes, and the crimson blood that seeped from the wound on her neck that got to Rhonda. She knew the girl had been a tormented soul in life, but even so, no one deserved such a violent and senseless death.

This time the knife had made one deadly slash, beginning at her left ear and ending just below her right one. The cut had almost decapitated the girl, and the wound was gaping and ugly.

Rhonda stared at the girl and the thought of turning away crossed her mind. The thought was fleeting, as turning was impossible. Helpless, she found her eyes drawn to the wound with a macabre fascination, and not looking was not an option. Besides, she had to somehow remain focused, look for the smallest clue, anything that might help her learn the identity of the girl and why she had been so brutally murdered.

From the savagery of the attack, Rhonda immediately tied it to the killing of the young preacher. It could have been the same weapon. The police had not found any leads at all as to the identity of the person who killed the preacher, but perhaps there would be something here, something that would link the two, something that would give Rhonda a beginning. She desperately needed a beginning.

The girl was fully clothed, albeit rather scantily, but there was no evidence of sexual molestation. *A lady of the night,* Rhonda thought, using an old fashioned term that she'd heard her father use, back when she was a child and the world was a simpler place. She didn't want to use the term hooker; it sounded too cold, too impersonal for this once pretty slip of a girl who lay with her lifeblood drained out on the dirty sidewalk.

Looking closer, Rhonda saw something strange on the girls left cheek. In the traces of blood that had somehow found their way from the neck wound, Rhonda saw what appeared to be the outline of lips. She bent closer, and then motioned for the photographer to get a picture.

She was sure it was the outline of someone's lips. Someone - the killer, perhaps - had placed a tender kiss on the girl's cheek, and it had been placed there after she was dead.

He's feeling something for the victims, Rhonda thought. *But what? Surely not remorse, more like pity. God, what kind of monster am I dealing with here?*

She was now certain that it was the work of one man, one killer, one man with a sharp knife and the ability to disappear into the background. A street person; maybe a homeless guy. No use in conjecture, just not enough to go on.

He'll strike again, she thought. *I have to figure out the pattern. He has to make a mistake.*

However, if he did make a mistake, Rhonda never found it. The days dragged by, and Rhonda was unable to figure out the killer's pattern, and he made not the first mistake. But he did strike again. And again.

May 2, Afternoon, The Boat docks

Joey "The Snitch" Mangrum was well known to Rhonda. He was a small-time hood, a sometime police informant, and had been busted half a dozen times in the past couple of years for petty theft and dealing drugs along River Street. He was strictly small potatoes, not important enough for anyone to want him dead, and yet, here he was, lying in the dirt and filth of the alley with a vicious puncture wound in his ribcage. The wound had found enough of his heart to stop its beating, and that's why Rhonda was called.

Another knife murder was not something Tucker wanted to think about this morning. She had other things on her mind, things that called out for attention, things that she knew she needed to take care of. As it had when she'd investigated the murder of the young prostitute, Rhonda's mind again turned to her daughter. Kristin was barely 20, and for the past few weeks she had been out there, somewhere on the streets. Rhonda didn't like to think about a serial killer running amuck in Savannah with Kristin unaccounted for.

Rhonda missed her daughter's smile, and the way she had of helping to ease the tension after a hard day at work. Kristin was as fair as Rhonda was dark, and by the time she was fourteen, she had grown a couple of inches past Rhonda's 5'6". She had been accepted to a dozen colleges, but had taken a couple of years off after high school, saying she wanted to 'find herself.' Rhonda pointed out that she was not lost, but it didn't matter. She just wished she'd come home. She didn't like her being on the streets. Especially not now.

Mother and daughter had not been getting along since Carl died, and even though Carl wasn't Kristin's natural father, he was the one who had raised her. Rhonda and Carl had married back in Memphis, 17 years ago this summer, and Carl was the only true father Kristin had really known. He'd passed away in September of last year; a heart attack at 46 had struck without warning. It had been Kristin who had found him on the floor when she got up that morning.

Kristin had spent the winter months grieving over Carl, taking flowers to the cemetery, questioning God and the universe, and then, a few weeks ago, she'd walked out the door and hadn't returned. Rhonda had searched, the entire department had searched, and it had paid off, in a kind of 'round about way. A street cop had found Kristin. He told Rhonda that she now and then slept on a bench down by the river, but that most of the time she lived in a rent-by-the-week cheap motel downtown. He reported to Rhonda that Kristin seemed fine, but from what he could learn she wanted to be left alone. Said she needed more time to work things out, and that she'd be home when she found what she was looking for.

That was almost a month ago, and Rhonda hadn't had any word from her since. So this alley was not where she wanted to be, not where she thought she should be. She wanted to be out searching, prowling Savannah's alleys and side streets until Kristin was safe in her arms. Instead, she was here, doing her job, staring intently at the face of a dead drug dealer. Deep inside she was ashamed that all she could think was that she was glad it wasn't her daughter.

Rhonda knew that Kristin blamed her for Carl's death. Kristin thought that Rhonda's job had put too much stress on Carl, and that he'd been trying to get Rhonda to take something in the private sector for the past few years. But Rhonda was dedicated to police work, and didn't want to look for anything else; it was all she knew, all she wanted to know. Carl wanted her to either step down or at least seek a desk job, but Rhonda had resisted. The situation had reached a crisis in August when a man named David Matthews had decided to kill his wife and his next door neighbor. Rhonda had been the first officer on the scene, and had almost lost her own life when Matthews ran out of his home shooting at everything that moved. Rhonda had been hit in the right upper chest, and the doctors agreed that a few inches lower might have been fatal. She had shot and killed Matthews, even after he wounded her, but that fact didn't carry any weight with Carl at all. It just made him more determined, and he reinforced his efforts to get her to walk away from the job.

She refused, and here she was a year later, working a vicious serial killer case, with Carl dead and Kristin missing. It was almost more than she could deal with, but her job was all she knew, and so, as she always had, she put the personal things aside and tried to focus on the latest victim.

Rhonda's left hand ruffled through her hair as she looked down at Joey Mangrum, small time crook and big time loser. Joey had been working the streets for several years now, but never in a big-time way. Mostly he sold a bit of weed, and now and then a bag of cocaine. It appeared as if it had been a coke deal that had gone bad that got him killed. Rhonda might not have tied his death to the others, had it not been for the rose.

Someone had placed a red plastic rose on Joey's chest, and the more Rhonda thought about it, the more convinced she became that Joey was another victim of the man Rhonda had dubbed *The Slasher*. The name wasn't very original, but it was accurate, and besides, it was all Rhonda could think of.

It all fit in. The killer used a knife, and Rhonda was willing to bet the marks would match the ones on the preacher and the girl in the alley. Joey wasn't robbed, in fact he had over $200 in his pants pocket, no doubt his night's earning from his drug sales. He wasn't mutilated like the preacher, nor slashed like the girl, but a gut feeling told Rhonda that the same killer had murdered him, and her feelings were seldom wrong.

Try as she may she couldn't figure out what the rose meant. It was plastic and looked like one of the roses that is sometimes found in a cemetery, a flower that will last awhile on a grave. She made a note to check the nearby cemeteries for clues, and was about to call it an afternoon when she noticed for the first time the smile on Joey's face. *Almost as if he had finally found some peace,* she thought. *Almost as if for the first time in years he was at rest.*

July 18, Morning, River Street

"Kristin, I can't take much more of this. There's one of the most psychopathic serial killers on the loose that I've ever seen, and you're just not safe out here on the street."

This was the first time Rhonda had spoken with her daughter in over two months, and the concern was heavy in her voice as she spoke. Heavy enough that she imagined her daughter could hear it, even over the less than great cell phone connection.

"I'm a big girl, mom, I'll be all right. I know and all my friends know he's out there, and we're being careful, but there's something really strange about this guy."

"Strange? Exactly how do you define strange? If you mean as in he's slashing throats coming and going strange, I'd say you and your friends are right. This guy is not strange, Kris, he's just plain dangerous."

"Yeah, mom, I know, but it seems he's only killing those who are so far down they're never going to get back up."

"What the hell is that supposed to mean, Kris? Do you think the people he's killed deserved it?"

"No mom, that's not what I meant, but look at who he's killed so far. Junkies, dope dealers, prostitutes. Many of them were helpless, most homeless, and all hopeless. He's taking out the ones who've hit bottom, Mom. It's almost as if they were asking him to do it."

"That's not entirely true, honey. How about the first one, the Preacher? He doesn't fit your profile."

"Well, maybe not exactly, but from what I've heard, Reverend Glover had his own demons he was dealing with. He was a recovering alcoholic, he'd lost his family, and from what I hear he may have been more than friendly with some of the boys that went to church there. Look, Mom, I'm just saying that I don't think he'll choose me. I don't have a drug habit, I'm not selling, and I think this guy will leave me alone."

"But honey, you're spending some of your nights on the street, sleeping on benches, and you know you don't have to do that. Just come on home, I love—"

"I know Mom, and I believe you, but I'm just not ready. I'm working it out, and I don't think it will take much longer, but I just have to have a bit more time. I'm sorry Mom, I really am, but please don't worry, I'll be fine."

"I'm doing all I can to catch this guy, Kris, and if you hear anything, anything at all, please call me. Please?"

"I will Mom, I promise I will. Look, I gotta go now, I have a couple of things to do."

"Ok, darling, but be careful. I love you."

"Love you too, Mom. Bye."

There was finality in the silence on the phone that Rhonda didn't like, a *something* that filled her with dread. *Damn it,* she wished Kris would just get it together. She might think she was safe, but Rhonda knew better. Even if her daughter was right about the killer, there were other crazies out there, others just as dangerous, maybe even more so.

August 27, Afternoon, River Street

For some reason, Rhonda didn't want to work the call that came in to her desk at 2:24 p.m. Last night a homeless girl had been beaten, kicked off the dock into the river, and had never surfaced. Her body had been found a half-hour ago, and Rhonda was needed at the docks to help with the investigation. She couldn't shake off the near paralyzing fear that permeated her every sense as she made the twenty-minute drive to the crime scene. Had her training not kicked in, she would have been in full-blown panic mode by the time she reached the river.

When she got out of her car, something made her stop, a feeling washed across her as if someone had just walked across her grave, and she knew, even before she saw the body, she knew.

Rhonda knelt beside the lifeless body of her only child and tortured sobs racked her body. She stroked Kristin's hair, pressed her lips to her hand, ran her fingers over her face. The feeling of sadness was overpowering, pressing down on her soul, wrenching the breath from her body in great gasps of fevered air. She couldn't stand to look at Kristin, didn't want to see her wet and dirty from the river's mud. Couldn't bear to think of her in this way, couldn't hold back the scream that started deep in her belly and rushed upward and out, reverberating across the Savannah River as time stood still.

"Rhonda, Rhonda . . . " It was Crane Elliott, her partner, and he was holding her close, offering her his strength until she could find her own, gently speaking her name as he tried to bring her back from whatever hell she had been in for the last two days. They were sitting in the funeral home's tent in the cemetery, and the minister had just completed Kristin's last rites. The coffin was closed, was being lowered, and Rhonda still hadn't been able to look at it.

"I know you don't think you can do this, Ron, but you have to. There was nothing you could have done about it, no way you could have prevented it. You know you won't catch her killer sitting here. You're gonna have to pull it together, get back out on the street and find whoever did this. You owe it to Kristin to catch them, Rhonda. Damn it, you owe it to yourself."

For the first time the words seemed to penetrate Rhonda's shell, get through the defensive wall she had erected when she knelt on the dock beside Kristin's body.

"You're right, Crane, you're right," she said. Her hand involuntarily touched the butt of the holstered Glock 9MM that pressed against her hip. "I'll find them, and when I do—"

"Yeah, I know, kid, I know. And I'll help. Nothing would give me more satisfaction than putting these guys down."

"We know for sure it's not the serial killer, is that right," Rhonda asked. "We know that?"

"Pretty sure about that one. No slash marks, no stab wounds, in fact, no wounds of any kind, except for the bruises where she was beaten. No, this wasn't him. This was more than likely a random killing, some high school boys beating up the homeless, you know they do that."

"Yeah, I know. I read the report where someone had seen some kids wearing high school jackets on the dock that night. Why would they do that, Crane, why?"

"They don't see them as humans, Ron, just as useless people not needed by anyone, and they think they can do whatever they want to, because nobody is going to give a damn."

"Well I give a damn, and I won't stop until I get these … monsters in my sights. You know, they're worse than the guy we've been looking for. I don't know why he kills, but these guys did this for fun. I promise you they won't be having any fun when I catch them. If I ever see them …"

September 29, Morning, Boat docks

Rhonda and Crane were looking at the two boys who had killed Kristin, but killing them was something Rhonda was not going to be able to do. Not unless they could die twice.

Their bodies had been found in an alley, slashed to death and propped against a wall. Nearby lay the stomped to death body of an old looking woman, shabbily dressed, more than likely homeless, more than likely killed by these two scumbags.

Seems they hadn't counted on the *Slasher* being there, and in a moment of extreme clarity, Rhonda saw in her mind's eye what had happened.

They'd come back to the docks; drinking beer, laughing, looking for another victim or two, someone easy, someone who wouldn't or couldn't fight back. They'd found the old woman, kicked and stomped her to death, laughed as the breath left her bleeding body.

Then they'd spotted the young girl sleeping on a nearby bench. Alone, unprotected, vulnerable. They'd turned their attention to her, hit her a few times, knocked her from the bench. Kicked her off the dock and into the murky water.

He watched them perhaps, hated them for what they were doing. Maybe he saw the homeless as his charges, his people, his congregation, and he meant to protect them when he could, and extract revenge if his protection failed. He'd held back, looking for the best chance to strike, and when the opportunity came, he took it. With the rage he was known for, he let the knife find first one of the boys, then the other. He dragged them into the alley, propped them up on the wall, and left them there. He went home then, wherever that was, to let the blood lust fade away, satisfied with his night's work.

Rhonda looked at the two corpses, saw the lettermen jackets with the big *S*, and instinctively knew these were the same two who had taken the life of her precious daughter. She squatted beside them, slapped first one and then the other, wiped the tears from her eyes and held back the scream. She shook off Crane's hand, leaned in close to the bodies, and spat on them. Without another word she stood up and walked away. Let someone else try to find the man who did this. She was glad they were dead.

Rhonda wandered the streets the rest of the night, drenched in sweat and wishing Savannah's sultry heat would let up a bit. She poked into every dive and back alley she could find, and then spent the next day doing the same. She was looking for a clue, any clue that might help her find the killer. Her problem now was that she wasn't sure if she wanted to arrest him or thank him.

She was now convinced that Kristin had been right. The killer was not randomly murdering innocent people. In fact, Rhonda now thought that the killer was convinced he was performing a service for his victims, and that he truly thought he was called to do this work.

Called to kill. That made him the most dangerous kind of killer, but still, Rhonda wasn't sure that he was wrong.

September 30, Evening, Talmadge Bridge

At a quarter after ten on the night of September 30, Rhonda stepped out of an alley on River Street directly into the path of the man she had been searching for all summer. She knew him immediately.

He looked at her but Rhonda knew he didn't see her. The look in his eyes told her he was lost in a world of his own, doing whatever he could to fight off the demons that were tormenting him. A bulge in his right trousers pocket might be the knife, but she couldn't be sure. Surprised, she saw the Bible in his hand and wondered if he thought he was on a mission from God.

She fell into step behind him, followed him as he walked along the river. He was oblivious to his surroundings, seeing nothing, noticing no one, listening to nothing except the siren song was playing inside his head. He mumbled to himself as he walked, and though Rhonda stayed as close as possible, she was unable to make out any words. She decided that what he was saying didn't matter, only where he was going and what he was planning.

In a matter of minutes she saw that they were headed for the Talmadge Bridge, and she wondered if he had spotted a potential victim there. Or maybe he was going to take his blade across the bridge, find another spot to work his miracles for the helpless people that he saw himself as championing.

She trailed along behind, not wanting to approach the man until she was completely sure he was the one. In her gut she knew it, but her gut feeling wouldn't hold up in court. She followed him out on the bridge, watched as he dug an object from his pocket and dropped it into the river, saw him lay the Bible down on the pavement.

Unable to move, she watched as he climbed the railing; saw the smile on his face as he stopped for a minute to carry on a conversation with an invisible companion.

She picked up the Bible and slowly inched along the bridge behind him. Her legs were trembling so that she had to will them to move, and she knew that whatever he was planning, there was no way she could stop it. She was only some 20 feet from the man when he stepped from the railing and dropped like a stone to the river below.

The only thing on the bridge, the only thing the man left behind was the Bible. Rhonda opened the book to the first leaf, saw the name Eddie written in what she was sure was blood. She was certain that it had been stolen from the preacher, although she didn't understand how she knew it.

Rhonda stared into the black water where Eddie had disappeared, ashamed at the feeling of relief that had crept into her mind. A small voice told her it was over, and Rhonda desperately wanted to believe it was so.

It was then that the Angel spoke to her.

The Angel's voice was a seductive whisper in her mind, sweet and invasive, a lover's voice, telling her to trust in him, that everything would be all right. For what seemed like an eternity the Angel occupied a back corner of her mind, murmuring in his low and hushed tones that tonight Rhonda herself might find the same rest that so many others had been granted.

Rhonda fingered the stained cover of the Bible, noticed that it fell open to a particular passage, a place in the book where someone had obviously spent many hours. There was only one passage outlined, and it too was colored in a dark reddish brown stain that could only be blood. Rhonda didn't understand how she knew it, but she was certain that this was passage that had guided Eddie's every more. She somehow knew that it was this passage that had procured the demons from the lower recesses of Eddie's tortured mind, and then brought the Angel to provide the reasoning for all of his later actions. In the faltering light from the bridge, she wept as she read the words;

"Come unto me, ye who burden and are heavy laden, and I will give ye rest."

Rhonda laid down the Bible, slowly climbed the railing, unsure of why but compelled to do so. On she went, one flagging step after another, seeking the last spot that had ever known the warmth of Eddie Danforth's existence.

She was surprised to see the Demons drifting about in the mist, and recognized them as the same ones that had twirled about Eddie's head, had perched on his shoulder and whispered their vile instructions. They seemed lost, desperate; their eyes searched the bridge and then the river, they screamed and wailed, moaning their sorrow over Eddie's sacrifice, and were never still.

And then Rhonda saw the Angel.

Hovering above the rails, Eddie's Angel rode the river mists, his wings dampened with Eddie's last tears, and he looked at Rhonda. Beside the Angel, Rhonda was sure she saw the face of Kristin, and that somehow made it all right. The Angel's voice had hushed, but now she could see that his eyes were filled with promise. Kristin smiled and beckoned to her.

The river called, Eddie Danforth's soul waited, and Rhonda was tired, so tired.

She smiled back at her darling daughter, stepped from the rail and wafted slowly on the river winds until she came into the arms of the Angel. She stared for a moment deep into the Angel's eyes, and there she saw the rest that Eddie had offered, and, like so many others, she accepted.

For the story of Eddie Danforth and his deadly silver blade, read REST: VOICES, published by the Amazon Shorts program. This is the story from the other side of the coin, the other perspective.

♦♦♦♦♦♦♦♦♦♦♦♦

E. DON HARPE, formerly of Nashville, now of Florida, is a songwriter, poet, and novelist. He has had a varied career, and his occupations include having been an engineer for a major appliance firm, a songwriter who has seen many of his songs recorded, and who for years ran his own music publishing company. Now retired, E. Don Harpe devotes his time to his family and his writing.

He is currently working on a series of fictionalized novels about the exploits of the infamous Harpe brothers. Called America's First Serial Killers, the Harpes hold a unique place in the history of America. The first book in the series, Born Wolf, Die Wolf, the Last Rampage of the Terrible Harpes was published in February 2006. The second book, Resurrection, Rebirth of the Terrible Harpes is also available from Amazon.

In September of 2007, Harpe was elected as the 2008 Secretary of Wizards of Words (W.O.W.), a literary non-profit group based out of Queen Creek AZ that is quickly becoming a leading online presence for new and established authors to showcase their work, as well as to grow each facet of their writing abilities.

Harpe is also the author of the Redneck Riviera stories, an ongoing series of humorous short stories concerning the adventures of an alien named JorG and his earthling friend Billy Joe White who attempts to guide him over the confusing terrain of contemporary southern culture.

He has a growing number of short stories published in places such as Amazon Shorts and Fictionwise, and his novel StormChilde is currently available as a seven part series in the Amazon Shorts program.

www.donharpe.com

TO JOIN WIZARDS OF WORDS:

please go to the WOW web site and click on JOIN.
Open to all writers – published and unpublished.

AS A MEMBER ...

1. You will receive special considerations and **registration discounts** to attend our annual WOW national conferences.

2. If you do not have a web site, you will receive a **full web page** on the WOW site with photos of you and your book covers, a bio and synopses of your books. If you do have a web site, we will provide a **link to your site** from our AUTHORS page.

3. You will receive a **complimentary e-copy** of David S. Rosenberg's **"The Compact Guide for the Creative Writer."**

4. You will receive a **free listing** of each of your books in **WOW's online book store**.

5. You will have access to the **members-only forums** on our message board - **WOW CHAT CAFE**.

6. You will have **voting rights** and are invited to participate in the annual business meeting at the annual conference.

7. You will receive **updates, announcements** and the WOW **quarterly newsletter** via email.

8. You are eligible to be included in the **annual anthology** and submit works to the **annual short story and poetry contests**.

2008 WOW WRITERS CONFERENCE
October 10-12

Friday - Days Inn - Scottsdale AZ
Saturday - Chaparral Suites – Scottsdale AZ
Sunday Morn – Annual Meeting – Days Inn

Banquet Keynote – David Morrell (*Best-selling Author – "Rambo" creator*)
Luncheon Speaker – Jerry D. Simmons
(*"What Writers Need to Know About Publishing*")

Fourteen Workshops in Two Days

1472181

Made in the USA